THIS DEED IS OURS

This Deed Is Ours

ISBN: 978-1-0682156-0-5
First Edition – May 2025

For more information, visit: www.jordandmartins.co.uk

A quiet thank you to those who supported me throughout this process - your time, ideas, and encouragement didn't go unnoticed.

To the people who shared suggestions, especially through TikTok and beyond, your input helped guide this story in the right direction.

And to everyone who believed in me, even in small ways - thank you. This has meant more than you know.

— *J.D.M.*

THIS DEED IS OURS

Jordan D. Martins

CHAPTER ONE

There was a weariness to the country that year, a kind of collective exhale that never quite refilled the lungs. Bills rose like floodwater, inch by inch, while pay stagnated with the stubbornness of old brick. Grocery aisles became a guessing game. Mortgage rates climbed, renters clung on and everyone, everyone was tired of pretending not to notice how tight things had become. People still smiled, of course. Brits were good at that. They queued, they cracked jokes about heating versus eating, they watched property shows about dream homes they'd never own. Quietly, though, most had made peace with the idea that comfort was no longer a given. That thriving was for someone else. In South London, tucked between a fried chicken shop and a vape lounge, a one-bedroom flat sat on the second floor above a nail salon that never closed on time. It rattled when the trains passed. It smelled faintly of nail polish remover on the hot days and inside lived a couple who, by many measures were doing just fine. Lena Hartley typed with one hand and scraped burnt toast into the sink with the other, she wore last night's hair, dressing gown hanging off one shoulder and had a video call pending in twelve minutes. Dan Kersey was still in bed. They weren't unhappy, not really, just paused. Like a film left running on mute. Lena rinsed the plate, more out of habit than purpose and set it beside the others on the draining board. The window above the sink framed a slice of grey sky the kind that made everything feel like Tuesday no matter what day it actually was. She checked the time on the clock. Eleven minutes now Dan still hadn't appeared. She padded across the narrow flat, stepping over a laundry basket and nudged a pair of his trainers out the way with her foot. The door to the bedroom stood half-shut, as if undecided. She pushed it open. He was awake, scrolling on his phone. Duvet pulled up to his waist, hair askew like tousled boyband member past his prime. He didn't look up.

"You working today?" she asked lightly, pretending she didn't already know the answer.

"Yeah," he mumbled. "Late start, need to finish the tasting notes from yesterday."

Lena nodded, in the early days, she would've teased him for forgetting things or teased herself for being the organised ones. Lately, they both just let things slide. Back at her desk, which was really just the end of the dining table shoved against the wall with a bookshelf laptop acting as a backdrop full of both the couple's collectibles. She checked her reflection in the black screen of her laptop, pinching her cheeks for colour. Rolling her shoulders back, she clicked into the video call. The screen lit up with a checkboard of familiar faces, some in home offices, some on sofas, one eternally backdropped by an unmade bed and a wall of fake ivy. Lena stayed dark for a moment, her camera icon safely off, and slipped off her dressing gown. She smoothed her hair quickly, raked fingers through the front to give it shape, then pulled a cardigan, clean-ish from the back of her hair.

"Morning" someone chirped through tinny speakers.

"Lena, you on?" questioned another.

"Yep, one sec" she called out, already reaching for a tinted lip balm she kept near her desk for exactly this reason. A dab on the cheeks too, just enough to look alert, professional, like she hadn't burned her toast or scraped it into the sink whilst still wearing pjamma bottoms. She tilted the screen up slightly, checked the lightly and forced her face into a breezy smile. Then, click. Camera on.

"Oh sorry," she laughed "Didn't realise my camera wasn't on"

The others barely blinked. Already talking KIPs and engagement statistics, campaign tweaks and content calendars but Lena knew what the little performance was. They all did it. They says, being 'oh' had nothing to do with being awake. She nodded along, unmuted when it was her turn and gave an update she could've recited in her sleep, probably had. When her screen blanked momentarily due to a connection glitch, she saw herself reflected back again, still smiling.

"Lena, can you hang back a second after this?" her manager's voice piped up just as the meeting began to wind down. "Just need a quick word."

Lena's stomach dipped, not in a dramatic way just a faint flutter of impending inconvenience. The others began dropping off the call with their usual chorus of "Cheers" and "Catch you later" until it was just the two of them. She sat up straighter.

"Right," said Marina, all chirp and efficiency.

"We've got a new client swinging by the office at twelve, last minute thing. Potential long-term campaign. Big deal if it lands, and I want you to be there for intros. You're great with these kinds of brands, and I think they'll really respond to your energy."

Lena hesitated, "Okay, but today's my home day, I've only just started,"

"I know, I know" Marina stream rolled, already checking something off on a clipboard that Lena couldn't see. "But work is work right? Company pays your salary, and all that…" It wasn't even malicious. Marina probably believes she was being reasonable.

"It's just that I'm, well, I'd need to get ready for a big meeting" Lena added.

"I'll send an Uber," Marina interrupted, typing audibly now. "Don't worry about the fare, it's expensed."

Lena's mouth opened to protest but her phone buzzed a second later. ***Your ride will arrive in 7 minutes.*** She linked at it. "I really don't mind just joining via call."

"No, no, face-to-face is better. You'll be great. See you soon" and just like that, Marina ended the call.

Lena sat there, camera off again, hair still halfway between bedhead and boardroom. Staring down at the countdown on her phone like it might slow down if she just refused to blink.

*"Seven minutes!?"*she cried, almost in disbelief that Uber was so quick for once. Lena shot to her feet, nearly tripping over the laundry basket. She grabbed her dry shampoo from the shelf by the mirror,

flipping her head over and spraying liberally, then ran for the bathroom. Dan was in there, toothbrush in one hand, scrolling his phone with the other.

"I need the mirror," she announced, already squeezing in beside him.

He moved aside, still brushing, watching her through the reflection. "What's going on?"

"I've got to fly into the office. Marina's sending an Uber. Big deal client or something." She shook her head, more at the situation than at him and scrubbed at her roots with the heel of her palm. "Of course it's today."

He gave a muffled, non-committal grunt and went back to brushing. She darted into the bedroom and yanked open the wardrobe, scanning for something, anything that said 'effortlessly polished' rather than 'rolled out of bed and cried in the shower.' Her hands landed on a black blazer, reliable, smart enough. She peeled off her cardigan and pulled it on, then shimmied out of her pyjama bottoms in record time, hopping into a pair of tailored black trousers that had mercifully survived the last wash. A honk echoed from the street below, Lena flinched, nearly knocking over the lamp.

"He's going to have to wait a minute" she muttered, jamming her feet into boots without socks.

She grabbed her laptop, slammed it shut, whilst she shoved it and the charger into her oversize tote along with her makeup bag and slung it over one shoulder.

"See you later" she called, already halfway down the hall.

Dan stepped out of the bathroom just as the door slammed behind her. he looked down at the side table, then back at the door.

"Lena, your badge…" he called, opening the door, but she was already gone.

He stood there a moment, holding her lanyard in his hand then shut the door and dropped it onto the kitchen counter with a sigh. Dan flicked on the TV, not to watch, really jus for background noise. One of those property shows Lena secretly loved but pretended to hate was playing, pastel kitchens, oak floors, couples pretending to care about plug socket placements. He slumped onto the sofa with a protein shake and his phone, absently scrolling through reels of people lifting, blending and renovating things. Facebook opened automatically, muscle memory. A video began auto playing, something about slow cooker meals or air fryer hacks, he didn't really register which. Midway through, the video paused for an ad. A bright, glossy promo filled the screen.

WIN A LUXURY FIVE BEDROOM TOWNHOUSE PLUS £250,000 OR TAKE £1,000,000 TAX FREE.
JUST £3 TO ENTER. NO STRINGS ATTACHED. LIMITED TIME ONLY.

Dan squinted. The picture showed an impossibly pristine kitchen, marble island, brass fixtures, some kind of indoor herb wall. Beneath it, bold text announced the property. A former Victorian brewery, fully restored, located near Chelsea embankment. He let it play for a few seconds then swiped up. 'Yeah right.' He thought. Probably one of those gimmicks. He'd seen loads lately, raffle houses hosted by this new company he'd never heard of prior to 2024, glossy nonsense for people with more hope than sense. He scratched his chest absently and went back to scrolling before he checked the time. If he didn't leave soon, he'd hit the mid-morning slog on the Overground. Dan turned off the TV, chucked the rest of his shake in the sink, and started gathering his things. A laptop bag, water bottle, jacket. He still hadn't found his work pass. Dan rummaged through the pile of post and takeaway menus by the front door, grumbling to himself. Gas bill, another pizza flyer, a folded leaflet from a dodgy looking car hire place in Camberwell. Finally, wedged behind Lena's expired Ouster card, he found his work pass. Jamming it into his pocket, trainers on, zip halfway up he headed out into the stairwell. Two flights down past the peeling paint, the faint scent of nail polish remover clinging to the walls. The door of the salon downstairs was already half open, the owner dragging out her A-board with one hand, phone cradled between her cheek and shoulder, shouting something cheerful in Vietnamese. Dan gave her a quick nod. Rye Lane was already buzzing. Someone was selling produce outside one of the local supermarkets. A man in a hi-vis vest was arguing loudly into his phone by the bus stop.

A cyclist swerved around a delivery van without so much as a glance. Peckham always sounded like it was mid-sentence. He crossed over toward Peckham Rye Station, dodging a puddle from last night's rain and spotted the old man who sat outside the shuttered betting shop. Same knit hat, same tattered rucksack. Just watching the world go by. He never begged, just existed quietly in the corner of it all. Dan gave him the usual nod and got one in return. Then he ducked into the station, past the smell of Greggs, past the coffee stand with the perpetually frothing machine and headed for the Overground platform.

Next train to Clapham Junction – 3 minutes.

He checked the time, if the change at Canada Water wasn't too packed then he might actually make it early, just maybe. The train pulled in with a metallic sigh, doors sliding open in a practiced rhythm. A chime sounded, followed by the familiar announcement.

Please mind the gap between the train and the platform edge.

Dan stepped on, joining the silent choreography of commuters shuffling into carriages with headphone cords, reusable coffee cups and faces already half switched off for the day. He found a spot by the door at first, but as the carriage emptied slightly at Queens Road Peckham, he slid into a recently vacated seat beside a man reading The Economist and a woman applying mascara with surgeon like focus. The carriage smelled faintly of damp coats and overly sweet coffee. At the next stop, a heavily pregnant woman stepped on, one hand resting on her belly with a purple 'Baby on board' badge clipped to the lapel of her jacket. She glanced around, that quiet scan of hope and reluctance all at once. No one moved, fortunately for her, Dan was already half way to his feet.

"Here take this." He said, giving her a quick smile and stepping aside.

She looked surprised, then grateful. "Thanks so much" she said, lowering herself into the seat slowly. Hand firmly placed on her belly.

Dan nodded and returned to his spot by the door, gripping the rail as the train lurched back into motion. A teenager yawned in front of him, someone near the far end coughed into their sleeve. The rhythm of the city had resumed, Dan opened his emails, pretending to check work things but mostly just tapping through junk so there wasn't any awkward staring. There was a new product update from a competitor, a chain reply about someone's birthday cake preferences and a newsletter he couldn't remember signing up about 10 ways to optimize your workflow. That was deleted without opening it. Once he reached Canada Water, the usual bottleneck formed. A polite crush of people, eyes glazed over, jostled without truly acknowledging one another. Dan slipped through, weaving past a woman with a pram and a man loudly narrating crpto advise into his AirPods. Once on the Jubilee Line, he settled in again, this time squeezed between two suits and a tired looking woman in her NHS scrubs. As the train shot into the tunnel, Dan caught his own reflection in the black glass of the window. He didn't look tired exactly, just automatic. Like everyone else on the commute. Somewhere between London Bridge and Waterloo, his mind drifted back to the ad. That absurdly perfect kitchen. He imagined walking into a place like that, marble counters and brass taps gleaming, a fridge that poured sparkling water or chips of ice. He imaged Lena there too, barefoot, coffee in hand, laughing at something he'd said. A different version of them, one that didn't live above a nail salon or argue over laundry baskets or feel vaguely exhausted all the time. By the time the train pulled into Westminster, Dan shook the thought off like rain. It was childish really, fantasies were easy however life, not so much. He stepped off the train with the crowd merging into the slow tide of people rising up the escalators like ants in expensive coats.

Lena's Uber crept along the Embankment at a snail's pace, heat blasting from the vents as though to make up for the cold, grey drizzle splattering the windscreen. Lena sat in the back, angled toward the murky light, her compact mirror balanced in one hand and concealer wand in the other. She'd managed to fix her hair into a low bun with a few rebellious strands framing her face deliberate, she hoped. The tinted lip balm had been replaced with real lipstick, the shade she kept for client meetings and exes she might bump into. With swift, practiced movements, she dabbed at her undereye circles, blended, brushed, swiped. The small rituals of transformation, by the time she dropped the last of her things back into her makeup bag, she looked if not boardroom ready then at least convincing enough to pass as someone who hadn't bolted out the door in a minor panic twenty minutes earlier. She tucked the makeup bag back into her tote and pulled out her notebook and phone, fingers already flicking to her notes app. Campaign angles, brand tones, potential engagement hooks. Marina had said it was a *big deal client* but hadn't given a name. Not even a sector. Lena frowned. What kind of manager sent someone into a meeting blind? She rifled through her memory checking through it, all sunshine and pressure. Still Lena wasn't the type to show up unarmed. She began mapping out generic pitches, adaptive social strategies and seasonal tie ins. She'd done it a hundred times before. Then she paused, not knowing the company wasn't just inconvenient, it could be potential catastrophic.

She exhaled slowly through her nose. "Okay," she muttered, scanning a few recent campaigns that had gone viral. Trends could give her a foothold. If she could anchor the meeting with something timely, they'd think she'd been prepping for days.

"Traffic's always murder on this stretch," the driver said suddenly, eyes flickering up to the review mirror.

Lena glanced up. "Hmm?"

"This road, ever since they started those works by Blackfriars. Don't matter what time of day, always backed up."

She offered a polite smile. "Typical London."

He chuckled softly, then went quiet again. The radio humming low in the background, some pop track dissolving into muffled chatter. The car inched forward. One more turn and they'd and they'd be there. Lena reached down to close her notebook when the radio cut into a local news segment.

'… and in lifestyle today, that viral house competition is back in the spotlight after one of last year's winners shared a tour of their million pound kitchen online. The competition, hosted by for profit fundraising company, Winspire, raising money on behalf of-'

Lena's fingers hovered over the handle of her tote, she caught only fragments, 'restored, Victorian brewery, tax-free cash alternative, life changing prize' but the name stuck, Winspire. The cab pulled to a stop outside, a sleek office building with glass panels and a discreet sign by the door.

"Here you go" the driver said.

Lena was already moving, "Thanks" she called over her shoulder, slinging her bag up and stepping out onto the wet pavement. She shut the door and hurried toward the entrance. Looking at her watch, the time was 12:03. She pushed open the door to the building and stepped into the lobby, which smelled faintly of fresh coffee and polished floors. She nodded to the receptionist as she passed, her shoes clicking against the smooth tile. The elevator doors opened just as she reached them and then she stepped inside, smoothing down her blazer and checking herself in the mirrored walls. The elevator chimed at the fourth floor and Lena stepped out into the airy, minimalist office. The scent of fresh flowers mixed with the faint tang of citrus from a nearby diffuser. Marina was already standing by a window, phone in hand, typing rapidly as if she were catching up on work. When she saw Lena, her face brightened.

"There you are!" Marina greeted her, her tone light but with a hint of urgency. "Glad you made it, we're just about to meet with the clients." She waved toward the open conference room, where a couple of her colleagues that were sleekly dressed sat at the top of the long table, papers nearly arranged before them. Lena nodded walking toward the meeting room. She wasn't sure what to expect. There had been no details about the company, nothing concrete to go on, except or Marina's vague comments. She felt the familiar rush of nerves at the back of her mind but pushed it back. She was good at this.

"Is everything ready?" Marina asked, pausing just before the door, turning to Lena with a raised eyebrow.

"What exactly am I walking into here? Who is the brand?"

Marina gave a quick, tight smile, tapping her phone screen as spoke to Lena.

"Oh right, the brand- *Eclat de Luxe*. You know, the one that just released that cult fragrance. *Velours Mystique*. They're looking for a new campaign and they want someone who can really make waves."

Lena nodded, finally letting the weight of it settle in. Eclat de Luxe. A name that carried weight within the luxury perfume world. They'd been on the radar for a while, but Lena hadn't worked with them before. She needed to bring her A-game.

"Okay" Lena said, pulling her laptop out of her bag and opening it as she walked into the conference room.

“Let me pull up the campaign presentation I worked on, I’ll be ready in a second.”

Marina gave her an approving nod. “Good, you’ve got this”

She gave her a quick pat on the back before stepping away to greet the clients. Lena quickly loaded the presentation, a campaign concept designed to highlight exclusivity and mystery, perfect for Eclat de Luxe. As she walked into the room, her nerves melted away. This was what she did, what she was good at and she was ready. Lena approached the conference table, connecting her laptop to the large display monitor. The screen flickered briefly before the campaign presentation loaded, and she adjusted her posture, trying to steady her hands. Marina took a seat at the table, with a few members from the design team, exchanging quick pleasantries with the clients who had already arrived. The Eclat de Luxe board members entered moments later, their presence immediately commanding the room. There were five of them, two women and three men, each impeccably dressed in tailored suits and exuding an air of quiet confidence. The assistant followed them in, a younger woman with sharp eyes and a well-coiffed bun. Without a word, the assistant moved around the table, placing a sleek, black velvet bag in front of each person. The bag had a subtle gold embroidery of the Eclat de Luxe logo, an elegant touch. As she handed one to Lena, the assistant’s movements were precise, almost ritualistic, as though presenting the brand’s newest creation. The assistant paused for a moment, giving a meaningful look to the group before she spoke.

“Inside,” she said with a quiet but sure voice. “Is the newest scent we are preparing for release. Velours Mystique was a hit but this…” She hesitated for a moment, a knowing smile tugging at the corner of her lips. “This one will take the market by storm.” Lena’s curiosity piqued as she carefully opened the bag. Inside was a sleek, minimalistic bottle, its glass a deep shade of midnight blue, with an iridescent shimmer that almost seemed to dance in the light. The top was silver, polished to a mirror like sheen and the scent already lingered faintly in the air. It was subtle yet intense, a blend of something floral, warm and undeniably seductive. The assistant gave a small nod, and as the group took in the bottles, she added.

"We've carefully chosen this scent to embody Eclat de Luxe's next phase, We hope that our new scent *La Cle* is the key within your campaign ideas.

Lena studied the bottle, the weight of the opportunity was now clear. This wasn't just another client, this was a brand on the verge of something bigger and she was about to present her vision for it. Her laptop screen flickered to life, showing the opening slide of her presentation. She could feel the eyes of the room turn toward her. It was her moment to make an impact. Lena took a deep breath, standing confidently in front of the large conference room monitor. She adjusted her blouse and, with a subtle nod, started her presentation. The screen behind her shifted to the first slide, an elegant, minimalist design with the Eclat de Luxe logo in gold.

"Good afternoon everyone," she began, her voice ready and steady.

"Thank you for giving us the opportunity to collaborate with such a prestigious brand. Today we're excited to showcase our vision for your upcoming launch. Velours Mystique's successor Le Cle." She paused for a moment to let the weight of her words settle in among the room.

"This scent, as you've just introduced, isn't just another luxury fragrance. It's a statement, it's a journey and we believe the campaign should reflect that." She clicked the remote and the screen changed to a visual of a luxurious, soft blurred imagery, glistening lights at night, draped velvet curtains and delicate floating petals. A sense of mystery and allure hung in the air.

"This campaign is built on three core pillars" Lena continued, her tone clear and confident.

"Elegance, intrigue and transformation" We want your consumers to feel like they're stepping into something exclusive, something more than just a fragrance. A symbol of refinement and timeless beauty." The next slide appeared, showing potential ad concepts, models draped in flowing goths, their faces partially hidden in shadow, gazing off into the distance with a look that was equal parts confident and enigmatic.

"We've chosen to lean into the brand's established identity, Luxury, opulence, sophistication but with an added layer of mystery and allure. These ads will focus on the sensory experience, playing with light and shadow, texture and colour."

Lena clicked again, and the slide changed to a mood board filled with deep jewel tones, dark metallics and imagery inspired by the night sky suggesting a shift from the softer, lighter tones of Velours Mystique to something more powerful and exclusive.

"Our creative direction," she said, gesturing toward the mood board, "takes inspiration from the scent itself. Deep, mysterious and a little unpredictable. We envision striking, minimalist sets, contrasts of light and dark, and luxurious textures that almost evoke the feeling of the perfume itself"

She glanced at the Eclat de Luxe team, watching for reactions. The board members seemed intrigued, their eyes shifting from the slides to each other, communicating silently as Lena continued.

"And of course," she added, "we can't forget the importance of digital and social media engagement. This campaign won't just be about print or TV ads. We're looking at a 360-degree approach, with targeted social media teasers, behind the scenes content, and interactive online experiences that immerse your audience in the world of Eclat De Luxe. A perfume this captivating deserves more than just a traditional ad. It deserves to be an experience." She clicked the remote once more, and the final slide appeared, statistic and analytics showcasing engagement projections, brand growth and potential ROI based on similar luxury brand campaigns.

Lena finished the presentation with a slide featuring an image of a perfume bottle, a clean, bold shot that captured it's elegance and mystery, surrounded by rich textures and soft lighting. She turned back to face the group, offering a confident smile.

"In short, we believe this campaign will elevate Eclat De Luxe to new heights, we're ready to create something that's as unforgettable as the scent itself."

Marina, who had been silently observing, nodded in approval. The board members exchanged looks, some smiling, others deep in thought.

"So, any questions?" Lena asked, her voice calm, despite the flutter in her chest. One of the board members, a middle aged man with sharp features, spoke.

"I think we're aligned on the overall vision, your idea's for the campaign align with what we were hoping for, but I do wonder how we can amplify the exclusivity of the brand without alienating our loyal customers."

Lena smiled, prepared for this question. She had anticipated it.

"That's a great point. The key is balancing the prestige while still making the brand feel accessible. We can focus on intimate, personalized experiences for our high end clients, while offering limited-edition collections to create that sense of exclusivity. This way, we maintain the luxurious feel but also invite customers to feel like they're part of something special."

Another board member, a woman with long dark hair and elegant glasses, nodded thoughtfully. "That sounds promising. What are your thoughts on the timing of the campaign launch?"

Lena glanced at the timeline slide she'd prepared and pulled it up on her laptop screen for everyone to see.

"We're looking at a full launch around late October, just in time for the holiday season. That gives us enough time for a build-up through exclusive teasers, pop-up events, and influencer engagement, culminating in a VIP event to reveal the full collection."

There were murmurs of approval from the board as Lena continued, confidently navigating the rest of the discussion. The questions were all about refining the details, but no one had any major objections. It was going better than she had hoped. As the meeting drew to a close, one of the board members, a man with a neatly trimmed beard and an air of authority, spoke up. "We're on board with the direction. Let's move forward and start aligning resources." Marina, who had been silently observing, stood up and walked to the front of the room, taking the lead with her usual poised demeanour.

"Well, I think we can all agree that Lena's done an excellent job here," she said smoothly, her tone warm but assertive.

"We're thrilled with the campaign direction, and I'm confident we'll have great success together. But before we jump into the work, I'd like to invite all of you to lunch." She turned to the board, her smile wide. "There's a new restaurant near Canary Wharf that's been getting rave reviews. It's on me. Consider it a small celebration before the real work begins."

The board members exchanged appreciative glances. "That sounds wonderful," one of them said with a smile.

Marina nodded, then turned back to Lena, her tone shifting to something more direct and commanding. "And you," she added, locking eyes with Lena, "get it done. Or get it ready for next week. We don't have time to waste."

Lena took a steadying breath, giving a quick nod in response. "Understood," she said, her voice firm.

With that, the meeting came to a close, the board members rising from their seats. Marina led them out of the room, and Lena followed behind, mentally preparing for the mountain of work ahead. The presentation had gone well, but as always, the real challenge was just beginning. As the door clicked shut behind them, Lena took a deep breath, gathering her thoughts before heading back to her desk. She pulled up her calendar, checking for the next urgent task meanwhile, across the city,

Dan was winding down his own day. The office had been a whirlwind of meetings, product testing, and last-minute adjustments, but it had been relatively straightforward. His team was working on a new line for one of the major UK retailers, and everything seemed to be on track. Still, the long hours and constant pressure were starting to wear on him. He glanced at his watch. It was already past six, and the thought of heading home to the cramped flat wasn't exactly inspiring. He rubbed the back of his neck, scrolling through his phone to check for any updates. No texts from Lena, it had been a couple of hours since she left for her meeting and he wasn't sure if she'd be home early or if she'd be caught up in more work. As the last of his colleagues filtered out of the office, Dan grabbed his bag and headed out, trying to shake the weight of the day. As Dan walked toward the elevator, his colleague, Imran, jogged up to him with a grin.

"Hey, Kersey, You and Lena up for dinner and drinks tomorrow night?" Imran asked, slinging an arm casually around Dan's shoulder. "It's Friday, and we've got that big showcase coming up with the company owner next week. Thought it'd be a good way to unwind and celebrate before the grind sets in." Dan hesitated for a moment, considering. It had been a long week, and while he wasn't sure if Lena would be up for it, he didn't want to disappoint Imran or his wife, who was always up for a night out. "I'll ask Lena," Dan said with a shrug.

"I'll let you know tomorrow morning." Imran nodded, giving him a thumbs up.

"Sounds good. Look forward to it, don't leave us hanging mate."

"Don't worry, I won't." Dan replied, forcing a smile as he made his way to the elevator, his mind already shifting back to Lena and the plans for the evening. As he made his way home, the hum of the city around him doing little to quiet his mind. The train ride felt longer than usual, but he couldn't shake the feeling of wanting to get home. As soon as he found a spot to stand, he pulled out his phone and sent Lena a quick message.

'Hey, are you home yet? Any idea what you want for dinner? x'

He tapped his fingers on the phone screen, while the train rattled along the tracks. After a few minutes, his phone buzzed with a reply from her.

Lena responded. *'I'm in an Uber, just turning onto our street now. I haven't decided yet, what do you feel like? X'*

Dan smiled, tapping out a response while the train passed through the tunnels. *'I was thinking pizza, or maybe a Chinese takeaway? Whatever your in the mood for x'*

He slipped his phone back into his pocket and looked out the window, the city lights flickering. After a couple of stops, his phone buzzed again with another message from Lena. *'Pizza sounds good x'*

Dan grinned, feeling a sense of relief and familiarity in the simplicity of it all. He quickly typed back before the train pulled into his stop.

'Perfect, I'll grab one on the way home. See you soon. x'

With that, he slid his phone back into his pocket and stepped off the train, walking home with the comfort of knowing it would be a quiet night with Lena. Dan stopped at the local Tesco Local on his way home, grabbing a pizza and six pack of beer, along with a few other essentials for the evening. As he made his way to the self checkout, he paused, remembering Lena's bottle of red. Turning back, he picked up a bottle of her favourite Merlot, the perfect accompaniment to their pizza. Satisfied, he paid and made his way home, ready for a quiet night in.

CHAPTER TWO

The morning slid in like a shrug, pale light across the ceiling. The slow crackle of the radiator, the soft rattle of Dan's teaspoon against ceramic. Lena lay still for a while, blinking at the corner of the wardrobe where one of her coats hung slightly off-centre. Her mouth was dry, that sour, woolly kind of dryness. A gift from the half bottle of red she'd polished off after dinner. Her head felt a touch too thick for the light outside. Not a hangover, exactly. Just, dulled. From the kitchen, Dan called gently.

"We're having dinner with Imran tonight."

She frowned. "Imran?"

"Colleague. From the new team. Invited us last minute just thought it might be nice."

Lena exhaled through her nose, not quite a sigh. She swung her legs out of bed and stood, the cold floor pressing up through her socks.

"You're always talking about work."

"I'll pay," Dan offered, a peace flag in the form of convenience. "Proper dinner me."

She gave him a look as she passed, already pulling her hair back into a bun. "From our one overflowing treasure chest of a bank account, you mean."

Dan grinned. “Exactly.”
She leaned down and kissed his cheek, warm, faintly stubbled before disappearing into the bathroom, leaving steam and the faint sound of her electric toothbrush behind. By the time she sat down to open her laptop, he was dressed and ready, in that smart-casual way he saved for Fridays. She glanced up at him as he slipped his keys into his jacket pocket.
“Meet me at work?” he asked, halfway out the door.
Lena nodded, eyes flicking back to her inbox. “Yeah. Text me where.”
She heard the door click shut. The flat sagged into quiet but not for long. A few seconds later, the latch rattled again, and Dan’s footsteps hurried back across the worn floorboards. Lena glanced up as he started rummaging through the stack of takeaway menus, bills, and crumpled letters on the coffee table.
"You already trying to get out of paying for dinner?" she called over her shoulder.
Dan grinned without looking at her, the corner of his mouth twitching. He found his wallet wedged under an old utility bill and held it up like a prize. "Wouldn’t dream of it," he said. He kissed the air in her direction, lazy, affectionate and was gone again, properly this time.
The door thudded closed. The kettle clicked itself off. Lena sighed, adjusted her laptop slightly and clicked into her browser. Deadlines. She pulled up her content planner first, a pink spreadsheet blinking with reminders. **#NewSeasonGlow**, **#SundayReset**, **#WeekendSelfCare** brand campaigns she needed to post on Saturday and Sunday. Not hers, she managed them for bigger names who couldn’t be bothered to schedule their own captions anymore. Still, it paid. She clicked into Canva. Half-listening to the world outside: a scooter tearing past, a baby crying two floors down, the endless low hum of city life that somehow managed to make the silence feel louder. She had three drafts to approve, five posts to schedule, and an overdue invoice to chase. Weekend plans, she thought dryly.

The flat faded behind him as Dan stepped out into the morning, shrugging his jacket higher against the chill. It wasn’t cold exactly, but the wind dragged yesterday's warmth out of the streets. He slipped his headphones in, thumbed a song at random from Spotify, something upbeat enough to kickstart him but familiar enough not to demand attention as he walked the short distance to the station. The train was late again. He boarded with the usual crush of elbows and backpacks, standing wedged near the door, balancing his coffee cup like an amateur tightrope walker. Someone's newspaper brushed his arm. A woman laughed too loudly into her phone, normal. As the city blurred by, he half-listened to the lyrics about getting out, starting fresh, something optimistic enough to make him smirk. It was still early by the time he reached his stop. He wandered into the corner coffee shop out of habit, shoulder to shoulder with other office bodies chasing caffeine. The line wasn't bad. He ordered a flat white without thinking, eyes flickering toward the pastry cabinet. Croissants, almond buns, a tray of custard tarts. His stomach growled but he hesitated. Sampling duty this morning. The companies new Christmas range, apparently. All tinsel-drenched mince pies and novelty puddings. Dan pocketed the thought of a pastry, waited for his name to be barked awkwardly by a teenager in a branded cap, and took his coffee back out into the thinning morning crowd. He walked the last few streets toward the office slowly, sipping, letting the buzz of London fold back around him. The building rose up in its usual concrete glory, stained glass doors, cracked pavement, the familiar half-lit corridor smell of microwaved noodles and printer ink. Dan shifted the coffee to his other hand and buzzed himself through, nodding vaguely to the receptionist who never looked up. The lights always flickered near the lifts, one overhead tube forever on the brink of giving out. He took the stairs instead, three flights, the same chipped edge on the second-floor banister catching his sleeve like it always did. Inside the office, it was warm in the way open-plan spaces always were, the heat of too many machines and not enough windows. Coats were piled on chairs, a few early birds hunched over their monitors, already lost in spreadsheets or Slack threads. Someone's Spotify bled faintly through tinny headphones. Dan passed the communal table, and headed for the kitchen corner. He peeled the lid from his coffee like it might contain more energy than it actually did. The trays were already waiting, stacked neatly beside the sink, each one marked in thick black Sharpie:

spiced, ginger & rum, vegan, boozy option. He let out a slow breath through his nose. Christmas in April. Of course. He pulled on the disposable gloves from the box on the counter and tied the branded apron around his waist with a practised knot. The fabric was thin and smelled faintly of whatever had been cooked last. Behind him, drawers opened and shut. Someone whistled. Footsteps padded across linoleum.

"You're early," came a voice over his shoulder, Jamie, from comms, in his usual oversized hoodie and lanyard tangle. "Trying to get first dibs on the truffle logs and pigs in blankets?"

Dan half-smiled. "Just needed coffee, and peace. Mostly coffee."

Jamie grinned and wandered off, already calling across the room to someone else. Dan stood for a moment, the tray in front of him, the silence creeping in now that the initial rush was over. He looked down at the samples, the sugar-dusted edges already sweating inside their foil cups. This wasn't what he pictured doing at thirty-two but it paid, very well and if he could get the bonus, get Christmas wrapped early, maybe they'd finally get ahead of the credit card. Lena could take that short course she kept bringing up and then brushing off. He popped one of the mince pies in his mouth, chewing absently. The filling was hot, sweeter than it should be. He made a note on the clipboard beside him, Pastry too dense. Cardamom harsh and reached for the next one. He made it through three more pastry samples, all variations on the same spiced-fruit theme before his mouth started to feel like the inside of a festive candle. The final Christmas range was due to be signed off by the end of next week. Today's tasting was part of a seasonal push. To get flavours locked in before the end-of-April marketing brief. Each tiny pie, each ginger biscuit twist, each sugar-dusted tartlet had been through at least five iterations already, cinnamon ratios, filling consistency, whether to edge the shortbread in dark chocolate or crushed candy cane. Dan logged every note on the shared spreadsheet: crust texture, sweetness balance, whether something had the right mouthfeel. A word he still hated saying out loud, even after four years in food development. Sometimes he tried to write comments that sounded like he cared. Other times, he didn't bother. He rinsed his mouth with cold water, reached for the next bite, something labelled Festive Clementine & Sloe Gin and chewed without looking up.

"You're not slowing down, are you?" came a voice behind him.

Dan turned as Imran approached, coffee in one hand, tablet tucked under his arm. He wore his usual soft blazer and slightly-too-long trousers, always a bit creased, always slightly warm-looking. Reliable.

Dan wiped his gloves on a napkin. "Powering through. Might never eat again."

Imran smiled. "We're still on for tonight?"

"Yeah," Dan said. "Lena's meeting me here. I promised her actual food."

"She'll like my wife," Imran said. "Sharp, very opinionated. Doesn't hold back."

Dan laughed softly. "Are you married to my girlfriend?"

They talked briefly about timings, parking, something about a bottle of wine. Imran made a joke about turkey-stuffed cannelloni being rejected last year, and Dan promised to forget that suggestion had ever existed. As Imran wandered back toward his desk, another colleague slid into view. *Joseph*. He wasn't on Dan's team directly, but they'd worked together during the Easter range. He carried a clipboard and a slightly wary expression, like he was always three seconds away from apologising for something no one remembered.

"Hi," he said, stopping near the table.

"Hey." Dan cleared a few empty cups from the tray, suddenly feeling like the apron made him look like a children's party caterer. "Want in on the sugar spiral?"

Joseph gave a tight smile. "Already been. Ginger and rum's strong this year."

"Too strong?" Dan asked, hoping to keep the tone light.

"No," he said quickly, eyes flicking to his, then down again.

"No, it's good. Just… memorable." Something hung in the air between them. Not tension, exactly. Just awkwardness. He lingered a moment longer, then gave a quick nod and moved on. Dan stood still for a second, eyes narrowing slightly. He went back to the samples, but didn't take another bite right away.

After his last bite, Dan rinsed the last of the foil trays, logged his final notes and peeled off the apron with a quiet grunt of relief. The sugar crash was setting in now, a syrupy lull behind his eyes. He glanced at the clock. Two hours until he needed to meet Lena downstairs. He debated doing a bit more work, then opened his inbox and stared at it blankly. Nothing urgent. Somewhere nearby, Joseph laughed too brightly at something. Imran's voice carried over the partition, talking about allergens and promotional flyers. Dan shut the browser tab and reached for his half-drunk coffee, now cold and bitter. He drank it anyway. He glanced at the time, then out the window, grey clouds drifting fast over the skyline, the day slipping past in slow inches.

Somewhere across the city, Lena was wrapped up her own kind of chaos, juggling six tabs and forgetting to eat again. The flat was warmer now, sunlight pooling across the scuffed wood floor, windows cracked just enough to let the city noise filter in. Lena sat cross-legged on the sofa with her laptop balanced against one knee, a half-eaten oat bar forgotten beside her. Her third cup of coffee steamed faintly on the table. She hadn't moved in about an hour. The final draft of Saturday's campaign post blinked back at her. Bright colours, big fonts, a carousel of curated skincare products she didn't actually use. She hovered the cursor over the *schedule* button, then clicked without thinking. Done. A breath slipped out as she leaned back, head tipping against the sofa. Her ponytail caught awkwardly beneath her shoulder, but she didn't fix it. A delivery van reversed somewhere down the street. A dog barked, sharp and bored. Two reels still needed editing, and Sunday's caption sat half-written in her drafts. It could wait. Maybe tomorrow. Maybe after dinner. Lena checked the time. Sat a moment longer. Then, with a small groan, she unfolded herself from the sofa and padded toward the bathroom. Water ran hot while her hoodie hit the floor in a soft heap. Steam curled up the tiled walls, fogging the mirror before she even stepped under the stream. The rush muffled the rest of the flat, the rest of the week, the weight behind her eyes. It was Friday. She was tired but she liked Imran, or what she remembered of him and if nothing else, it would be nice to eat something that hadn't come from the freezer. A towel wrapped snug around her chest, she wiped a clear patch in the mirror and met her reflection. Not bad. Tired, but not bad. She moved into the bedroom, brushing fingertips across the hanging row of shirts and jeans, pausing at the black dress she kept for nights that weren't fancy, but still deserved effort. Tonight felt like one of those. The towel dropped to the floor as Lena pulled open her top drawer, fingers brushing past everyday cotton and old gym socks until they found what she was looking for, deep red lace, soft and slinky. She smiled to herself, slipping into the lingerie, smoothing the fine straps over her shoulders, adjusting the band until it sat just right. Perfect. No one else would know but Dan might, *eventually*. She sat down at the vanity, towel-twisted hair dripping onto her bare knees. Quick strokes of the brush, a little styling cream raked through then the careful heat of the hairdryer. Her hair fell into soft, deliberate waves, framing her face. Not too much, effortless enough to look like she hadn't tried. She kept her makeup simple, a flick of liner, a hint of highlighter across her cheeks, the kind of soft-focus polish that said Friday night without shouting it. Standing, she slipped into the black dress, the familiar weight of it sliding into place over silk and skin. It hugged her waist, skimmed her hips, the neckline dipping just enough to draw the eye without begging for it. Before she reached for her boots, Lena caught herself in the mirror. Impulse flickered. She picked up her phone from the bed, turned slightly, one hand on her hip, angling the camera just right, enough curve, enough shadow, the lace peeking out from the fall of black fabric where the dress hadn't yet been zipped. *Click*. She grinned at the image, flirty, cheeky, but still tasteful and opened WhatsApp. Sending him a *view once image.*

"Depending on how good dinner is tonight... you might get dessert x"

Winking emoji, She hit send. Tucked her phone away and zipped up the dress properly, still smiling.

Across the city, Dan's phone buzzed on his desk, a low vibration against laminate and leftover crumbs. Dan glanced around, the office chatter low and harmless and flipped the screen up.

WhatsApp: Lena sent a view once image.

He tapped it open casually, shielding the screen instinctively as the photo loaded. The breath he didn't realise he was holding left him in a sharp exhale. The image vanished after a heartbeat, burned into memory. A slow, wide grin spread across his face. He set the phone face-down, cleared his throat, and tried to look interested in the festive cupcake discussion Jamie and Joseph were having two desks over. *'Focus, mate. Just get through the next hour.'* Dan leaned back in his chair, already thinking about later. About Lena in that dress. About what might be waiting once dinner was done. Maybe it was going to be a very good night after all. He had just started shutting down his computer when Imran appeared at the edge of his desk, a lowball glass in hand, the kind with weight, half full of something amber and neat. The ice clinked as he tilted it slightly.

"You all set?" Imran asked. His jacket was draped over one shoulder, tie already loosened like he was halfway into the evening.

Dan nodded, sliding his laptop into the canvas bag beneath his desk. "Just about."

Imran took a sip, watching him with a faint smile. "You sure that's what you're wearing?"

Dan looked down at himself, smart-casual, nothing dramatic. "Should I be worried?"

Imran's grin widened. "Only if you're allergic to expensive things. I booked somewhere my wife's been nagging me about for weeks. Had to check my credit card limit before I hit confirm."

Dan gave a short laugh, half-surprised. "You didn't mention this was one of those places."

"You'll be fine," Imran said. "Just act like you belong and don't question anything on the wine list." He turned, heading for the lift, voice trailing behind him. "And for god's sake, don't order a lager."

Dan watched him go, then let out a slow breath. Dinner somewhere like that wasn't exactly in the plan, not when rent was looming and the joint account had dipped below the comfortable line again. The real focus was next week. If the supermarket pitch landed, the exclusive supplier deal they'd been pushing for all quarter, it would mean a serious step up. A name on a contract. A bonus he could actually use. He was ready. The pitch was solid. Feedback had been strong. He pulled on his coat, checked his phone, and swung the bag over his shoulder. The office was thinning out, lights dimming as the last few screens flickered.

Outside, the air had cooled just enough to lift the edge of Dan's collar as he stepped onto the pavement. Across the street, Lena was waiting. She stood beneath a soft-glowing streetlamp, the hem of her black dress catching in the breeze. Hair styled in gentle waves, makeup flawless without trying too hard, she looked like she'd been poured into the evening. Not overdressed, not showy. Just right. Dan crossed toward her, a small, involuntary smile tugging at his mouth.

"You look…" He paused, leaned in, kissed her lightly. "You smell divine."

Lena arched a brow, amused. "Sample from a client. It's not out yet, thought I'd give it a trial run."

He gave a low whistle, still looking at her. "You could sell it single-handedly."

She smirked, slipping her arm through his. "I usually do."

A few paces ahead, Imran stood on the curb with his wife, petite and elegant, her coat a soft cream that didn't look cheap. She was curled into him, laughing at something he'd said. The kind of couple who knew how to present themselves, close, unforced.

"Ah, there they are," Imran called, spotting them. "Perfect timing."

As Dan and Lena joined them, he gestured. "This is Zoya, my better half."

"Lovely to meet you," Lena said, offering her hand.

Zoya returned it with warmth. "And you. I've heard good things."

"Only good?" Lena teased.

Zoya smiled. "So far."

Imran glanced at his phone. "Our ride's just around the corner."

Moments later, a black Mercedes pulled up, clean, quiet, nothing flashy but clearly not cheap. They climbed in, Dan and Lena in the back, Zoya and Imran up front. The restaurant was tucked down a quiet side street in Marylebone, all soft exterior lighting and tall, frosted windows. The name was etched discreetly into the glass, the kind of place that didn't need to shout. Inside, it was all warm tones and low light, cutlery that clinked softly and service that moved like choreography. Not a single glance was thrown at Dan's boots or Imran's unbuttoned collar. If anything, they fit in just fine. They were seated near the back, the table already set with polished glassware and bread plates that looked like ceramic art. A waiter filled their glasses without asking. Water arrived with lemon slices. Everything moved smoothly. Menus were handed around. Orders placed. Conversation picked up like it had already been flowing. Zoya leaned toward Lena as the starters arrived, voice warm but inquisitive.

"So where are you two living?"

"Peckham," Lena said, pausing to butter her bread. "Just off Rye Lane. It's loud, but we like it. We're renting for now, trying to save for a deposit."

"Oh, you're braver than me," Zoya said, with a laugh. "We almost moved south once. Couldn't handle the trains."

"They're not great," Lena admitted. "But the flat's decent, and there's a little park nearby. Enough space to breathe, you know?"

Zoya nodded. "And are you thinking of staying?"

"For a while," Lena said. "We're planning ahead slowly. Mortgage, maybe even a dog. One thing at a time."

Dan listened quietly, sipping his wine. He glanced at Lena, something soft flickering behind his eyes. The mains arrived, delicate, delicious, plated like art. The wine flowed steadily. Imran and Dan talked shop now and then, careful not to dominate the table. Zoya recounted a disastrous client pitch from the week before, which had them all laughing. The waiter returned without needing to be called. It was the kind of evening that felt effortless, until the bill, at least but that would come later. For now, it was warmth and full glasses. Easy company. A night that, for once, felt a little bit like the life they were all aiming for. The waiter returned with a warm smile, a polished notepad in hand.

"Would anyone care to see the dessert menu?" he asked, his eyes drifting to Lena first.

She glanced across the table. Zoya gave a little shrug, already half-reaching for her wine. Imran nodded politely, and Dan gave a short laugh.

"Why not," he said. "Let's see what indulgence looks like tonight."

The menus came quickly, thin, dark leather covers with elegant embossed lettering. Inside: delicate descriptions of crème Brulé, winter puddings, and a rich chocolate fondant that boasted a molten centre timed to the second. The kind of things you tell yourself you don't need, then order anyway. Conversation picked up again, casual and looping, as each of them took turns scanning the menu.

"Did you sort that issue with the menu?" Imran asked, reaching for his water glass.

Dan wiped the corner of his mouth with a napkin.

“Finally, said it was an ‘administrative oversight.’ Took three emails and two calls to hear that.”

“That sounds about right.” Imran shook his head, amused. “Classic.”

Zoya leaned in slightly toward Lena. “How’s work going? You’re still managing the content campaigns, right?”

Lena nodded, setting her dessert menu down.

“Yeah. Still wrangling brand accounts for influencers who wouldn’t know their own passwords if their lives depended on it. But it pays. I’ve got a shoot tomorrow actually, ‘Sunday Reset’ nonsense. Candles, linen robes, faux-spontaneous smiles.”

Zoya chuckled. “I’ve seen those. Always makes me feel like I should be steaming oranges in a ceramic bowl.”

“You’d be amazed how many bowls of oranges I’ve moved around for the perfect shot,” Lena said. “Dan caught me trying to arrange ‘casual’ laundry the other day.”

Dan lifted his eyebrows. “It wasn’t casual. It was staged chaos.”

They all laughed, warm and honest, the kind that settled easily after two courses and a shared bottle of wine. The restaurant around them hummed softly, cutlery, low conversation, the faintest thread of jazz. The desserts, when they came, were works of art. Zoya’s pear tarte tatin glistened under its glaze, Imran’s selection of sorbets came nestled in tiny silver cups, and Dan’s chocolate fondant let loose a perfect river of molten richness as his spoon broke the surface. Lena picked the fig tart, not out of hunger, but curiosity, and finished nearly all of it. As the final bites disappeared and the wine ran low, the warmth between them softened into something quieter. That lull just before a night turns toward its end. The waiter returned, a discreet slip in hand.

“Whenever you’re ready,” he said.

Dan reached for it, but Imran was faster, already pulling out his wallet.

“No, let me,” Imran said.

Dan shook his head, holding up a hand. “Split it.”

“You got the wine.”

“Exactly. You get mains and dessert. Call it even.”

The two men exchanged glances, a brief, silent negotiation.

"You're insufferable," Imran muttered, relenting with a grin.

"Yet here we are," Dan replied.

As the card machine beeped and receipts were printed, Lena leaned toward Zoya with a half-smile.

"They always do this?"

"Every single time," Zoya said, swirling the last of her wine.

"It's like a soft-bellied duel." Lena laughed.

"God forbid one of them pays without making it into a noble sacrifice."

A few minutes later, they rose from the table, coats collected, scarves untwisted from chair backs. The restaurant doors swung open with a soft hush of air, and the cold welcomed them like a returning guest. Marylebone at night shimmered with subtle elegance. Golden light spilled from lampposts and shopfronts, cobbled side streets curling into shadow. The restaurant's windows glowed behind them, opaque with condensation. Across the road, a florist's wreaths hung in a window, deep reds and evergreens wrapped in twine. The faint scent of woodsmoke hung in the air. Zoya pulled her coat tighter around her. "This street always feels like a movie set."

"It's too quiet to be real," Lena agreed.

"Or too expensive to be honest," Dan muttered, earning a nudge in the ribs from her elbow.

Imran's phone buzzed. "That'll be ours."

A sleek black Uber rounded the corner, headlights soft against the wet road. Imran opened the door for Zoya, then turned back briefly. "Thanks for coming. It was good. Let's do it again, next time, our place."

"Looking forward to it," Dan said.

Zoya leaned in and kissed Lena's cheek. "Lovely to meet you properly. We'll text soon, yeah?"

"Definitely."

The door shut softly, and the car pulled away, red lights glowing against the rain-damp tarmac.

Lena and Dan stood on the pavement alone, their breath fogging faintly in the air Their own Uber was still a few minutes away, typical. The silence was different now. Not awkward. The world around them thinned out. A cyclist passed, a dog barked twice from a nearby mews, a man stood across the road lighting a cigarette under a streetlamp. Time seemed to slow, caught in the hush of an expensive postcode at rest.

"That was… really nice," Lena said, voice low.

Dan looked sideways at her, hands tucked into his pockets.

"You seemed happy."

"I was." She paused, then glanced at him.

"Thank you, for dinner." He shrugged slightly.

"You don't have to thank me."

"It wasn't exactly a cheap night."

He gave her a soft look, one corner of his mouth lifting. "You deserve it."

Lena smiled, not wide, not showy. Just a curl of something genuine. "You always say that."

"And I always mean it."

She reached for his hand, threading her fingers through his in the pocket of his coat. It was a quiet intimacy, one no passer-by could see. Warm, steady, familiar. She leaned in and kissed him, slow, lingering, just enough pressure to make it count. Their Uber pulled up just as they broke apart. Dan opened the door for her.

"After you."

"Charmer," she said softly, brushing past him into the car.

He climbed in after her, the door clicking shut behind them. As they pulled away, Lena looked out the window, watching the streetlamps blur, the wreaths and windows retreating behind them. A good night. The kind that almost made her forget the rest of the week. Almost. The Uber moved smoothly through Marylebone, tyres hushed against the road as the city blurred by outside. Lena leaned her head back against the seat, eyes half-lidded, the wine still warm in her blood. Dan sat beside her, one leg angled toward her, one hand resting loosely on her knee. The air in the car was quiet, no music, just the low thrum of the engine and the occasional turn signal clicking like a metronome. Outside, London unfolded in soft, cinematic fragments. Townhouses with lit windows like silent stage sets. A cyclist weaving through the narrow gap between taxi and curb. Neon signs from late-night chemists and wine shops flickering against the misted glass. The lights along Oxford Street were still strung up in hopeful strands, even if

Christmas had long passed. A black cab pulled alongside them at a junction, a woman inside laughing into her phone, eyes crinkled in the passing light. They cut through Soho next, glimpses of people spilling from bars, coats unbuttoned, collars up against the breeze. A man with a guitar stood on a corner, strumming something slow and bluesy, his case open for coins. Lena watched him disappear behind the glow of a noodle bar. Everything felt just a little unreal, the wine, the glow of the streets, the steady hum of movement carrying them forward. By the time they crossed the river and wound toward Peckham, the roads had quieted. South London moved slower at night, not asleep, but hushed. A fox darted across Rye Lane ahead of them, bold and street-smart. They passed shuttered barbershops and chicken joints still flickering with fluorescent buzz. An off-license kept one light burning behind foggy glass. Home was close.

The Uber pulled up just off Rye Lane, slowing to a halt between the flickering sign of the vape lounge and the ever-lit front of the chicken shop. The windows of the nail salon below their flat were dark but the “Open” sign still glowed lazily in red, as if the staff were trying to will another walk-in before close. A damp heat clung to the pavement, bin bags stacked by the alley, the smell of fried batter hanging in the air. Dan slid out of the car first, then turned to help Lena. She stepped out carefully, blinking against the fluorescent haze of the street.

“Two glasses too far,” she mumbled, steadying herself against him.

“I told you not to finish Zoya’s wine.”

“She offered.”

They made their way toward the entrance wedged between the vape lounge and the salon’s fire exit, an unmarked metal door that always stuck at the base. Dan gave it a shove with his shoulder while Lena fumbled through her bag for the key. Once it clicked open, a waft of chemical citrus and old concrete greeted them, the signature scent of the stairwell. The hallway bulb was out again, casting the first few steps into gloom. The hum of the street faded behind them.

“God, I forgot how many stairs this place has,” Lena groaned, heels in hand now, climbing barefoot.

Her tights caught slightly on the edge of the concrete as she moved. Dan’s voice floated up behind her.

"Just think of it as cardio." Dan said

"Cardio shouldn't smell like acrylics and damp."

The second floor landing welcomed them with its usual creak. Their door was covered in scuff marks from years of deliveries and had a sticker someone had tried to peel off, half a love heart, faded. Lena unlocked it in two turns. Inside, the air was warm and familiar, a mix of lingering incense, dust, and the faint ghost of the laundry detergent she'd used earlier. She'd made a last-minute attempt to tidy: the coffee table was clear except for one mug and a crumpled tissue, the sofa cushions rearranged into something that vaguely resembled order. The kitchen counter still held two empty mugs and a wilting banana, but it wasn't chaos. Just lived-in. Dan kicked the door shut with his heel. His jacket hit the back of the sofa. Lena dropped her shoes by the door and turned toward him. They stood there for a second, flushed and breathless from the climb, wine-flushed, Friday-loose, staring at each other like they hadn't kissed in weeks. Then she stepped forward and kissed him hard, hands gripping the sides of his face. He caught her waist, pulled her closer, stumbling back into the tiny living space until they hit the edge of the sofa. She laughed against his mouth, biting back a gasp as they broke apart just enough to breathe.

"Bedroom," she murmured.

Dan nodded, dizzy. They half-tripped their way down the short hallway, one bedroom, barely wide enough for two people, knocking into the frame as Lena reached back to shove the door open. Dan landed on the bed with a soft thud, one hand catching the crumpled throw beneath him. The bedroom light, one low bulb in a paper shade, cast soft shadows across the far wall. The curtains were still open a crack, letting in the muted glow of the streetlamp below, the occasional headlight washing silver across the floorboards. Lena stood above him, still, the room's hush suddenly electric. She reached behind her and slowly tugged the zipper down. The black dress slipped over her hips and fell in a slow, deliberate drop to the floor. Beneath it, the red lace clung like a whisper, delicate straps, scalloped edges, sheer in all the right places. The kind of thing you didn't wear unless you wanted to be remembered in it. Dan's chest rose, mouth slightly open.

"Holy…" he breathed.

Lena stepped forward, straddling his legs at the edge of the bed. She leaned down, pressing her mouth to his, slow at first, exploratory then deeper, her fingers already in his shirt buttons. She kissed like she was anchoring herself to him, threading through the wine and the adrenaline and the laugh she'd nearly choked on coming up the stairs. His hands moved instinctively, finding her back, her hips. She was warm, skin flushed from the wine, from the walk, from the anticipation she'd been nursing since she'd hit send on that photo hours earlier. Dan's shirt came off clumsily, one button giving way with a soft POP. Lena didn't care. She wanted skin. Contact. She slid her hands over his chest, nails grazing down his stomach, feeling him tense beneath her touch.

"You're" he started, but her mouth was already on his again..

She kissed him hard, pulling him into her, letting the weight of the evening, the wine, the want all push to the surface. Then she pulled back slightly, her lips brushing his jaw, her breath warm against his ear. Her fingers curled into his hair, guiding him downwards. Wordless, certain. Dan hesitated just a second, not out of doubt, but reverence, then followed her lead, lowering himself between her thighs as she fell back against the mattress with a soft gasp. The sheets were cool, but her skin burned. She reached for the headboard without thinking, back arching as his mouth met her. Dan's touch was careful but hungry, like he couldn't quite believe she was real. That this was real. That Lena, precise, dry-witted Lena, had planned this, had slipped into something she knew would leave him speechless. Her hands threaded into his hair. He moved with purpose, coaxed by her quiet sighs and the way her legs tightened around him, hips tilting instinctively. Every sound from her was encouragement. Every breath, every shift, a response.

They'd done this before, yes, but not like this, not with this kind of intention. Lena gave in to the sensation, the building pressure, the swell and release, like waves breaking one after the other. She felt herself unravel under him, breath catching on a whisper that never fully formed and still they moved. The bed creaked beneath them, the sheets twisted around their feet. Her laughter, then his. A moment of silence as she pulled him up to her again, mouths crashing, fingers frantic at his belt. The sound of a drawer handle clattering. A condom packet tearing open. The whisper of lace sliding away. When they finally came together, skin against skin, tension breaking in a wave that rolled through them both, it was with that dizzying kind of closeness that made everything else go quiet. Just them, moving as one. Mouths pressed to shoulders, fingers curling, hearts loud in their chests. Time bled out around them.

After, they lay tangled in the warm wreckage of the bed, Lena's head against his shoulder, Dan's fingers tracing lazy circles over her hip. Her hair was damp against his chest, their bodies still knotted, reluctant to separate. She let out a long, slow breath, her eyes half-lidded.

"That," she said, voice rough, "was definitely worth dessert."

Dan laughed softly, one arm tightening around her.

"You planned that," he murmured.

"Maybe."

He kissed her temple, lips warm against her skin. "I love you, you know." She didn't say anything right away. Just shifted closer, eyelids fluttering shut.

"I know," she whispered. "I do too."

The streetlamp cast its slow glow through the cracked curtains. Somewhere below, a siren wailed far off, fading into nothing. The room smelled like candlewax and sweat and cheap wine, and it felt, for one rare moment, like everything was still. Like they were safe..

CHAPTER THREE

The flat was heavy with sleep when Lena stirred, warm sheets tangled around her bare legs, the faint thud of a train passing in the distance rattling the windows. She blinked into the muted midday light leaking past the gap in the curtains. Dan was still beside her, one arm thrown across his face, his chest rising and falling in the deep, even rhythm of someone not quite ready to face the day. Lena smiled lazily to herself, stretching one arm out across the bed, feeling the soreness in her thighs, the ache of last night lingering. It wasn't often they got a full Saturday without alarms, without obligations biting at their heels. After everything, the long week, the late dinner, the wine, the way they'd fallen into each other like gravity, the lie-in felt like an earned indulgence. Eventually, the scent of the city started to creep through the cracked window: faint nail polish from the salon below, fried oil from the chicken shop two doors down, something sharp and metallic from the passing trains. South London wrapped around them like a worn-out coat. She rolled out of bed eventually, padding barefoot across the cold floorboards to the tiny kitchenette. Dan grunted into the pillow behind her, shifting but not waking. Coffee first, she decided. Always coffee first. The cafetière hissed and sputtered as she pressed it down. She set out two mugs, pouring the dark liquid with steady hands, letting the ritual of it nudge her into wakefulness. A glance at her phone told her she had an hour before she needed to head out for the photoshoot. Enough time to drink this slowly, maybe even shower. The message from the photographer popped up just after she took her first sip:

Running a little late. 1:30pm start instead. Studio just off Hackney Downs.

Lena sighed into her coffee. Hackney wasn't exactly next door. She'd need to catch the Overground and hope it wasn't delayed. Again. Still, it gave her a little breathing room. Behind her, Dan finally stirred, groaning as he sat up, raking a hand through his hair.

"Morning," he croaked, voice gravelly from sleep and too much red wine.

"Afternoon," she corrected, smiling over the rim of her mug.

He scrubbed a hand over his face, looking around the messy living room like he was surprised it hadn't cleaned itself overnight. Then he caught her eye, and for a second, the lazy grin from last night flickered back.

"You walking funny yet?" he teased, voice low. She threw a balled-up sock at him from the laundry pile.

"Asshole," she said, laughing. "Go make yourself useful, you're on croissant duty."

He groaned dramatically, but dragged himself up, pulling on the pair of jeans crumpled at the end of the bed. They moved through the flat like orbiting planets, brushing past each other, stealing lazy touches, trading yawns and smiles. No rush. Just the luxury of time. Dan returned with the croissants, slightly squashed from the paper bag, still warm enough to melt the butter she dropped onto them. Lena had moved to the sofa by then, one knee tucked under her, her mug cradled in both hands like it anchored her to the morning. The radio hummed softly from the kitchen, one of the stations that played lo-fi remixes of old soul tracks before noon.

"Got the good ones," Dan said, holding out the bag like a peace offering.

She peeked inside, nodding approvingly. "You always say that, they're never not the good ones."

They ate in easy silence, broken only by the crisp flake of pastry and the muffled shout of someone arguing below their window. The flat felt cocooned from the outside world, warm, lived-in, faintly scented by coffee, cheap fabric softener, and the ever-present hint of nail polish from downstairs.

"You sure you don't want to go out?" Lena asked, licking sugar from her thumb. "It's weirdly decent out there."

Dan leaned back with a satisfied sigh, the stretch of his limbs taking up half the sofa.

"Tempting. But I've made a promise to myself to be profoundly unproductive until at least noon."

"Living the dream."

He grinned without opening his eyes. "Manifesting my full potential."

Lena's phone buzzed against the armrest, a sharp reminder of reality. She glanced at it and groaned.

"That your cue?"

"Client pushed the shoot to 1:30. Hackney Downs," she muttered, already calculating how long it would take to drag her gear up three flights of stairs. "Sounds like hell."

"It is. But the invoice makes it slightly less hellish."

She stood, brushing pastry flakes from her lap, and wandered toward the bedroom. The familiar sounds of zippers and hangers followed, a little disorganized, a little rhythmic. Dan stayed put, flicking lazily through channels until he landed on a home renovation show he'd already seen three times. Background noise. Something to fill the space. When Lena emerged again, she looked sharp and tired all at once, high-waisted jeans, a black utility jacket, hair pulled back in a ponytail still fighting stray wisps. She dabbed a finger at the corner of her eye, blending eyeliner, then glanced over at Dan, still horizontal. "You going to do anything today?"

"I'm thinking about it."

"Dangerous." She leaned down, kissed him once, slow, brief, then slung her bag over her shoulder.

"See you in a bit," she said.

"Don't forget your umbrella," he called after her.

"Looks like it might spit."

"I've got my hoodie. I'll survive."

The door clicked shut behind her. Dan listened to the sound of her steps fading down the stairwell, then exhaled into the stillness she left behind. The flat sighed with her absence. He closed his eyes, arm draped over his head again and for now, that really was enough.

Outside, the air had that stillness particular to late Saturday mornings, like the city hadn't fully decided whether to wake up or stay hungover. Lena stepped onto the pavement, tugging the zip of her jacket higher as a chill threaded down the back of her neck. It wasn't cold, not properly, but the breeze had a bite to it. The usual blend of smells hit her nose as she walked, engine fumes, last night's takeaway spilling from bins, and the metallic tang of train tracks not far off. She turned the corner past the vape lounge and the fried chicken shop, the door already open and pumping out a low thrum of bass and fryer oil. The rhythm of Peckham moved around her, early shoppers dragging wheeled trolleys behind them, stallholders arranging fruit into pyramids too perfect to last, a cyclist weaving past with one hand on his phone and the other barely gripping the handlebars. By the time she reached the station, the crowd had thickened. Not the weekday rush, no suits, no commuter scowls, but weekend traffic. Slow-moving, chatty, half-asleep. A couple in gym gear stood yawning at the entrance, arguing quietly over whether to get smoothies before or after their Pilates class. A kid whined about missing the train while his mum scrolled, oblivious and there he was. As always. Slumped in his usual corner near the Oyster card top-up machine, the homeless man Lena had first noticed months ago, wrapped in a coat three sizes too big and sipping something steaming from a battered paper cup. His presence was almost comforting in its constancy. He wasn't aggressive, didn't shout or rattle coins. Just watched the world pass with tired, hollow eyes. She nodded to him, as she always did. A small, silent gesture. His head dipped in return. The platform was busy, but the Overground came quickly. Lena squeezed into a carriage, one hand clutched around a rail, her bag thudding against her hip with every jolt of the train. The windows rattled, the orange poles were sticky with invisible grime, and somewhere further down, someone's phone was blaring out music tinny through busted speakers. She tuned it all out. Let the rhythm of the journey lull her into a quiet focus. By the time she stepped off at Hackney Downs, the sky had brightened a little, not quite sun, but a suggestion of it behind gauzy cloud. The streets felt looser here, less frantic. Fewer shouting pedestrians, more cafes with wide windows and chipped paint, more dogs being walked by people who looked like they had creative jobs and disposable income. The studio was just off a side street lined with lampposts covered in gig flyers and handwritten ads for drum teachers and flat shares. Her client was already outside when she arrived, Nora, a lifestyle blogger-turned-wellness-brand, all flowing linen and curated warmth. She wore big sunglasses and hugged Lena like they'd known each other for years.

"Lena, You're a dream. Come on in, the lighting in here is tragic, we're going to need every bulb we've got."

The building was a repurposed unit with high ceilings and brick walls trying hard to be rustic. Lena followed Nora inside, rolling her sleeves up before she'd even unzipped her jacket. The space was cluttered with folded yoga mats, houseplants wilting in mismatched pots, and a faint smell of eucalyptus that never quite covered the damp.

"Ring lights?" Nora asked, gesturing vaguely toward the gear bag on Lena's shoulder.

"I've got them."

"Thank god. I want soft glowy 'morning-after-your-best-sleep' energy. Not 'hospital lighting in an interrogation room."

Lena chuckled, already setting the stands in place and adjusting the angles by instinct. As she worked, Nora flitted around in bare feet, smoothing her dress, fluffing a pillow, checking her reflection in her phone camera like it was a trusted advisor. Lena barely had to ask what she wanted, she knew the drill by now. Natural, relaxed, but absolutely controlled. Light that looked accidental but took twenty minutes to get right. Photos that whispered authenticity and screamed money. She flicked the switch on the first light. A warm halo flooded the corner of the room. There it was. That sweet spot.

By the time Lena had her ring lights positioned and the first test shots flickering across the camera screen, Dan was already weaving through the swelling current of people at Borough Market. The air was thick with the smell of grilled meat, spice, and sweet syrup, a warm haze that wrapped around him like a memory. Even on a day like this, greyish sky, hint of rain, a bit too much wind, the market thrived. It always did. It was loud, alive, and vaguely overwhelming. Tiled walkways slick with the morning's drizzle. Voices tumbling over each other, baristas shouting names, tourists pointing at pastries, locals negotiating with butchers like it was a dance they'd rehearsed. Dan moved slowly, letting himself be pulled by instinct. A bakery stall glistened under a cloud of powdered sugar. Nearby, a man roasted chestnuts over an open drum, the metal hissing with every crack. Street food stalls spilled from the arches, Moroccan wraps, Ethiopian stews, glistening duck legs over sticky rice, Spanish tortillas the size of wheels. He paused at a Thai stall, watching them toss noodles with theatre, flames licking the air, fish sauce hissing into hot pans. He ordered pad kra pao, extra chilli, and stood by one of the high wooden tables to eat it, chopsticks clumsy but determined. The heat hit him right behind the eyes. It was perfect. A text buzzed on his phone. Nothing urgent. He left it. Afterward, he wandered. No real destination. Just the kind of aimless exploration that felt like rebellion against the rest of the week. He passed a cheese stall and lingered, accepting a toothpick sample from a guy in a waxed apron who spoke passionately about rinds and cave-aging. He made a mental note to come back for a wedge of something sharp. Eventually, he stopped at a fresh pasta stall and bought a box of handmade tagliatelle, sealed in brown waxed paper. Two portions. Enough for dinner. Then grabbed a small tub of wild mushroom sauce and a wrapped loaf of crusty sourdough, practical and thoughtful, without trying too hard. He wasn't sure if Lena would be starving or emotionally drained by the time she got back, but carbs always softened the landing. As he queued to pay, he overheard a nearby vendor talking about a new property competition, something about a house in the Cotswolds, five million pounds, plus cash on top. The voice was faint under the buzz of the crowd, but the numbers caught his attention. He didn't turn. Just filed it away. The bag in his hand was warm from the bread. He smiled faintly to himself and made his way out through the stone archways, back into the blur of the afternoon.

Back in Hackney, just as Dan stepped out through the arches of Borough Market and into the churn of late-afternoon foot traffic, Lena was adjusting her lens again, one eye squinted against the viewfinder, the other half-listening as Nora changed outfits behind a draped linen screen. The shoot had found its rhythm. The light outside had softened slightly, casting warm tones through the high windows of the studio. Nora emerged in a pale blue wrap dress and sat cross-legged on a stool that had definitely not been made to sit on comfortably. She fluffed a cushion behind her, took a sip from a bottle of green juice, and exhaled like she was about to share a secret.

"So, get this," she said, repositioning her legs as Lena fine-tuned the exposure.

"You know that prize draw thing going viral today? The Townhouse one?"

Lena nodded without looking up. "Think I scrolled past it this morning. Fancy townhouse, golden hour filter, some influencer doing a slow-mo spin in the hallway?"

Nora pointed at herself with a smirk. "Guilty. That was me."

Lena dropped the camera slightly, blinking. "Seriously?"

"Yeah, quick gig. They hired a few of us to make it look effortless. 'Just woke up in my multi-million-pound dream home' energy. You know."

Lena gave a dry smile. "You're good at that."

"Thanks, babe. Place was actually incredible, though. Marble kitchen. Built-in wine cellar. The staircase alone had its own echo."

"I could've done a better job on the edit," Lena muttered. "Music was off, pacing was choppy. And who cuts a property tour before the bathroom reveal?"

"I told them that!" Nora laughed, clearly delighted. "But they just want clicks, not polish."

Lena crouched again, camera in hand. "No offence, but if you're selling a fantasy, at least commit."

"Tell me about it. You should pitch to them or better yet, take over."

"Maybe I will," Lena said, lining up the next shot. "Ready?"

"Born ready." The shutter clicked twice, then three times, the rhythm clean and calm. But Lena's thoughts lingered behind her focus now, caught somewhere between the artificial serenity of the scene in front of her and the gaudy dream home sitting on someone's feed.

The walk back from Borough Market was unhurried. Dan moved with the lazy rhythm of a man without a deadline, pasta and bread in one hand, the scent of garlic and sourdough still lingering around his jacket. The crowds thinned as he left the market behind, trading the chaos of food stalls for the worn-out quiet of Southwark side streets. He'd just crossed the road near The Royal Oak when he caught sight of someone leaning against the low brick wall beside the pub's entrance, cigarette in one hand, pint in the other, sunglasses half-on despite the dull sky.

"Kersey," the man called out, grinning. "Bloody hell."

Dan blinked. "Robbie?"

Robbie Baxter let out a bark of laughter, dragging on his cigarette before flicking ash toward the kerb.

"Didn't think I'd see your hungover face again outside a place like this. Thought you'd still be in recovery from Jack's stag."

Dan stepped closer, laughing. "You mean your fault I can't look at rum anymore without gagging?"

"You were off your face," Robbie said, eyes twinkling.

"Kept calling the DJ 'Dad.' Pretty sure you tried to snog him too."

"Pretty sure I did," Dan shot back. "But I stand by it, great jawline."

Robbie winked. "You had a very good night."

Dan shook his head, grinning. "Jesus. What are you doing out here? Thought you moved to Bristol."

"I did. Still there. Down for the weekend, seeing mates, catching up. Smoking too much. Celebrating, technically."

Dan raised a brow. "Celebrating what?"

Robbie stubbed the cigarette against the wall, flicked it toward the drain, and lifted his pint. "Won fifty grand and a Range Rover."

Dan laughed, then paused. "Come again?"

"One of those prize draw things online," Robbie said, taking a casual swig. "Entered on a whim months ago. Thought it was a scam. Got an email this morning, turns out I'm a runner-up. Tax-free. Full payout. Car, too. The fancy kind with doors that close themselves."

Dan blinked. "You're not winding me up?"

"Swear down," Robbie said. "Signed the paperwork. Told my boss to shove my next shift. Felt fantastic."

Dan leaned on the wall beside him, adjusting the weight of the shopping bag under his arm. "I've seen those ads. The houses are always ridiculous. Thought it was all bollocks."

"Same. But someone's got to win, right?" Robbie lit another cigarette, cupping the flame against the breeze.

"And they've just launched a new one, Cotswolds mansion, apparently. Five million. Quarter mil cash or a million lump sum instead. £3 to enter."

Dan let out a low whistle. "Jesus."

"Not bad for a few quid and a bit of wishful thinking." Dan took the offered pint and clinked it lazily against Robbie's.

"Well, cheers to beating the system." Robbie smirked, exhaled a plume of smoke, and nodded toward the bag.

"Dinner?"

"Yeah. Just grabbing something decent for me and Lena. Figured carbs are safer than surprises."

"True. She still puttin' up with you?"

"Somehow."

They both laughed, and for a moment, the years peeled back. Just two blokes outside a pub, shooting the shit but behind Dan's easy smile, a thought had already started to take root. Dan didn't rush off. He and Robbie slipped inside The Royal Oak, the noise of the street muffled instantly by thick brick walls and the hush of worn familiarity. The pub was old in the way only certain London pubs managed to be, not curated or made to feel old, but genuinely aged. The wood panelling was dark and scuffed at knee height, the windows streaked slightly from years of condensation and conversation. A mismatched collection of chairs surrounded solid oak tables scarred by time and the bottoms of pint glasses. The bar gleamed from constant use, polished not by staff but by hands, elbows, and decades of habit. Copper lamps hung low over booths near the back, their light warm and amber, casting everyone in a gentle glow that made even the worst hangover look forgivable. A blackboard above the bar listed today's guest ales in smudged chalk. A bored spaniel dozed under a table in the corner, leash looped around the leg of a stool, one paw twitching in a dream.

They took their pints to a quiet corner, slumping into an old leather booth that sighed under their weight.

"Remember that night in Brighton?" Robbie said, taking a sip.

"The one with the karaoke and the magician?" Dan barked a laugh.

"Oh god, yes. Didn't someone lose a shoe?"

"You did. You threw it at the magician and shouted, 'do something useful with that.'"

Dan shook his head, grinning into his pint. "No regrets."

They chatted for another half-hour, slipping in and out of stories from their twenties with ease, the cheap hostels, the band they almost started, the girl Dan nearly moved to Dublin for. It was the kind of conversation that carried a lightness they hadn't felt in years. But beneath it, Dan could feel something new, not envy exactly, but awareness. Robbie, a man who once lived off Rustlers burgers and borrowed lighters, had just been handed fifty grand and a car for doing almost nothing and now here Dan was, sipping a second pint and wondering what £3 might buy him next.

As the sun was setting on Hackney Downs later that afternoon. The shoot had wound down to its final frames. Nora posed barefoot on a vintage armchair, one leg curled beneath her and the other extended just enough to show off her anklet. The ring light cast a soft glow on her cheekbones, and Lena caught the moment, click, click, click, before lowering the camera.

"That's a wrap," she said, pulling the viewfinder away.

Nora stood, stretching theatrically. "God, you're a magician. I actually look alive."

"You'll look even better after a bit of Lightroom and strategic shadow removal."

Nora laughed, collecting her jacket and bag. "I need to dash, my Uber's outside. You good to pack up solo?"

Lena waved her off. "Go. I've got this."

Nora leaned in for a quick hug. "You're a legend." and just like that, she was gone. The space felt immediately different, not eerie, just… still. The kind of silence that pressed against your ears. Lena stood for a moment, letting it settle, then rolled her shoulders and began unscrewing the light stands. The studio, emptied of chatter and laughter, returned to its raw state. Bare-brick walls. Concrete floor. Exposed beams catching the last of the afternoon light. Halfway through unplugging the second ring light, she froze. A sound. The faint creak of the front door. Lena straightened slowly, listening. Nothing followed. No voices. No returning footsteps. Just the slow tick of the heater cooling beside the back wall.

"Nora?" she called, already knowing the answer.

No reply. She walked to the entrance, her boots echoing too loudly in the empty space. The door was closed. Latched. No one there. A gust of wind, maybe or the old hinges shifting with temperature. She'd heard stranger things in older buildings. Still, a ripple of unease slid across her back as she returned to her equipment, moving a touch faster now, hands brisk with movement. She told herself it was nothing but when she finally slung the gear bag over her shoulder and stepped outside, locking the door behind her, she paused.

The street was quiet, too quiet for a Saturday. No dog walkers. No delivery vans. The usual café two doors down had its blinds drawn. The light had gone colder, flatter. As if something had shifted while she was inside. Lena scanned the pavement once, adjusted her bag, and began walking toward the station but that feeling, a tightness in her gut, didn't lift.

Back at the pub, Dan checked the time discreetly as Robbie launched into a story about nearly missing his flight to Lisbon because he stopped for a full English on the way to Gatwick.

"…and then the bloody check-in desk was closed, but the guy at security used to work with my sister, so…"

"I hate how your life works out," Dan said, laughing. "But I should probably head off. Got dinner to throw together before Lena gets back."

Robbie held up a hand, already reaching for his wallet.

"Come on, one more. I owe you for the stag disaster alone."

Dan shook his head, easing out of the booth. "Tempting. But I'll hold you to it next time. Preferably when there's no magician involved."

They exchanged another quick grin, the kind that lingered just a second too long, then clapped shoulders. Dan slipped out into the afternoon air, the chill kissing his face as the pub door swung shut behind him. As he walked, the idea of the competition flickered back in his mind like an ember catching the wind.

Lena's boots tapped steadily along the pavement, her bag heavier than it had felt earlier. The streets were still quiet, a kind of hollowed-out calm that made every passing car sound louder, every rustle of plastic against a railing feel deliberate. She passed the café again, blinds still drawn. As she turned onto the main road, a sliver of doubt crept into her stomach. Not fear, not quite. Just awareness. The kind that prickled the back of your neck and made you pull your jacket closer without knowing why. She resisted the urge to glance behind her too soon. Instead, she adjusted her strap, kept walking, eyes focused forward. The station wasn't far. She could already see the familiar cracked blue paint of the sign through the trees ahead. Another footstep behind hers. Faint, delayed, not an echo, not quite synced. She stopped, nothing. The street behind her was empty, just a few parked cars and a discarded takeaway bag tumbling gently in the wind. She stood, brushed her hands off. Forced herself to keep moving. Halfway to the crossing, she looked back over her shoulder. Thinking she caught a glimpse of a shadow, she exhaled through her nose, forcing a small laugh. Just nerves. Leftover adrenaline. The building creaking, the long shadows of the day getting into her head. Still, she picked up her pace. Just slightly and that tight knot in her gut. It didn't loosen. Lena pulled her jacket tighter as she turned onto the main road, the weight of her gear bag dragging slightly against her shoulder. The light had shifted again, that late-afternoon grey that London wore so often, soft but unsympathetic. She passed shuttered shop fronts and shuttered expressions. A group of teenagers sat slouched at a bus stop, all hunched shoulders and quiet laughter. One glanced up at her and looked away again. Nothing out of place and yet, There was that feeling again. Not fear, not exactly. Just a pressure in the air. Like the weather was about to break, or like someone was watching from just out of view. She walked on. The street narrowed between buildings. A plastic bottle rolled into the gutter behind her, catching her attention just long enough to make her glance back. Empty. Just the stretch of pavement, the same graffiti-tagged wall, the same rusty bike chained to the same lamppost. Still, she didn't slow down. She passed a salon with its blinds still down, the shop where someone was sweeping leaves from the threshold without looking up, the alley she ignored on instinct. Her footsteps landed harder now, breath slightly too shallow for the pace. She knew better than to call it paranoia. Intuition had saved her more than once. The station appeared up ahead, blue sign, chipped paint, three people standing outside in loosely spaced silence. Relief didn't bloom. It simply waited. Lena didn't look back again..

Once Lena stepped out of Peckham Rye Station, the familiar rush of city life pressed in around her. The street was noisy in that comfortable, chaotic way, buses hissing past, the clatter of heels on pavement, someone selling phone cases on a foldout table near the newsagent. She adjusted the strap on her shoulder and took a breath, trying to shake off the last threads of unease. It had been nothing, it had to have been. A creaky door. A shadow at the wrong angle. Her own imagination folding in on itself after a long shoot. She turned the corner just as someone rounded it from the other side, and for a split second, she startled. Then she saw the carrier bag in one hand, the crusty loaf poking out of the top, and the familiar slouch of his jacket. Dan.

"Hey," he said, surprised and grinning. "Look who I've found."

Lena didn't smile right away. Relief, more than anything, flooded her face.

"You okay?" Dan asked immediately, adjusting the weight of the bag and taking a step closer.

She nodded, then stopped, swallowing hard.

"I don't know. I've had this weird feeling since I left the shoot. Like someone was behind me. I thought I heard the studio door go after Nora left, went looking, nothing. Then walking to the station, same thing. Nothing there. But it felt… off."

Dan's expression shifted, the smile fading but not entirely gone. He scanned her face, then glanced briefly down the street behind her, more out of instinct than suspicion.

"You're alright now," he said gently, stepping in to press a kiss to her temple. "I'm here."

Lena let her body lean into his for a moment, grounding herself. The city noise wrapped around them, trains overhead, a burst of laughter from a group by the chicken shop, the hum of buses idling. They started walking, shoulder to shoulder, heading home. Dan carried the shopping. Lena matched his stride. By the time they reached the flat, the city outside had started to settle, the low hum of early evening threading through the cracked windows and floorboards. Dan unlocked the door with one shoulder pressed to the frame, the smell of fried chicken from down the road still clinging to the hallway behind them.

Inside, the familiar warmth wrapped around them. It wasn't much, just a second-floor flat above a nail salon, but it was theirs. The cushions were a bit saggy, the kettle clicked twice before it boiled, and the radiators whined like ghosts. But it held them. Dan dropped the shopping bag onto the counter and got to work. Pasta boiling, sauce gently warming. He sliced the bread in uneven hunks and stuck them under the grill. His movements were easy, relaxed. Comfortable in the space. Lena moved toward the coffee table, pushing aside a magazine and a spare USB cable. She pulled out the half-stuffed folder of bills from under the tray and opened her laptop, dragging her legs up beneath her. There it was. The usual, council tax creeping up again. The latest energy bill higher than expected, and that damned broadband charge that never matched what they originally signed up for. She didn't say anything at first. Just let the numbers do their quiet haunting.

Dan looked over from the stove. "Bad?"

She gave a small, tired sound. "Not catastrophic. Just… everything's creeping. Rent, bills. Food. Even the sodding water bill."

Dan stirred the sauce, then turned the heat down. "We'll manage."

"We always say that."

"We always do."

Lena sighed, clicked open the budgeting spreadsheet she only half-maintained.

"I've been thinking. About our savings, the mortgage fund. It's slower than we planned. I'm not saying we're failing, but…"

"But we're treading water," Dan finished for her.

She nodded. There was a pause, the soft bubble of boiling pasta, the grill ticking behind them. Dan cleared his throat, half-turning from the cooker.

"So, listen… at the pub, I ran into Robbie Baxter."

Lena raised an eyebrow. "Didn't he move to Bristol?"

"He did. He's in town for the weekend. Turns out he entered one of those prize draw things. You know, win a mansion for a few quid."

"Oh god," Lena muttered. "Those things."

"Right?" Dan said, grinning. "But get this, he didn't win the house, but he got a runner-up prize. Fifty grand. And a bloody Range Rover."

Lena blinked. "You're joking."

"Dead serious. Showed me the email and everything. It's real."

She leaned back slightly. "That's mad."

"They've launched a new one already," Dan added casually. "Five million pound house in the Cotswolds. Comes with £250k, or a million tax-free instead. Three quid to enter."

Lena let out a short laugh, somewhere between disbelief and amusement.

"And here we are, debating whether to cancel Spotify Premium."

Dan came over with two plates of steaming tagliatelle, setting them down gently. "I'm just saying. People win. Why not us?"

Lena stabbed her fork into the pasta, watching the steam curl off the surface. "Because we're not the kind of people who win things."

"But maybe we're the kind who try." There was a beat of quiet. Lena tilted her head.

"If we're doing it, we're doing it properly. Ten entries. Twenty-five quid." Dan raised an eyebrow. "Ten?"

She shrugged. "It's either a laugh or a long shot. Might as well commit."

He grinned and grabbed his phone from the windowsill.

"I'll get the wine. You handle the gambling."

As she reached for her laptop and started typing in the URL, Lena smiled, just a little, over the rim of her fork. Maybe it was ridiculous. Maybe it was a waste but it was theirs to hope for. Lena clicked through the glossy homepage, all slow-motion drone shots and smiling families holding keys. Your Dream Home Awaits, the banner read, arcing above a pristine country home framed by lavender and stone.

Dan leaned over her shoulder, sipping wine, his chin brushing against her temple.

"Look at that staircase," he murmured.

"I'd fall down that in style." She snorted, nudging him gently.

"You'd trip before the second step."

They scrolled past testimonials and prize tiers, down to the bright yellow Enter Now button. Lena glanced at him. "Ready?"

Dan raised his glass. "To optimism."

She entered their names, selected ten entries, and hit confirm. Just like that, done. They stared at the confirmation screen for a moment, both quiet. Ten entries. Twenty-five pounds. A dream stretched impossibly far, but just close enough to imagine the shape of it. Lena shut the laptop and leaned back into the sofa. Dan slipped an arm around her shoulders. Outside, the streetlights flickered to life, casting golden puddles on the wet pavement. The trains rumbled overhead. Somewhere below, the scent of lacquered nails drifted up from the salon. The city carried on. And in their little flat above the noise, they let themselves believe, just for a minute, that maybe something was about to change.

CHAPTER FOUR

The cab smelled faintly of petrol and takeaway. Lena sat with her coat draped over her lap, smoothing a crease from her dress with the side of her hand. Outside, central London passed in quick, reflective flashes, shopfronts, couples crossing against the light, someone holding a giant balloon shaped like the number five. She checked her phone. Two missed calls from the junior exe. One text from Zoya. 'Don't let them dull your sparkle, own it' Lena half-smiled. She didn't have time to reply, Tonight was the launch. The *Le Cle* Campaign she'd been eating and breathing for weeks, endless calls, edits, emails pinging in at all hours. She could still see the mood board taped to their fridge, curling at the corners. Dan had signed off work early. He'd closed the big supermarket deal two weeks ago and was still riding the high. He said he'd meet her at the venue. She reached for her lip gloss, dabbing it on without a mirror. The car slowed. The hotel loomed into view, tall glass, gold signage, two doormen waiting like punctuation marks. Lena breathed in and stepped out.

The lobby carried the kind of silence that cost money, thick carpet underfoot, music low enough to be tasteful but engineered to loop. Polished marble floors. Gold hardware on the doors. The perfume's branding had been worked into everything: frosted acrylic signs by the lifts, white orchids arranged to look incidental, but weren't. Dan stood at the edge of the bar, one hand resting on the counter, his drink untouched. The room felt curated, too smooth to be casual, too warm for comfort. Soft lighting picked up the edges of mirrored columns, and the air smelled faintly of the product, something floral, clean, deliberately unobtrusive. He recognised a couple of people, faces he knew from photos Lena had shown him or names she'd mentioned in passing. Probably agency staff or brand people. They looked busy, or at least good at pretending to be. He shifted his weight slightly, resisting the urge to check his phone. Then she walked in.

Lena stepped through the revolving door without breaking pace, her coat folded neatly over her arm, trousers pressed, blouse crisp and light under the glow of the lobby lights. There was something about the way she moved, unrushed, assured, that caught more than just his attention. Even here, surrounded by people dressed to be noticed, she stood out. Her gaze swept across the space once. Not searching, just registering. Her posture barely changed when she spotted him, but he felt it. The brief lift of her chin. The smallest shift of focus. Dan set his glass down and waited as Lena made her way over to him. She'd only taken a few steps when one of the brand owners, he couldn't remember the name, called out to her from near the entrance to the private lounge. Polished, mid-fifties maybe, in a navy blazer and a watch that probably cost more than their rent. He greeted her like they were old friends, arms open, voice too loud for the room. Dan watched her pause, just briefly, before turning and stepping toward him. He couldn't hear every word, but he caught the tone, praise, mostly. Something about the visuals. The rollout. A gesture toward the screens looping campaign footage overhead. Lena smiled, polite and still, nodding once. Then another voice cut in. Sharper, lighter. Her boss. The same one who always managed to pop up in conversations she hadn't started. The two shook hands like they were equals. Her boss was already talking over her. Dan could tell from the rhythm, too quick, too confident. Taking credit in real time. The brand owner looked at Lena, then. Just for a second. A flick of something that might have been apology, or respect. She smiled like it didn't bother her, offered a quick, *'Excuse me a moment,/* and stepped away, leaving them mid-sentence. Dan watched as she took a champagne flute from a passing tray, turned without hesitation, and started toward him. Now she was smiling properly. Lena took the glass without breaking stride, fingers slipping neatly around the stem. The champagne fizzed, pale gold under the overheads. She didn't glance back, but she could still hear her boss's voice, bright and pointed, pitched to carry just enough to seem important. The brand owner had smiled at her like he knew. One of those looks. Quick, almost imperceptible. The kind that didn't need words. She let it go. The room was warming up now. Voices layering into a soft rise, music weaving just beneath. The scent of the perfume hung in the air like a filter, sweet but not cloying, floral with a thread of something deeper. They'd spent two weeks arguing about the balance of notes. It didn't matter anymore. It was here. Bottled. Branded. Packaged and poured into the hands of a woman in a silk co-ord, now posting a photo beside the display board like she'd built the whole thing herself. Lena reached Dan, holding his gaze as she handed him the second flute from the tray she'd caught.

"You found the only quiet corner," she said.

He smiled, and it was real. "Didn't feel like competing for air."

She took a sip. The bubbles caught slightly in her throat but didn't sting. For a moment, neither of them said anything. It didn't feel tense. Just, full. Like silence earned, not stretched.

"Boss already taking the credit?" Dan asked, voice low.

"Of course." She glanced sideways at the lounge.

"She came in late, but she'll still be the one they quote tomorrow." Dan didn't respond. He didn't need to. The silence held.

They stood close enough for their coats to brush. Hers was still folded over her arm, slightly crushed where she'd held it at the elbow too long. The lights dimmed. Just a fraction but it was enough to shift the room. Conversations began to hush. A cue built into the schedule. A new track faded in something orchestral and dramatic but carefully branded. One of the event staff moved toward the centre stage, mic in hand, ready for the formal welcome. Lena exhaled through her nose, quiet. She didn't move, but her weight shifted forward slightly, like she was preparing herself. Dan tilted his glass, touching hers without clink.

The night unfolded in careful sections timed speeches, photo calls, curated chaos. Branded hashtags ran as ticker tape across the screens near the bar. A white-gloved bartender served a themed cocktail in tiny glass bottles that no one actually drank. The agency's exec team rotated the space like clockwork, making sure every major guest got their moment. Lena did her part. She posed, she smiled, she answered questions she already knew were coming but the sharpness of the lead-up had started to dull. Her name was on the campaign, somewhere buried in the metadata but no one said it aloud. It was fine. She wasn't here to be noticed. She was here because it had worked. From a distance, she caught Dan watching her. Not performatively just present. It grounded her more than the drink ever would. The speeches wrapped. The music picked up again. Conversations turned looser, voices louder. Somewhere near the back wall, someone popped a bottle too close to a spotlight and got gently told off.

At some point, Lena stepped out onto the hotel's terrace balcony, just long enough to check her notifications and breathe in the cold. When she returned, Dan handed her another glass, already half-full.

"Think you survived," he said.

She gave a soft hum of agreement, then glanced toward the venue's main doors.

"Let's not stay much longer," she said and just like that, it was done.

Morning arrived slow and golden. Sunlight pushed through the thin gap in the curtains, casting soft lines across the bedroom wall. The air carried the early warmth of a June morning, not hot, just settled. A breeze moved somewhere out of reach, stirring the hem of the blinds. Lena lay still, her body relaxed in a way it hadn't been for weeks. No alarms. No shoot lists. No panicked agency messages asking if a caption had been approved. Just quiet. From the other room came the sound of cupboard doors opening and the low rustle of a cereal packet being tucked away. Dan was up. She could hear him moving light-footed, familiar, not bothering with shoes. She sat up slowly, stretching once, then swung her legs over the side of the bed. Her toes met the cool patchwork of the wooden floor, still uneven in places. The flat always felt smaller in daylight but not worse for it. Just honest. In the kitchen, Dan was poking at the toaster, two slices already browned and stacked on a chipped plate. The kind of bread they'd settled on lately soft, own-brand, nothing fancy. They'd trimmed back gradually. Less brunch, more bulk buys. Fewer 'treats' that added up when no one was counting. It had been working. The savings looked better. The goal felt closer. He glanced over his shoulder as she entered.

"Hey," he said. "Figured I'd get something going before we head out."

She nodded, stepping past him toward the kettle. "What time were you thinking?"

"Late morning? Before traffic turns hellish." She didn't answer straight away. Just reached for a clean mug and poured hot water over the teabag she'd dropped in out of habit. They'd planned the Surrey visit two weeks ago. Her mum's suggestion. Just a night. Long enough to feel polite, not long enough for questions. Lena sipped, leaning against the counter. The kitchen smelled like toast and fresh air. She didn't know if she was ready to leave the quiet behind just yet.

The Surrey air had a quietness that didn't exist in London. Not the heavy kind built from noise held back, but something cleaner, natural. Like the space between leaves on trees or the breath before speaking. Lena leaned her head against the passenger window as they pulled up to the house. Her mother's garden was tidy in the way that suggested it never stopped being looked at flowerbeds neat, hedges trimmed, pots swept of petals. A flagstone path led to the door, the doormat was new. Dan parked with one wheel brushing the curb. As he killed the engine, neither of them moved to open the doors immediately. They sat for a moment in the stillness. The front door opened before they knocked. Her mother stepped out, cardigan hanging loose at the elbows, smile already halfway formed. She pulled Lena into a soft, practical hug, then gave Dan a look that meant welcome without fuss. Inside, nothing had changed. Not really. A new rug in the hallway. A different light fixture in the kitchen. But the smell was the same clean linen, wood polish, something faintly floral. The same framed photos lined the wall leading up the stairs, slightly askew in the same places. The kettle was already boiled. A cake Victoria sponge, dusted with sugar sat beneath a glass dome on the counter. Lena didn't need to ask if it had been bought that morning. Of course it had. They drank tea in the sunroom with the doors open, letting the June air drift in. Her mother talked about the neighbour's new car, the council's plans to redo the pavement on the south end of the village, the twins from church who were now apparently running a YouTube channel. It was pleasant, in the way that smallness can be when it isn't forced. Dan asked the right questions. Lena let herself sink into the familiarity of it, the edges of her day softening for the first time in weeks.

In the afternoon, they walked. Her mother insisted "It'll clear the city from your head" and led them down the old footpath that skirted the cemetery and curved back through the green. Lena had walked it as a teenager, headphones in, eyes low, impatient to be elsewhere. Now, it felt like borrowed space. A place unchanged while everything else had shifted. That evening, dinner appeared with little ceremony but perfect timing. Roasted lemon chicken, thin potatoes layered so tightly they held together like tiles, a salad of herbs Lena hadn't thought to buy in years. Her mother poured a cold Sauvignon and filled their plates without asking if they were hungry. They ate slowly, surrounded by the low murmur of Radio 4 playing quietly from the next room. Afterwards, Lena helped dry the dishes while her mum scrubbed the pans. Dan offered once, then vanished to the living room with a second glass and the soft sound of sports commentary filling the silence. Later, they climbed the stairs with the kind of shared quiet that came after wine and warmth. Her old bedroom had been painted since she'd left. The pink stripes were gone, replaced with something neutral. Greige. The bookshelf still stood, untouched in one corner, the spines of old novels tilted like they were waiting to be picked back up. A childhood mirror leaned behind the door. There were fresh sheets on the bed, corners tucked too precisely to be casual. Lena peeled off her jumper, folded it neatly on the chair, and slipped between the covers. Dan opened the window just a crack. The night outside was dark in the way only countryside could be, deep and whole, not interrupted by light pollution or restless traffic. They didn't speak. Sleep came easily.

By morning, the house felt even quieter. Her mother was already up, soft radio, cupboard doors gently opened. The smell of fresh toast and filtered coffee drifted up the stairs. Lena pulled on yesterday's jumper and joined her in the kitchen. The table was already set. Cutlery in place, a small dish of butter, eggs steaming gently in a ceramic bowl, strawberries sliced into a glass dish. Her mum had even brought out the floral mugs Lena secretly hated as a teenager. Dan wandered in ten minutes later, hair damp, phone in hand, yawning into his sleeve. They talked plans for the day. Her mum had booked a table at a new place in the village. She'd heard it was minimalist, everything served on those silly grey plates but the food was meant to be good. Lena leaned against the counter, chewing a piece of toast and watching the sun shift across the tablecloth. Then her phone rang. It was her upstairs neighbour, Mrs. Patel. She almost didn't answer. But something about the timing felt off.

"Hi?" she said, brushing crumbs from her jumper.

"Oh, Lena. I'm so sorry to bother you, dear, but I didn't know what else to do." Her voice was tight, fast.

"There's a man outside your flat. Dressed in all black. He's been standing there for nearly fifteen minutes now. Not knocking. Just… there. Watching. I thought he might be council or one of those people from the energy firms but he hasn't moved. Not once."

Lena blinked. "What does he look like?"

"Tall. Pale. Long coat. He looks like, well… it's silly, but he looks like the kind of man who asks questions. I thought maybe… debt collector? I'm sorry."

Lena didn't speak. Her pulse had slowed. Not from calm, but from focus. The way it did when something wasn't adding up.

"Thanks, Mrs. Patel. I appreciate it." She hung up.

Dan had stopped eating. He was watching her now. He'd heard enough to know. Lena turned to her mother, carefully setting her phone down on the table.

"I think we need to head back. Something's come up."

Her mother paused, knife halfway through a croissant. "Is everything alright?"

Lena nodded, too quickly. "It's probably nothing. Just something at the flat." Her voice didn't sound like hers.

Within fifteen minutes, they were packed. Apologies made, hugs given, the car reversing back down the gravel drive. The sun was still out, the sky still clean, but something had shifted. The quiet they'd found had turned sharp. Neither of them spoke for the first ten minutes of the drive. The roads blurred past in long, familiar stretches of countryside. Fields broken by dry stone walls. Petrol stations with peeling signage. The kind of journey they'd done dozens of times, but never like this. Neither of them spoke for a while. Dan kept one hand on the wheel, the other resting loosely in his lap. His eyes stayed fixed on the road, jaw set just slightly. Not tense exactly but focused. Like a man trying not to get ahead of himself. Lena sat angled toward the window, her arms crossed lightly over her chest. She watched hedgerows blur past, then village signs, then roundabouts she could name without thinking. Her phone sat in the cup holder, screen facing up. Still. Quiet. She hated that she kept glancing at it. They passed a pub she used to know, The Cricketers. New signage now. Painted navy with gold lettering. A group of cyclists stood outside with drinks, sun catching on their helmets. The normalness of it made her stomach twist. She finally spoke. "It's probably nothing."

Dan didn't answer immediately. "Yeah," he said eventually. "But it doesn't feel like nothing."

Another few minutes passed. The motorway signs reappeared. Guildford, then Croydon. A low hum of traffic picked up as the lanes narrowed. Then Lena's phone lit up. *Mrs. Patel – Upstairs Neighbour*

She picked it up before it finished the first ring. "Hello?"

"Oh, I'm sorry again, Lena but I thought you should know. There are more of them now."

Lena sat forward slightly, blood thick in her ears. "More?"

"Yes two others. One with a camera. A proper one. Not a phone. The tall man's still there but now they're speaking quietly. That kind of speaking where they want you to see but not hear. I saw from the stairwell. The way one of them gestured toward your front door."

Lena swallowed. "Did they try the buzzer?"

"No. Not yet. I've stayed in the stairwell. I don't want them seeing me watch. I-I think I recognise the man. The one with the coat. I think he was on telly. You know that programme, Cant Pay, We'll Take It Away. You don't think they're from something like that, do you?"

Lena blinked slowly. "What?"

"I just wondered if… well, I don't mean to pry, but are you and Dan… behind on anything?"

No," Lena said too quickly. Then softer: "No, we're not."

Mrs. Patel gave a sound somewhere between a sigh and an apology. "Alright, love. I just thought… better to say something. It didn't look good."

Lena thanked her and hung up. The silence in the car was tighter now.

Dan didn't look over. "What was that?"

"She said more people are there now. One with a camera. She thinks one of them might be from that bailiff show."

Dan's knuckles tightened slightly on the steering wheel. "That's ridiculous," he said. "We're not in debt."

"I know."

"Council would've written. Utilities too."

Lena stared ahead.

"It's not council. They haven't rung the buzzer. They're just standing there apparently."

Neither of them said it, but the thought hung between them like condensation on the inside of glass, what if this has nothing to do with money?

The traffic thickened the closer they got to Peckham. Buses wheezed through junctions. Pedestrians shuffled past zebra crossings without looking. The high street was its usual mess of music, fried food, and shouted conversations bleeding out of shopfronts. Dan turned off early and found a space two streets down from the flat, just inside the resident zone. Neither of them commented on it. Lena clicked her seatbelt free, her jaw tense. The street looked normal. People carrying corner shop bags, a man pacing on speakerphone outside a barber's. There was nothing that gave the morning's call weight. No camera crew. No strange men in long coats. No vans parked at odd angles. Still, neither of them relaxed. They walked the rest of the way in silence. The flat's exterior loomed, familiar aged brick scuffed white door, a keypad with worn digits. Dan punched in the code. The door opened with its usual click and a gentle mechanical groan. Communal hallway, empty. Same scuffed skirting board. Same old smell of bleach and warm dust. The stairwell echoed under their feet. Their steps sounded louder than usual. Lena found herself holding her breath slightly on each landing. The third floor was quiet. No one at the door. No note. No van. No noise. Dan unlocked the flat. The inside smelled the way they'd left it, linen, cheap hand soap, and something faintly metallic from the kitchen sink. Nothing was touched. Lena drifted into the hallway and checked the floor under the letterbox. Nothing. No papers, no folded forms, no stamped warnings. She opened the front door again. Empty corridor. She typed quickly on her phone. ***Nobody's here. No letter. All quiet.*** The message went through. Read almost instantly. No reply. She stared at the screen for a few seconds longer than necessary, then locked it and dropped it on the kitchen counter. Dan flicked the kettle on. It rattled faintly as it began to boil.

"Tea?" he asked.

She nodded. They didn't say much as they moved around the space. Familiar motions, half on autopilot. Mugs. Teabags. Milk from the half-used carton. The kettle clicked off. Outside, a horn sounded in the distance. The television buzzed slightly as it turned on, audio still muted. Dan handed her a mug. She took it without speaking. They sat on opposite ends of the sofa, both holding their drinks, neither drinking yet. The knock came at the door. Sharp, precise. Three times. They froze. Not heavy. Not aggressive. But deliberate. Dan turned his head toward the hallway. Lena's hand tightened around the mug. The knock echoed a second time. Lena set her mug down slowly on the coffee table. Dan was already standing, head tilted toward the hallway like he was trying to listen through walls. Neither of them spoke. A third knock followed, steady, not rushed. Dan moved first, crossing to the door, shoulders set with the kind of tension that looked casual from a distance. He paused before the handle, glanced toward Lena, then leaned forward to the peephole. Silence stretched.

"Well?" she asked, quietly.

Dan didn't answer at first. He straightened slowly, blinking like he wasn't sure how to translate what he'd just seen.

"There's… three of them." He stepped back slightly.

"That guy in black's still there. Long coat. Same as Mrs. Patel said. Another with him, holding a clipboard or something and someone behind them with a proper camera."

"Camera?" Lena echoed.

Dan nodded. "They're already filming."

Lena moved in beside him, looking through the lens briefly. The peephole curved everything at the edges, but the centre was sharp enough: the man in the coat stood closest, face unreadable. Next to him, a shorter man with a lanyard and tablet and behind them, the cameraman, shouldered rig, red light blinking steadily and then just to the left Mrs. Patel appeared. She stepped out from the stairwell, weaving carefully between the camera rig and the coat. Her hands weren't clenched, not like before. She looked almost… conflicted. Not afraid, not confused. Just aware that something was happening, and unsure how the people on the other side of the door would take it. Her eyes met Dan's through the slim pane of frosted glass. Dan opened the door. Only slightly at first, enough to see clearly. The man in the coat gave a quick, professional nod.

"Daniel Kersey?" Dan blinked.

"Yes?"

The man smiled. A rehearsed smile. The kind used in press launches and press briefings. "And Miss Hartley?"

Lena stepped into the frame beside him. "Yes," she said cautiously.

The cameraman adjusted his grip, already rolling. The man with the lanyard tapped his tablet. A soft chime played.

"Apologies for the surprise," the tall man said.

"We've been trying to reach you for a few days. Phone numbers weren't connecting, and our emails bounced. You've been shortlisted for a prize in the Winspire property giveaway."

Lena's stomach dropped. She blinked at him. "What?"

"You've won," the man said plainly.

"You've won the house." Dan turned toward her. Not laughing. Not smiling. Just stunned. Mrs. Patel leaned slightly toward them from the side, her voice lowered like she wasn't sure if she was allowed to speak.

"They told me just now," she murmured. "In the stairwell, said you'd entered months ago."

Lena didn't answer. Her thoughts were already trying to climb out from the wrong direction. The man gestured toward the camera.

"With your permission, we'd like to continue capturing your reaction. We usually do it on the doorstep. You were the chosen entry for the Rosehill House prize draw."

Still, neither of them spoke. The man hesitated, then softened his voice.

"This is the good kind of news."

Lena let her eyes flick to Dan. His mouth opened slightly. No words yet. Then, finally.

"You're serious?" he asked. The camera's red light blinked on, steady and cold. The man smiled again.

"Very." The camera light blinked steadily now, trained on their faces. A subtle whirring sound came from the stabiliser, too faint to be heard over the blood rushing in Lena's ears. The presenter or whatever title the man in the coat had held the silence like he'd been trained for it. He gave them a moment. A pause calibrated for drama. Then he stepped forward slightly, smile widening.

"Congratulations again," he said, gesturing toward the camera with an open palm. "We're here today on behalf of the Winspire Foundation to announce that you, Daniel and Lena, are the official winners of the Rosehill House prize draw."

The camera tilted in slowly. Lena felt her cheeks stiffen with the beginnings of a smile she hadn't fully committed to. Dan let out a short breath, part laugh, part disbelief. His hand moved instinctively to rest on her back, just between her shoulder blades. The presenter went on, voice pitched like velvet.

"Out of over seven million entrants across the UK, your ticket Entry 190243-6 was selected at random as the winner of this season's dream property."

Lena blinked again. She hadn't even remembered the number. She barely remembered entering. He turned to the camera.

"Rosehill House is a six-bedroom Georgian property on four acres of private land in the Cotswolds, fully renovated, furnished, and mortgage-free. This is one of our most exclusive properties to date."

Lena heard herself laugh. A small one, nervous and awkward. It didn't feel real, not the camera, not the presenter, not the red light blinking like a heartbeat. Dan leaned closer to the mic. "Sorry, this is… this is mad."

The presenter nodded, clearly used to disbelief. "It's a lot to take in. You're not the first to be stunned." He stepped slightly to the side, giving the camera a clean view of both of them. "Now, for the final moment. This is where we usually ask the big question."

Lena's brows furrowed. The presenter smiled wider, like he was waiting for them to realise.

"Because" he said gently, "as with all our high-tier draws, you have a choice."

Dan's eyes narrowed slightly. "A choice?"

The man nodded. "You can either accept the house," he said. "Rosehill. All of it. Transferred to your name, full ownership, freehold, no strings." He paused. "Or you can take the cash alternative."

Lena tilted her head. "Cash?"

The man nodded again. "One million pounds. Transferred to your bank account within ten working days."

The air around them changed. Behind the camera, someone gave a subtle nod, probably a signal. Another camera operator stepped to the side, getting a wide shot of the hallway. Lena could feel the tension tighten behind her ribs, not fear, but pressure. The weight of options. The sharp pivot from dream to decision. The presenter held his hands together.

"We don't need an answer this second," he said softly. "But we'll ask again on camera in a moment. We understand it's a life-changing decision."

Dan didn't speak. His jaw tightened faintly. Lena looked past the lens toward the stairwell, toward Mrs. Patel, who stood just behind the banister. She gave a small nod, lips pressed into something unreadable, something between encouragement and caution.

"Would it be alright if we filmed a celebratory shot?" the presenter asked. "Just you two, hugging, maybe a little jump or something? We usually wrap the doorstep with that. You can decide the rest inside."

Dan looked at Lena. His hand was still on her back. She gave a nod.

"Alright." The presenter stepped away. The camera operator reset. Dan leaned in, kissed her temple, and gave the smallest shake of his head, half amazed, half stunned. Lena let herself laugh properly this time. He pulled her in, arms wrapping tight, and she pressed her face into his chest as if to centre herself.

"Okay, on three," someone called gently. "One…"

Lena looked up, eyes locked on the camera's glassy eye.

"Two…"

They gripped each other tighter.

"Three!"

The confetti cannon was small, discreet, fired from the hands of the assistant beside the banister. A soft spray of gold and white flakes burst above their heads and fluttered down. They both laughed, real now and Lena raised her arms instinctively as the flakes landed across her shoulders, in Dan's hair, on the floor at their feet. The cameraman swept close for a final pass. Behind them, the smell of nail polish lingered faintly in the hall, remnants from the salon downstairs. The walls were thin, the floor uneven in places. A damp mark near the ceiling in their bedroom hadn't dried since March. They stepped back inside. The door closed gently behind them. Inside, their flat was silent. Dan rubbed his hands through his hair, knocking away the bits of confetti.

"Jesus Christ," he said, finally.

Lena nodded, leaning against the wall.

"They said seven million. Dan gave a small, breathless laugh."

"What the hell do we do now?"

The knock came again gentler this time. A polite tap. The presenter reappeared in the doorway, the camera behind him but not speaking yet.

"We don't need a full sit-down interview," he said.

"Just the one answer. That final moment. So we can cut it clean."

Dan nodded slowly. Lena looked toward the kitchen. Their mugs sat half-full on the counter. The clock above the hob had frozen three minutes slow again. A post it note on the fridge read "milk" in Dan's handwriting. They looked at each other. No words passed between them, just the kind of look shared in quiet, decisive rooms. The kind of look where the answer is already there. Dan turned toward the camera.

"We'll take the house," he said.

Lena nodded in sync beside him. "Yes. The house."

CHAPTER FIVE

The morning after didn't feel like a new beginning. It felt like a gap. Quiet, shapeless, and slow. The flat was still. The air inside carried the faint scent of last night's takeaway. Something garlicky with too much sauce and barely eaten. Lena stirred beneath the covers, blinking against the faint morning light bleeding through the edge of the blind. No alarm had gone off. Her phone was face-down on the floor beside the bed, exactly where she'd dropped it. She lay still for a moment, listening. No footsteps above. No music from the nail shop below. Just the soft groan of pipes warming up and the shuffle of Dan moving around the kitchen. She sat up slowly. The duvet had twisted around her legs. Her back ached faintly from sleeping in the same position too long. It didn't feel like the morning after a life-changing win. It felt like the morning after something unexplainable. The kind of surreal hangover that made you question your own memory. She padded barefoot into the living room. The overhead light was off, but the blinds were half-open, throwing a pale square of brightness across the cluttered coffee table. Dan was at the table, laptop open, coffee cooling beside him. He looked up when she entered but didn't smile.

"Morning," he said, voice rough.

"Hey," she murmured.

She made her way to the kitchen, filled the kettle, and let it boil. The silence between them wasn't uncomfortable, just muted. Like neither wanted to say it first: We won a house. Instead, she reached for the mugs. The one with the chip and the slogan she hated. The one Dan's sister had given them as a joke. Everything felt too familiar to be matched with something so unfamiliar. Behind her, Dan clicked something on his laptop. The screen reflected blue across the corner of his glasses.

"I was thinking," he said, "we should tell your mum today."

Lena didn't answer immediately. She poured the water and watched the tea bags darken. "Yeah," she said finally. "I'll call her after we go out."

Dan raised an eyebrow. "We going out?"

She handed him a mug. "We've been saying we'd try that place on the corner for months."

He gave a faint smile. "Celebration breakfast?"

She shrugged. "Or just coffee that isn't in a chipped mug."

Lena took her tea into the bedroom, leaving the door slightly ajar. The flat still held that faint scent of old paint and fabric softener, layered now with the quiet dust of lived-in corners. She stood by the wardrobe, staring at her clothes like they might answer for something. None of it felt right. Most of what she owned had been bought with compromise, on sale, work-appropriate, easy to repeat. She skimmed past blazers, knit jumpers, a dress she hated that Dan secretly liked. Then she found it. Navy. Cinched at the waist. Structured enough to say "put together," soft enough to feel like her. It wasn't designer, just a well-cut high street number that looked like it could be. She slipped it on without ceremony, smoothing it over her hips, and stepped in front of the mirror. The effect was subtle, but satisfying. A clean line down the spine. A soft V at the neck. She added her gold hoops, a sweep of liner, and a trace of colour on her lips that made her look like she hadn't slept badly. Behind her, she heard the wardrobe door creak open. Dan had wandered in shirtless, towel-draped over one shoulder, hair damp and curling slightly at the fringe. He didn't speak, just stood behind her a moment. Brushing his teeth and watching her through the mirror like it wasn't the first time he'd caught himself staring.

She glanced at him over her shoulder. "Are you planning on wearing actual clothes today or…?"

He grinned, toothpaste in the corner of his mouth. "I'm still considering my options." He ducked back out.

She watched him go. Fifteen minutes later, he reappeared as she clipped on her necklace. Jeans fitted at the waist, a charcoal jumper rolled at the sleeves, clean white trainers. He smelled faintly of her shampoo combined with his aftershave.

Lena tilted her head. "You're scrubbing up for a coffee?"

Dan gave her a look. "You're in a dress and lipstick."

"High-low balance."

"Right." He took her in again, longer this time.

"You look like you've already made it."

She raised an eyebrow. "And you look like you'd follow me into whatever meeting I made it to."

He stepped in close, thumb brushing the fabric at her waist. "Maybe I would."

For a second, everything else, the emails, the flat, the camera crew still echoing in their heads fell away. It was just the two of them again, in that soft middle place between chaos and calm. Dan kissed her cheek, slow and familiar.

"Come on. Before we overthink it." She grabbed her bag, still half-packed with receipts and chewing gum, and followed him into the hall.

The stairwell smelled of floor cleaner and nail polish remover. Someone downstairs was burning incense again, too much of it, a headachy mix of rose and something metallic. They walked in sync without speaking. Two streets up, the café stood like a perfect little diorama, glass, tile, trailing plants, and wooden stools too nice to sit on for long. Inside, it smelled of roasted beans and money. The kind of place you didn't order, you requested. A barista with a plait and sleeve tattoo nodded them toward the window seat. Lena sat down carefully, smoothing her skirt. Dan slid in beside her, not across from her, close enough that his knee brushed hers.

"This what winning a house tastes like?" he asked, glancing at the menu.

She smirked. "Feels more like pretending to be the kind of people who win houses."

He leaned in a little, voice low. "Pretend better. I think the couple two tables down thinks you're famous."

She didn't look. Just raised an eyebrow. "They probably just think you're punching."

Dan exhaled a short laugh. "You think I don't know that?"

For a moment, it was easy. Soft. Just them. Her hand brushed against his on the table and didn't move. The coffees arrived in glass tumblers without handles, dense and warm to the touch. Dan leaned back, resting his arm along the back of the bench seat, fingers grazing the top of Lena's shoulder. She didn't move away. Outside, the sky had that soft, unspecific grey London wore best, neither bright nor dark, just hanging there. The window caught their reflections faintly in the glass, two people who looked composed if not exactly settled.

Lena stirred her coffee slowly, the spoon tapping against the edge.

Dan nudged her ankle with his. "Do you think they'll give us a welcome mat?"

She glanced up. "What?"

"Like a monogrammed one. 'D & L, est. 2025' in some terrible font."

Lena gave a quiet laugh, shaking her head. "If they do, I'm setting it on fire."

He took a sip. "Rebellious."

She tilted her head. "Just selective about aesthetics."

They sat like that for a while, nursing overpriced drinks and letting the silence sit comfortably between them. Around them, the café filled slowly. Two girls at the bar with matching tote bags, a man in an expensive coat scrolling endlessly on his phone. Everything felt curated. Dan tapped the side of his cup, thoughtful.

"It's weird," he said after a moment. "The flat already feels like it isn't ours anymore."

Lena didn't reply straight away. She looked at her coffee, then out the window. "I know what you mean."

She reached for her phone out of habit, thumb brushing across the screen. There it was two new emails. One marked Winspire –

Congratulations. The other: ACTION REQUIRED – Completion Pack Enclosed. Her chest tightened, just slightly.

"They've emailed," she said.

Dan sat up straighter. "Already?"

She opened the first one. The header was slick, white text over gold, too bold to be tasteful. The body read like a press release. Congratulations again on being selected as the winner of the Rosehill House Grand Prize… We're thrilled to welcome you to the Winspire community… It went on for a while. She skimmed. The second email was more direct.

Subject: ACTION REQUIRED – Completion Pack Enclosed
From: Winspire Legal & Property Transfer
To: L.Hartley@…
Dear Miss Hartley and Mr. Kersey,
Please find attached your Completion Pack, which includes:
The property transfer form
Confirmation of deed
Bank detail verification
Media release form
These documents must be completed and returned within five working days to avoid delay.

We are scheduled to film your Welcome Home feature in two weeks. Confirmation of attendance is required.

Failure to complete these steps may result in forfeiture.

Best wishes,
The Winspire Team

Lena passed the screen to Dan. He read it in silence.

"Five days," he muttered.

She nodded. "And follow-up filming. At the new house." Dan leaned back slightly, pushing a hand through his hair.

"I know this was part of it," he said. "But it suddenly feels… corporate."

She finished her coffee, setting the empty glass down gently. "It is corporate."

He glanced out the window. "Still doesn't feel real."

"No." She paused. "But it is."

They sat quietly for a moment more, watching the world pass by outside the glass. Someone wheeled a pram past. A cyclist paused at the lights, foot on the pavement. Nothing around them had changed but everything in their inbox had. Lena scrolled back up to the top of the email and read it again. Not because she hadn't understood it, but because she needed to see the words land twice. Welcome Home Feature, Five Days Forfeiture. Each line felt like another inch of rope around their ankles. Nothing sinister. just tight. Binding. Across from her, Dan picked up the congratulations email and read it aloud in a flat, exaggerated voice.

"We're thrilled to welcome you to the Winspire family…" He paused.

"Your story will inspire countless others." He looked up at her.

"Inspire them to do what? Sign away their personal data for a scented candle and a lanyard?"

Lena smirked. "You didn't seem this cynical yesterday."

"Yesterday we hadn't seen the terms and conditions." He leaned on one elbow.

"Do you think they'll let us change the wallpaper?"

"Probably," she said. "I think they'll send a follow-up letter."

Dan cracked a smile. "God. What if it smells like one of those show homes? All faux leather and artificial fig. I'll riot."

He reached across the table and brushed his thumb lightly across her knuckles, just once. "At least we'll riot together."

She looked down at his hand. It was warm, familiar, the only part of this that felt normal. Outside, the weather had shifted. Light drizzle softening the pavement, fogging up the window edges slightly. The streets looked greyer now. People moved faster. The spell of their quiet moment cracked just slightly. Lena sat back.

"We should head back." Dan nodded.

"We've got five days to figure out how to move our entire lives into a PR campaign." They stood slowly, easing into coats and scarves, brushing stray coffee grounds off their sleeves. As they stepped outside, the air was damp and faintly metallic. The kind of London day that soaked into your bones before you realised it.

Back at the flat, the space already looked different. Not physically, nothing had moved. But it was like the walls were watching now. Expecting something of them. Dan pulled a stack of flattened cardboard boxes from behind the sofa. Lena kicked off her boots and tied her hair up before tugging open the hallway cupboard. Within five minutes, they were both elbows-deep in '*should we keep this?*' territory. Half-used candles, old paperwork, wires with no known origin.

She held up a tangled phone charger. "Is this yours?"

Dan barely looked. "Probably, but if I haven't used it since last year, bin it."

She dropped it into a pile of cables they were pretending had future value. The flat had that kind of quiet that came with productivity, the zip of duct tape, the thud of books into boxes, the occasional sound of Dan talking to himself when he couldn't find the masking tape. Lena knelt in front of a box of miscellaneous kitchen things when her phone began buzzing against the sideboard. **Mum**. Before she could wipe her hands, Dan reached across and picked it up.

"I'll get it." He swiped and answered, tucking the phone between his shoulder and ear.

"Hi, Trish… yeah, it's Dan." Pause. "Yeah. Mad, right?"

Lena sat back on her heels, watching him pace slightly across the kitchen tiles, one hand gesturing aimlessly as he spoke.

"No, we didn't know. Honestly, we thought it was some kind of prank. You should've seen our faces… Yeah, they turned up with cameras. Like doorstep-style."

She could hear her mum's voice on the other end, sharp, excited, slightly disbelieving. Dan laughed.

"No, we haven't seen it in person yet. They said we'll visit in two weeks. No, we've not packed. We're-" he looked at the half-folded mess around them "starting now."

He winked at Lena, who raised her eyebrows and pointed at a box labelled '*Tupperware*' Dan nodded along, still listening.

"Yeah, we'll come down before we go. Promise. Lena's just, hang on, I'll put her on." He handed her the phone with a grin. "Brace yourself."

Lena took the phone from his hand with a glance that said: don't you dare disappear. Dan smirked faintly, stepping around a half-packed box as she lifted the phone to her ear.

"Hi Mum," she said, drawing out the words just enough to soften the oncoming barrage.

Dan crouched by the pile of miscellaneous kitchen gear, chipped mugs, an orphaned lid, a garlic crusher neither of them remembered buying and tried not to listen. It was impossible, of course. Trish Hartley's voice projected even through the tinny speaker, cutting through the air like a butter knife through warm toast.

"I know, it's mad," Lena said, turning slightly away, her tone a practiced blend of patience and disbelief.

"No, they haven't shown us the interior yet… Just photos. Yeah, it looks big and clean. Yes, a bit like a film set."

Dan wrapped a second layer of tape around the box and set it aside. His knees cracked as he stood. Behind Lena, the room looked untouched by excitement. The same scuffed sofa. The TV stand missing a drawer knob. The framed print of Brighton Pier they'd never bothered to hang properly. The kind of space that clung to them even as they tried to peel away from it. Lena nodded along.

"We're coming down before the move. Promise. It's just, there's a lot to sort. Yeah. Packing and paperwork. No, they didn't mention if there's a cleaner. I don't think a cleaner is the point."

Dan caught her eye and raised a mug he'd just unearthed from a lower cupboard. "Yours or mine?"

She mouthed, *Bin it.* He dropped it in the discard pile with a quiet thunk. Most of their kitchen could be replaced with two shopping bags and a Tesco run. The kettle, a couple of plates, the pan with the loose handle. The furniture stayed. So did the rugs, the lamps, the bookshelf that bowed in the middle but wasn't theirs to take. Lena had wandered slightly toward the bedroom, pacing in small loops as she tried to land the call politely. Dan leaned against the wall and listened to the rhythm of her voice. There was something grounding about it. Even in disbelief, even under pressure, she stayed measured. He admired that.

She came back in a few minutes later, phone in one hand, sigh in the other.

"She's already Googling nearby garden centres," Lena said, dropping onto the edge of the sofa. "Says she wants to help with 'the outdoor flow'."

Dan blinked. "We don't even know if it has a garden."

"She says if it doesn't, we'll need planters."

He laughed softly. "Of course."

Lena leaned forward and picked at a stray thread in her skirt. "She means well."

"I know," he said, sitting beside her. "She's just trying to make it real."

Lena didn't answer. Her fingers kept worrying at the thread. The flat felt smaller again. Not claustrophobic, just on the edge of being packed away. Like a theatre set after the final show. Dan looked around and saw it properly for the first time: the parts that were theirs, and the parts that never had been. The blue lamp with the frayed shade, landlord. The creaky dining chairs. landlord. The sagging double bed with one leg propped up by a book, also landlord, and not even one of their books.

"We don't actually have that much to move," he said aloud, more to the room than to Lena.

She looked up. "No. Just everything that feels like us."

The light had faded into that greyish blue dusk that crept in early this time of year. The windows reflected more of the room than the street outside now. Lena flicked on the lamp by the sofa and immediately winced.

"Too bright," she said.

Dan adjusted the dimmer, casting the room in a warmer glow. It made the flat feel smaller, but kinder. They'd made it halfway through a box of books before realising the cutlery drawer was empty.

"Where did you pack the forks?" Lena called from the kitchen.

Dan didn't answer immediately, just stood in the middle of the room, staring at the four identical boxes labelled "Kitchen – misc."

He crouched by one and started peeling tape.

“Too early,” he muttered. By the time they found the forks, one of their better pans, and the soy sauce bottle that had somehow ended up wedged inside a winter boot, it was nearly eight.

Dinner became a thrown-together stir fry eaten cross-legged on the sofa, bowls balanced on knees, the TV humming in the background. A documentary about abandoned amusement parks played quietly, the flickering images catching on their faces like candlelight. They didn’t talk much, just passed the soy sauce back and forth, trading glances when the show took strange turns. It was nice. The kind of nice that made you forget there was still paperwork waiting on the table. Eventually, Lena wiped her mouth with the back of her hand and nodded toward the laptop.

“Let’s do it.” Dan opened the emails again.

They read through everything twice. Then again. Each field of the form felt heavier than it should have, like signing their names was a kind of small surrender. He watched Lena read the media release form, her brow furrowed.

“It’s basically saying they can use our faces forever,” she said.

Dan clicked the box. “Guess we’ll be famous.”

“I’d settle for anonymous homeowners with a quiet life.”

“Not in this story.” He replied.

They finished just after ten. The forms uploaded. The progress bar filled. A polite ‘Thank You’ message flashed on screen, and then it was done.

Dan sat back in the chair, rubbing his eyes. “Think that counts as adulting?” Lena leaned her head against his shoulder.

“I think that counts as not losing a house over laziness.”

They turned off the lights and left the kitchen half-tidy. A couple of mugs on the counter. The rest of their life, still in boxes.

Two Weeks Later

The Uber slowed as it turned off the main road, the tyres crunching over gravel. Outside the window, low brick walls gave way to open fields stitched with winter branches. The sun was bright but cold, casting everything in harsh, photogenic light. Dan adjusted the collar of his coat and glanced sideways at Lena, who was rechecking the address on her phone.

"Why are we coming here?" he asked.

She nodded. "Producer sent it this morning. Said we'd meet here first before heading to the property."

The house ahead was sleek and square, set slightly off the road, with slate tiles and tall glass panes that caught the sky. A black car already sat in the drive. The kind of car that suggested a well-pressed itinerary and no margin for lateness. The Uber rolled to a stop. Dan stepped out first, tugging at his jacket as the wind bit across the open space. Lena followed, brushing her hair back from her face as they approached the front door. Before they could knock, it swung open.

"Mister Kersey, Miss Hartley. Perfect timing." Miles Fenner stood there in a navy coat that probably cost more than their combined wardrobes, holding a clipboard and smiling with precision. His hair was immaculately styled, his teeth a shade too white, and his voice had the smooth clarity of someone used to calling 'action' on set.

"We've got a lot to cover," he said, stepping back to let them in.

"And a perfect window for soft natural light. Let's make the most of it, shall we?"

The house Miles led them into was all clean lines and curated neutrality. Taupe walls, brushed brass, mid-century accents carefully chosen to suggest wealth without edge. The kind of space where no one actually lived but everyone wanted to film in.

"This way," he said, glancing over his shoulder just long enough to check they were keeping up.

Lena caught Dan's eye and gave a half-smile. He couldn't tell if it meant 'This is Insane' or 'Behave.', possibly both. They followed Miles through a sitting room lit like a boutique showroom and into a smaller back lounge set up like a casual interview space. Soft lighting, a sideboard with still-wrapped croissants, water bottles arranged with military precision.

"Take a seat," Miles said, gesturing to the cream sofa.

"We've got makeup coming shortly. Just touch-ups, don't worry. Nothing theatrical." He checked his watch, then clapped his hands softly, a cue to someone off-screen they couldn't see.

"As you know," Miles began, flipping open a leather folio, "today's just a light orientation shoot. A few close-ups. A little b-roll of you both entering the property. Natural reactions, smiles, that sort of thing."

Dan nodded, though his mouth was dry. The sofa was too deep, like it wanted to swallow them whole.

"We'll film you walking up the drive, opening the gate, that first look. Try not to look at the camera unless prompted. Just soak it in, be yourselves but the version you'd want televised."

Lena gave a polite laugh. Dan wasn't sure if it was real. A young assistant in black jeans and an oversized blazer stepped in with a small makeup case. She introduced herself as Harper, offered warm greetings, and got to work dusting translucent powder across Lena's cheeks, then tapping a balm across Dan's forehead. She moved like someone used to working in silence, adjusting a strand of hair here, smoothing a wrinkle there.

"Perfect," Miles said, eyes already on the next item in the folio.

"Now, before we head to set…"

He slid two folders onto the coffee table in front of them. Inside: printed copies of the same documents they'd already submitted digitally. Property transfer. ID confirmations. Media permissions.

"These are for your records and for signature on camera. Just ceremonial, but legally required to film. We like to capture the moment you 'accept' the keys, even though the paperwork's already done."

Dan flipped through the pages. Each one printed on thick, ivory paper. Each one feeling somehow more real than it had on screen. Lena signed first, her pen barely scratching against the weight of the page. Then Dan. Miles collected the papers like they were precious artifacts and nodded, satisfied.

"Wonderful. Shall we?"

They followed him back out through the house and into a waiting black SUV parked in the circular drive. A second vehicle already had a small camera crew prepping in the backseat. Miles didn't ride with them, just gave a two-finger wave as they climbed inside.

The SUV was silent inside. Not just quiet, silent. Engine barely a murmur. Doors shut with a soft, padded thud. Even the tyres seemed to glide instead of grip. Lena sat upright, her seatbelt still twisted slightly from how she'd rushed it over her shoulder. Dan leaned back, one elbow braced on the window frame, watching the trees fold past in blinks. For the first ten minutes, no one spoke. It felt too formal, like they were guests in someone else's morning. The car pulled away from the shoot location and wound through a sequence of increasingly narrow lanes, hedges crowding the edges, the odd cottage set back behind dry-stone walls the colour of warm ash. The further they drove, the less familiar everything became. London slipped away in layers, petrol fumes. Corner shops, train lines. Then came the wide, high fields, grazing sheep and thick clusters of woodland, all bowed under the weight of late-winter green. Signs for villages they'd never heard of. Laybys with single picnic tables. A phone box that looked more like a relic than a service. Dan glanced over. Lena was still staring straight ahead, one hand resting on the centre console between them.

"You alright?" he asked.

She nodded, then shrugged. "It feels like we're being driven into a dream sequence."

Dan gave a dry smile. "A scenic abduction."

The car crested a hill, revealing a ribbon of road unspooling through a valley flanked by woods. Low stone walls bordered wild fields, peppered with daffodils even this early in the season. A small sign flashed past Stanton Glebe.

He turned back to Lena. "Did you catch that name?"

She nodded. "Sounds made up."

But it wasn't, none of it was. That was the strange part, it was all real. The cottages, the greenhouses behind wrought iron gates, the inns with crooked signage and stacked logs outside the doors. Even the air smelled cleaner, like moss and soap and cold. They passed a pub called The Bent Stag, that looked like it hadn't changed since 1780. An elderly man in a waxed jacket was walking a spaniel down a muddy path. Someone was burning wood nearby, smoke lifting in grey threads above a garden wall. Dan exhaled slowly, tapping his thumb against the door handle.

"We're not in Peckham anymore."

"No," Lena murmured.

"We're not."

The SUV turned again, this time onto a long, tree-lined drive. Gravel whispered under the tyres as if reluctant to announce them. Ahead, something large began to emerge through the branches. Not just a house. An estate.

The trees opened like a curtain. The SUV curved gently to the right, cresting the last rise of the long drive. Ahead, the house came into view. If you could call it a house. It looked more like something lifted from a period drama's establishing shot. Stone and symmetry and time itself, wrapped in a warm summer hush. The lawn stretched out in a perfect rectangle, too flat, too green, like someone had taken a ruler to it. At its edges, the hedges had been shaped into tidy pyramids, their bases dusted with crushed gravel. Wisteria curled along the front façade in full bloom, violet strands drooping like lazy confetti under the weight of July. Every windowpane was immaculate. Tall, old glass that reflected the sky like water.

Dan sat forward, mouth parted. "Jesus Christ."

Lena said nothing. She was already staring, hand resting lightly against the door as if unsure whether to open it or just keep looking. The car rolled to a stop. For a moment, everything was still. Then the front door opened. Miles Fenner stepped out, coat immaculate, his clipboard tucked under one arm. His smile was small but sharp, like a blade honed for hospitality. A woman followed, tall, camera-friendly, in a coat the colour of clotted cream. The presenter. Her heels made no sound on the gravel as she walked. Behind them, the camera crew were already in place. A drone lifted from the lawn with a soft mechanical whir. Dan and Lena stepped out of the SUV like they were waking into someone else's memory. The air was warmer out here, clean and thick with lavender. Lena smoothed her skirt with one palm, her eyes never leaving the building. The house stood three storeys tall, with low extensions tapering off either side like wings. Its stone was honey-coloured, softened by weather but untouched by decay. Ivy clung lazily to one side wall, and the long sash windows gleamed with the kind of polish no one could afford to maintain in real life. Beyond the garden walls, a conservatory glinted through the trees. Further off, the slate roofs of stables curved around a private courtyard. The pool, half-hidden from the drive, shimmered like it belonged on the cover of a magazine.

Dan glanced at Lena, then back at the house. "It's… a bloody estate."

Miles approached with a deliberate pace. His shoes didn't scuff, didn't slip. Just clicked lightly, crisply, like punctuation.

"Mr. Kersey. Ms. Hartley," he said, offering his hand.

"Welcome to Rosehill." Lena shook it.

"This is…"

"I know," Miles said smoothly.

"It's a lot. You'll have time to explore shortly. But first, a small surprise."

The presenter stepped forward. Her smile dialled to exactly the right wattage for national broadcast. In her hands, a black leather briefcase. She looked to the camera first, then turned to them.

"We want to make sure that your new life in the Cotswolds is exactly how you dreamed it to be," she said, voice bright but measured.

"That's why we're giving our Grand Prize Winner £250,000 in cash to help them settle in." She clicked open the case and turned it toward them.

Inside, neat rows of thick cash bundles. Real money. Tangible. No oversized cheques or fake press props, just a quarter of a million pounds, lined up like it had been waiting for them all morning.

Lena blinked. "That's… actual cash."

Miles smiled faintly. "Of course. It's yours."

Dan gave a stunned laugh that barely made it past his throat. "Is this real?"

"Every bit of it," the presenter said. "The house is fully furnished, too. You may find a few items aren't quite to your taste, but it's all yours. No usage restrictions. No 'please preserve' clauses. Redecorate, remove, resell. This isn't a showcase property anymore."

Dan looked up at the house again, really looked at it. "We can just… live here?"

Miles handed him the key. It was brass. Heavy. Old-fashioned, like something from a manor. "You already do," he said.

Lena looked back toward the car, then at the camera crew, then down at the briefcase.

"We don't have a safe," she murmured.

The presenter's laugh was velvet. "Then the first trip into town is on us."

Dan squeezed her hand without thinking. The house stood there in the background, unmoving, unchanged. Perfect. Patient. Waiting. A soft voice behind the camera called,

"Ready when you are." Lena flinched.

She hadn't even noticed the crew repositioning. One man was crouched behind a monitor. Another was shifting the reflector board slightly to catch the sun on their faces. Miles turned slightly, addressing them without really looking.

"We'll have you both sign the ceremonial copy now, just for the feature. You've already signed the legal paperwork, of course, but this is for continuity."

He produced a crisp white folder from under his arm and handed it to the presenter, who opened it like it was the Ten Commandments. Inside, two printed forms. Blank, clean, bearing their names in heavy serif font. Dan took the pen first. He looked down at the lines and hesitated, not because he doubted it, but because it all felt so staged he wasn't sure what expression to wear. He signed anyway. Lena followed, barely remembering how to shape her signature. The presenter smiled wider.

"Perfect." A nod from behind the camera.

Someone whispered, "Hold for champagne."

A beat later, a young woman emerged from behind the hedgerow, carrying a tray of coupe glasses and a chilled bottle glistening with condensation. The glasses looked antique, etched glass, gold rims. She offered the presenter one first, then Lena, then Dan, then Miles. The bubbles fizzed softly, catching sunlight like powdered gold. The presenter raised her glass with theatrical timing.

"To new beginnings," she said, eyes on the camera.

"To Rosehill House." They all clinked.

Dan's glass was cold against his fingers. He took a cautious sip. Real champagne, not prosecco, not sparkling wine. Actual, crisp, expensive champagne. The presenter turned slightly toward the lens.

"And cut." The moment snapped in half.

The director behind the camera gave a quiet "great" and stepped back to adjust something. The drone hummed higher above the treetops, repositioning for a wide shot of the lawn. The presenter turned back to Lena and Dan, her voice dipping an octave.

"That was perfect," she said, suddenly more human.

The performance melted just slightly, replaced by something brighter, unfiltered, off-script. "God, this place is unbelievable, isn't it?"

Dan gave a slow nod, still holding his champagne like it might vanish if he looked away. The presenter's grin widened.

"Come on. You've got the keys. Let's show you what you've actually won." She passed her empty glass to an assistant and motioned for them to follow.

Her stride was quick, already halfway up the path before they could gather themselves. Cameras adjusted in her wake, picking up B-roll as the trio approached the stone steps.

"No scripts now," she called over her shoulder. "You can actually react."

Lena reached over and squeezed Dan's hand, her palm slightly damp. He didn't let go. The door stood tall, the brass handle already catching the light. Dan stepped forward, fit the heavy key into the lock, and turned. It opened easily and the house, their house awaited.

The door opened inward with a muted creak, the kind that came not from age but from weight. Dan stepped in first, Lena just behind, and for a moment neither of them said a word. The entryway smelled of polish and stone. Cool air coiled upward from the flagstone floor, carrying a faint trace of lavender and something earthier. Like old plaster or sealed wood. Sunlight filtered in through the window above the door, cutting soft lines across the parquet. To the left, a narrow passage curved toward the ***boot room***, a space that felt more like a curated gallery than a place to shake off mud. Woven baskets beneath a built-in bench. A row of pegs holding pristine coats in neutral tones. Even the floor tiles looked deliberately scuffed, like a lifestyle magazine's idea of rustic. The ***lounge*** opened wide to the right. A grand, pale room with generous windows and high moulded ceilings. The furniture was luxurious but stiff: oversized armchairs, a pale green sofa that looked antique but un-sat-on, coffee table books that had never been opened. An abstract seascape hung above a limestone fireplace, and fluted lamps framed the space like theatre lights set to *casual elegance.* Lena moved into the room slowly, brushing her fingertips along the top of a console table.

"Do you think we're allowed to sit down?"

Dan shrugged, still holding the key in his hand like he didn't know where to put it. "You heard them. It's ours."

She sat, the sofa dipped just slightly. *"Feels like I'm trespassing in a showroom."*

Dan joined her, their knees barely touching. The camera crew lingered in the hallway, catching wide shots through the open doorway. No instructions, no commentary. Just observation. That made it worse somehow.

Beyond the lounge, a short hall led to the ***game room***. All polished oak panelling, a low-slung leather sofa, and a full-sized billiards table beneath a moody pendant light. Framed vintage prints hung in a tight grid, each one capturing some curated, masculine past. A walnut bar cart gleamed by the wall, stocked with untouched decanters.

Dan let out a low breath. "I've never owned anything with decanters in it before."

"You still don't," Lena murmured, eyeing the glassware.

"We own this house. Not whoever they dressed it for." He nodded, quiet.

The space looked like it belonged to someone named Charles who smoked cigars and wore cufflinks but it was theirs now. Somehow. A few more paces down the hall, and the house opened up into the real showpiece: the ***kitchen***. The shift in scale was dramatic. A vaulted ceiling stretched above sleek beams. At the centre, a vast island of white stone anchored the room, surrounded by modern cabinetry in muted charcoal tones. Four woven bar stools sat precisely aligned. The brass fixtures caught the overhead lights like jewellery. The far wall was lined with open shelving. Ceramic dishes, shallow bowls, matching glassware, everything just slightly mismatched enough to look casual. A double range sat under a wide, pale stone hood. There was a corner bench with soft linen cushions, and a second prep sink sat under a wide window that overlooked the south lawn.

Lena stepped forward slowly, eyes widening. "Okay… this is ridiculous."

Dan turned a slow circle, hands on hips. "This is three of our flat. Just this room."

She opened a drawer. Inside, utensils still wrapped in paper. The kind no one had touched yet. Dan opened a cupboard. All the mugs matched. There were no takeaway menus pinned to the fridge. No half-used jars. No evidence of life. Not yet. They lingered in the kitchen longer than expected. The space just kept revealing itself, quiet alcoves, deep drawers, hidden power sockets beneath the island ledge. Every time Lena thought she'd mapped the room, something else surfaced.

"Feels like it shouldn't all be one room," Dan said quietly, testing the touch-latch on one of the cabinets. It swung open silently to reveal a built-in coffee machine. "Feels like a café. Or… a movie set."

As if summoned by the word, Miles Fenner appeared in the archway.

"Funny you say that," he said with a smooth smile, hands clasped behind his back. "The kitchen was actually the last part to be completed during the renovation. Took longer than expected to source the stone, hand-cut from a quarry in Oxfordshire."

Dan turned slightly. "The whole house was redone?"

"Top to bottom," Miles nodded. "Converted by Winspire's architectural partners before the prize went live. Structurally, it's eighteenth-century, much of the original timber framing is preserved but the interiors were updated just this past spring. Insulation, electrical, water pressure, you won't find a better upgrade in the postcode. Probably the entire county."

Lena leaned against the back of one of the stools. "Was it always a family home?"

Miles gave a small smile. "Judging by the size, I'd assume so. Though you'd be surprised how many people buy homes like this just for weekends."

Dan glanced around at the space, still trying to take it in. "Right. Just a little weekend place with a cinema and a pool."

Miles laughed softly, polished but sincere. "Speaking of, would you like to see it?"

He gestured down the corridor. They followed, past a tucked-away ***utility room***. Neatly folded towels, stacked detergent pods, an iron still in its packaging and into the ***cinema room***, which felt like it belonged in a private hotel. The walls were painted a deep, velvety navy. The ceiling was a soft matte black. Rows of oversized armchairs stepped gently downward toward a full-width screen larger than anything they'd ever owned, flanked by panelled acoustic walls. There was no cheap surround setup here. Everything felt embedded, seamless.

"There's surround sound," Miles said, "built into the panelling. Also hidden acoustic insulation in the ceiling. Temperature-controlled."

Lena ran her hand along the velvet armrest of one of the chairs. "This is insane."

Dan stayed at the back, arms loosely crossed, eyes scanning the room. "This is nicer than any cinema I've paid to go to."

Miles nodded, pleased. "It's ready to go. The tablet by the door controls lighting, blinds, audio. There's a hidden snack drawer too. Help yourselves."

He stepped toward the hallway again, pausing at the threshold.

"We'll give you a moment," he said. "The crew's shooting exteriors. No rush. When you're ready, we'll head upstairs" and with that, he was gone.

Silence settled in like warm fabric. Lena eased into one of the chairs, her posture slackening. Dan sat down beside her. Neither of them spoke at first. They just looked around, wide-eyed.

"I don't think I've processed a single thing since we turned off the A40," she said finally.

Dan gave a quiet nod. "I feel like we're squatting in a Bond villain's weekend place."

She let out a quiet breath of a laugh. The armrests were warm from sunlight that had already moved on. Everything around them was new and untouched. And yet somehow, the weight of ownership was already starting to press against their ribs. This was real. They just didn't know how to be real inside it yet. When they emerged from the cinema room, the house felt brighter like someone had lifted the veil between them and daylight. Miles was waiting near the base of the staircase, his hand resting lightly on the banister.

"If you're ready," he said, tone gentler now, "we'll head up."

The staircase was wide but not ostentatious. Stone steps softened by a thick runner, the kind that quieted your footsteps even if you weren't trying. The banister was original wood, polished by years of imagined hands. It creaked once, softly, under Lena's touch. At the landing, the corridor unfolded in two directions. One wing stretching toward a collection of closed doors, the other toward a set of grander double doors with an ornate brass keyhole. Miles led them toward the latter.

"This is the main bedroom," he said, pushing the doors open with an effortless motion.

The room exhaled luxury. Soft natural light poured through twin sash windows, spilling across the pale carpet and catching the subtle textures of cream and sage-green linen. The bed was a statement piece, solid, understated, dressed in layered fabrics and too many pillows. An upholstered bench stood at the foot, perfectly aligned. Flanking the room were matching nightstands, each topped with ceramic lamps in soft grey glaze. Lena stepped inside slowly. The space seemed to muffle sound.

She brushed one finger along the edge of the windowsill. "I've stayed in boutique hotels that looked like this. For a night."

Dan wandered toward the far end of the room where another door led into a ***dressing room***, a walk-in wardrobe, really. Floor-to-ceiling cabinetry lined both sides. Mirrors, backlit shelving, drawers with leather pulls. Everything smelled faintly of cedar. He opened one of the doors. Inside: padded hangers, a lavender-scented sachet, and a set of empty shoe cubbies. No clothes. No imprint of a previous owner. It really was ready for them. Miles stepped to the side.

"Through here is the en suite," he said. "If I may." He opened the adjoining ***bathroom*** door.

The room was elegant, minimalist, expensive. A freestanding bath sat beneath a wide window that framed the rolling green beyond. The floor was warm wood, the walls a muted plaster pink. A pair of marble sinks rested on a carved black-lacquered cabinet, and the fittings were all burnished gold. Lena leaned slightly on the doorframe.

"I feel like I shouldn't be allowed to use any of this."

"It's all functional," Miles said lightly. "Though I do recommend the bath in the evening. The sunset through that window is something else."

Dan blinked. "You've bathed here?"

Miles smirked faintly. "No. But I've heard the brief."

They continued down the corridor, passing a smaller **utility closet**, then reaching a string of guest rooms. Each decorated differently, as if styled for different catalogues of wealth. One was pale blue with built-in shelving and sea-grass accents. Another in dusky rose and cream. All of them neatly made. All of them waiting. The furnishing covered in dust sheets to protect it.

"This floor has five bedrooms total," Miles explained. "Main suite, plus four guest rooms. There's also a attic, but we'll leave that for another day, it's dry, clean, good for wine. Not much else."

Lena opened one of the guest room doors and peeked in. Soft carpet. A low bench under the window. Matching prints on the walls.

Dan leaned close behind her. "We could get lost just deciding where to sleep."

She gave a soft hum in agreement but didn't move. The air up here was warmer, more still. Quiet in a way that wasn't silence. Just contained, like the house was holding its breath. They climbed the narrow set of stairs to the second floor, where the air grew thinner and cooler, filtered through older plaster and thicker stone. The steps creaked more here not from age exactly, but from the house reminding them this part had been lived in longer. Less polished. Less posed. The top floor opened into a single bedroom tucked neatly under the eaves. Sloped ceilings met above a central bed dressed in muted ochres and white. The far window was deep-set, framed by thick walls and a wide sill. Outside, hedgerows rippled across a patchwork of fields.

"This is the highest point in the house," Miles offered, stepping carefully inside. "It stays cool in the summer, surprisingly warm in the winter. Often used as a studio or a quiet retreat." Dan wandered over to the sill.

"I'd write something up here," he murmured.

Lena leaned into the doorframe, arms folded loosely. "You've never written anything."

"Then I'd start." Dan replied.

The walls were quiet here. There was no hum from the power systems. Just the faint sound of trees moving far below. They didn't say much else. The house didn't ask for it. Miles let them linger a moment, then guided them gently back down. They passed each level again, footsteps echoing differently in every corridor, light shifting across walls they were only beginning to recognise as their own. By the time they returned to the ground floor, the film crew was packing up. One of the camera operators gave them a soft smile. Another was folding a reflector into its case with quick, efficient snaps. The presenter, now in trainers and a long coat, greeted them just inside the kitchen archway with a warm clap of her hands.

"There you are," she said, cheerful but with a note of finality.

"Just one last thing." She stepped aside as an assistant handed her a branded envelope and a final document sleeve, this one gold-foiled with their names printed across the front. "Officially, this makes it yours," she said.

"And before we wrap, one more question for the video's closing line." She held up a mic. "We'd usually ask if you're staying tonight or heading back to London. No pressure, of course. Transport's arranged either way."

Dan glanced at Lena.

"We'll take the lift back," she said softly.

He nodded. "We've still got a few things to pack."

The presenter smiled. "Understood. Your driver's already waiting at the gate."

An assistant stepped forward with a final gesture, another ornate key thick key on a leather fob. Lena took it, warm from the presenter's hand.

"That's yours also" the presenter said. "No backups. No returns."

She gave a parting grin and stepped away to speak with the crew. Dan turned toward the front door, but Lena held back. She looked over her shoulder once more at the vaulted ceiling of the kitchen, the polished brass, the faint scent of lavender still lingering in the air. Then she stepped forward and, without a word, locked the front door behind them. The key clicked once. Twice. Firm. Final. She slid it into her coat pocket and turned toward Dan.

"Let's go home," she said and they walked back down the long gravel path together, leaving the house sealed, silent, and waiting

CHAPTER SIX

Over the next week, the flat slowly hollowed itself out. Lena packed in stages, first the obvious things, then the emotional ones. Scarves she never wore but always meant to. The chipped mugs. Their decent kitchen knives. Each day, another drawer closed for the last time. Dan took care of logistics. Work calls, forwarding addresses, the dreaded change-of-address form that never quite covered everything. His office had agreed to hybrid. Tuesdays and Fridays in person, the rest from home. Lena's manager, more curious than concerned, signed off a three-month remote trial.

"You'll have to send pictures," she'd said. "That part of the country's supposed to be charming."

They drove down to Lena's mum's place in Surrey one evening with a small suitcase and a bottle of supermarket red. It was a quiet dinner. Her mum asked all the right questions, most of them twice. At the end of the night, she hugged Lena a second time at the door and whispered,

"Don't forget to visit us from your estate."

Back in Peckham, the flat grew sharper around the edges. Dust behind the bedframe. Scuffs where the table had been. The nail salon downstairs stopped playing music at 10 p.m., but the scent of acetone lingered in the walls. Their lives shrank into canvas bags and taped boxes, everything they truly owned fitting into the boot and back seat of Dan's car. By the time the landlord came round, there was almost nothing left. He arrived late. Keyring jangling, clipboard under one arm, reading glasses pushed onto the bridge of his nose like they gave him more authority.

Dan opened the door and stepped back. "We're ready."

The landlord walked in like it still belonged to him and in fairness, it did. The sofa, the bed frame, the lamps. All his. All included in the rent. Still, he frowned like something had been taken from him.

He ran a hand along the kitchen counter. "Hmm. Bit of wear here."

Lena said nothing. He opened cupboards, looked under the sink. Made a show of checking the blinds.

"You didn't report this crack in the tile," he muttered. "Could've got worse."

Dan nodded once. "Didn't."

The man sniffed and scribbled something on his sheet. Then he paused by the hallway radiator. "Bit of damp here."

"It was there when we moved in," Lena said, voice even.

"Hmm. Doesn't say that on the inventory." She didn't reply.

Neither did Dan. The inspection lasted twelve minutes. He clicked his pen twice.

"We'll be in touch about the deposit," he said on the way out. "Depending on cleaning fees."

"Sure," Dan said, already locking the door behind him. They didn't push, didn't challenge. They just allowed him to have his moment.

They carried the last two bags down the stairs, through the narrow hall, past the door with the faint polish smell behind it. The car was already heavy with their lives, bin liners of clothes, boxes of mismatched kitchen things, one overfed houseplant that had never quite died. Dan opened the boot. Lena squeezed in the final bag.

He looked up at the building. "Doesn't feel like ours anymore."

Lena ran her fingers along the car door. "I don't think it ever really did."

They slid into the seats, closed the doors, and pulled away. No one waved. No one watched them go. South London peeled itself away street by street. Flats gave way to shopfronts, then to warehouses, then to scattered housing developments that blurred together like a sketch someone had rushed to finish. By the time they hit the motorway, the rain had started light, aimless. The kind that settled into glass slowly, turning everything beyond the windscreen into a smear of grey and green. The satnav counted down the miles. Lena watched it quietly. Neither of them said much until the roads narrowed and the sign came into view:

Welcome to the Cotswolds.

The drive up to the house was quieter this time. Less performance. No camera crew. no presenter. Just tyres crunching along gravel and the hum of an engine trying not to sound tired. The house rose before them exactly as they remembered it. Gold-stone and symmetrical, ivy hugging one side like a sleeping arm. The windows were blank, reflective. Still. Lena reached into her coat pocket and pulled out the key.

Dan killed the engine. "You want to do it?"

She nodded, already halfway out.

At the front door, she slid the key into the lock, twisted but it didn't click. The door pushed open with the gentlest resistance, like it had been waiting. She paused.

Dan came up behind her, frowning. "Didn't lock it?"

"I did," she said, too quickly. "I double-checked."

He stepped inside, flicked on the hallway light. "Maybe you weren't used to the key yet. It's stiff."

"I remember locking it."

Dan glanced back at her. "Could've stuck. Might've just looked locked."

Lena didn't reply. The hallway looked untouched. Still polished. Still pristine. No signs of movement. But the air felt looser, somehow.

Like a window had been cracked somewhere and the whole house was just slightly out of breath. They dropped their bags by the stairs, still zipped and dusty from the road. Dan rolled his neck once and reached for the banister. "Quick sweep?"

She nodded. Upstairs, everything was where it had been. The main bedroom sat in perfect stillness, light shifting softly across the duvet. Doors closed exactly as they'd left them. Drawers untouched. The second-floor guest rooms were just as neat. Not a pillow out of place, no footprints on the carpet. By the time they reached the dressing room again,

Dan looked unconvinced. "Nothing's been touched."

Lena didn't answer. She was already halfway down the stairs.

The kitchen still gleamed under soft recessed lighting. The air smelled faintly of lavender and warm plaster. But the far end of the room, the large double doors leading out to the pool terrace and guest house was ajar. Not wide. Just enough for a hand to pass through. A few brown-edged leaves had blown inside, caught in the groove of the stone threshold. One of them moved slightly in the draft. Lena froze.

"I shut that," she said. "When we were looking around with the presenter. I shut it."

Dan came to her side and studied the door.

"Maybe someone opened it during filming. One of the crew. Could've been getting drone footage."

"I didn't see anyone go out." Lena replied, her face expressed unease.

"Neither did I. But we weren't watching the whole time, were we?" He pushed the door closed with a soft click and turned the lock once. "There."

Still, Lena stared at the leaves for a moment longer before brushing them away with her foot. The silence of the kitchen returned. Just the low tick of the clock on the wall. The faint hum of the fridge. Dan exhaled and leaned on the counter. "Well… home sweet home."

She managed a small smile, but it didn't quite land. The house no longer felt staged but it didn't feel lived-in either. Just large, watchful. The kind of quiet that didn't settle, it lingered. Still, they moved through it like they belonged. They unpacked slowly, shedding coats and shoes, dragging the bags into the boot room where they'd decide what needed storing and what would just collect dust. Dan cracked a window upstairs, said the air needed circulation. Lena opened the fridge, found a welcome bottle of wine still untouched from the handover shoot. She uncorked it without ceremony and poured two glasses. They sat in the lounge later, the same pale sofa they hadn't dared to sit on before, surrounded by the hush of expensive things. The television stayed off. No music. No laughter from a neighbour's window. Just the low sound of wind threading through the hedges outside and the house, solid and clean, locking in every breath they made.

The next few hours passed in soft, disjointed rhythms. They didn't plan a system, they just moved. One room at a time. The boxes were unpacked faster than they'd expected, mostly because there weren't many. No sofas to lift. No wardrobes to manoeuvre. Just clothing, kitchen items, cables, a few books, and the ghost-trails of their former lives folded into bubble wrap. Dan took a few things upstairs, shirts, chargers, their worn duvet from the flat even though the house already had nicer linen. Lena filled kitchen drawers on autopilot. They didn't speak much, only small remarks passed between them, *"Where do you want this?" "God, we have too many mugs." "That drawer sticks."* At some point the sky outside shifted. Pale blue fading into the cooler tones of early evening. Dan stretched, arms above his head, spine clicking faintly.

"I'm gonna move the car into the garage," he said. "Feels weird having it out front like it's just visiting."

Lena nodded. "I'll start setting up the study. Might as well get my desk sorted."

He kissed the top of her head as he passed. "Call if you need me or scream dramatically. Whichever."

She rolled her eyes and smirked, but her fingers paused briefly on the drawer handle. The ***study*** sat just off the main corridor, tucked behind a frosted glass door with a soft latch and a slightly warped hinge that clicked when you opened it too fast. The room was beautiful. Cold, but beautiful. Large sash windows framed the far wall, currently closed and dappled with the shadow of a tree that stood somewhere just beyond view. The desk was already in place. An old oak piece with brass handles and shallow drawers, set dead-centre beneath a mid-century light fixture that hummed faintly when turned on. There were built-in shelves to the left. Mostly empty. A few decorative hardbacks, a glass paperweight, a brass magnifying glass that looked untouched. The carpet was low-pile, dark grey. Minimal, almost commercial. Lena set her box down near the desk and exhaled. She began pulling out her things. Laptop charger, pens, a small notepad with half-used lists still stuck between the pages. A framed photo of her and Dan from some holiday years ago where they both looked a little sunburned and too caffeinated. She placed it on the corner of the desk, then adjusted it twice. Her fingers brushed the drawer handle. Something about it felt, colder than expected but not in a way she could justify. Just cold. She opened the top drawer. Empty, aside from a neatly folded notecard tucked against the back. She hesitated. Then picked it up. Blank. Just a square of thick paper, cream-coloured, with a slightly embossed border. No writing. No markings. No smell. Not new, not old. Just there. She set it aside and kept unpacking. The room didn't feel bad, exactly. It just didn't feel quite like hers. Something about the angles. The way sound carried or didn't. The way the tree's shadow shifted slightly across the carpet even though the wind outside had stopped. She plugged in her laptop. The charging light flickered once. Then stayed solid. Dan's voice echoed faintly from somewhere near the garage. A door closed. Distant, but definite. Lena looked around the room again, her boxes now mostly empty, the desk starting to resemble something familiar, and let out a slow breath. Just a new space. Dan reappeared just after seven, wind-ruffled and flushed from the cooler air outside. He walked in through the boot room, shaking his keys lightly and giving the door an extra pull behind him before locking it.

"Car's tucked away," he called toward the hallway. "Garage door took me a minute to figure out, but it's fancier than I am, so I'll adapt."

He wandered into the kitchen and paused, hands on hips, surveying it like a man about to perform a ritual. The island gleamed, the brass taps caught the soft pendant lighting, and the double oven sat there, silent and state-of-the-art, waiting to be worshipped. Dan grinned.

"Alright, let's see what this place can really do."

He unpacked the small bag of groceries they'd brought with them. fresh pasta, garlic, a tin of tomatoes, and an overpriced olive oil Lena had thrown in '*for the vibe.*' The fridge had a few basic essentials left behind from the Winspire shoot, along with the rest of the wine, and some unlabelled condiments that looked suspiciously artisanal. He switched on the stove. It responded instantly, sleek induction heat, backlit controls, a soft hum instead of a roar. Even the sizzle of garlic in the pan sounded expensive. He was plating the garlic base when Lena reappeared, still holding her phone out in front of her like a tour guide. Her mother's voice carried through tinny but clear.

"…and that's your view from the kitchen?" Lena turned the camera to the wide pane that framed the back garden and guest house.

The sun had dipped lower now, throwing the lawn into amber relief. Shadows reached long across the flagstones.

"Yep," Lena said. "Apparently there's heating under the terrace tiles."

"Good God," Trish muttered from the screen.

"You'll be ruined forever. You'll never be able to visit us again."

Lena smiled, wandering closer to the island. "We'll make time. You and Dad should come stay."

Dan looked up, dusting oregano over the sauce. "Definitely. Bring an overnight bag or five. We've got enough bedrooms for a small army."

Trish's voice perked. "Oh don't tempt us, Daniel."

Dan leaned against the counter, tossing a wooden spoon between his palms.

"We were actually saying we could do something bigger. Maybe host a barbecue once we're a bit more settled. Get a few people down. You lot, some of mine. It'd be nice."

Lena glanced at him, surprised but pleasantly.

"We could. I mean, if we don't mind people traipsing through our enormous countryside retreat."

"Exactly," Dan said. "It's wasted on just us."

From the phone, Trish was already planning dates.

"End of the month could work. We'll bring wine and your father's newest hobby is slow-cooked ribs, so brace yourself."

Lena laughed, angling the camera away so Trish didn't see Dan dramatically miming regret. "I'll let you know once we've got furniture on the terrace."

They said quick goodbyes and Lena ended the call, letting the silence settle back into the room.

Dan poured her a glass of wine without asking. "So… garden party?"

Lena took the glass, leaned against the counter beside him. "I like the idea. Might make it feel more lived-in."

Dan nodded, stirring the pot. "Exactly. Put some history into the walls."

He tasted the sauce, frowned slightly, then reached for a pinch more salt. The whole kitchen smelled warm now, garlic, tomato, something like rosemary. The kind of smell that made a space feel claimed. Lena looked around the room again. The high ceilings, the soft light, the door to the terrace now firmly locked. She exhaled. "We'll need citronella candles."

Dan raised his glass. "And maybe a fire pit." They clinked, softly.

Outside, dusk had finally settled. The sky burned low behind the guest house. Shadows deepened across the lawn and somewhere, in the silence behind all this newness, the house watched on. Later, the dishes dried and stacked, the wine low in the bottle, they drifted toward the ***cinema room*** almost without speaking. Dan led the way, flicking on lights as they passed through the darkened hallway. The panelled walls greeted them like old friends. Rich navy and deep oak, the floor a soft hush beneath their bare feet. Inside, the room felt different in the dark. Not ominous, just deeper. Quieter. The kind of quiet that came from thick insulation and money.

Lena lowered herself into the nearest velvet armchair and curled one leg beneath her. "This still doesn't feel real."

Dan sat down beside her, stretching out, glass in hand. "Nope. Still feels like we're about to be told we've overstayed our welcome."

She smiled faintly. "Or that someone else is about to come in and claim it."

Dan clicked the tablet from the wall mount and swiped through the interface. It was smooth, responsive. The lights dimmed with a soft blink. The screen hummed awake. The curtains pulled tighter over the window with a mechanical sigh.

Lena blinked. “This room is smarter than we are.”

Dan raised his eyebrows. “I accept that.”

He tapped into the streaming service. The screen filled with thumbnails: films they hadn’t thought about in years, glossy new releases, an eerily on-point *‘Recommended For You’* row.

“I’m picking something terrible,” he said.

“Of course you are.”

“Something comfortingly dumb. So we don’t have to think.” He scrolled, stopped and smirked.

“This?” Lena glanced over and groaned.

“You’re unbelievable.” He pressed play.

The film loaded. The lights dipped lower. Then he paused it again.

“There was supposed to be a snack drawer,” he said, already standing.

Lena watched him with an arched brow. “You’re seriously investigating?”

He was already checking the side table. Then the one across the aisle. Nothing. Then the third one, nearer the projector controls. He tugged gently, and the drawer slid open with a neat click. Inside, three glass jars. sweets, hard mints, some kind of sugared almonds and a packet of popcorn still sealed, best-before date safely months away.

Dan held it up triumphantly. “This place. I mean…”

He carried the finds back over, dropped into the seat beside her, and passed her one of the jars. They unspooled slowly into the film. Wine drained. The room glowed softly around them, velvet and gold, soft carpet, the kind of sound system that made everything feel close. At one point, Lena glanced at the doorway, the only visible exit and for the briefest moment had the oddest sensation that someone had just left the room before her eyes adjusted. She blinked. Just the hallway beyond, silent and perfectly still. She leaned back into the chair and reached for the popcorn as Dan laughed at some idiotic line on-screen. The house didn’t creak. It didn’t breathe but it watched quietly as they fell into their first night of pretending this life already belonged to them. The film ended in the usual avalanche of credits, white on black, with music too dramatic for the quiet that lingered in the room. Dan stretched his arms above his head, letting out a long breath that bordered on a groan.

"Okay. That might have been terrible enough to be perfect."

Lena smiled but didn't answer. She was staring at the last few names scrolling past on the screen, barely seeing them.

"More wine?" he offered.

She shook her head. "Think I'm good."

He stood anyway, collecting their glasses, padding barefoot out toward the kitchen with the sleepy confidence of someone beginning to believe they lived here. She remained seated, curled into the armchair, one hand resting lightly on the edge of the throw blanket she hadn't realised she'd pulled over her lap. The projector powered down with a mechanical sigh and the soft ambient lights returned, stretching shadows up the navy walls like vines. Lena stood slowly. Her body felt too quiet. She gathered the empty popcorn packet, dropped it in the small side-bin tucked beneath the control panel, then stepped into the hallway. The corridor was darker than she expected. The motion lights hadn't come on, and for a moment she wondered if she'd missed a switch. The stillness felt thick. Like the air was just a little slower here. more reluctant. She headed toward the main bathroom off the hall to wash her hands and splash her face. The tap was silent-smooth. She watched the water swirl down the marble basin, the mirror catching only the top of her head at this angle. She turned the tap off and paused. Somewhere above her, the faintest sound. Like a floorboard, It didn't repeat. She stayed still a moment longer, hands braced on the counter, watching her breath fog the corner of the mirror. Then she wiped it away with the side of her wrist and left the light on as she stepped back into the corridor. The hallway remained empty. Silent. The house exhaled softly around her. Dan was back in the kitchen, rinsing the wine glasses and humming some unplaceable tune under his breath.

He glanced over when she reappeared. "Hey. I forgot to ask, how's the desk setup?"

Lena shrugged. "Functional."

Dan dried a glass. "You sure? You look…"

"Just tired." He tossed her a dish towel.

"Let's call it then." They shut the kitchen down together, checked the back doors again, flicked off switches, dimmed the pendant lights. The house transitioned into its overnight setting like it had been trained to. One by one, the spaces went quiet.

Upstairs, they changed slowly. The main bedroom felt even bigger at night. The bed, once impressive, now looked comically oversized for just the two of them. Like something that belonged to a hotel they couldn't quite afford . Lena brushed her teeth in the en suite while

Dan leaned against the frame of the dressing room door, watching her in the mirror. "You think we're gonna get used to this?"

She glanced at him through the reflection, toothbrush half-raised. "Used to what?"

"This. Waking up in a house that feels like it costs more per day than our flat did in a month." He responded.

She smirked around the bristles. "That's not a real stat."

"Feels true though."

She spit, rinsed, wiped her mouth with a towel that still smelled faintly like whatever luxury brand Winspire stocked. "I think we'll forget eventually. That it wasn't always ours."

Dan didn't reply. Just nodded once and went to switch off the wardrobe lights. They climbed into bed without ceremony. The sheets were smooth. Cool. The duvet heavier than expected. Lena rolled to her side, back to Dan, her arm tucked beneath her head. His hand found her waist, resting there lightly.

Outside, the countryside had gone black. No hum of traffic. No sodium streetlights. Just the vast absence of city. They lay there a long time without speaking. Then, softly

"I thought I saw someone earlier," Lena said.

Dan's hand stilled. She felt him shift slightly.

"Where?"

"Cinema room. Right as the movie started. Just for a second. In the doorway." He was quiet for a beat longer than she wanted.

"Could've been a shadow," he said eventually. "Light from the screen or something."

"Yeah," she murmured. "That's what I thought."

He kissed her shoulder once, then settled again, but she didn't close her eyes. Not yet. She stared at the faint outline of the ceiling above them. At the small blink of the smoke alarm. At the shadow of the open en suite door where a soft green light still glowed from the mirror controls. The house was quiet. Too quiet to tell if it was listening.

Sometime after midnight, Dan stirred. It wasn't a sound that woke him. Not exactly. Just a change in the air, like the weight of the room had shifted slightly while he slept. He blinked into the darkness. The house was silent. Truly silent. No hum of passing cars, no heating pipes adjusting in the walls. No neighbours on the other side of a shared floorboard. Just stillness. The kind you could fall into if you weren't careful. He rolled onto his back and listened. Lena breathed steadily beside him, her shoulder just grazing his arm beneath the covers. Her face was turned toward the open window. The thin curtain barely moving. He stared at the ceiling. The red LED from the smoke alarm blinked once. Then again. His eyes adjusted slowly. The room looked unchanged. He considered getting up, just to check the kitchen, or the garage, or the back door again. But the feeling passed almost as quickly as it had come. Not fear. Just… awareness. That they were no longer surrounded by sirens and footsteps and streetlights. That every sound out here was theirs to make or to miss. He exhaled softly and turned onto his side, facing Lena. Outside, something shifted. A bird, A branch? He couldn't tell. His eyes flicked to the door of the en suite, still cracked open slightly, the mirror light faintly pulsing in standby and then, lower, barely visible against the wall. A notecard. Similar to the blank one Lena had pulled from the study drawer. It was resting on the floor now. Just outside their bedroom door. Dan stared at it. Not moving. Not breathing. Just paper. Silent. Still. As though it had been placed there or had moved all on its own.

CHAPTER SEVEN

The morning after unfolded slowly, with more quiet than light. Dan woke first. The soft weight of the duvet held him down for a moment before his eyes adjusted to the muted grey slant seeping through the curtains. The air felt thick like the silence had a weight to it. He stayed still, listening. No birdsong. No hum of the pipes. Not even the wind. Just the soft tick of his pulse and Lena's quiet breathing beside him. She was turned to the pillow, one hand curled loosely near her chest, her shoulder exposed to the chill. He didn't wake her. Didn't speak. Just eased himself upright, careful not to shift the mattress. He rubbed a hand over his face and looked finally toward the doorway. The notecard was still there, sitting dead centre on the floor like it had chosen its spot deliberately. He hadn't touched it the night before. He couldn't bring himself to but now, in the hush of morning, he rose. Crossed the room and picked it up. *Blank*. Exactly as it had been. He turned it between his fingers. The paper was smooth but not entirely empty. There was a faint roughness, like something had been written and then erased. Not words. More like the impression of them. A pressure that left no ink but remained in texture alone. He squinted closer, tilting it toward the light. For a heartbeat, he thought he saw the curve of a letter, a lowercase "e" or a curled number but then it was gone. He slipped the card into the top drawer of the nightstand and closed it softly. By the time Lena stirred and stretched, the light had warmed slightly. Outside, mist clung low to the grass, giving the hedges a wet sheen that looked more like sweat than dew. The house hadn't made a single noise. No floorboard creaks. No boiler clicks. The kind of silence that felt deliberate. They met in the kitchen in wordless synchrony. Dan reached for the coffee press; Lena flicked the kettle. Cups were found. Milk, forgotten, then retrieved. It wasn't habit so much as instinct like their bodies moved through the space out of muscle memory, not choice.

Lena tilted her head toward the wall. "Clock's stopped."

Dan followed her gaze. The kitchen clock, mounted above the pantry door, sat frozen at 3:17. Its second hand pointed straight down like a warning. Unmoving.

"Battery might've gone," he said. "Thought this one was meant to be wind-up."

He stepped closer and checked behind it. There was no battery slot. No keyhole either. Just smooth backing. He didn't take it down. Just stood there a second longer than needed, hand resting on the edge of the wall.

"I don't remember seeing it before," Lena said.

Dan looked at her. "What, the clock?"

She nodded. "Don't think it was here during filming."

Dan shrugged, but not convincingly. They drank their coffee by the wide kitchen windows, staring out at the garden. The lawn looked untouched, like no one had ever walked across it. The trees beyond the hedge barely moved. Even the clouds above seemed still.

"Quiet out here," Dan said.

Lena sipped slowly. "Too quiet."

Later that morning, Lena moved through to the study with a box tucked under one arm. The door opened with its usual soft click and its usual resistance but something about the pressure felt different, like the room pushed back, just slightly, before letting her in. Sunlight poured across the oak floor in a neat rectangle. Warm, but dustless. Too clean, she stepped inside, glancing at the desk then stopped. The photo. The one of her and Dan in Sicily. It had moved. Only slightly. Tilted, perhaps. Not where she'd left it. She'd positioned it precisely the night before, centre-right of the desk, next to the notepad. She always set things with purpose but now it leaned subtly toward the lamp, like it had shifted under its own weight. Her gaze dropped to the drawer beneath it. It was ajar. Half an inch, if that. But it had been shut. Firmly. She remembered pressing it closed with her knuckles. Lena reached out. Slid it open. The blank notecard was no longer there. Her skin prickled. She pressed the drawer shut again. This time with the flat of her palm, slow and deliberate. Then turned to the shelves and began placing a row of books with more force than necessary. The spines thudded into place. Order. Weight. Control. She didn't look back at the photo. Behind her, the door eased itself a fraction more closed than it had been when she entered.

Around midday, the doorbell rang. A soft chime. Pleasant. Barely loud enough to register. Like it was part of the house. Dan answered it. On the step stood an older woman in a pale raincoat, her silver hair swept into a bun that had softened with time. She held a small woven basket and a polite smile.

"Just wanted to welcome you properly," she said. "I'm Anne, Anne Winter, from the house just at the end of the lane."

Dan stepped aside slightly. "That's lovely. I'm Dan. This is Lena."

Anne passed the basket to Lena. Inside, a sourdough loaf, a jar of dark chutney, and two lavender sachets wrapped in muslin.

"The bread's fresh from the village," Anne added. "The lavender's from my garden. Helps with sleep."

Lena smiled, though her fingers lingered on the sachets a beat too long.

"That's very kind of you."

Anne looked past them into the hallway.

"It's nice to see the place full again. It's been too quiet." She didn't elaborate. Just offered another polite smile.

Dan thanked her again, made a few gestures of neighbourly warmth, and Anne excused herself. Her boots made no sound on the gravel as she walked away. They stood in the doorway for a moment longer after she left.

"Friendly," Dan said.

"Too friendly?" Lena asked quietly.

She looked down at the sachets again. They smelled faintly of lavender but something else, too. Something slightly sour beneath the sweetness. She didn't mention it. That afternoon, Dan settled into the study with his laptop and headset. His calendar filled the screen; the taskbar blinked with notifications.

Across the house, Lena stepped into the guest house. It smelled clean. New. Faintly of varnish and cotton but the air was colder than outside, sharper, like it hadn't been disturbed in years rather than weeks. She ran a hand along the hallway wall as she passed, fingertips grazing the plaster. When she flicked the bathroom light on, it buzzed softly before settling into a weak yellow glow. *Drip. Drip. Drip.* The tap wasn't gushing, just a single drop every few seconds, landing in the basin with a sound far louder than it should've been. She tried tightening the handle. It resisted. Moving to the back door, she nudged it open. Damp air drifted in. The grass outside was thick with dew. Then she saw them, Footprints. Leading across the lawn from the guest house toward the kitchen terrace, soft, shallow impressions in the damp grass. Barely visible but there, They stopped halfway. No return path. Lena stared. The air felt thinner now like her breath had to push harder to escape her lungs. She walked back to the main house without looking behind her. Inside, the air felt heavier. She locked the back door with more care than usual, pressing the bolt in until it clicked. The silence had a texture now, dense, unmoving. Like the house was listening. Somewhere deeper inside, she could hear Dan shifting boxes. She slipped off her shoes, placed them neatly beside the bench, and crossed into the hallway.

Dan reappeared a moment later, brushing dust from his sleeves. "Guest house okay?"

She nodded. "There's a dripping tap in the bathroom. I'll sort it later."

Dan moved past her to the bottom of the stairs, pausing with one hand on the banister.

"Still feels like we haven't actually arrived," he said. "Like it's waiting for us to leave."

She didn't reply right away.

"I saw something," she said at last.

Dan turned slightly.

"Footprints," she continued. "Outside the guest house. They led halfway across the lawn. Then stopped."

His brow furrowed. "Could've been from the film crew."

"They weren't there before," she said. "And they don't lead back."

Dan opened his mouth, then closed it. He didn't argue. But he didn't agree either. "Let's keep an eye out," he said eventually.

"We've got a lot to do anyway." Lena nodded, though her chest still felt tight.

They spent the next hour in different corners of the house. Dan adjusted his home office setup, mumbling to himself about cables and extensions. Lena quietly reorganised the kitchen drawers, Neither said much. The silence between them wasn't uncomfortable but it wasn't warm, either. It just filled the space, slow and steady, like fog through an open window. At some point, Dan passed through the living room with his phone and a car key.

"Quick trip to the garage," he said. "Found a charger I forgot in the boot."

Lena raised a hand in vague acknowledgment. She was standing at the far kitchen window, watching the trees shift slightly in the distance. The shadows between the hedges never looked the same twice. When Dan returned, winded from hauling an old storage box inside, he was trying to play it off.

"Remind me next time not to pack the toolkit under the gym weights."

He set the box down with a thud just as Lena's phone buzzed on the counter. A message from her mum. Just a photo of a kitten they'd seen in a shop window the week before. No words. No context. The kind of message only a parent sends to remind you they're thinking of you. Lena smiled faintly. Replied with a heart. Then looked out the window again. Still no wind. Still that sense of something just at the edge of knowing. By late afternoon, the air in the house had thickened. Dan stood in the hallway, jacket half on, phone in one hand.

"Let's head into town. Grab supplies. Get out of our heads for a bit."

Lena didn't argue. She pulled on her boots quietly, tucking one foot into the heel with her thumb. She didn't ask what they needed. Didn't check the fridge or the list pinned beside it. They both already knew: bread. Milk. something warm, something familiar, something to do. Outside, the light had flattened. Clouds hung low over the fields, grey, soft-edged, unmoving. Like the sky had paused mid-thought. The gravel shifted under the tyres as they pulled away. The lane curled out in slow turns, hemmed by overgrown hedgerows and dips where old stone markers leaned into the grass. They passed a rusted gate with no fence, a pair of blackbirds frozen on a wire. There were no signs. No cars. No sound. Just open road and the distant rhythm of the tyres over damp tarmac.

Dan drove in silence, one hand on the wheel, the other resting loose on the gearstick. Lena watched the landscape pass. The occasional tree. A broken post. A ridge of bare earth like something had been dug and forgotten. She didn't know how long it took to reach the town. Time stretched differently here. Like the roads weren't measured in distance, but in stillness. The town revealed itself slowly. First a single red post-box, half-swallowed by ivy. Then a squat building with too-clean windows but no life inside. Then, at last, the high street, a short run of stone façades, every window square and watching. It wasn't empty. Just... paused. They parked beside a crooked bench with flaking green paint. Across the road, a green grocer's sign swung gently on its hinge, the lettering faded to soft brown. **Everley's**. Inside the shop, it was warmer, dim, narrow. The wooden floor creaked softly underfoot. Shelves were stacked with local produce. waxed cheese, jam jars with floral fabric lids, soap cut into rough blocks. It smelled of lavender and root vegetables. Sweetness beneath earth. The man behind the counter looked up as the bell above the door gave a tired chime. He had the broad-shouldered build of someone used to lifting crates. His sleeves were rolled. Hair combed back with care. No apron. No name tag.

"You'll be from the old place," he said. Not quite a question.

Dan paused. "Just moved in."

The man nodded slowly. Like that confirmed something. "Rosehill."

Lena picked up a basket. The name echoed too sharply in her ears. It wasn't what she called the house. It wasn't even printed anywhere they'd seen. Not on the contract. Not on the post. She didn't ask, she didn't want to. They moved through the shop slowly. Eggs. A jar of jam, A jar of dark mustard with a handwritten label that bled slightly at the edges. Lena reached for a box of herbal tea, her usual blend but halfway to the basket, she changed her mind and put it back. Her fingers brushed another box behind it, identical, but colder. As though it had just been placed there. The man didn't hover but he watched. When Dan brought the basket to the counter, he began ringing the items through in silence. The till made no sound. No mechanical clunk. No beep.

"You'll get used to it up there," the man said at last.

Dan glanced at Lena. "Used to what?"

The man smiled faintly. It didn't touch his eyes. "The quiet. It gets into your bones."

He packed the items into a paper bag and folded the top with precise corners. No receipt, no goodbye. Outside, the air felt colder. A breeze had picked up too sudden to be natural. Lena stepped off the curb and paused at the corner, her gaze caught by a narrow offshoot of road that curled past the old church. There was something about the curve of it, like it wanted to be followed, like it led to something it wasn't ready to show.

Dan pointed to a nearby shop with hand-painted lettering: **Books & Maps**. "Want to check it out?"

She nodded. Anything to delay returning. Anything to keep moving. The door stuck slightly before giving way. Inside, the air was thick with dust and paper. Books leaned in precarious towers. Maps hung from rods above the doorway. A small electric heater buzzed in the back, throwing out more noise than warmth. A woman sat behind the till. Her glasses perched on her head, a paperback open in her hands. She didn't look up. Just nodded once, like she'd been expecting them. Lena drifted toward the fiction shelf. Her hand fell on a worn copy of *Rebecca*. The edges were soft. The cover sun-faded. It looked older than the shelf it sat on. As if it had always been there before the shop. Before the town. There was comfort in the stillness here. Not peace, exactly, but steadiness. The kind you feel in old libraries or empty museums. Places that remembered more than they said. Dan picked up a local walking guide, not for the text, but for the map folded in the centre. The woman behind the counter wrapped it in brown paper and tied it with twine, all without speaking.

As they stepped back into the street, the breeze had sharpened. Awnings fluttered faintly. Light bent around the shopfronts in subtle ways. They passed two men smoking outside the pub. Both turned just enough to watch them go. Not hostile. Not curious. Just aware.

"Late lunch?" Dan asked, Lena nodded.

Her stomach had begun to ache without her noticing. They found a café tucked between a florist and a second hand shop. Its windows were slightly fogged at the edges, the sign in chalk paint above the door reading simply: ***The Cracked Teacup***. Inside, the light was golden and low. Not dim, but diffused, like a photograph aged by hand. A woman stood behind the counter, wrapping a sandwich. She looked up as they entered. Red hair, tied back neatly. No smile, just a glance that measured them.

"Just the two?" she asked.

Dan nodded. "Yes, please."

"Take a seat. I'll bring the menus."

The tables were mismatched. Wood, metal, painted, bare. Each had a small ceramic vase with dried flowers. The jazz playing from a tucked-away speaker wavered between notes like it couldn't quite commit to the melody. They sat near the window, the glass slightly warped. The woman returned with two small menus clipped to wooden boards.

"Soup's carrot and coriander. Got sandwiches. Cake. Tea."

She didn't linger. Lena looked over the menu without reading it. Her eyes followed the names but didn't connect them to hunger. Outside, a young couple passed by hand in hand. Neither looked toward the café. Neither spoke. They ordered two soups and lemonades. When the food came, the woman said only:

"Carrot's strong today. Let me know if it's too much." Then she paused.

"You staying nearby?"

Lena answered, "Not far."

"You don't sound local."

"No." added Dan.

The woman studied her for a beat longer. Then nodded.

"Hope the place is treating you kindly." She left them alone.

Dan leaned in slightly. "Do you think she knows about Winspire?"

Lena shook her head. "If she did, she'd have said something."

They ate slowly. The soup was rich and hot. The lemonade cloudy, slightly bitter. The kind of food that tried to warm you but never quite made it to your hands. As they left, the woman raised a hand in farewell.

"See you around." There was no warmth in the phrase. Just inevitability.

Outside, the sky had begun to lower. The wind dropped off as suddenly as it had come. The town looked unchanged. But the air had shifted. As though something had registered them. Dan loaded the bags into the boot. Closed it gently. Braced his hands against the car and looked skyward. The clouds were thicker now, packed close like insulation. Lena turned once to glance back toward the town. The buildings stood in the same order, same size, same shape but something about the angles felt different now. Less inviting. More exact. They drove in silence. The lane twisted back through the trees, the hedgerows darker now. They passed the broken gate again. This time, it was open. Just slightly. Enough to register in the periphery. As they reached their property, the gate at the edge of the drive creaked on its hinges. There was no wind. Dan parked. Cut the engine. Neither moved to get out. The house stood still. Wide and patient. The windows caught the last of the grey light like half-lidded eyes. Lena opened her door first. The gravel crunched underfoot, sharper than before. The chill bit at her collar. Inside, the temperature had dropped. Not cold. Just... emptied. Dan dropped the bags onto the counter with more care than usual.

"I'll unpack," he said. "You okay?"

She nodded, eyes already flicking toward the stairwell like it might move. Neither of them said it out loud. But the house felt different. Like it noticed they'd gone and now it was listening again. Lena stood by the kitchen window while Dan unpacked the bags, the soft rustle of paper and the clink of jars sounding far too loud against the hush. She watched the terrace lights flicker on in the garden, one, then another, casting shallow pools of yellow that didn't quite touch the hedge line. The trees remained unmoved. Still. Like props on a stage.

"I should've told you earlier," Dan said, setting the loaf on the counter. She turned slightly.

"Told me what?" Lena questioned.

He didn't answer right away. Just opened a drawer, found the cling film missing, and let out a soft breath. Then he leaned back against the counter, hands flat to the surface.

"There was a card," he said. "Yesterday. When we first arrived."

Lena blinked. "What kind of card?"

"Just a notecard. Blank. It was outside our en-suite door when I woke up. Middle of the floor." He didn't look at her. "I thought maybe it fell out of your stuff while we unpacked or maybe it was from the crew."

Lena furrowed her brow, confused a she was sure she left it in the draw. "That's weird, it was in a draw in the study maybe I put it in my pocket and it fell out" she said finally, "Probably from the moving boxes."

Dan didn't push. The pendant light above the island cast a wide, pale circle across the counter. The marble looked colder than it had that morning, grey-veined and flat, like polished bone. Lena poured water into the kettle.

"Tea?" she asked.

"Yeah. Please." Dan replied.

The kettle clicked softly, steam rose curling slow. Vanishing fast. Upstairs, a single floorboard groaned. A long, low creak, then silence. Neither of them looked up. They drank their tea standing, like it wasn't worth sitting for. The mugs warm in their hands. The kitchen clock still frozen at 3:17.

Eventually, Lena moved to the sink. The glass in front of her was just reflective enough to catch her outline but not clearly. Not in a way she liked. The terrace lights flickered again. The glow now hazier, less yellow, more white. It made the grass look flattened, like something had pressed it down. She stepped upstairs a moment later, toothbrush in hand, and crossed into the landing bathroom. The door clicked behind her. The mirror held her reflection too still. For a second, it didn't move when she did. She paused, blinked and waited then brushed her teeth, one hand gripping the edge of the sink a little too tightly. The window beside her was cracked open half an inch. The latch still down. The air that slipped through was cold and still. Below, the terrace lights cast faint halos onto the stone slabs. The hedges curved like sleeping animals. That was when she saw it.

The garden gate, the one leading down the narrow path between the main house and the guest building creaked open. Slow, careful. One hinge stuttering in the cold. There was no wind. It swung wider. Then paused. Lena didn't breathe. Didn't blink. Just watched. The gate stayed open for a moment. Still. Then, as if nudged by an invisible hand, it began to close again. The latch didn't catch. It stayed ajar by an inch. She didn't move, not until she felt Dan behind her, his presence first, then his reflection.

"You okay?" he said, his tone hushed. She didn't look away from the glass.

"The gate just moved," she said.

Dan leaned in slightly, squinting through the dark. "Could've been a fox."

"It opened and closed."

He didn't respond. She flicked off the light and stepped into the hall. Her heartbeat didn't slow, her skin felt too tight over her ribs.

She moved quietly down the landing, the floor cool beneath her feet. The hallway light was off, but the bedroom door remained open, casting a faint spill of amber from the bedside lamp. Dan had retreated there already, his silhouette shifting faintly behind the fabric of the duvet. Lena hovered in the doorway.

"Will you go and check it?" she asked, her voice low but steady.

Dan sat up, rubbing the back of his neck. "The gate?"

She nodded once. He didn't argue. Just swung his legs over the side of the bed and slipped his feet into the old trainers by the wardrobe. The floor creaked once beneath his heel.

"I won't be long," he murmured, more to the room than to her.

Downstairs, the house had gone still again. Each step echoed faintly as he crossed the hallway and passed through the kitchen. The terrace lights were still glowing outside, duller now, their halos blurred by mist. He unlocked the door, the bolt stiff in his hand, and stepped out into the cold. The garden air had turned damp, thick with the smell of moss and earth. His breath fogged in front of him. Somewhere in the distance, a fox barked once, brief and sharp but the trees didn't move. Dan made his way across the lawn toward the side path. The grass gave slightly underfoot, leaving dark impressions behind him. The gate stood still. Closed. Firm, undisturbed. He frowned. His memory had been clear. He hadn't imagined the way Lena had described it the groan of the hinge, the gap, the pause but now, it sat shut. Like it had never moved. A breeze slipped past him, cold across the back of his neck. He turned nothing, no branches moving, no sign of life beyond the hedges. He exhaled slowly and turned back toward the house but just as he stepped onto the last flagstone leading up to the kitchen door, he stopped. There were footprints. Not his. Pressed neatly into the earth right outside the window. Facing inward. Like someone had stood there. Watching, waiting. They were faint, partially dried but visible. Two prints. Too narrow for boots. Too light for work shoes. Dan stared at them. The breath stilled in his lungs. He reached out automatically to steady himself against the glass and froze. There, in the reflection of the moonlight sky, a handprint. On the outside, smudged. Not his, not Lena's. Fingers splayed slightly, Palm distorted by the texture of the glass. Too clear to be old. He stood motionless for a beat. Then slowly reached for the handle and slipped back inside. Locked the door behind him. Drew the curtain. The house swallowed him like it hadn't noticed he'd gone. Footsteps above, Lena.

"Is everything alright?" she called down, her voice more careful now.

"All fine," he called back.

He didn't mention the handprint, didn't mention the footprints and didn't mention the gate. Just climbed the stairs slowly, past the unmoving clock, through the humming hallway light. When he entered the bedroom, Lena was already tucked in. Dan sat on the edge of the bed and rubbed at his wrist, noticed a faint smear of earth across his skin. He wiped it off on the hem of his T-shirt and pulled back the duvet. As he lay down, the covers still held Lena's warmth but something else lingered beneath it. A faint waft of lavender. Like a memory that hadn't been made yet. He stared at the ceiling a long while before closing his eyes.

CHAPTER EIGHT

They woke to movement, not loud, not sudden. Just soft enough to be mistaken for the settling of the house, the kind of shift old floorboards made when warmth met cold air but then it happened again. A faint, rhythmic sound. footsteps, slow. confident. Lena blinked against the muted light, lashes sticking slightly. The bedroom held its usual hush, thick with the insulation of morning. She reached across the bed. Dan's side was already empty. The duvet still faintly warm. Somewhere downstairs, a cupboard clicked shut. She sat up slowly. Dan's voice didn't call out, no kettle boiled. no music played. Just the low creak of movement below. She wrapped the throw from the end of the bed around her shoulders and stepped out into the hallway, feet bare, breath held. The house didn't feel empty. It felt occupied. In a way it hadn't before. By the time she reached the top of the stairs, Dan was already standing in the hallway below, halfway between the banister and the kitchen door. He didn't turn when she appeared, just tilted his head slightly, like he wasn't sure what he was hearing either. Then came the sound of rubber gloves snapping. Dan stepped forward. They found her in the kitchen. A woman, mid-forties, short dark hair tucked beneath a patterned headscarf, pale yellow gloves halfway up her forearms, she was crouched by the under-sink cupboard, rearranging bottles with the calm efficiency of someone who'd done it a hundred times before. She glanced up casually as they entered.

"Oh…sorry. Didn't mean to disturb," she said, rising. "I usually come earlier, but the lane was muddy. Hope it's alright."

Dan blinked. "Sorry, who are you?"

"Clara," she said simply, peeling one glove off with a practiced tug.

"Clara Sheen. I'm with Winspire's property rota. They've got me down for Tuesdays, usually mornings, but I try not to wake anyone."

Lena stood in the doorway, still wrapped in the throw, pulse thudding in her neck. "You're the housekeeper?"

Clara gave a warm nod. "Part-time, yes. Just upkeep. Bathrooms, kitchen, that sort of thing. Only for the first few months, part of the prize package."

She smiled again, like it was all perfectly normal.

Dan glanced at Lena. "Did you know about that?"

Lena shook her head slowly. "No one mentioned…"

"There should've been a slip in your welcome folder," Clara interrupted, already turning back to the cupboard.

"Right at the back. Most people miss it." She moved like someone who belonged. Like someone who'd always had a copy of the keys.

Dan stepped aside and scratched his jaw. "Right. Well... since you're here."

Clara smiled again. "I won't be long." and just like that, she resumed her cleaning, clinking bottles, checking cloths, humming faintly to herself.

Lena remained still in the doorway, arms folded tighter around herself. She hadn't unlocked the door that morning, neither had Dan. Dan didn't move at first. He stood with one hand braced on the counter, eyes fixed not on Clara, but on the fridge door like if he focused hard enough, he could remember a detail that would explain her being there. A memory, a voice message. Something but there was nothing. Clara worked methodically behind him, completely unbothered. A bottle clinked. A cupboard shut. The hum of her low tune curled faintly through the room like steam. Lena stayed in the doorway, the throw still wrapped around her.

"We didn't hear the door," she said, almost to herself.

Clara didn't look up. "Winspire gave me a key. I've been cleaning for this place for months" She paused, wiped her hands on a striped cloth. "You'll find it's all in the agreement. Paragraph thirteen, I believe."

Neither of them responded. Dan gave a slow nod that didn't quite reach belief. Then turned, opened the drawer by the fridge, and pulled out a spoon just to do something.

"Right. Well. I've got a few things to prep." Clara offered him a smile.

"Won't be in your way." He said as left the room.

Lena watched him go, then turned back to Clara, who was now rearranging glass jars beneath the sink like she'd lived there her whole life.

"Do you come in through the back?" Lena asked.

Clara didn't miss a beat. "Whichever's easiest, usually. I knock if the car's gone. Otherwise I let myself in, just the way they trained us." She glanced up, that same pleasant expression softening her features. "I can text next time, if you'd rather."

Lena offered a tight smile. "That'd be great." but the smile didn't reach her eyes. She lingered a second longer, as if expecting Clara to offer something, an apology, maybe or at least a reason but there was only the sound of a cloth being wrung out and the squeak of the cupboard door closing again. Lena turned, heading back toward the hallway. The floor creaked just once under her heel. By the time she reached the stairs, she could hear Dan already in the study. The door half-shut. The low murmur of a headset call. A different kind of silence had settled over the house now, one filled not with absence, but presence. The sense that someone else's routine had been folded into theirs without consent. She went upstairs. Closed the bedroom door behind her. Pulled on a jumper and brushed her hair back with the flats of both palms then she sat on the edge of the bed, staring at her phone screen without unlocking it. Just watching the black surface reflect her face. For a long moment, neither of them made a sound, her, or the house and downstairs, Clara began to hum again.

Dan returned to the study with the weight of a man already late. His coffee had gone lukewarm. The house still smelled faintly of lavender and polish. Clara, still humming faintly somewhere behind the walls. He closed the door with a soft press of his palm and stood in the centre of the room for a moment, looking around like something had shifted in his absence. His eyes scanned the desk. Laptop, notepad, wireless mouse, his phone, charger cable all in place. The USB drive however wasn't there, though it had been. He was sure of it. He crouched to check the drawers. Nothing. Lifted the cushion of the chair, even patted his back pockets. Still nothing. A hot edge of panic bloomed behind his ribs. The USB held the backup version of the supermarket Christmas campaign deck. A duplicate, yes, but the only version with the original mock-ups intact, the ones his art director had begged him not to overwrite. If he didn't have it today, he'd be reworking three weeks of layouts from memory. Dan raked a hand through his hair and turned slowly in the room, eyes scanning the bookshelves. There, tucked neatly between a framed postcard and a glass paperweight was the USB. Upright, balanced. Placed as if deliberately displayed. He stared for a moment before he picked it up. No dust, n static. Just his own breath behind his teeth. He didn't remember putting it there, he would never have put it there. Dan returned to the desk, plugged it in, and told himself it didn't matter. Told himself that maybe Lena had moved it or Clara before they realised she was there.

The screen lit up and his calendar expanded like a map of the week's pressure points. The entire morning was carved out for client work, end-of-year strategy, digital placements, social rollout. The deck was due in twelve hours. Final sign-off by Friday. He double-checked the rendering specs for the branded assets, then clicked into the main call. Eight faces. Two black boxes. One bored junior designer sketching on a sticky note. Dan adjusted his posture, flicked on his camera, and smiled like everything was under control. The call blurred quickly into demands. Adjust the layout, change the font, we want something festive but not *too* festive, something nostalgic but modern, something unique but recognisable. Something that didn't exist, not really. They talked about chestnut stuffing like it was currency. Someone from marketing wanted to know if the pigs-in-blankets could be *reframed* as "cultural indulgence." Another asked if the cinnamon brand video should have snow, or just *snow energy*. Dan blinked twice, then smiled again. “We can mock up both.” Laughter, approval. The grim warmth of being compliant enough to pass. He muted himself and rubbed his temple. Outside the window, the light had turned soft. The garden stretched beyond the hedge like a painting with no frame. Golden-edged and strangely still. The kind of view that made you forget there was a camera watching your face. Dan let his eyes follow the bend of the path toward the old tree line, where the branches split apart like fingers. For a moment, it looked like something moved, just beyond the hedge. A flicker of shape, then gone. He blinked before he focused again. Back inside, the Wi-Fi hiccupped. The call froze. His screen pixelated, voices stuttered. The familiar hollow of digital silence echoed for half a second before his camera feed cut to static. Then flashed back and for a moment, just a single, breathless moment. He saw someone behind him. Not clearly, not distinctly. Just the vague outline of a figure standing in the reflection behind him. By the bookcase. His chest tightened, Dan turned, fast, chair scraping wood. The study door was closed. No one was there. Only the faint tremble of the curtain where the heater clicked on. He stared for another few seconds, then looked back to the screen. The call had resumed. Someone was sharing slides now. His camera still frozen, he clicked it off and kept it that way. The meeting ended with a half-hearted promise to ‘*circle back*’. Most of them logged off without saying goodbye. Dan stared at the empty call window until it vanished, leaving his desktop scattered with half-edited assets and an untouched checklist.

He leaned back. The chair creaked. Another alert buzzed in the corner of the screen, this one marked *Private: H. Tredwell calling*. He hesitated then clicked accept. A new call window opened. Just one of his managers, Helen, on the other side. Mid-forties, razor-sharp. She wore a navy turtleneck and that same clean, practical expression she always had like she’d been prepping three steps ahead of him since last Tuesday.

“Dan,” she said, voice smooth through the headset. “Got a minute?”

He nodded. “Just wrapped the client deck.”

“I know. I’ve seen it.” She paused. “Looks solid. Could use some polish on the layout slide, but I’ll give you line edits by morning.”

"Appreciate it."
She tilted her head slightly. "How's the new place?"
Dan smiled, more out of reflex than pleasure. "Big. Quiet."
Helen gave the faintest flicker of amusement. "Good for focus then."
He didn't answer. Her tone shifted subtly.
"Listen, I wanted to run something past you. The team's trying to finalise the print samples by Friday and the board review's been moved forward."
Dan sat straighter. "Forward?"
"To Wednesday."
"That's…" He checked the date. "That's two days."
"Yes." Helen folded her arms. "We're behind on testing some of the layout variables. Colour calibration's off in the festive range. We need someone senior physically there, mocking things up alongside design. Coordinating adjustments. Fast."
Dan didn't ask who else she'd called before him. Helen continued,
"I know you're hybrid. I know this wasn't the plan but if you could be in the office by tomorrow, say midday, I can get you a desk in the lower suite. The rest of the team will be there."
Dan exhaled through his nose. He looked around the room, at the wall of quiet books and the USB "Yeah," he said after a beat. "I can do that."
"Good. I'll let people know you're coming in. Bring the drive, obviously."
"Obviously." Dan replied, trying not to roll his eyes.
The call ended with a professional nod and a blink. Just like that, he was due back in the city. Out of this strange, pulsing quiet, back into fluorescent lights, long tables, coffee that tasted like deadlines. Dan closed his laptop. The quiet reasserted itself instantly, like the house had been holding its breath. Somewhere upstairs, a floorboard creaked. He rubbed the bridge of his nose. He hadn't told Helen about the internet hiccups or the reflection, or the way the garden looked like it was waiting. Instead, he stood and stretched. The mug on his desk was empty. He didn't remember finishing it.

Upstairs, Lena was pulling clothes from hangers. Silks and knits. The sound of sleeves brushing one another in soft murmurs filled the room. The light had shifted, cloud-soft and pale through the tall windows. She folded a scarf into thirds, paused, and unfolded it again. At first, she thought it was lint. Just a thread but as she tugged a sweater free from the back of the wardrobe, she noticed two dry, curled leaves tumbled to the floor near the en suite. Crisp, speckled, brown around the edges. Lena stared at them, slowly crouched. One leaf still had a twig attached, snapped clean, like it had come from a hedge. Not a tree. She hadn't packed leaves. She picked one up, turning it gently between two fingers. The texture crinkled in her grip. She rose, crossed to the waste bin, and dropped them both inside. Then closed the wardrobe door, a little too firmly as stepped back into the hallway. The silence greeted her like a known scent, warm, familiar, just a little wrong. The kind of silence that remembered things. She turned toward the stairwell and paused. One of the guest bedrooms, the one at the end of the hall, stood open. Just slightly. The door had been closed that morning. She was sure of it. They hadn't even properly taken off all the dust sheets for their families pending arrival yet. Lena took a step forward. The hallway stretched out in front of her like a sentence waiting to be finished. Long and narrow, the wood beneath her feet carried the chill of the shaded side of the house. The kind of cold that didn't change with weather. A stillness settled there, weightless but watchful. Lena moved slowly, her footsteps soundless against the floorboards. The air felt more concentrated at this end of the hall. Like it had been gathered and stored. She paused halfway, glancing back toward the light pooling weakly from the stairwell. It looked too far. The shadows stretched longer than they should. The guest bedroom door at the very end stood slightly ajar. Not flung open, just enough to let the room breathe. Enough to suggest someone had been in and meant to return. She didn't remember it being like that earlier. She would've noticed. They hadn't even opened that room. It had been one of those *later* spaces, one of those *'we'll get to it eventually'* boxes on the mental list. She was sure of it, she took a step closer. As she did, a gust of light wind passed through the hallway. No movement from behind her, no sound. Just a sudden shift in air pressure, like a door had been opened on the far side of the house. Her arm prickled with goosebumps. The door, she noticed, was more used that the others. The brass handle, worn smooth at the top, had a faint blue tint in it, like something that had been handled by too many people over too long a time. The paint around the frame had cracked into faint spiderwebs. She placed her hand gently on the handle. Cold metal, smooth. The kind of cold that wasn't just temperature, it was absence. The door opened inward with a reluctant sound, not quite a creak. More like breath escaping from a long-held chest.

The guest bedroom was dim. The curtains were pulled halfway closed, leaving a bar of dusty light across the foot of the bed. Everything was neat. Too neat. The kind of neat that felt like staging, not living. The bedspread was tucked so tightly it might as well have been ironed into the frame beneath the light dust sheet. A glass vase sat on the dresser, empty but for dust. Then her eyes adjusted. A figure stood near the far wall. For a split second, she thought it was a reflection, some angled trick of mirror and light, but no. It was someone. A woman. Standing with her back to the door, examining something small in her hands. ***Clara.*** Still in the same pale apron, still humming. That same soft, tuneless melody she'd had earlier. The kind of sound that didn't fill a room, just curled around it. Her silhouette was calm, unmoving, framed by the weak window light that turned her shape to something almost painted. Lena opened her mouth to speak, but no sound came out. Clara didn't turn. Didn't startle. Just said softly,

"I was just dusting. Thought I'd freshen the edges while it's still early enough for the light." Her voice was friendly, lilting. Like the start of a conversation in a quiet waiting room.

Lena took a step further in. "This door was closed."

Clara nodded, still not facing her. "I know. But these old houses…" she trailed off, examining the small framed photo in her hand. "They breathe differently. You close a room and it opens again when you're not looking. Like lungs, really."

Lena blinked. "We haven't been in here."

Clara turned then, slowly. She smiled but it wasn't a smile made for photos. It was older than that, calmer. One that didn't require effort. Her eyes scanned Lena like she was trying to place her, not like a stranger, but like a dream she'd half remembered. "It's a good room," Clara said. "South-facing. Always feels warmer than the rest."

Lena glanced around. It didn't feel warm. The corners were dim. The furniture had the kind of stillness that came from disuse, not peace.

"There are leaves in the wardrobe," Lena said, half without meaning to. Clara didn't seem surprised.

"Sometimes the outside gets in. One way or another." Lena looked to the bedside table, where the photo frame had been replaced.

She couldn't see the image clearly. Just the suggestion of a shape. A figure, maybe. The edges were blurred with age. Clara followed her gaze.

"You can't always tell who they are," she said. "Faces change over time. Paper fades. But the rooms remember."

There was a silence then. A thick one. Lena stepped back, just a fraction. Her hand hovered near the edge of the doorframe, as if she needed to remind herself there was still a way out. Clara didn't move. She simply glanced toward the wardrobe, then to the corner where a small crack in the wall ran like a vein from ceiling to skirting.

"All these old houses," she said, quieter now, "have hidden corners."

Lena frowned. "What do you mean?"

"Spaces that were built, but not planned. Rooms behind rooms. A hallway that doesn't meet its door. Places that feel like drafts but aren't."

And then she moved, not rushed, not abrupt. Just walked past Lena with slow, quiet steps, shoulders relaxed, apron brushing the air as she passed. Lena turned to follow her path down the hallway, but it was empty. No sign of movement, no creak of the stairs. Just the steady hum of the hallway bulb and the muffled sound of Dan's keyboard somewhere below. Lena remained in the doorway a moment longer. Then she stepped back into the hall. Closed the guest room door with a firm click and stood very still. Lena stayed in the hallway long after the door clicked shut. Her hands hovered, uselessly, at her sides. It was the kind of stillness that didn't come from calm, but from confusion. Like her body hadn't caught up with her brain yet. She ran a thumb across the ridge of her palm, grounding herself in the sensation. *"All these old houses have hidden corners."* The words curled through her again, echoing where they shouldn't. She replayed them as she made her way down the hallway, brushing her fingers once against the wall as she passed, as if checking for seams she hadn't noticed before.

In the office, Dan was exactly where she'd left him, headphones on, shoulders tense, eyes narrowed at the second monitor. His fingers moved rapidly over the keyboard, pausing every now and then to switch tabs, cross-reference slides, open folders layered with digital stickies. The low murmur of a client voice drifted faintly from the headset, tinny, brisk. Lena leaned on the doorframe, watching him without interrupting. The strain in his brow was subtle, but it was there. His work face. The one he used when he was trying not to seem stressed, trying to manage the expectations of too many voices through too many screens. He caught her eye for a second and gave a tight-lipped smile. She didn't mention Clara, not yet. Instead, she retreated into the bathroom, splashing cool water on her face and breathing slowly until the sharp edges of the encounter dulled. The mirror fogged slightly at the bottom, despite the cold. She wiped it with her sleeve. Her reflection blinked back, tired and faintly unsatisfied. The kind of face that looked like it had more to say than it ever managed to. Dan had switched calls. The voice was American this time, bright, clipped, corporate.

"No, no, if we swap the mulled pear for the clementine glaze, we'll hit the allergen margins for packaging compliance. Yeah. The supermarket's legal flagged it in last year's range, hang on, let me pull the document."

He was already opening a third folder, clicking into a tab marked *Seasonal Pitch FINAL_FINALv3*. Spreadsheets bloomed across the screen. He scanned them like scripture. This was the season, after all, the holiday menus, the November packaging trials, the thousand overlapping deadlines that would culminate in glossy promotional reels and soft-focus ads playing on televisions by the end of the month. His team was split across two time zones and three teams, packaging, brand strategy, digital retail. Dan, as usual, was floating between all of them. '*The glue guy,*' someone had called him once. He wasn't sure if it was a compliment. On a good day, it was problem-solving. Creativity, market insight. On a day like today, it was firefighting.

The afternoon wore on. Meetings blurred into one another. Slideshows bled together. The Christmas branding mock-ups, reindeers, copper foil, frosted scripts, filled the lower monitor while his email spat out feedback from four different managers with contradictory suggestions. Outside, the light had changed again. The edges of the lawn looked blurred by fog. It clung to the lower glass panes in the French doors. Movement caught his eye, Clara. Still in her pale apron, a tote bag slung over one shoulder. She moved at a steady pace, heading up the gravel path. Her figure blurred slightly at the edge of the mist, then sharpened again when she passed under the bare branches at the drive's entrance. She didn't look back, she didn't wave, she just walked. Disappearing in the same quiet way she'd appeared. Dan checked the time. Half four. She hadn't said goodbye. He leaned back, stretching his shoulders. The ache at the base of his neck pulsed like a metronome. He stood to fetch another coffee, hesitating just a moment before stepping into the hallway. Upstairs, Lena had finally gathered the nerve to do something normal, she pulled a fresh jumper from the wardrobe, folded the one she'd been wearing, and paused to sniff it for that faint musty smell the guest room had left behind. Nothing. Deciding on a short walk, she tugged her coat from the hook by the door and stepped outside, breathing in the cooler air with purpose. She circled the garden once, letting the tension bleed from her limbs. It helped. A little. By the time she returned, dusk had settled fully over the house. She reached the front door, digging for the key in her coat pocket, except it wasn't there. She tried the handle, Locked. From the inside. She stilled. The porch light buzzed above her head. Inside, she could hear the muffled sound of Dan's footsteps upstairs. A faint creak of the floorboards. The hallway light flickering as someone passed beneath it. She knocked, twice and waited. Something cold pressed at the base of her spine. A sensation without shape, without reason, then the door opened. Dan stood there, confused, mug in one hand.

"I didn't lock it," he said automatically.

Lena didn't answer right away. Her hand hovered near the edge of the doorframe, like she was bracing herself.

"I didn't either," she replied. and for a moment, they simply looked at each other, each holding something unsaid, something quietly unsettling between them.

Dan stepped aside to let her in, his expression still slightly furrowed. "I've got to head into the office tomorrow," he said as she slipped past him. "Mock-ups. Final tasting meeting for the Christmas range. Jules wants everything reviewed in person, something about supplier confidence."

Lena glanced at him as she pulled off her coat. "You said you wouldn't have to go in this month."

"I said I *hoped* I wouldn't," he corrected, offering a half-smile that didn't quite land. "But they're panicking again. Everything's two weeks behind and someone in packaging keeps sending the wrong template."

He took a sip of his coffee, then looked toward the study.

"Just a couple of hours. I'll be back before dinner, *maybe…*"

Lena nodded, not arguing. She watched as he disappeared down the hall, the soft thud of the door closing behind him. The kitchen was quiet again, but not still. The hum of the fridge, the tick of the stopped clock, the occasional creak of the overhead pipes all worked in disharmony. Lena let them settle around her as she pulled ingredients from the fridge, a bag of spinach, a block of feta, a handful of fresh pasta coils from their shop trip the day before. The chopping was methodical. Familiar. The scent of garlic warmed the air. Dan's voice echoed faintly from the study, too distant to make out words, just a cadence of stress. The sound of a man fielding expectations through a screen. Lena stirred the sauce slowly, her other hand braced on the countertop. Her shoulders ached in that low, restless way that made it hard to stay indoors. By the time the pasta was simmering, she was already eyeing her coat again. She found the key hanging from the hook by the side door, the spare, long and brass, with a slightly tarnished loop. It hadn't been there earlier. She couldn't remember leaving it there. Still, she took it.

The air outside had changed again. The wind had dropped entirely, leaving a hush over the property like snow had fallen, though the sky remained dry. She zipped her coat to the collar and stepped down the stone path that skirted the garden, her boots soft against the earth. The hedgerows curved gently along the far end of the lawn. Beyond them, the fields opened like slow exhalations, rolling, uneven, tufted with patches of pale grass and long-forgotten furrows. The sky had begun to shift toward its golden hour hues, bathing the field edges in coppery light. It was beautiful, in a quiet, serious way. Lena walked with slow steps, one hand brushing the wooden post of the gate as she passed. She paused near the rise at the edge of the garden, where the ground sloped down toward one of the fields they hadn't yet explored. The view was expansive, distant hills softened by haze, a thin ribbon of trees stretching toward the east. It was the sort of view that made you feel both isolated and watched, like you were standing inside a painting that remembered you. A soft wind tugged at her scarf. In the distance Lena's eyes began to adjust to something in the distance, A figure, far across the field. Still, upright. Too far to see details, too far to be certain. Lena stopped walking. Her breath caught, not in fear, exactly, but in recognition. The figure didn't move, didn't shift its weight. Just stood, like a lone tree set against the open land. She squinted into the distance, lifting a hand to shield her eyes. The sun broke suddenly through the clouds, just for a second casting a beam of light directly toward her. The glare was blinding, gold and white and too sharp to face. She turned her face slightly, blinked. When she looked again, the figure was gone. Just gone. The field was empty. Lena's heart ticked harder in her chest. She stared at the spot where it had been, willing her eyes to adjust. The grass wavered softly. The wind rose again, gentle and indifferent. She took a step back, then another before she turned slowly, gaze still flicking over her shoulder toward the field every few paces, half-expecting the figure to reappear, to step out from behind a tree that hadn't been there before or emerge slowly from the tall grass but nothing moved. Nothing followed. As she re-entered the garden, the terrace lights flicked on behind the kitchen glass. Automatic. Still, they startled her. She slipped the brass key from her pocket and moved toward the front door, brushing her hand against the ivy along the brick arch as she passed. She reached for the handle out of habit and paused. Locked. Again, from the inside. Her brow tightened. She tried again, just to be sure, but the bolt was drawn. She hadn't locked it. Dan hadn't come outside, she'd have seen him or heard the door and Clara had already left, she was certain of it. Lena stared at the door a moment longer. Her breath came slower now, each exhale condensing faintly in the air. A long minute passed before she moved toward the side entrance, sliding the key into the lock and stepping back inside. The house greeted her with warmth, but not welcome. The lights hummed low. The hallway held that faint smell of polish and heat-dried wood with a lingering smell of lavender in the air. It was only when she heard Dan's voice again from the study that her shoulders dropped a little. She slipped off her coat and made her way toward the kitchen, her mind still trailing back to the field.

In the study, Dan had finally collapsed into the high-backed chair after a day of firefighting deadlines. His second coffee sat cold beside him, untouched since noon. The rest of the day had been a whirlwind of muted chaos. He'd bounced between Teams meetings, each one overlapping with the last, marketing briefs, supplier updates, last-minute allergens list reviews. The new Christmas menu was already behind schedule and every stakeholder seemed to want something different. *Bigger branding, warmer flavours, sustainability cues but make it festive.* He was expected to be three people at once, brand storyteller, logistics wrangler, and miracle worker. Slides blinked on his monitor. Notes scrawled across PDFs in red. His voice had started to lose its sharpness around four o'clock. Now, hours later, his muscles were tight from sitting too long, and his cursor hovered over the last bullet point in a deck that no longer made sense to his eyes. A soft knock came at the door. Lena stepped in, her hair loose around her shoulders, cheeks slightly pink from the cold.

"Dinner's ready," she said. "Spinach pasta. Thought I'd try that balsamic glaze."

Dan nodded, scrubbing a hand over his face. "Give me ten minutes?"

She lingered a moment. "Everything alright?"

"Yeah. Just tired." He gave her a small smile. "Tomorrow should be easier."

Lena didn't reply straight away. Then: "Don't work too late."

When she left, Dan leaned back in the chair, letting the silence settle for a breath before leaning forward again. His fingers moved with less urgency now, the intensity of the day giving way to tired momentum. He adjusted the layout of the presentation deck for the morning, fixed a misaligned slide, rewrote a product descriptor that had been bugging him since lunch. *Aromatic winter glaze with hints of star anise.* Too much. He scaled it back. Outside, the terrace lights had dulled to an amber glow. His reflection hovered faintly in the glass beyond the monitor, warped by the pane as if a second version of himself were watching. A soft tap came at the door again, barely a knock, more like a nudge. Lena stepped in holding a plate, the warm scent arriving a moment before she did.

"Didn't want to wait," she said with a small smile. "Eat while it's hot."

She set it down beside him, spinach tagliatelle twisted in soft ribbons beneath roasted cherry tomatoes, the balsamic glaze slick and dark across the top. Steam coiled in gentle spirals. Dan pushed his laptop aside.

"You're an angel."

"Just hungry," she murmured, but her voice had softened.

He watched her leave again before turning back to the food. The pasta was perfectly warm, the sweetness of the tomato cut just enough by the glaze. It anchored him in the moment. Reminded him that dinner still happened. That evenings still existed. As he ate, he let his gaze drift to the study window again. No movement. Just the hedges holding their shape against the dark. When the plate was clean, he set it carefully aside and turned back to the screen. A final glance at the checklist. Then, out of habit, he opened his inbox. Dozens of flagged threads blinked at him, Packaging update needed by COB, Urgent: Taste panel reschedule, Marketing deck revisions. He skimmed them with a practiced eye, marking two for tomorrow. Then he clicked over to *Drafts*. There it was. A single new message.

No subject. No recipient. Just one line in the body of the email.

Hello Daniel.

He stared at it. The timestamp said it had been created two hours ago. He hadn't written it. He hadn't been in his email two hours ago.

Dan moved the cursor toward the delete key, but didn't press it. Instead, he read the words again. Just three syllables, but they rang in the silence like a note struck and left to hum. He closed the laptop.

CHAPTER NINE

The kettle clicked off. Steam curled in delicate whorls above the countertop, catching the faint slant of morning light through the narrow kitchen window. It was early not rushed, but not slow either. The kind of morning that moved with its own gravity. Lena stood barefoot on the tiled floor, one hand resting on the edge of the sink, her phone held loosely in the other. She hadn't planned to check it. Hadn't wanted to. But her thumb moved with a mind of its own. Missed email. Delivery delay. Two ads. One story view and then a direct message.

Tom Calder

Sent last night. 23:33PM

No typing dots. No follow-up. Just one message: Saw you and Dan in that

Winspire ad. Congrats on the house, looks amazing. Mad seeing your face

pop up like that.

Nothing else. The words sat there, black on white, impossibly casual. As though they hadn't spoken in over a year. As though their last conversation hadn't ended on a silence that still echoed. Lena's thumb hovered. For a moment, she considered replying. Then her jaw tightened. She exited the app. Paused, reopened it and then deleted the message. The toast popped from the toaster, startling her. The house still smelled of garlic from last night's dinner, the scent caught in the crevices of the air like smoke that hadn't quite lifted. She buttered her toast with mechanical precision, placed it on the plate, and didn't eat it. Behind her, Dan stepped into the kitchen, tugging his coat sleeve straight. His overnight bag sat near the door, already zipped and upright. He looked rested, but only just.

"Train's in an hour," he said, voice thick with morning.

"Do you have everything?" she asked without turning.

"Think so." He poured coffee into the two mugs waiting by the kettle.

The smell rose sharp and grounding. They stood for a beat, backs angled, silence leaning in like a third presence. Lena took her mug, wrapped both hands around it, and finally turned.

"About yesterday…" she said.

"The front door?" Dan guessed, cutting her off gently.

She nodded. "It was locked again," she said. "From the inside, I told you, you said you didn't lock it."

"I didn't," he replied, not meeting her eyes.

He added sugar to his mug, one spoon, then a second. A habit she thought he'd dropped.

"It doesn't make sense," Lena continued. "I would've seen you if you'd come out."

Dan sipped his coffee. "Maybe Clara locked it on her way out."

Lena didn't respond. Dan exhaled. "I'm not saying you imagined it."

"But?"

"But… it's an old house. Things stick, latches turn weird. Wind pressure. That sort of thing." He tried a smile. "Old houses get under your skin."

She didn't smile back.

"I'll be back tomorrow afternoon," he added. "Straight from the office."

Lena nodded. She wasn't sure if it was agreement or dismissal. Dan finished his coffee, rinsed the mug and grabbed his bag.

“I’ll text when I’m on the train.” He said as Lena followed him to the front door. The morning air beyond was cold and pale, mist still curling along the drive. He turned. Kissing her gently. “Try to relax today.”

She managed a small nod. “Safe trip.”

Dan gave one last glance back as he stepped outside. Lena stood framed in the doorway, arms folded, coffee cooling in her hands. She didn’t wave. He loaded his bag into the car. Started the engine. She didn’t close the door until the car had vanished entirely from view.

Later that morning, Lena dressed slowly, tugging a soft wool cardigan over her long-sleeved top, her hands moving with the measured pace of someone still inside their thoughts. She pulled her hair back loosely, letting strands fall where they wanted. Her lips were slightly chapped. She dabbed a little balm on, then paused at the mirror in the hall, eyes fixed not on her reflection, but on the room beyond it. It still smelled faintly of balsamic glaze from the night before, a trace of normalcy clinging to the air. The kitchen clock, dead still at 3:17, caught her eye as she passed. She ignored it. A small canvas tote waited by the front door, filled with errands she’d half-decided to run, post office, milk, maybe something sweet from the bakery in town. She didn’t feel like doing any of it, but the house had begun to feel too thick with stillness. A walk would help. It had to. She zipped up her coat, pulled on her boots, and paused by the small brass key hanging on the hook. The spare. Still slightly tarnished. Still warm from the last time she held it.

Outside, the air had the crisp bite of midwinter sunlight, bright, but cold. The gravel crunched softly beneath her steps as she made her way through the front garden, the frost underfoot beginning to soften. Her breath clouded the air in steady intervals. For a moment, she turned toward the kitchen window, imagining Dan still at his desk even though he was miles away now. She pictured him sipping bad office coffee, forcing smiles through screen calls, adjusting slide decks with his tired fingers. The image softened something in her chest. Her eyes flicked toward the fields beyond the hedge, almost without thinking and stopped. There, again. The figure. Further off than before, standing just beyond the dip of the closest field. Upright, still. Oddly still. From this distance, it could've been a scarecrow. A lone fence post, something explainable but Lena knew what she'd seen. Knew the shape, the weight of it. The way it seemed to belong and not belong all at once. The latch clicked softly as she slipped through, and the sound felt louder than it should've in the hush. Her boots flattened patches of frost-tipped grass as she made her way along the gentle incline, every footstep sharpening her pulse. The figure was still there. Upright, still. Facing in her direction. A man, she could see that now. Not old, but not young either. Wearing a thick coat and something slung over one shoulder, a satchel maybe. He wasn't moving, just standing at the edge of the field, like he'd been waiting. Lena slowed as she approached, her breath visible now in short, steady clouds. The sunlight curved low behind her, long shadows stretching between them. When she was close enough to speak without raising her voice, she stopped.

"Hi," she said, her voice more casual than she felt.

The man turned his head slightly, just enough to show she had his attention. His expression was unreadable, neutral, like someone trying not to give anything away too soon.

"Didn't mean to alarm you," he said. His voice was low, careful.

"Didn't think anyone walked in the fields." Lena studied him.

His features were ordinary enough. Soft-edged in that countryside way, weather-lined, but not old. Dark curls visible beneath a hood, stubble along his jaw. His eyes were the only thing that struck her, grey-blue, sharp and assessing. Watching her more than looking at her.

"I saw you yesterday," she said. "Out here."

A flicker passed across his face, faint, but not nothing.

"Must have just been passing through." He said calmly.

"You live nearby?"

He hesitated, then offered a nod. "Close enough."

That wasn't an answer, not really but something about the way he said it didn't feel aggressive. Just evasive.

"You walk the fields often?" she tried, shifting her weight.

"Not really." He glanced sideways. "But sometimes I find places worth walking, I'm a dog walker."

They stood in silence for a moment, the breeze threading between them.

"I'm Lena," she said eventually, folding her arms for warmth. "Myself and my partner, we own these fields now."

He gave a nod. "Elliot."

She waited for a surname. It didn't come.

"Nice to meet you," she offered, though her tone held caution.

Elliot looked toward the house in the distance, just visible through a veil of low sunlight.

"Rosehill's a quiet one, I heard there were new residents" he said.

"You know it?" she said, her arms remained folded for warmth.

"Everyone around here does." He didn't elaborate. Just looked at her again, like he was trying to decide something. Lena took a half-step back, but not out of fear. It was more instinct, like giving space to a fox in the hedgerow. Measured distance. Mutual awareness.

"I should get to town," she said. "Errands to run."

He nodded once. "Course."

She turned, walking back the way she came, conscious of not hurrying. As she reached the gate, she glanced back. Elliot was still there. Still watching but when the sun shifted again and she blinked against the glare, he was gone. Not vanished. Just not there anymore. Lena slipped back through the gate, fingers tight on the latch until it clicked shut. The sound echoed for a moment longer than it should have. The wind stirred, tugging lightly at her coat, but the chill was already settling deeper than her skin. She rubbed her arms once, casting a glance over her shoulder. Nothing but the field behind her, gold-tinged and empty. She pulled her scarf higher and pressed forward. The path that led to town weaved gently alongside the property's boundary wall, trailing through a low dip before rising again with the landscape. Lena moved steadily, her boots scuffing damp leaves, her breath visible in soft huffs. She kept her eyes ahead now, not lingering on the hedgerows or the gnarled trees that leaned slightly toward the lane like they were listening. Her thoughts circled tighter around Dan, how quiet he'd been that morning, how quickly he'd left. She missed him already. It was a vague ache, but it pressed in behind her ribs. The walk helped. It always did. Something about the rhythm of movement, the sensation of being small against a wide sky, cleared the static from her thoughts. By the time she rounded the bend where the stone wall dropped away and the open view of the village unfolded before her, her muscles felt looser. Her breath steadier. Everley wasn't large. Just a single high street with neatly kept shopfronts, most painted in muted tones that looked almost washed out by the pale light. Lena passed the crooked post-box, its red chipped and faded, and the familiar bench with flaking paint outside the grocer's. The place looked the same as it had on their last visit, paused. As if someone had left the scene between takes. She crossed to the opposite side of the road, boots tapping softly against uneven flagstones. The café sign came into view: *The Cracked Teacup*. Its windows were slightly fogged, like before. A warm smudge of yellow light glowed behind the glass. Lena paused, then pushed the door open. The bell chimed a dull, pleasant note and warm air wrapped around her shoulders.

Inside, the atmosphere was nearly identical to their last visit. Mismatched tables. Dried flowers in bud vases, the same low hum of jazz from a speaker tucked somewhere behind the counter. It smelled faintly of orange peel and cinnamon. The woman behind the counter, red hair tied back, same calm expression, glanced up.

"Just you today?"

Lena nodded. "Yeah."

"Anywhere you like."

She chose a corner table, halfway between the frosted window and the little bookshelf near the till. As she peeled off her gloves, a voice caught her attention. Smooth, precise, female.

"Shame, really," the voice said. "They had such lovely bone structure, the Harrows and to go out like that, such a waste."

Lena glanced over. A woman, well-dressed, early forties perhaps, was seated alone at the next table, stirring tea with absent-minded elegance. Her lipstick was dark and her coat expensive. She caught Lena's glance and smiled.

"Sorry, small town gossip," she said, not sounding sorry at all.

Lena offered a polite smile back. "No worries."

The woman tilted her head. "You're the new tenant up at Rosehill, aren't you?"

Lena blinked. "News gets around this village fast."

The woman extended a gloved hand across the small distance between them.

"Louise Hale. I handle probate properties and estate law in these parts. Well, try to."

Lena shook her hand. Firm grip, cold fingers.

"Lena. Nice to meet you."

"Likewise."

Louise's gaze flicked briefly to Lena's coat, her boots. Her smile lingered.

"And how are you settling in?"

"We're, getting there," Lena said, careful.

Louise leaned back slightly. "That house has history. You must feel it."

Lena hesitated. "We're still figuring out the heating."

Louise laughed lightly. "Aren't we all."

Their conversation stalled when the café woman arrived to take Lena's order, a tea, black, no milk, and Louise turned back to her phone but the impression lingered. Like the scent of someone's perfume long after they've left a room. Cora arrived moments later with a delicate clink of porcelain. She set Lena's tea down with care, then glanced between the two women.

"Everything alright here?"

"All fine," Louise said, voice sugar-sweet.

"Just admiring the new homeowner." Cora's brows lifted slightly.

"Didn't realise you two were the lucky winners at Rosehill," she said, directing the comment at Lena with a warmth that didn't quite reach her eyes.

"You and Dan, is it?" Lena blinked, her smile faltering a touch.

"Yeah... Dan."

"Funny," Cora added, collecting a nearby tray of empties. "You didn't mention it last time."

Before Lena could think of a reply, Cora was gone, moving briskly toward the counter. Louise's smile sharpened, just for a moment, like the edge of a page being turned.

Meanwhile, Dan's train slid into St Pancras with a soft, hydraulic sigh. He stepped onto the platform, breath fogging faintly as he adjusted the strap of his bag and tucked his coat tighter around himself. The city greeted him with its usual chilled indifference, grey light falling in diagonal slants across the glass roofing, commuters slipping past in fast, silent streaks. He blinked hard, resisting the urge to rub his eyes. The fields outside Everley had felt like another world entirely, this was momentum again. Noise. Schedule. Purpose. By the time he'd reached the station exit, his phone buzzed with the day's first Teams notification.

Helen Tredwell: Quick huddle before print. You in?

He replied with a thumbs up and tucked the device back in his pocket, exhaling into the cold. The streets of King's Cross were already busy, men in camel coats, women in leather gloves, the sharp scent of roasted coffee trailing from kiosks. Dan let the city pull him in, let its rhythm override the strange stillness of the past few days. The creative studio was on a quiet street just off Charlotte Road. All exposed brick and matte black trim, minimalist signage with a fingerprint scanner beside the entry. He buzzed in, climbed the stairs two at a time, and pushed through the door into the familiar mix of warm lamplight, soft jazz, and the faint chemical tang of printing toner.

"Dan's here!" someone called from behind a monitor, and half a dozen heads lifted in brief greeting.

He offered a quick wave, dropped his coat on the back of a chair, and immediately slipped into the flow of conversation.

"Prints are on the drying rack."

"Jules wants your eyes on the clementine layout."

"Can we swap the matte for gloss before noon?"

"Have you got the revised mock-ups for the fig jam label?"

Dan fielded the barrage with polite nods, already scanning the desktop for the USB drive he'd brought from home. His desk had been cleared except for a steaming cup of black tea, someone remembered his order, and a stack of colour swatches marked ***Festive Range, Batch 6***. He plugged in the drive, clicked into the main folder, and pulled up the current version of the Christmas campaign. Clementine glaze, star anise drizzle, copper-foil script. It was all there. Half the team still wanted snowflakes. The other half insisted on elevated heritage warmth. He leaned in, switching rapidly between screens, his fingers flying across the keyboard. The city buzzed behind the windows. Conversations rose and fell around him. Still, beneath it all, he felt that hum of disquiet. Like something had been left open back at the house, like the air hadn't fully cleared.

The scent of machine-brewed coffee clung to the corridor as he passed the communal kitchen, the low hum of chatter seeping from open meeting rooms. Everything here felt unnaturally fast, screens flicking, bodies moving, doorways opening with purpose. The pace of it pulled at him, urgent and caffeinated. He hadn't even unzipped his coat before Imran waved him down the hall.

"Studio Two," Imran said.

"Joseph's already in there. Mood boarded the hell out of the projection wall." Dan rolled his neck once, then followed. The meeting room was flooded with white light. Joseph Hill stood at the head of the table, all dark slacks and crisp confidence, laser pointer in one hand and an untouched oat latte in the other.

"Finally," Joseph drawled, barely looking up. "We can begin."

He sank into a seat beside Imran as the screen shifted, slides flipping through the new campaign rollout with tight animation. Hero shots of turkey crowns and blood-orange spritz. Snow-dusted table settings. Overlaid text in elegant serif. *Where Christmas Comes Home.*

"We're three weeks behind visual approvals," Joseph said, clicking to the next slide.

"Legal flagged the packaging alignment on two SKUs. The mulled syrup photos need to be retouched, we want shine, not sweat and the vegan Wellington? Don't even get me started. That mock-up looks like a doorstop in a pastry coat."

Dan rubbed his brow. "We talked about bringing in a new stylist."

"Not in budget," Imran muttered.

"We're reallocating to influencer touchpoints." Joseph clicked again.

"Speaking of which, Dan, your tasting notes from last week? Gorgeous, but we're pushing for more romance in the copy. Less 'indulgent savouriness,' more 'fireside comfort.' Can you rework by EOD?"

"Sure," Dan said, though the words tasted like cardboard.

The room pushed on, notes, metrics, critiques. PowerPoint warfare with the slow-burning urgency of a boiling kettle. By the end of the hour, Dan's back ached and his list had doubled. As the others filtered out, he stayed behind to gather his charger cable and notepad.

"You alright?" Imran asked, pausing at the door.

Dan gave a dry laugh. "Depends. Do we count still breathing as a win?"

Imran smirked. "In this place? Gold star, mate."

They shared a brief, tired look, the kind that said *same storm, different buckets* and then Imran left. Dan leaned against the table's edge, checking his phone. One missed call. *Mum.*

He stepped into the corridor and answered.

"Darling," her voice came through with a slight crackle. "Are you still working? I won't keep you."

"All good, Mum. Just stepped out."

"Wanted to check about the party next weekend. You and Lena are still coming?"

"Of course," he said.

"Wouldn't dare cancel on you."

"And Lena, how is she? Are you treating her well?"

There was a pointed lilt to the question. Dan smiled faintly.

"She's good. Beautiful, stronger than I deserve." A pause.

"And are you... thinking of proposing yet? Not to pressure. But you're not getting any younger, love."

He pinched the bridge of his nose, though he was smiling.

"I've actually got a bit of time tomorrow before I head back. I was thinking of popping into Hatton Garden."

Her gasp was soft and satisfied. "Oh, Dan. She's going to love that."

"I hope so."

They exchanged a few more pleasantries before she said goodbye. As soon as the call ended, he opened Lena's contact and tapped to call.

She answered on the second ring, wind curling faintly through the line.

"Hey," he said.

"Miss me yet?" Her voice was warm.

"Terribly. I'm in town, hunting for treats. Thought I'd stock up before your grand return." He chuckled.

"Anything for me? Chocolate sauce? Squirty cream?"

"Wouldn't you like to know," she teased, laughter softening the line. "Let's just say I'm one step ahead of you."

"God, I love you," he murmured.

"Love you too," she said. "Now go impress those overlords."

"Always." He ended the call and leaned briefly against the wall, letting the noise of the office slide past him like water.

For a moment, all that existed was the echo of her voice and the faint taste of possibility on his tongue. The wind had picked up by the time Lena left the café. A fine mist had begun to cling to the edges of her coat, softening the outlines of the shopfronts as she made her way through town with the bag of wrapped pastries nestled into the crook of her arm. The street had grown quieter, and the sky overhead had shifted again. Its earlier golden hue traded for a pale silver, dense with the suggestion of late afternoon. Her conversation with Louise still lingered, nestled uneasily in her thoughts. She replayed it without meaning to: the way Louise's eyes had narrowed slightly when she mentioned the Harrow family, the odd cadence of her voice when she'd asked how long Lena and Dan planned to stay up at Rosehill. It hadn't sounded like casual curiosity, more like a loaded question dressed in local manners. Lena's boots tapped a steady rhythm along the footpath as she turned off the main road and began the slower ascent toward home. Her mind wandered, not to Clara this time, or the guest room, or even the door that had locked itself. It wandered to Dan. To the way his voice had sounded on the phone. Warm, playful, grounding. She pictured him tomorrow, hunched over a counter with a jeweller's loupe, pretending to know the difference between diamond clarity levels. The thought made her smile. The hedgerows grew taller as the path narrowed, the soft hush of nature swallowing the last few distant sounds of the village. Just beyond the bend where the road curved slightly into a patch of untended woodland, she paused. Movement. To her left, just beyond a row of ash trees, a figure walked through the undergrowth. A figure, tall, lean, a silhouette carved from soft greys and greens. He moved at a slow pace, like someone familiar with the path beneath him. At his side, a dog trotted. Black or dark brown, it was hard to tell, its shape blurred between the trunks. The figure stepped lightly, his coat skimming the edge of the brambles without catching. He didn't look at her. Lena stopped walking. The figure continued for a few more paces, then paused, head turning slightly as if sensing her but before she could call out, he moved again, slipping through a gap between the trees where the brush grew denser. In seconds, he was gone. The dog that was with him, too. As though neither had ever been there at all. Lena stayed still a moment longer, her eyes on the place where the figure had vanished. There was no sound, no snap of twigs, no rustle of leaves. Just the steady hush of wind through winter branches. She exhaled and adjusted the bag of pastries in her arm as she kept walking. The house came into view slowly, its pitched roof and tall chimneys rising like watchtowers against the pale sky. From a distance, it looked serene. A postcard of countryside peace but Lena knew better now. She saw the way the windows never caught the same light twice. How the ivy along the left wall never seemed to grow or shrink. The symmetry of it all. Too perfect, like a painting hung slightly askew, but you couldn't tell until you stared long enough. She let herself in through the side door. The air inside greeted her with a warmth that had no temperature to it, just presence. Familiar now. Unnerving in its quiet. In the kitchen, she unpacked her bag slowly. A jar of salted caramel. A half-dozen brown paper parcels tied in string. A new brand of tea she hadn't tried before, the label handwritten in looping calligraphy. As she reached for the cupboard, the scent of something faint and herbal brushed her senses, lavender, maybe or old wood. She paused. Then shook it off. Just Clara's polish, lingering. Just a long day. She pressed the kettle switch and stood by the counter, waiting for the water to boil.

Far away, beyond the hills and the trees and the winding roads, the city pulsed on. Dan rubbed his jaw as he stepped into the open-plan coworking space adjacent to the creative wing. It was quieter here, the kind of quiet that came from too many people wearing noise-cancelling headphones. He grabbed a stool near the back and fired up his laptop again. Still forty unread emails. Half of them from Jules. The other half from a supplier asking if they *could explore edible glitter options for the panna cotta line*. He didn't respond, not yet. His shoulders slumped for the first time all day. From the window, the city looked smeared by drizzle. Below, a red bus hissed around a corner, headlights blurring against the glass. Somewhere on another floor, someone was laughing. Not cruelly. Just freely. Dan closed his eyes for a moment and imagined the sound echoing in the halls at home. Then opened them again, the agency wasn't done with him yet. Another sip of lukewarm coffee, that could possibly not even be his, that was abandoned on the side of his desk which did little to revive him, but it gave him a reason to stay seated. Jules' topmost email blinked open. A revised tagline: *Taste the Tradition*. Another pivot. Another inch away from what they'd agreed yesterday. Dan exhaled slowly and adjusted the layout. Snowflake swapped for fir branch. Kerning tightened, the changes were minor but chipped away at the design like limescale on tile, quiet and constant. The ambient lights above dimmed as dusk crept in. Most of the studio had emptied. Chairs sat pushed in, headphones coiled neatly on desks. He saved the files, uploaded the latest build. Slid the USB into the interior pocket of his bag with a care that suggested it was made of something more fragile than plastic. His jacket clung damply to his shoulders by the time he stepped into the street. Mist hung in the air, not heavy enough for rain but thick enough to find every fold of his collar. City light bled upward into the cloud cover, staining it the colour of old paper. A cyclist passed too close, wheels whispering along the slick pavement. Dan didn't flinch. The walk to the hotel was short, four blocks through a corridor of shuttered cafés and glass doors humming with after-hours light. His room, charcoal walls, a compact desk, bed tucked too neatly, welcomed him with the faint, clinical hush of all hotel rooms. Generic comfort. The smell of bleach over citrus. He stood at the foot of the bed for longer than necessary, bag still slung over one shoulder, then set it down and crossed to the window. Brick wall, no skyline, no moon. Without turning on the TV, he dropped onto the mattress. Let silence wrap around him, then reached for the kettle, filled it with tap water and flicked it on. The knock in the pipes came low and slow, like something shifting deeper in the building. It reminded him of home. Not his childhood home, the one now filled with boxed-up things, but the new one. The strange one. Rosehill. He didn't notice the kettle click off. Didn't move to pour the tea.

Back at Rosehill, the sky had deepened to a heavy violet, thick with low clouds and the promise of frost. The kind of cold that didn't show itself through temperature alone, but in the stillness it left behind. Lena moved quietly through the kitchen, the faint hum of the refrigerator the only sound accompanying her. She switched off the under-cabinet lights, checked the bolt on the back door one final time, and glanced once through the glass, just enough to confirm the terrace lights were on and the garden was empty. Her movements were slow, methodical. The kind of rhythm one adopted in unfamiliar houses, even after weeks. Upstairs, she folded her jumper neatly on the armchair by the window and peeled back the duvet. The bedroom light was low, soft and golden, but still cast long shadows beneath the chest of drawers. She didn't look too long. She didn't linger. Climbing into bed, she glanced at her phone, still no messages from Dan. She hesitated, thumb hovering above the screen. Then, quietly, she typed:

21:36
Lena: *Night love. Hope it's not too grim in the city. Miss you. x*

She added a small heart, deleted it and then added it again. Then turned the screen over and placed the phone face-down on the nightstand. The duvet was warm now from her body heat. The silence around her wasn't loud, exactly, but present. Settled. She let her eyes close slowly, lashes brushing her cheekbones, and allowed sleep to reach her before her mind could protest.

Across in the city, Dan sat propped against the headboard of the hotel bed, the light from his laptop casting long shadows against the opposite wall. The screen was angled slightly down, illuminating only the lower half of his face as he reviewed the mock-ups one last time The slideshow looped again, copper ribbon overlays, sprigs of rosemary, reworded product titles designed to evoke "intimate holiday charm." He wasn't even sure what that meant anymore. He reached for the glass of water beside him, half-drank, and refreshed his inbox without much expectation. Still open. Still there. The draft.

No Subject.
No Recipient.
Just the context of the email, **Hello Daniel. xx**

He hadn't written it. That much he was certain of now. The timestamp didn't align with anything on his calendar. No auto-save quirks. No accidental template leftover. It sat in his drafts, still bolded. Still waiting. He hovered the cursor over it again, thumb tapping absently against the trackpad. A moment later, he reached for his phone instead.

22:43
Dan: *Goodnight gorgeous, can't wait to see you tomorrow! Miss you x*

He waited, watched the screen. No typing bubble, no read receipt. A faint hiss from the hallway vent broke the silence. He glanced toward the door, but nothing moved. The window beyond showed only darkness, city less and hollow. It reminded him of the back field at Rosehill. That same depthless black. That same feeling that something might be standing just beyond the frame. He placed the phone back on the nightstand. Let it lie face up. Then closed his laptop.

CHAPTER TEN

The morning arrived without light. Just the suggestion of it, a greying at the edges of the window, a thinning of the shadows. Lena stirred before the birds did. The duvet had slipped from her shoulder, her skin prickled against the chilled air. Her phone, face-down on the bedside table, blinked silently. She reached for it with the groggy caution of someone expecting bad news. A reply. A response from Dan reading '*Goodnight gorgeous, can't wait to see you tomorrow! Miss you x*' sat unopened, sent just before midnight. She rolled onto her back and stared at the ceiling. The faint hush of the room pressed in a little tighter this morning. Not heavy, just too still. She climbed out of bed slowly, the floorboards cool beneath her feet. The hallway beyond their bedroom stretched long and quiet. Familiar now but not comfortable, something made her pause. A strange, quiet unease she couldn't name. The pattern of the boards looked wrong. Not dramatically, just subtly as if two planks had traded places in the night. As if the wood itself had shifted when no one was watching. She shook the thought off, but her pulse had quickened. Downstairs, the kitchen was wrapped in early dimness. The overhead bulbs flickered once before holding steady. Her gaze dropped to the window above the sink, the one she was sure she'd locked last night. It was ajar. Barely, an inch, at most. Enough for a draft. Enough for something else. A faint breeze stirred her fringe as she stepped forward. A few leaves had blown in, crumpled, brittle, like they'd been carried from far further than the garden. She bent down, pinched them between two hands, and dropped them into the compost bin without ceremony. Lena reached for her phone again. Her thumb hovered, he thought about the window. About the night before. But what was there to say?

Lena: *Hope work's OK. Weird morning here again. Xx*

She hit send, then set the phone down and turned toward the kettle, flicking it on without thought. The sound of it boiling didn't fill the room. It just sat in it. Humming low, like something thinking behind a door. The cab jolted slightly as it turned off Euston Road, the rumble of early traffic pressing faintly against the windows. Dan sat hunched in the back, one hand wrapped around a takeaway coffee, the other idly scrolling through his phone. His shirt was wrinkled from the rushed hotel ironing job, his coat collar still slightly damp from the drizzle outside. The city looked half-awake, grey-faced buildings blinking into life, shop shutters yawning open, cyclists weaving through gaps with the grim focus of routine. Dan's eyelids felt thick, like the night hadn't properly ended. The bed at the hotel had been fine. Just fine. But sleep had evaded him in broken, weightless intervals. His phone buzzed.

Lena: *Hope work's OK. Weird morning here again. xx*

He read it twice. Frowned faintly. Then tapped out a reply, pausing halfway.

Dan: *All good. Running late. Can't wait to be home. x*

He didn't ask what she meant by weird. He didn't want to invite the weight of it, not when he was about to walk into Jules' lion's den of seasonal mock-up reviews and last-minute slide chaos. But the message stuck with him. Clung behind his ribs. He imagined her in the kitchen, barefoot, arms crossed, tea cooling beside her. That look she got when something didn't sit right. The cab pulled up. Dan slid out, nodded at the driver, and took the stone steps two at a time into the agency building. The warmth of the lobby hit him like a radiator blast. Coffee machines hummed. Someone coughed in the stairwell. Familiar noise, familiar pace but something about it felt distant now. Like the beat had shifted by half a second. In the lift, he adjusted his tie. Checked his reflection. The mirror didn't lie, exactly, it just didn't look like him this morning. Not fully. The doors opened. Jules was already waiting. She stood near the boardroom glass, her hands clasped in front of her like she'd been pacing.

"You're late," she said, without turning.

Dan offered his best "I fought traffic" smile. "Train was chaos."

Jules didn't care. "We're going in hard today. We've got three brand execs and a taste director in from Manchester. I need you sharp."

"I'm always sharp," Dan replied, already slipping into rhythm.

The meeting room was a slow spiral of feedback. The panna cotta samples were a hit, except the elderflower one. The mince pie branding was 'too nostalgic,' whatever that meant. Dan fielded questions with half a mind while his thoughts wandered back to the draft email from the night before. *Hello Daniel. xx.*

It still lingered, He hadn't told anyone. After the third set of mock-ups, Joseph Hill cornered him by the drinks table.

"We need to talk re: budget flow for the rollout," Joseph said, voice low and clipped.

"Now?" Dan replied, glancing toward the ongoing meeting.

Joseph nodded. "You've been slipping, Dan. Just saying."

Dan's jaw flexed. "I've moved house. I've not slipped."

Joseph leaned closer. "That's not what the numbers say or the feedback on your last two client calls."

Dan stared at him. "If you've got something to say, say it."

Joseph gave a tight smile. "Maybe I will." He walked off.

Dan exhaled through his nose. His phone buzzed again. Another message. This time from Imran.

'Private chat after lunch? Something weird is going on with the doc access logs.'

Dan didn't respond. He glanced at the clock, nearly noon. He checked his emails, his inbox looked like a spreadsheet had exploded. Dan found Imran on the mezzanine level near the tall windows, halfway through a protein bar and tapping something into his tablet. He looked up the moment Dan approached.

"You got my message?" Imran asked, lowering his voice.

Dan nodded. "What's going on?"

Imran shifted his weight, glancing behind them before leaning in.

"Someone's been accessing the packaging files from an external location. The file paths pinged three logins last night, between e and three a.m."

Dan frowned. "Who the hell's working at that time?"

"No one on payroll," Imran's voice dropped lower. "What's weird is... one of the accesses was tagged with your ID."

Dan blinked. "I was asleep, I'm never awake at that time."

"I figured." Imran held out the tablet, flicking to a log entry.

"It pulled your saved layout folder. The *second* FINALv5. The one with the allergen note changes."

Dan stared at the screen. His name. His login. Timestamped at 03:12 a.m.

"I didn't touch anything," he said. "I wasn't even logged in."

"Which is why I thought you should know," Imran said. "It's not public-facing yet, so no client risk, but it triggered the activity alert on the back-end."

Dan raked a hand through his hair.

"Do you think it was someone internal?"

Imran hesitated. "Could be, could be someone spoofing logins or someone had your laptop?"

Dan didn't reply, his mind flashed to the house. The study, The faint smell of lavender, the cold screen glowing with the words *Hello Daniel. xx.* He'd never closed that email, never hit send.

Imran studied him. "You good?"

"Yeah," Dan said. "Just... weird week."

Imran didn't push. "If you want me to run a deeper trace, I can. Might take a few days."

"Do it," Dan said.

"But keep it quiet." A nod. Imran was already tapping into a new thread. Dan lingered by the window for a moment after Imran left, staring at the blur of London traffic beneath. It felt miles away from the house. From Lena but part of him was already there again, in that hush of shadowed hallways and locked doors that weren't supposed to be locked.

At Rosehill, the silence had a different flavour that afternoon. Less stillness, more waiting. Lena had finished her tea an hour ago but hadn't moved far from the kitchen. A quiet sense of unsettled energy pulled her toward the upstairs hallway again, back to the west wing she'd barely explored. Not since the room with Clara. She opened the door opposite the one she'd found Clara in days before. It was darker here, the curtains were drawn, though a narrow shaft of light sliced in at the corner where the rod hung unevenly. The room looked untouched. Furniture draped in old white sheets, their corners yellowed with age. A tall dressing table stood near the far wall, its mirror clouded and speckled with dust. She stepped in, floorboards gently groaning beneath her feet. The air was cooler. Stiller. She reached out and tugged one of the sheets aside, beneath, the dressing table was surprisingly elegant. Carved legs, a shallow drawer, tarnished handles. As she adjusted the mirror slightly, something caught her eye behind it, a subtle seam in the wall. Just off to the side. She frowned, stepped back, and realised the table was blocking a small built-in cupboard door. Almost invisible beneath the wallpapered panel. Curiosity flared, she dragged the dressing table aside with some effort, coughing softly as dust puffed into the air. The cupboard door was barely a foot wide and half as tall as a regular one, more of a crawlspace or storage hatch than anything practical. A small brass latch held it closed. It opened with a soft click. Inside was dry, empty, save for a single cardboard box and a thin layer of time-stained linen. She crouched, tugged the box toward her. The cardboard was soft at the edges, the colour faded. Inside: old papers. A dried pen. A cracked porcelain trinket box and a photograph. It wasn't labelled. A black-and-white image, slightly curled at the edges. The house. Rosehill. Clear as day, though the garden had looked different then, less wild, more trimmed. And in the foreground: a man and a woman, arms looped, dressed in wedding attire. The man looked stiff but smiling. The woman's face had a strange quality, not blurred, but somehow hard to pin down. Not quite looking at the camera, not quite looking anywhere. Lena turned the photo over. No names. No date. Just a faint pencilled word in the corner. **Harrow.** She stood slowly, her skin prickled. Something about the photo made her feel, watched. She carefully placed back into the box, slipping the picture into her pocket as she pushed the cupboard closed, and stepped back into the hallway. A beat passed, then she went to grab her coat.

Dan finished the last of his follow-up notes with a tight jaw, eyes dry from staring too long at bright screens and clipped-font documents. The meeting with Joseph still hovered in the back of his mind like a bruise, visible only when pressed. He closed his laptop with a slow exhale and glanced out the tall office window. The city shimmered beneath a drizzle-smeared sky. The light had begun to soften, London gold at its most forgiving. He checked the time. Just enough. Downstairs, the lobby lights flickered a polite farewell as he crossed into the street and hailed a cab. The ride was short, just a few turns past a florist with wilting dahlias and a bookstore he once swore he'd go into. The cab dropped him near a discreet corner shopfront, the window display delicate and almost old-fashioned. Pale velvet boxes, glass domes, a soft wash of yellow light that gave everything inside a kind of gentle glow. He pushed the door open. A small bell rang, the shop was silent except for the tick of a vintage clock on the back wall. An older man, dressed in charcoal grey with a subtle sheen to his waistcoat, appeared from behind a curtain.

"Good afternoon," he said. Not warmly, not coldly. Just, correctly. "Looking for something in particular?"

Dan hesitated, then nodded. "An engagement ring."

A brief flicker of understanding passed behind the man's eyes. He stepped aside and gestured toward the left display case, where rings nestled against silk like secrets waiting to be chosen.

"Something classic?" the man asked. "Or something that surprises?"

Dan moved closer. The glass reflected back a quieter version of himself, creased shirt, tired eyes, hair flattened slightly by the rain.

"Something she'll remember," he murmured. "Something that feels like her."

The man nodded once. Then lifted the lid to a narrow, navy box. The ring inside was simple, but not plain. An oval diamond, faintly rose-cut, flanked by two smaller stones that shimmered with a pale fire, moonstone, maybe, or a delicate opal. The band was slim, but not fragile, etched with the faintest detailing that caught the light only when tilted just so. Dan stared at it.

"That one," he said, before he could overthink it. "That's the one."

"It's handmade," the jeweller said softly. "One of a kind."

Dan nodded. "That's perfect."

The ring was boxed and tied with a ribbon so smooth it barely made a sound. When Dan left the shop, the city air felt different, brighter, even as the clouds thickened. He tucked the small box into his coat pocket, fingers brushing the velvet once before letting it go. For the first time in days, his thoughts didn't race. They settled, landed. The weight of the decision wasn't pressure. It was gravity. He was ready.

Meanwhile, back in the countryside, Lena tugged her scarf tighter as she reached the outer curve of the village road. The sky above was low and flat, the air still as breath held in a chest. Her boots struck the earth with a rhythm that grounded her more than the walk itself. She'd stuffed the photo, house, bride, groom, into her bag before leaving. There had been something about it. The way the groom's face blurred at the edges. The subtle tilt of the bride's smile, like she knew something the camera didn't. As she turned onto the main street, the scent of coffee and burnt sugar drifted from The Cracked Teacup and there he was. Miles Fenner. Seated inside, back to the window, gesturing sharply across the table. Cora Bell sat opposite him, arms folded, mouth thin. It wasn't a friendly conversation. Even through the glass, Lena could feel the friction. Miles leaned forward, a finger pressing to the table like punctuation. Cora's expression didn't shift. Lena slowed her pace, pretending to glance into a bakery window next door. She could hear her pulse behind her ears. They didn't see her, or if they did, neither acknowledged it. She moved on quickly, the sharp edge of curiosity now tempered by something else, unease.

The estate agent's door opened with a jingle of brass bells. A gust of warm air brushed her face. She stepped inside, eyes scanning for Louise. It was time for more answers. The office smelled faintly of laminate paper and something floral, synthetic and not quite pleasant. A small brass heater clicked faintly in the corner. Behind the desk, Louise Hale looked up from her monitor, her reading glasses perched at the tip of her nose.

"Lena," she said with a small smile. "Back again?"

Lena returned the smile, polite but cautious. "Hope you don't mind."

"Not at all." Louise gestured to the seat opposite. "Take a pew. What can I help you with?"

Lena slid into the chair, her bag resting in her lap like a shield. For a moment, she didn't speak, he quiet of the office stretched gently, enough to be felt, not enough to be uncomfortable. Then she reached into the bag and pulled out the photo.

"I found this," she said, setting it down on the desk. "In the house. Tucked away in an old cupboard behind a dressing table in one of the unused rooms guest rooms, I was taking off all the dust sheets."

Louise leaned forward, her expression sharpening just slightly. She took the photograph gently between her fingers, examining it as if it might crack. Her eyes narrowed at the image.

"Hmm," she said after a moment. "That's… not one I've seen before."

Lena watched her closely. "Do you know who they are?"

Louise gave a small shake of her head.

"Not personally. but, " she tapped the corner of the photo, where the base of the front steps and the lower edge of the rose trellis were visible. "That's definitely Rosehill. No mistaking it."

"And you're sure the place has been empty all this time?" Lena pressed. "No one mentioned anything in the paperwork. Just that it was previously unoccupied."

Louise hesitated, just long enough to be noticed. Then she folded her hands on the desk, the photo resting between them. "Look, most of what I know is second hand. Records on Rosehill have always been a bit…sparse. Some of the paperwork's been lost, especially around the time of the fire."

Lena's breath caught. "Fire?"

Louise nodded slowly. "Nearly twenty years ago. The back portion of the house was damaged, nothing too structural, mostly interior, but after that, it just sat. No tenants, no sale attempts. Just left."

Lena blinked. "I thought it was listed."

"It was," Louise said. "Through private agencies only. Winspire took over the listing about six years ago. Spent a fortune refurbishing it, even then, no buyers. Eventually, they just added it to the prize portfolio. You'd be amazed how many of those houses are won because they can't be sold." A pause. Louise gave a small, dry smile. "But that's the dream, isn't it? A house with a story."

Lena tried to smile back, but it didn't quite form.

"And the previous owners?" she asked. "Do you know who they were?"

Louise glanced toward the filing cabinet beside her desk.

"I can check what's in the archive, but honestly, love, if you're looking for peace of mind, I'd just enjoy the place. All houses creak. All old ones hold a bit of history."

Lena nodded and thanked her but as she stepped back outside, the damp air curling around her again, the weight of the photo in her coat pocket felt heavier. Twenty years. A fire but this picture was unburnt? She glanced back once at the office window. Then started the slow walk home.

As the sun began to set, The train rocked gently as it pulled out of Paddington, the lights overhead flickering once before settling into their usual hum. Dan sat by the window, one leg stretched out, the other jittering faintly beneath the table. His bag was tucked between his boots, heavier than it had been that morning. The ring box inside felt strangely alive, like it had a pulse. Outside, the city blurred into industrial shadows, rows of warehouses, bridges, brief flashes of graffiti. Then came the softer edges of suburbia, and eventually the darkness of the countryside swallowing everything but the carriage lights. Dan closed his eyes for a moment, letting the sound of the train fill his ears. There was a comfort to it. A kind of rhythm. He checked his phone. One message from Jules, nothing urgent. One from Imran, a meme about Joseph and his 'budget emergencies.' and one from Lena.

Just a photo: two candles flickering on a table, the edge of a wine glass catching the light. No caption. No emoji. Just the image. Dan smiled faintly, thumb hovering over the keyboard.

Dan: *On my way. Can't wait. x*
He hit send and slid the phone back into his coat pocket. The train slowed as it reached his stop. He stood, stretching stiff shoulders, and retrieved his bag. The platform was near-empty, just two figures walking toward the parking lot, their footsteps echoing into the cool evening air. Dan made his way to the car. The metal was cold beneath his palm as he unlocked it. He dropped into the driver's seat, started the engine, and let the heater tick on. For a long moment, he just sat there. The lights in the distance cast long, stretched reflections across the car hood. He breathed out, reached into his bag, and touched the velvet box once, just a light brush, as if to remind himself it was real. Then he shifted into gear and pulled onto the road.

Back at the house, Lena peeled a strip of wax paper from the top of the brie and placed it on the board with the rest of the cheese. Her hands moved with quiet confidence, slicing apples, arranging olives, setting out bread. The table was already laid. Two plates, linen napkins folded neatly, the cutlery gleaming beneath the low light of the kitchen pendants. A bottle of red breathed beside the sink, uncorked half an hour ago. She glanced at her phone, Dan wouldn't be long now. The house was quiet, still. The kind of stillness that followed the flick of every switch, the lights were on in every room that bordered the kitchen. Not out of forgetfulness, out of instinct. Out of that same silent logic that made you check under beds or pull shower curtains fully open. It was protection however ridiculous that sounded. Lena leaned on the countertop, the sleeves of her jumper pushed to her elbows, the wine glass in her hand still untouched. Her eyes kept drifting to the window above the sink. The garden beyond was pitch black now, reflecting only the warm gold of the kitchen lights back at her. But still. That feeling. The one that prickled at her neck like static. She turned on the radio, soft jazz, low volume, and tried to shake it off. The scent of rosemary from the slow-roasted potatoes mingled with the wine and wood polish. It should've felt cosy and in some ways, it did but something beneath it gnawed. Familiar now. Less fear, more knowing. Her phone buzzed on the counter. She reached for it absently, expecting Dan but it wasn't. Another Instagram message. From Tom. She stared at it for a moment before opening.

Instagram Notification
Direction Message from Tom Calder
Are you not going to offer me a tour of your new house?

No punctuation, just that. Lena's mouth went dry. Her thumb hovered over the screen. She clicked to his profile, no new stories, no visible activity. Just that one message. Sent four minutes ago. She locked the phone and set it down slowly, face-down on the counter.

"Is he losing it?" she whispered aloud, the room too quiet to swallow the sound.

The jazz track ended. A new one began, this one slower. Dreamier. Lena straightened her back, shook her head as if to clear it, and turned to light the candles on the table. Their flames danced upward with a quiet enthusiasm, casting shadows that wavered against the walls. For a flicker of a moment, the house felt, almost right. The kind of right that lived in movies and wedding brochures. She closed her eyes. Took a breath. Tonight, it would be fine. Tonight, she wanted to believe in ordinary things.

Meanwhile, Dan flicked on the headlights and turned down the narrow road that led to Rosehill. The trees leaned in tighter here, their branches clawing over the single-lane track like bent fingers. The tyres crunched over gravel, the soft curve of the drive finally coming into view. His eyes found the house. Lit from within. A golden hush. He pulled in slowly, cut the engine. For a few seconds, he sat there, fingers still curled on the steering wheel. Listening, watching. Then he stepped out into the cold, the gravel crunching softly beneath his boots. The cold kissed his cheeks, sharp but bearable , the kind that made you glad to be heading indoors. The house loomed ahead, bathed in low amber light from every window on the ground floor. It looked peaceful, lived-in. Almost warm. Through the kitchen window, he spotted her. Lena stood at the counter, her back to the window, sleeves rolled, hair tucked behind one ear as she poured something into a dish. Her movements were steady, graceful in that distracted way she had when cooking, focused, but humming beneath it. He smiled. Took a step closer. Steam fogged the lower edge of the glass. He couldn't see her face, but the curve of her shoulder, the soft bend of her neck, that was enough. She looked like home. Dan moved quickly, quietly. Not through the front door, he looped around, stepping softly onto the path that led to the side entrance. His key slid into the lock without a sound. The door creaked faintly as he eased it open, but the radio and the oven fan muffled the noise. He slipped inside. The house wrapped around him like memory. He didn't go straight to her. Instead, he moved with purpose toward the study. The lights were off. Everything was as he'd left it, almost. There was a faint scent in the air again. Lavender. Just a trace. He ignored it, crossed to the bookshelf. His fingers found the hollowed book spine near the back, the one he'd clocked weeks ago, a novelty decoy gift from an old Secret Santa. Tucked behind it, wrapped in a soft black cloth, he placed the ring box. Deep enough it wouldn't be found unless someone knew. His pulse thudded. It felt heavier than it had earlier, more real. He closed the shelf. Smoothed the spine. Exhaled, then he made his way back into the hall.

The kitchen ahead was warm, lit by the soft glow of pendant lights and flickering candles. The scent of dinner lingered, rosemary, caramelised onion, a hint of garlic. Lena stood at the stove, stirring something in a copper pot. Dan's eyes drank her in for a moment. The slope of her shoulders. The faint sway to her hip as she shifted her weight, her silhouette wrapped in a thick-knit jumper. He padded forward quietly, the floorboards soft beneath his steps. Three strides. He reached her, in one smooth movement, he slid his arms around her waist from behind, pressing his chest to her back. She screamed. Not loud, but sharp. Instinctive, her whole body jolted against his, the spoon clattering into the pot with a dull thud. She twisted in his hold, breath caught in her throat, hands half-raised to defend, then saw him.

"Dan!" she exhaled, swatting at his chest. "Jesus, what the hell are you doing?"

He grinned, arms still snug around her. "Surprising you."

"I could've stabbed you."

"You were holding a wooden spoon."

She glared but the corners of her mouth twitched. "You absolute arse."

He leaned in, pressing a kiss to hers. "Missed you too."

She let out a breath, resting her forehead briefly against his collarbone before pulling back just enough to look at him properly.

"You scared the life out of me."

"I know." He tilted his head, eyes crinkling. "Sorry."

"No, you're not."

"Not really, no." he replied.

She huffed, but her arms slid up around his shoulders anyway, drawing him in. Their bodies found each other again in that quiet, natural way, not urgent, just relieved. As if everything stressful could pause for a moment inside that embrace.

"I was starting to worry," she murmured. "Your train ran late?"

"A little. Weather's rubbish. Traffic too."

She nodded, then pulled away, gesturing toward the table. "Dinner's nearly ready. Go sit. I'll pour."

Dan lingered just a second longer, watching her as she moved, something softer in his eyes now, something fuller. Then he slipped off his coat and joined her at the table, the flicker of candlelight catching in his smile.

Dinner passed in a way that almost made Lena forget. The table had been set with care, mismatched plates arranged purposefully, candles flickering down the centre in stubby glass holders. She'd even tucked a sprig of rosemary beside each napkin, the scent subtle but grounding. Dan noticed it immediately, running his thumb gently over the leaves as he sat.

"Nice touch," he said, pulling out her chair for her.

Lena smiled, pleased in that quiet way she had when something landed.

"I figured we deserved something that didn't come out of a box."

The food was simple, honest, roasted aubergine layered with torn basil, a side of warm focaccia drizzled in olive oil, and that salted caramel tart she'd picked up in town, still chilled in its brown paper box. They ate slowly, their conversation unhurried. No work talk, no odd occurrences. Just shared glances, the occasional soft laugh, and a few bites fed from fork to mouth across the table. Dan's hand found hers as they finished dessert. His fingers brushed hers lightly at first, then settled.

"This," he said. "You. Here. This makes it all feel real."

Lena looked down at their hands, thumbs grazing.

"You mean the mortgage-free madness we've been dropped into?"

He chuckled. "I mean the parts that matter."

The room held a different kind of quiet now, not the still, eerie hush that sometimes crept through the halls, but the cocooned kind. The sort that wrapped around candlelight and clinking glasses.

Lena leaned back slightly, her lips curling into something playful. "Well, now that we've had our lovely grown-up dinner, what's next?"

Dan's eyes narrowed with a glint. "Is that a suggestion?"

"Depends," she murmured. "Are you going to surprise me again? Or can I see this one coming?"

He pushed his chair back without answering. Came around to her side of the table. Bent down, slow, hands resting on either side of the chair.

"I think," he said, voice low, "we both know how this ends."

She tilted her chin toward him. "And how's that?"

His kiss was the answer.

It was gentle at first, just a press, a familiarity but it deepened quickly, the weight of distance and delay finally shedding from their shoulders. She stood, pressing against him, hands slipping under the hem of his shirt. He hissed softly against her mouth as her fingers grazed skin. They didn't make it far. The hallway light was still on, their plates half-cleared but they barely noticed. By the time they reached the bedroom, they were breathless with laughter between kisses, limbs tangled in the loose choreography of rediscovery. Her jumper hit the floor. His shirt followed. They moved with the kind of urgency that wasn't rushed, just overdue. Their hands mapped familiar skin like it had changed in the days apart. The cold of the house faded beneath the warmth they built together, one kiss at a time and when it was over, they lay in the half-light. Lena's head on Dan's chest, his arm loose around her waist. For once, nothing moved. No noises crept.

No cold settled. Just the slow rise and fall of breath. Lena drifted first, her exhale catching slightly before sleep took her, her hand resting against Dan's ribs. Dan lay awake longer, listening to the rhythm of her breath. Letting it steady something in him. He watched the shadows shift across the ceiling, not quite ready to close his eyes. Not yet.

CHAPTER ELEVEN

The morning light was almost too kind. It spilled through the gauzy bedroom curtains like warm silk, casting long golden shapes across the wooden floorboards. Lena stirred first, blinking slowly, her limbs draped over Dan's like ivy. For a moment, she didn't move. She just breathed. The house, this house, felt still. No tapping, no creaks, no sense of something hiding just beyond the walls. Just her and Dan, tangled, warm, quiet. He shifted beside her with a low groan, pressing his face into the pillow.

"What time is it?"

"Saturday o'clock," she murmured, curling closer.

"No alarms. No meetings. No emails." Dan gave a sleepy chuckle.

"Don't jinx it." She kissed his shoulder and slid out of bed, wrapping herself in the cardigan draped over the nearby chair. It smelled like laundry detergent and home.

Dan followed a few minutes later, barefoot and shirtless, hair tousled beyond repair. In the kitchen, he declared himself 'Breakfast Commander' and began rustling through the cupboards in search of ingredients. Lena perched at the island, sipping from a fresh cup of coffee, elbows on the counter, watching him. The house looked different in daylight. Gentler. The stone walls held the sun well, and even the old beams seemed to gleam slightly, as though shrugging off their shadows.

"You sure about eggs?" he asked, holding up a carton.

"Positive. And toast. Crispy."

"Aye aye, General." He cracked an egg too fast.

A small splatter hit the counter, but he wiped it with his sleeve before she could say anything. The second egg opened neatly, the third, not so much, a fleck of red in the yolk that he flicked aside with barely a blink. Lena watched in silence, her coffee cooling in her hand. They ate at the table by the patio doors. Sunlight stretched across the grass outside. Everything looked bright, normal, even joyful. After clearing the plates, they wandered into the living room and collapsed onto the couch, limbs entangled again, feet tucked beneath a shared blanket. They put something on, some chaotic cook-off show that neither of them really paid attention to. Mostly they just lay there, lazily scrolling through their phones, letting the weight of the past few weeks melt off.

Evcntually, Dan nudged her side. "Should we use the pool?"

She glanced out the window. The water shimmered like polished glass. "You're serious?"

"Come on. We've been here how long and haven't touched it? Might be the only dry day we get before winter hits."

Ten minutes later, they stepped outside wrapped in towels, barefoot and laughing. Lena shrieked when she dipped a toe in the water, it was colder than it looked, but Dan dove in without hesitation, surfacing with a grin and hair plastered to his head. They swam lazy laps, floated under the sky, let the chill tingle their skin and make them feel alive. At one point, Lena lay on her back, arms stretched wide, eyes closed. Silence, but not the kind that held menace, just the vast, open kind.

"I'm glad we're here," she said quietly.

Dan didn't answer at first, then: "Me too."

They towelled off, breathless and dripping, and headed back inside. The moment they stepped over the threshold, Lena hesitated. It was nothing, just a feeling. Like stepping into a room seconds after someone else had walked through it. Lena shook the water from her hair with a towel as they stepped into the hallway. The wooden floor felt cool beneath her feet, the house air sharp against her damp skin. She gave Dan a soft shove toward the stairs.

"Shower first," she said. "You smell like pond."

"Romantic." He leaned in like he might kiss her, then tugged at her wet towel instead. She laughed, pulled it tighter, and vanished into the bedroom to dress.

Upstairs, the shower hissed to life. She changed slowly, easing into a jumper and leggings, moving without urgency. Her limbs felt loose, her mood light. She passed by the kitchen clock on her way past. **3:17,** but when she reached the kitchen and glanced at the same clock again from a different angle, it read **3:19**. She blinked. She must've lingered longer than she thought, still, the slight disorientation settled in her gut like a stone dropped in water. Dan joined her a few minutes later, dressed in joggers and a clean T-shirt, hair still damp and spiky. He had his phone in one hand, scrolling.

"So," he said, "you know what we haven't done?"

"Rewired the house?" she offered.

"Funny. I meant order things. For next weekend. The family gathering" She snorted.

"Right, and here I was trying to forget about my mother's pending arrival."

They sprawled out in the living room again, laptops open this time, occasionally lifting their heads to compare items.

"Do you think we need candles?" Lena asked, tilting the screen toward him.

"Too moody. Go for those outdoor plates instead."

"Plates it is."

"Maybe a new kettle? Ours screams like a banshee. Don't want our parents judging..."

"That's just her voice," Lena said, and Dan rolled his eyes.

They ordered a few practical pieces, throws, a ceramic fruit bowl for aesthetic, a better doormat and checked out with next-day delivery. By the time they were done, the afternoon light had softened to gold. Long shadows stretched across the kitchen tiles. Dan shut his laptop with a soft click.

"Come on," he said. "Let's walk, make the most of the weather."

Lena hesitated, glancing toward the back window. The trees swayed gently. Nothing strange, nothing wrong. She nodded.

"Okay," she said. "Let's go."

They grabbed jackets, locked the door behind them, and stepped into the woodland path. The path into the woods was soft beneath their shoes, layered with last season's leaves and new spring shoots pushing up from the earth. It wound behind the house, past the thinning hedgerow and into a stretch of tall beech trees that leaned together like old conspirators. Lena zipped her jacket up to the collar. The air was cooler here, shadowed, but not cold. Just shaded. Birds rustled somewhere up high, nothing dramatic, just movement. Distant and ordinary. Dan walked beside her, arms swinging gently, his eyes on the path ahead.

"This is nice," he said after a while. "I keep forgetting we own some of this."

Lena nodded. "It doesn't feel like London anymore."

He glanced at her, eyebrow raised. "You say that like it's a bad thing."

She shrugged. "No. Just different, like we're in someone else's story."

Dan didn't answer, and the conversation fell into a comfortable hush.

For a while, they just walked. Then, quietly, Lena said,

"I didn't tell you, I found a photo."

Dan looked over. "What kind of photo?"

"In one of the guest bedrooms. Top drawer. It was old, faded, scorched at the edges. A woman, a man but the faces were scratched out. Then a name Harrow."

Dan stopped walking. "Scratched out?"

She nodded. "Deep, too. Like… whoever did it really meant it."

He ran a hand down the back of his neck, processing. "And this was just lying around?"

"In a cupboard. Wrapped in fabric. Like it was supposed to be forgotten."

They walked a few more paces before Dan said, "And you're just now telling me?"

"I wasn't sure it meant anything, but it stuck with me."

He frowned. “Okay, so, how did you come across the contents of this cupboard?”

“I was exploring, removing dust sheets and I saw it” she said. “I just… needed to get out the house. While you were in London. I went into town. Stopped by the estate agency.”

Dan stopped again. “Wait, you spoke to an estate agent?”

Lena nodded. “I met one the day before in the café, Louise. I asked her about the house. About who lived here before.”

He blinked. “Why?”

“Because I wanted to know if we were losing our minds or if something bad actually happened here. And if it did, I wanted to know what kind of bad.”

Dan’s expression shifted, surprised, maybe a little uneasy. “So? What did say?”

“She said the house was unoccupied for over a year. Because the previous owners… died. A fire. What a tragedy.”

A pause settled between them. The wind moved through the trees again, a soft rustling above.

“I should’ve told you sooner,” Lena added. “I just forgot with dinner and you know...”

Dan looked ahead down the winding path. “Don’t apologise.” He reached for her hand. “You were just trying to figure it out. That’s all.”

She squeezed his fingers once. “I know.”

They walked on, following the worn path as it curved between trees, over a shallow ditch filled with moss and waterlogged leaves. Sunlight speckled through the canopy above, gold spots drifting across their skin like dust motes.

For a while, it felt simple, quiet. The good kind of silence. Lena slowed as they reached a fallen tree. It looked old, half-crumbled, rotted down the middle, a twisted skeleton of roots exposed and dry. Dan stepped over it easily, holding out a hand to help her across. She took it without hesitation.

“Maybe we should bring a picnic next time,” he said. “Make a day of it.”

Lena smiled. “And risk poison ivy on your arse? Brave.”

“Reckless, actually,” he said, but his voice was light.

They moved on. The trees thinned slightly as they entered a clearing, the canopy breaking into a wide patch of sky. Blue and cloudless. The sun fell over them like a warm sheet, and the scent of bark and damp wildflowers filled the air. Then Lena saw her. Not far ahead, perhaps twenty feet away, just off the main path, stood Anne. She wasn't walking, she wasn't gardening. She wasn't doing anything, just standing, watching something. Her clothes were the same as before, tidy, neutral colours, well-fitted. Her hands hung by her sides, empty. Her gaze locked on them as they approached. Lena slowed instinctively. Dan's pace faltered, then caught up with hers. Anne didn't move, didn't smile. Didn't even twitch. Her eyes were sharp, focused. Not confused or startled. Just looking. Lena raised a hand, small, polite, not wanting to startle her.

"Hi Anne," she called gently. "Lovely day."

No response. Anne's expression didn't change. She didn't blink. After a long second, she turned, slow and deliberate, and walked away into the trees without a word.

Dan exhaled. "Okay. That was weird."

Lena didn't answer. The warmth of the sun felt thinner now, like it was bleeding away between the branches. They continued in silence, following the bend in the path until it looped back toward the deeper edge of the woods. The ground dipped slightly, softening beneath their steps. That's when they heard it, paws against earth, rapid and rhythmic. Elliot emerged from the undergrowth, three dogs in tow, trotting ahead of him in practiced formation. The white spaniel was up front, followed by a scruffy mutt and a sleek brown labrador. Elliot kept a steady pace behind them, his hoodie pulled up and eyes ahead. Lena raised her hand again.

"Hi Elliot!" Dan joined in, louder.

"Afternoon!"

But Elliot didn't look their way, didn't wave, didn't stop. He walked straight past grunting as he did so, with the dogs, who didn't bark, didn't veer, didn't acknowledge them at all, except the spaniel, who hesitated just for a second as she passed Lena. Her ears twitched. She gave a soft whine, almost like recognition, and then followed the pack.

Lena turned to watch them go. "Did he not hear us?"

Dan frowned. "He looked right through me"

They stood there for a moment, the path behind them empty again. The wind shifted in the trees, and somewhere above, a branch creaked.

"I think I'm done walking and being friendly to the neighbours," Lena said softly.

Dan nodded, they turned around and made their way back toward the house. The sun had started its slow descent by the time they reached the house again. The light had changed, warmer, more golden, casting long, lean shadows across the lawn. The windows reflected a dull amber, and the stone exterior glowed faintly in the soft hush of early evening. They rounded the curve of the path, chatting quietly about dinner, when Lena slowed.

"There's someone at the door."

A man stood facing it, hand raised like he'd just knocked. He was tall, in a navy jacket, dark jeans, and heavy boots. One hand held a small brown parcel, the kind Amazon didn't bother wrapping anymore.

Dan called out. "Hello?"

The man spun around, clearly startled. "Oh, sorry," he said, adjusting his grip on the package. "Thought I heard someone coming inside."

Lena frowned. "There's no one in."

The house behind him was still. The porch light wasn't on. No windows glowed. Just empty glass and drawn curtains. The man looked back at the door, as if doubting himself.

"Right, must've been the wind or something. Sorry." He extended the parcel, awkwardly. "I've got a parcel here for you."

Dan took it. "Thanks. Appreciate it."

Without further word, the man turned and jogged down the front lawn, not the drive, heading toward a white van parked out on the road, a good fifty yards away. Too far, really, for what should've been a straightforward delivery. Dan watched him go, parcel in hand.

"Why did he park so far?" Lena questioned.

"Maybe he didn't think he could drive up the path," he offered. "We could've had guard dogs."

Lena cocked her head. "If we did, wouldn't you feel safer driving up than walking?"

Dan paused, then nodded. "Fair point."

He shifted the box under his arm. "I'm a city boy, born and raised. These country folk are different."
She gave him a look. "Are you implying I'm different?"
He turned to her with a crooked grin. "Obviously."
Before she could fire back, he jogged out of arms reach.
"Dan!"
But he was already laughing, fumbling for the keys. Lena hung back a moment, watching the van disappear behind the trees. The man didn't look back.

Inside, the house was cool again. Shadows clung to the corners of the hallway. Lena stepped in first, quietly, and ducked behind the archway just past the stairs. She waited, footsteps, a creak. Dan, still chuckling, entered a few seconds later, juggling the parcel and the keys.
"Lena?"
She waited another beat, then jumped out. "Boo!"
Dan jolted back, nearly dropping the box. "Jesus!"
But it wasn't just the jump, his face had gone pale, expression shifting, something beyond startle.
"What?" Lena asked, laughing but uneasy. "You alright?"
He stared at the staircase for a moment.
"I thought I saw you on the stairs," he said. "Just, out the corner of my eye."
She turned slowly. The stairs were empty. Still, Just the hallway, the door, and the settling silence of home.
"Wasn't me," she said softly.
Dan gave a breathy laugh and rubbed the back of his neck. "No. Course not."
But he didn't take his eyes off the landing. Dan didn't say much after that.
He carried the parcel through to the kitchen while Lena checked the post left in the porch basket, mostly takeaway menus and a glossy flyer offering chimney sweeps at *special winter rates.* The kind of thing no one ever actually asked for, but always seemed to appear. By the time she joined him, Dan had unpacked the parcel, something they had ordered before moving in, a patterned throw, a set of rustic-style

mugs, and the ceramic fruit bowl. It was all neutral, unobtrusive, things designed to make the house feel just lived-in enough.

"You want to cook or shall I?" he asked, eyes on the packaging.

Lena leaned against the doorframe. "If I say you, is that sexist?"

"Not if I offer first." He raised his hands. "I volunteer as tribute."

She smirked. "Fine. But I'm picking the music."

They settled into a rhythm. Dan chopped vegetables with exaggerated flair while Lena queued up a mellow playlist, something acoustic and nostalgic, and set the table. The air filled with the comforting smell of onions, garlic, and a slow simmering sauce. Dinner was a simple pasta dish, eaten by candlelight more out of habit than romance. Neither of them spoke much while they ate, but it wasn't a strained silence. Just the easy quiet of two people who'd already said enough for one day. Afterwards, Lena rinsed the plates while Dan dried. She flicked a bit of water at him; he retaliated with a dish towel snap. It was nothing, and everything. The kind of night you forget until later, when you remember what peace used to feel like. Later still, they curled up on the sofa with mugs of tea. The TV was on, but neither of them watched it closely. Lena's legs were stretched across Dan's lap, her socked feet warm beneath the throw they'd just unwrapped. He rubbed slow circles on her shin with his thumb.

"I like nights like this," she said softly.

Dan nodded. "Yeah."

"Even with… you know."

He didn't ask what she meant. He didn't have to.

"We're still us," she added.

He looked at her then, really looked, and gave a small, tired smile. "Yeah. We are."

By the time they got into bed, the house had cooled again. Dan opened the window slightly, letting in the crisp air. Lena curled up under the duvet and pulled it to her chin.

"Do you ever think," she murmured, "that houses keep memories?"

Dan, brushing his teeth in the ensuite, paused mid-motion. "Like ghosts?"

"No. Not ghosts. Just, impressions. Like heat in the walls."

He spat, rinsed. “Maybe. I think places remember what we bring to them too.”

Lena closed her eyes. “I hope that’s true.”

Dan slipped into bed beside her, wrapping an arm across her waist.

“Then let’s make sure it remembers this…”

She smiled into the dark. Outside, the wind picked up just slightly, nothing dramatic. Just enough to whisper against the glass.

CHAPTER TWELVE

The rain had started sometime during the night. Not the dramatic kind that came with thunder and the shudder of rooftops, but the persistent, quiet kind. The kind that settled in, soaked through, and made everything feel slower, dimmer. still. Lena stirred under the covers, the muted light leaking around the edges of the bedroom curtains casting everything in soft greys and blues. Her limbs felt thick, like she'd been sleeping too long or not quite right. The air in the room was cool. damp. She could hear the steady tick-tick-tick of droplets against the windowpane. Sunday. She rolled onto her side and stared at the wall for a while. There was no urgency to get up. No pressing sense of wrongness. Just a foggy, lethargic quiet hanging in her chest. Downstairs, she could hear Dan moving. The soft scrape of a chair, a cupboard closing. A distant sizzle. Lena sat up slowly and rubbed her face, then wrapped herself in the cardigan at the foot of the bed. Her legs ached faintly as she stood, like she'd gone for a run in her sleep. She padded barefoot down the hallway and descended the stairs, hand sliding along the rail. The smell hit her halfway down. Eggs, sausages, toast. Something rich and buttery. Ordinarily, it would've been comforting. Today, it made her stomach

lurch. Dan looked up from the hob as she entered, spatula in hand, hair sticking up at the back.
He grinned. “Morning, sleeping beauty. You want coffee?”
She hovered in the doorway, swallowing hard. “I don’t think I can eat.”
His expression flickered. “You alright?”
She gave a small shake of her head. “No. I don’t know. I just feel... off. Dizzy. Nauseous.”
He immediately turned down the heat on the stove. “You want to lie down?”
“I just need a minute.” She replied.
Dan crossed the kitchen and gently touched her elbow, steering her toward one of the stools. She sat down slowly.
“You think it’s something you ate?” He questioned.
“Maybe, or the weather. I don’t know. It just came on suddenly.” She replied.

Dan filled the kettle and flicked it on.

“We should get you checked out. Register with the local surgery tomorrow.”

“I will,” she said. “I’ll do it first thing.”

He raised an eyebrow. “We still haven’t registered?”

She managed a faint smile. “No. But I’ll sort it. I’ll put you down too.”

He nodded. “Thanks.”

The kettle clicked behind him. Outside, the rain continued to fall in soft, relentless sheets, streaking the windows and blurring the garden into nothing but shapes and greys. Dan leaned against the counter, watching her.

“You sure you don’t want anything? Even toast?”

She shook her head again. “I think I just need to rest.”

Dan didn’t argue. He simply brought her a glass of water and guided her gently to the sofa.

The living room was dim and cool, the only light coming from the grey smudge of sky outside. Lena pulled the throw from the back of the couch around her shoulders and lay down, tucking her knees close. Dan placed the water on the coffee table, turned on the small lamp by the sideboard, and stood for a moment like he wasn't quite sure what to do next.

"Do you want anything else?" he asked.

She closed her eyes. "Just stay close."

He did. He moved through the house with deliberate quiet, keeping to the kitchen and hallway, checking in every half hour. The TV stayed off. So did the radio. The only sound was the distant hush of rain against glass and the occasional creak of old floorboards adjusting to the change in pressure. Sometime around midday, he made a pot of peppermint tea and brought it in without asking. Lena sat up slowly and accepted it with both hands, grateful for the warmth even though her stomach still turned uneasily. Dan sat beside her, one arm draped along the back of the sofa, close but not crowding. He didn't press her to talk, didn't ask more questions. Just stayed. A quiet presence. Something fixed and familiar in a house that didn't always feel like it belonged to them. She dozed off eventually, lulled by the tea, the steady patter of the rain, and the weight of exhaustion she couldn't quite name. Dan sat with her until she shifted and murmured in her sleep, then gently eased himself away to make soup from whatever was left in the fridge. The afternoon passed in the way Sundays sometimes do, slow and soft and a little formless. Time felt strange, Not lost, exactly, just muted. When Lena woke again, the light had shifted. It was still raining. Dan brought her soup in a chipped bowl, handed her a hot water bottle wrapped in a clean tea towel, and smiled like he didn't mind any of it.

"Thanks," she said, voice rough.

"You're allowed to have an off day," he replied. "Especially with my cooking."

She gave a weak laugh and leaned her head on his shoulder as he settled beside her again. They spent the evening curled up with a film they didn't finish. Dan stroked her hair absent-mindedly. Lena stared at the television long after the screen had gone dark, her eyes unfocused. By the time they climbed into bed, the rain had slowed to a whisper. The wind had dropped completely. The house was still. Not silent in a menacing way, just quiet. As though it, too, was resting. Dan kissed her temple and tucked the duvet around her shoulders. He watched her for a few minutes, then reached into the drawer where the ring was still hidden. He didn't open it. Just touched it. Lena's breath had already slowed, her face turned toward the wall. Dan lay back and closed his eyes. For the first time in a while, nothing felt wrong and that, somehow, was the strangest feeling of all.

That night, the house held its silence like a breath not yet released. Dan flicked off the lamp and eased in beside her, the duvet rustling softly between them. Lena turned toward him, tucking her face into the crook of his neck. His skin was warm. Familiar.

"Think it's just a bug?" she murmured.

"Maybe," he said, voice low. "Or your body just telling you to slow down."

She hummed faintly. "I didn't think I was pushing."

"You've been adjusting. We both have."

She didn't reply, but her fingers curled gently against his chest. He pulled her in closer. Outside, the rain drummed steadily on the roof. Inside, sleep came in waves, shallow at first, then deeper. By the time the house sank into the earliest hours of morning, only the faint shifting of wood and distant rustle of the garden gave any sign of movement.

The following morning, Lena woke to pale grey light. The rain had eased overnight, but everything outside was still slick and dripping. The garden glistened with leftover water, and a low mist clung to the lower hedges like an afterthought. Dan was already up, shower running. She lay still for a moment, gauging her stomach. It felt better, not fine. Not quite normal but manageable. Her skin was clammy, her throat dry, but the churning had softened into something duller. Less urgent. By the time she made it downstairs, Dan was in the kitchen dressed in his work-from-home uniform, button-down shirt on top, joggers on the bottom, mug in hand.

"You look slightly more alive," he said.

"Don't get used to it." There was a bluntness in her tone.

"Still off?"

"Less than yesterday. I'm going to call the local GP. Get us registered."

He nodded and kissed her forehead on his way past. "Good idea. Let me know what they say?" She sat at the kitchen table, laptop open, the kettle steaming beside her. The process was slow, forms, confirmations, uploads. By the time she clicked *'submit'*, her head was starting to throb. She called the surgery and, after being on hold for six minutes and forty-two seconds, a bored-sounding receptionist finally answered.

"We have a registration pending, Miss Hartley," the woman said.

"If it's urgent, we recommend calling 111. Otherwise, we can offer a routine appointment tomorrow afternoon."

"Right," Lena murmured. "No problem. Tomorrow works."

She hung up and stared at the table for a moment. The nausea had crept back in. Not sharp, just persistent. Like the sense of someone watching you from across a crowded room. She went to the sink, filled a glass, and drank it slowly. Dan reappeared from the hallway, phone to his ear, mouth moving silently as he pointed toward his laptop with an apologetic wince. She waved him off, already halfway to the sofa with a blanket slung over one shoulder.

By mid-morning, the first wave hit again, brief and vicious. She darted to the downstairs loo, gripping the sink edge after. Sweat prickled at her hairline. The rest of the morning moved in disjointed fragments: lie down, sit up, sip tea, feel worse. Dan checked in every hour between meetings, each time looking a little more concerned. He offered toast, she declined. He asked again, quietly, if she wanted him to call someone. She said no.

"It's easing," she lied.

By lunchtime, the rain had started again. Dan stood in the kitchen with his headset off, staring out at the garden.

"Maybe it's the house," he said.

"All this weird weather. We're not used to it."

Lena looked up at him from the sofa. "You think the rain gave me a stomach bug?"

"I think…" He trailed off, rubbing the back of his neck. "I think we've had a lot of strange days, and maybe now it's all just catching up."

She nodded faintly. "Yeah. Maybe."

But inside, she wasn't convinced. Not that it was the house. Not that it wasn't. Just not sure anymore. The rest of Monday passed in slow, manageable hours. Lena drifted in and out of sleep, curled on the sofa beneath a blanket, the rain still whispering at the windows. Dan kept the day running in quiet loops around her, his headset on and off, typing in bursts, appearing with tea or crackers or a new water glass before disappearing again. By late afternoon, the nausea had dulled just enough for Lena to sit upright without bracing for the next wave. Her muscles ached faintly, but the fog in her head had lifted a little.

Dan leaned over the back of the sofa, one hand brushing her hair. "Dinner?"

"I think I could try something," she murmured.

"Something beige?"

She smiled. "Beige sounds perfect."

He made risotto, plain, buttery, soft. It was warm and comforting and didn't turn her stomach for once. She managed a small bowlful, each spoonful slow and deliberate, as if her body was relearning how to accept food. Dan watched her the whole time with cautious optimism, like she might vanish if he blinked too long. Afterwards, they cleaned up together, quietly. No music, no distractions, just the clink of dishes and the hum of the dishwasher. Then a short, uneventful hour on the sofa again, half-watching a rerun of something neither of them remembered choosing. By 9:30, the house had taken on that soft hush again. Rain, the occasional groan of floorboards. The ticking of the hallway clock. Dan helped her upstairs without fuss. She was steadier now, but still pale around the eyes.

"Big day tomorrow," he said, pulling back the duvet for her. "Doctor Wren sounds proper, doesn't he? Like he lives in a tweed suit."

"If he turns up with a monocle, I'm walking out."

Dan kissed her forehead. "Deal."

She was asleep within minutes. Dan stayed awake a little longer, staring at the ceiling. Listening. The house had been kind today or quiet, at least but that didn't always mean peace.

The following morning, Lena's stomach rolled before she was even fully awake. She pressed her hand against her side, breathing slow through her nose. It passed after a minute. Then returned, not as sharp as yesterday, but just enough to anchor her down again. Dan had already left the bedroom, she could hear the kettle and the low clack of keys from the living room. She managed a shower, got dressed slowly, and sipped water in place of breakfast. The nausea faded again around mid-morning, but hovered like a shadow in her ribs. By the time her appointment rolled around at 2:00, she was steady on her feet but drained. The clinic was tucked in behind a stone terrace on the edge of town, ivy curling up its front. Inside, the waiting room was clean and bright, with posters taped to the walls and a faint antiseptic scent lingering beneath the scent of someone's too-sweet hand lotion.

"Lena Hartley? Room Three." the receptionist called.

She stood, smoothed her coat, and followed the hallway down to Room Three. Dr. Jasper Wren smiled as Lena entered Room Three, standing slowly to greet her.

"Miss Hartley," he said warmly, offering a hand.

"You found us easily enough, I hope?" His voice was soft, honeyed, with the kind of charm that belonged to a bygone era.

He wore tweed, of course, the collar just slightly scuffed with age, and the room smelled faintly of worn leather and tobacco that clung gently to his sleeves. A man who hadn't quite let go of the past, and didn't intend to.

"It's Lena," she said, shaking his hand. "And yes, no trouble."

He gestured to the seat across from his desk, already jotting something in her file.

"So," he began, flipping a page. "Nausea, appetite loss, fatigue… all began roughly forty-eight hours ago?"

She nodded. "It's been… on and off. Worse in the morning. It eases, then comes back. No fever, no stomach bug symptoms."

Dr. Wren gave a small hum of thought. "Stressful week?"

Lena hesitated. "We've just moved. It's been, a change."

"Ah, yes." His eyes flicked up, bright behind wire-framed lenses.

"The Harrow place, isn't it?" She nodded. He didn't press.

"Well," he said, pen tapping against the file. "I'll ask a few routine questions, and then we'll run a quick test today just to rule some things out. Any chance you could be pregnant?"

Lena blinked. Her mouth opened, then closed.

"I… my cycle's a little irregular. Sometimes. But I wasn't… "

"No trouble," he said gently. "It's something we always check, particularly with nausea this early in the day."

She nodded slowly. "Alright."

He handed her a small test kit with a discreet gesture and directed her to the restroom just down the corridor. Lena moved on autopilot, hands colder than they had been moments before. When she returned, Dr. Wren was by the window, hands folded behind his back, gazing out at the mist-shrouded village rooftops. He turned as she entered, offered that same warm smile, but it didn't reach as far as before.

"I'd rather not dance around it," he said kindly, slipping the results onto the desk.

"It's positive." Lena sat down, carefully, like the floor had shifted beneath her.

"Oh," she said.

"It's early," he added. "And no cause for alarm with your symptoms, they're consistent with the first trimester. Nausea, fatigue. The appetite will come and go."

She nodded, slowly. The room felt too warm. Too quiet.

"I'll get you booked in with our midwife," he continued, already writing.

"And you'll want to start taking folic acid if you haven't already."

"I haven't," Lena said faintly.

Dr. Wren paused then, pen hovering. "You weren't expecting this?"

She looked up. "No. Not at all."

He nodded, gently. "It has a way of catching people off guard."

Lena gave the smallest laugh, breathless and frayed at the edges. "Yeah. I guess it does."

As he guided her back toward reception, his tone returned to polite normalcy, next steps, leaflets, a reminder to get plenty of rest. But before she reached the door, he stopped.

"There's no shame in being surprised," he said softly. "Sometimes it's just the housewarming gift life sends in unmarked boxes."

Lena gave a tight smile. Outside, the village was still cloaked in mist.

The drive back felt longer than it should have. Mist clung to the trees, thicker than it had been when she'd left. The roads shimmered faintly with leftover rain, and the house loomed ahead like it always did, stoic, unmoved, indifferent to what came through its door. Lena pulled up and sat in the car for a moment with the engine off, keys resting loosely in her hand. The silence inside the vehicle felt artificial, like a seal keeping the truth from fully reaching her. She stepped into the house and locked the door behind her with quiet fingers. No one greeted her, just the stillness, and the faint thrum of a laptop fan coming from the office down the hall. Dan was in a video meeting. She could hear his voice, clipped and polite, through the wall. Lena moved to the living room, dropped her bag onto the armchair, and folded herself onto the sofa. She tugged the throw around her shoulders and switched on the TV without looking at the screen. The light flickered over her face, dancing with the static blur of daytime nonsense, a quiz show, maybe. Something bright and meaningless. She tucked her knees up. Let the sound wash over her. Let it anchor her. Her hand drifted to her stomach, no bump, no change. Just the idea of it, *Pregnant*. The word echoed without landing. She should've felt something, joy, shock, tears. But what she felt instead was pressure. A quiet, blooming pressure in her chest. Why was she scared? They had a house. A beautiful house. They were safe, weren't they? Dan adored her. He made her tea and risotto and joked about guard dogs. He was everything she could've asked for and yet Lena swallowed hard, eyes fixed on nothing. The timing, the silence, the way the house seemed to pull her further inward, like a pocket folding in on itself. She wasn't unhappy. She knew that but she wasn't happy either. She was floating. Dan's voice rose slightly from the office, laughter, maybe. He was still working, still normal. Still on the outside of what she'd just found out he wrapped the blanket tighter, pulled her feet beneath her, and turned the volume up two clicks. The quiz show host shouted a question. Lena didn't hear it. She closed her eyes and let the room hum around her.

Later that night, The house was darker than usual. Not just in lighting. Dan had only turned on the bedside lamp before bed, but in feeling. Like the walls were waiting. Lena stood in the doorway of the bedroom, watching him sleep. He was curled on his side, one arm beneath the pillow, his chest rising and falling in steady rhythm. His face, softened by sleep, looked younger, unbothered. Unaware. The faint glow from the hallway pooled across the duvet in long, honeyed streaks. She didn't move. Her hand rested against the frame. She had brushed her teeth. She had washed her face. Gone through the motions. And yet she hadn't stepped fully into the room. Not yet. The words pressed against the back of her throat.

She could tell him now. Wake him gently. Say it softly. Watch his face shift with wonder or confusion or fear or joy. They could lie here and talk about it in whispers until the morning rose behind the curtains but something held her back. She didn't know if it was doubt, or timing, or fear of changing something by naming it aloud. Once it was spoken, it would be real. A part of the world. A part of *them*. She stepped inside quietly and moved to her side of the bed. Slid beneath the covers without disturbing him. The sheets were cool against her legs. The silence deeper here. Dan shifted slightly in his sleep and let out a breath. Lena turned onto her side, propping her head on one hand, watching him in the low light. She studied the slope of his shoulder, the dark edge of his jaw, the familiar rhythm of his breath. She smiled, faintly. Soft, tired, terrified.

"I'm pregnant," she whispered to the dark.

The room didn't answer. Only the quiet reply of rain beginning again at the windows.

CHAPTER THIRTEEN

Over the next few days, Lena's morning sickness had eased somewhat. The house remained a place of calm, no creaks or things moving. Except, the clock in the kitchen that remained with no batteries had changed from **3:19** to **3:21** and then **3:23** over the next few days. The power sourced remained unknown. Clara had attended to complete the housework and she was surprisingly efficient when left to her own devices.

The morning sky was a washed-out blue, streaked with pale clouds and the promise of a weekend that might actually feel like spring. Birds flitted between the hedgerows, and sunlight spilled across the kitchen tiles in a way that almost made the house look warm. Lena stood at the sink, rinsing out two mugs. She moved quietly, deliberately. Every cupboard was already in order. Towels had been folded and laid out in the guest rooms the night before. The shopping had arrived by 9 a.m. sharp. She was out of things to do, and it was still early. Dan breezed in behind her, freshly showered, hair still damp, sleeves rolled up. He kissed the back of her neck in passing and went straight for the coffee machine.

"You've been up ages," he said. "Finishing touches again?"

"I like to be ready."

He glanced around at the spotless kitchen, the vase of fresh tulips on the counter, the stack of clean plates. "You're terrifying when you're efficient."

She smiled faintly. "You'll appreciate it when your mum walks in and doesn't find a smudge on anything."

Dan groaned. "Don't jinx it."

He poured his coffee, leaned against the counter, and took a slow sip.

"They'll love it here," he said after a pause. "The house, the space. You. All of it."

Lena nodded, her hands drying the mugs automatically. "Yeah."

He watched her for a moment longer than usual. "You okay?"

She looked up, then back down at the towel. "Just tired."

Dan set his mug down and moved to her side, slipping his arm around her waist. "You've been brilliant this week. Honestly. I know having everyone here at once is a lot."

"It's fine," she said.

"It'll be good. You'll love it." He chuckled.

"Speak for yourself. My mum's bringing half London and two types of chutney."

Lena smiled, but it didn't reach her eyes. She pulled away gently to fold the towel. Dan didn't press. He grabbed his coffee again and wandered toward the living room. Upstairs, the spare beds were made. All the dust sheets removed. Cases of sparkling water were lined up neatly in the pantry. Everything was in its place, except the truth.

Dan had just drawn her into a soft embrace near the patio doors. The sun was climbing higher now, spilling through the glass, catching in Lena's hair as he tucked a loose strand behind her ear. His fingers lingered a little longer than they needed to.

"You sure we have to let them in?" he murmured. "We could lock the doors and pretend it's haunted."

Lena gave a soft laugh. "Don't tempt me."

Dan leaned in and kissed her, slow, steady. Familiar and for a brief moment, the house felt like theirs again. Not a prize, not a performance space. Just home. The sound of gravel crunching outside broke the moment. Dan groaned theatrically.

"Showtime," Lena exhaled. "Here we go."

Through the front windows, a silver Audi pulled up beside the main house, followed by a smaller blue car that looked like it hadn't had a proper wash in six months. Her parents. Right on time. Dan opened the front door while Lena smoothed her jumper and stepped out, the early spring air cooler than it looked. The gravel popped underfoot. Her mum was already climbing out, sunglasses perched on her head despite the cloud cover, a floral scarf fluttering behind her like a flag of personal flair.

"There she is!" her mother called.

"Oh, look at this place, Lena, it's like something out of *Country Living*! Have you *seen* this driveway?"

"Oh didn't I tell you? We're booked for a shoot with them next week" Lena replied sarcastically.

Her dad climbed out more slowly, closing the car door with unnecessary care. He gave a polite nod in their direction, then turned to retrieve a modest suitcase from the boot, saying nothing.

Lena braced herself. "Mum. Dad. Hi."

Her mother swept her into a hug before she could finish blinking, all perfume and enthusiasm.

"Oh darling, look at you! You look so well. Have you put on weight or is it the haircut?"

"It's the house, I've not had a haircut, nor have I put on weight mum." Lena said, half smiling.

Dan shook hands with her dad, who gave him a small nod of approval, his version of warmth. Then came a brisk hug for Lena, firm and brief.

"We've put you both in the guest house," she said, gesturing to the smaller building tucked neatly across the lawn.

"Plenty of space, and you'll have some privacy."

Her mother raised an eyebrow. "The guest house? Very Downton of you."

"I thought it might be… easiest," Lena replied, careful not to glance at her father.

"Might be nice to have a bit of space," he muttered, already heading toward the boot for a second bag. Her mother turned back with a warm, sharp smile.

"Well, I think it's perfect and look at those windows! You've really landed on your feet with this one, Daniel."

Dan chuckled. "All her doing."

They all turned as the next car rolled up the drive, a deep red SUV with loud music pulsing faintly through the windows. It parked confidently beside the Audi. The doors opened in a flurry of movement. Dan's mum emerged first, short, stout, immaculately dressed in a navy pea coat and boots with a muddy hem.

She beamed, "Right, I'm not hugging anyone until I've had a cuppa!"

From the passenger seat came Dan's younger brother, Theo, hair bleached at the tips, a small ring in one nostril, and beside him, his boyfriend Rory, tall and soft-eyed, clutching a bouquet awkwardly like he wasn't sure who it was for and last, climbing out of the backseat with a scarf around her shoulders and a tote bag packed to the brim, *Brenda*. The neighbour who helped raise Dan after his dad left. A second mother in all but name.

"Oh," Lena whispered. "They brought *everyone*."

Dan turned to her with a boyish grin. "Told you."

She didn't say it aloud, but she felt it deep in her chest: there were too many moving parts now. Too many voices. Too many expectations and still, the biggest thing hadn't been said.

Lena led her mother across the lawn toward the guest house, her father trailing behind at a polite distance, wheeling his own case. The air was crisp, still damp from the week's rain. A breeze tugged gently at the scarf around her mother's neck as she peered up at the cottage with an approving little hum.

"Well, this is rather lovely, isn't it? I thought 'guest house' meant a converted garage. This is practically its own property."

"It was renovated before the handover," Lena replied, unlocking the door.

"Everything's new inside."

She stepped aside to let them through. The space was clean and modern, soft grey furnishings, pale oak floors, tall windows that looked out over the rear hedges. Neutral and non-threatening. Like a show home, staged for tranquillity. Her mother dropped her handbag on the neatly made bed without waiting for an invitation.

"Honestly, this is *exactly* what you needed, darling. I always said London made you look pale. This country air suits you."

Lena offered a faint smile, folding her arms. "Glad you approve."

Her father gave the room a perfunctory glance, then muttered something about unpacking and headed down the short hallway toward the second bedroom without another word. Her mother sighed, too loudly.

"He's never impressed by anything. You could win a castle and he'd complain about the moat." Lena pretended not to hear it.

"I'll give you some time to settle," she said, stepping back toward the door. "We'll start lunch soon."

"You're cooking?" her mother asked, arching an eyebrow.

"We're keeping it simple."

"Well, let's just hope *he* doesn't burn anything." Trish said bluntly.

Lena smiled, sharper this time. "It's handled."

She stepped out, letting the door click softly shut behind her. Back at the main house, Dan was elbow-deep in bags and laughter. His mum had already taken control of the kitchen, rearranging things without asking, and Theo was halfway through explaining the speaker system to Brenda like it was state-of-the-art tech.

"Honestly, Daniel," his mum called over her shoulder,

"Do you not own any Yorkshire Tea?" "We have Earl Grey," Dan offered weakly. Brenda patted his arm. "That's not tea, love. That's leaf-flavoured perfume." Rory was trying to figure out which room was theirs, and Theo was already opening drawers just to see what was inside them. Lena returned to find chaos unfolding neatly across every surface. Dan met her eyes with an almost imperceptible shrug: *What did I say?* She smiled, despite herself. "Everyone good?" he asked, crossing to her. "Settled," she said. "More or less." They stood close for a moment, two hosts, holding the fort. Then Lena cleared her throat. "Alright. Let's get this over with."

The living room had been tidied for the occasion, blankets folded, candles lit, the *best* mugs pulled from the cupboard. A plate of biscuits sat untouched in the centre of the coffee table. Lena had even lit the wax burner. She couldn't smell it anymore, but she hoped it was something neutral. Vanilla or fig. The families merged slowly, like oil and water in a single jug. Her mother took the best armchair. Dan's mum perched on the ottoman like she owned it. Brenda brought over her knitting from the car. Theo and Rory stayed just out of reach, examining the bookshelves with half-interest, whispering.

Introductions were made. Polite nods exchanged. Dan's mum was all smiles.

"So lovely to *finally* meet you both. Lena's told us… well, very little, actually, but I've filled in the gaps."

Lena's mother smiled thinly. "Likewise. We don't see her often enough these days."

Brenda extended a hand across the coffee table. "I'm no relation. Just a hanger-on. Dan's unofficial aunt."

Her mother shook it with a touch of hesitation. "How nice."

Dan passed around mugs. "Sugar, anyone?"

His brother made a loud snort behind him. "Yes, please. This room needs it." The silence that followed wasn't quite uncomfortable but it was aware of itself. Lena watched it all from the edge of the room, arms folded, legs crossed, smiling when expected.

The room buzzed with overlapping pleasantries and tiny power struggles. Everyone performing, everyone watching, everyone deciding what kind of weekend this would be and underneath it all, resting against her ribs like a stone in her coat pocket, sat the truth. She hadn't told him, not yet. Dan slipped out through the French doors with a crate of barbecue tools tucked under one arm and a bag of charcoal in the other. The spring sun had finally made good on its promise, warming the stone patio and casting sharp shadows across the grass. Behind him, the low murmur of conversation continued, rising and falling like polite tide. His mother followed not far behind, arms full of towels and good intentions.

"Thought I'd help get the loungers sorted," she said.

"If I wait for Theo, I'll be waiting till Christmas."

"Much appreciated," Dan grinned.

Together, they unfurled striped towels and draped them over the loungers near the pool, the corners flapping gently in the breeze. His mother tucked one with practiced precision, smoothing the edges like it mattered. Dan focused on the grill, stacking charcoal into a neat mound before flicking the ignition. The flames caught quickly. Satisfying. Controllable.

"Got your hands full this weekend," she said gently, glancing toward the house.

Dan chuckled. "Bit of a circus."

"Good circus. Though I imagine you're still figuring it all out."

He didn't answer, just flipped open a packet of skewers and laid them out on a tray. Chicken, peppers, halloumi, stacked like offerings to the gods of bank holiday weather.

"You seem happy," she added.

"I am," he said, and meant it.

Still, his eyes drifted toward the kitchen window. Lena hadn't come outside yet. Lena remained by the living room doorway as the families settled into their new seating arrangements, now comfortably softened by caffeine and chatter. Her mother and Brenda exchanged stories about markets and herb gardens. Her father made conversation with Rory about estate architecture, and Theo had taken it upon himself to change the living room playlist from classical to something vaguely retro-funky. It was going surprisingly well. Lena couldn't relax into it, but she could observe it. That was enough.

"I'll get the wine," her mother said suddenly, rising with flair. "Let's loosen everyone up a little more, shall we?"

She disappeared into the kitchen with the air of someone seeking a crown. Lena drifted toward the open doors, standing just beyond the threshold, watching Dan laugh with his mum as he carefully turned the skewers. The sun caught in his hair. He looked easy out there, in control. She wrapped her arms around herself and didn't move. Her mother reappeared, triumphant, carrying a tray with six glasses balanced and a bottle of white under her arm. It clinked gently as she moved, heels ticking softly on the stone as she crossed the patio.

"Glasses for the grown-ups," she sang lightly. "God knows we've earned it."

She passed them out one by one, Brenda, Dan's mum, Theo and Rory, her husband. Smiles all around. A toast was half-mumbled, half-raised.

Finally, she reached Lena. “Here you go, darling, crisp, not too sweet.”

Lena looked at it, hand frozen halfway to take it. Then she shook her head.

“I’ll pass, thanks.”

Her mother blinked. “It’s one glass.”

“I know. I just don’t want any.”

Something in her tone must’ve landed, because the moment stretched a little longer than it should have. Dan looked over from the grill. His smile didn’t drop, but it wavered. Her mother paused, wineglass still hovering, then gave a breezy laugh and turned back to refill her own.

“Suit yourself,” she said, dismissive. “More for me.”

Lena sat down beside Brenda and tucked her hands beneath her thighs, gripping the fabric of her jeans. The sun was warm. The food smelled good. People were laughing but all she could feel was the sudden thump of her own pulse behind her eyes.

The late afternoon had slipped into something golden and lazy. Plates had been passed around, the first skewers devoured and replaced with burgers and grilled veg. Wine flowed freely, except into Lena’s glass, which sat untouched in front of her. The warm hum of overlapping chatter filled the garden. Dan’s mum leaned back in her chair with a theatrical sigh and a second glass in hand.

“Well, if Lena won’t drink her wine, I suppose I’ll take one for the team,” she said, grinning. “Unless there’s something we should *know*, hmm?”

The group chuckled. Brenda smirked into her glass, even Theo let out a low, playful “Ooh.”

Lena forced a smile. “I’m just not in the mood.”

Her mother, from the far end of the table, piped up far too loudly.

“I *did* say she looked like she’d put on weight this morning.”

Silence, not dramatic, but sharp, sudden. Forks hovered halfway to mouths. Dan’s eyes moved to Lena. Something shifted in his expression, concern, confusion, then something else. A question, unspoken but heavy in the air. Lena’s stomach tightened. Her mother looked pleased with herself, sipping her wine like it was a punchline.

Dan leaned in slightly, brow furrowed. “Lena?”

She looked around the table. Every face turned toward her now, each reaction held just behind the eyes, mild amusement, thinly veiled discomfort, Brenda's hand slowly stilling over her napkin. She hadn't planned to do this here. Not like this but there was nowhere else for it to go. She drew in a breath.

"I'm pregnant." The words landed like a soft thud, not explosive but final.

Dan blinked. "Wait, what?"

Lena turned toward him, eyes wide and wet.

"I found out two days ago. I was going to tell you. I just, there was never a moment."

His mum gasped, hand over her chest. "Oh my *god*. Are you serious?"

Her mother's smile dropped, wine glass lowering. "Oh."

The table stilled. Dan stared at her, something unreadable moving behind his eyes. "You're… sure?"

Lena nodded slowly. "Doctor confirmed it the other day."

A beat passed. Then another. Dan let out a breath and half-laughed, more from shock than anything else.

"Jesus, okay. Wow. I mean… that's big."

"It is," she said quietly.

He ran a hand through his hair, eyes flicking down to the table before returning to hers. "I wish you'd told me sooner."

"I didn't know how."

He didn't answer right away. Just nodded, slowly. Processing. Then, quietly, he reached under the table and took her hand. Everyone else resumed breathing again. Rory clinked a fork against his glass in mild panic.

"So… dessert, anyone?"

Brenda was already standing. "I'll put the kettle on."

Just like that, the moment passed but the air around them had changed. Lena looked down at their hands, his fingers wrapped around hers, firm and steady. But inside, something still trembled. Dan stood, dusting the crumbs from his hands as the table slowly returned to life after Lena's announcement. Conversation was awkward in places, overcompensating in others, but the tension had started to melt back into the grass beneath them.

"I'll grab dessert," he said, lifting the empty tray.
"Everyone stay put."

As he stepped inside, the noise of the garden faded behind him, the scrape of chairs, glasses being refilled, his mum asking Brenda if she thought Lena's mother would notice if they swapped the wine for Ribena. He didn't go straight to the kitchen. Instead, he veered left, into his study. The air was cooler here. Still. The bookshelves lining the far wall stood like quiet witnesses, their spines shadowed in the late afternoon light. He knelt down near the bottom shelf, where the hollowed-out hardback sat tucked between a pair of forgotten thrillers. The book looked untouched. The cutout section crisp. Clean but when he opened it, the ring wasn't inside. Dan stared at the empty hollow, his chest tightening. He stood quickly, eyes scanning the room like someone had broken in, then dropped to his knees again to check beneath the chair, behind the radiator, the edge of the skirting board, nothing. His breath caught. His hands moved faster now, rifling through cushions and drawers, flicking books aside with more force than necessary. Then he stopped. There, on the opposite bookshelf. Between *The Art of War* and *How to Cook Everything*. The ring box. Sat neatly. Upright. As if it had been *placed* there. Dan stared at it. He didn't remember doing that, didn't remember moving it. Not even in passing. His hand hovered, hesitant for the briefest second, before he picked it up and checked inside. Inside the ring remained. He slid it into his pocket. *You're tired,* he told himself. *Probably moved it after too much wine and forgot.* He went to the fridge, retrieved the pavlova and berries, and plated everything carefully, almost ritualistically. The ring weighed heavy in his pocket. He balanced the tray, took a slow breath, and stepped back outside. The garden had settled into golden-hour ease. Shadows were long now, stretching across the patio. Glasses clinked gently, laughter was quieter, but genuine. Dan placed the dessert down in the centre of the table, passing slices around, offering seconds before most had finished their first. Lena caught his eye. There was something behind her gaze, hesitancy, maybe, or just that lingering ripple from earlier.

He reached out, brushed her wrist gently. "You okay?" She nodded.

He stood. "Can I have everyone's attention for a second?"

Chairs creaked. Heads turned, Lena looked up at him, brows knitting faintly.

Dan extended his hand. "Lena, come here a moment?"

She rose, barefoot on the warm stone, the breeze lifting her hem. Her hair was half-loosened now, her cheeks softly flushed from the sun and the spotlight. She moved to his side, confused but smiling. He took both her hands in his, turning toward the table.

"I know this weekend was meant to be about bringing our families together. To show you all the house, to thank you for helping us get here, through jobs and rent and long phone calls about floor tiles."

A few quiet chuckles followed.

"But the truth is, I've been planning something else. Something I hoped might make this place feel a little less like a prize, and more like a beginning."

He turned to Lena, eyes full. "I love you. You're brave and stubborn and terrifyingly organised and I still don't know how I landed you."

She gave a small, breathless laugh, eyes beginning to gloss.

"I knew, pretty much from the moment you dragged me out of that estate agent's office by the elbow, that I wanted to build something with you. A life, a home, something with roots." He paused, his voice softening.

"And I know… the timing's strange and maybe not perfect but life isn't clean like that." He reached into his pocket and then, slowly, he knelt.

The ring box opened with a soft snap. The stone caught the last of the sun, glinting like a secret.

"Lena Hartley," he said, "will you marry me?"

Lena stared at him. For a heartbeat, two, she didn't breathe. The world had gone still: the birdsong hushed, the breeze stilled, every chair around the table suspended in a moment of quiet disbelief. d and then, softly, her breath hitched.

She covered her mouth with one hand. "Yes," she whispered.

Then louder, surer: "Yes, Dan. Of course I will."

The applause was instant and mismatched, chaotic and heartfelt. Theo whooped. Brenda clapped politely with the grace of someone trying not to cry. Rory had already pulled his phone halfway out for a photo but wisely slipped it back in. Dan rose, and Lena met him halfway, arms wrapping tight around his neck as he pulled her into him. The kiss they shared wasn't showy. It was real. Slow. Anchored.

"Jesus," he murmured against her cheek.

"I was not expecting today to go like this." She laughed, wet-eyed and breathless.

"Neither was I." He slipped the ring onto her finger.

It fit perfectly, her mother was the first to break the moment.

"Well," she said, adjusting her sunglasses where they didn't need to be.

"It's about time."

Dan's mum beamed. "You do realise this means a wedding with two strong-willed mothers involved? You poor sods."

Lena just smiled and leaned her forehead against Dan's chest. For the first time in days, she let the weight of everything soften. Even if just for a while.

As the night drew to a close. The house had quieted. Wine bottles emptied. Shoes kicked off at odd angles near doors, suitcases left half-unpacked for tomorrow. The guest rooms glowed dimly behind closed doors. Out in the garden, a single citronella candle guttered near the loungers, forgotten. Upstairs, Lena lay in bed beside Dan, the sheets light and cool against her legs. They hadn't spoken much after the last guest had turned in. Just brushed their teeth, exchanged tired looks, climbed under the covers.

Now, in the hush of night, she lay on her side, facing the moonlit wall. Dan's arm wrapped around her from behind, warm and steady. His hand settled gently against her stomach. Protective, reverent.

His voice was low, laced with exhaustion and something else, something deeper. "You said yes."

She smiled into the pillow. "I did."

"Still mean it?"

"I do."

A pause. Then, softer: "I'm still getting my head around everything," he said. "The baby. The ring. Your mum saying you looked fat."

Lena laughed quietly, eyes still closed. "She's lucky I didn't throw a bread roll at her."

Dan kissed the back of her shoulder. "You handled it like a queen."

They lay in silence for a while, the rhythm of their breathing syncing. The only sound was the occasional creak of the old beams, like the house was settling too. Lena opened her eyes, just enough to glance down at her hand. The ring caught a glimmer of moonlight from the window. It looked perfect there. Unreal, like it belonged to another version of herself, one that wasn't still trying to piece together how she felt. Dan's hand stayed on her stomach. She covered it with hers, fingers lacing. The baby, the ring, the house. It was all happening and in that moment, she let it.

CHAPTER FOURTEEN

It was sometime after three when Lena woke to the sound of footsteps. Not heavy, just light enough to question. Soft, rhythmic creaks crossing the upstairs landing. The kind a person might make if they were walking barefoot, careful not to wake a sleeping house. She blinked into the dark, heart quickening, unsure if she was awake or somewhere between. Dan's breath was steady beside her, arm draped over her hip, undisturbed. Another creak. Closer this time. Lena held her breath, eyes fixed on the outline of the door. Nothing followed. Just the usual silence, thick and rural. She told herself it could've been the pipes. The house shifting. An echo. Still, it took her a long time to fall back asleep. The morning light was pale and cold. Spring had retreated again, replaced by low clouds and a sting of wind through the windows that made the house feel older. Lena entered the kitchen to find her mum already up, robe tied tightly around her waist, warming her hands near the kettle.

"You alright?" Lena asked.

Her mum glanced over her shoulder, slightly startled.

"Did you hear it too?"

Lena frowned. "Hear what?"

"I got up in the night, about three, maybe later. Went to the bathroom and saw someone walking down the front steps. Out of the house." Lena stiffened. "Dan?"

Her mother shook her head. “Too small, moved differently. Didn’t look like him at all. I thought maybe one of the others… but then I checked the windows. Everyone’s cars were still there.”

Lena felt the room narrow. “Why didn’t you wake anyone?”

Her mum sipped her tea. “I thought it might’ve been a dream. You know how these old houses get.”

Lena didn’t answer. She just stared at the French doors, the garden beyond looked grey, uninviting. Still. At breakfast, the table was lively enough. Dan made eggs, Rory handled toast. Brenda brought down a jar of homemade chutney no one asked for but everyone appreciated. Between bites, she glanced over at Lena, eyes sharp despite her usual softness.

“Place like this remembers things,” she said, unprompted.

Lena looked up. “What do you mean?”

Brenda tilted her head. “Houses this old. They keep little echoes of what’s come before. Like footprints that don’t wash out.”

Theo chuckled. “Alright, Miss Marple.”

But Lena wasn’t laughing. After breakfast, the group went out for a walk, something to clear the heads and stretch the legs. Dan led the way through the woodlands, Rory chatting with Brenda, Lena trailing behind with her mother, who was still talking about wanting to visit the farm shop before they left. They returned around midday, mud on their boots and hands tingling from the cold.

It was Dan who noticed it first.

“Our bedroom window’s open,” he said.

Lena looked up. The second floor. Their window. A wide gap in the glass where there shouldn’t have been one.

“I swear I closed it,” she murmured. “Maybe the wind?”

But she was already shaking her head. Dan jogged up the stairs to check. When he returned, he looked pale.

“There were footprints on the carpet. Barefoot.,,”

Lena didn’t speak. She just reached for the doorframe to steady herself. Something in the house had shifted again. And this time, it wasn’t letting go so easily. Lena didn’t return upstairs. Not yet. The house felt wrong again, just off-centre. As though everything had been moved a fraction of an inch while no one was looking. She stayed by the doorframe, one hand resting lightly on the wood, her eyes drawn up toward the landing. Dan had gone quiet since coming back down. He'd explained what he saw, bare footprints on the carpet, too light to be his, and then hadn't said much else. He poured himself a coffee and sat in the dining room, scrolling through his phone like he wasn't really reading anything. The others milled around the kitchen, slowly gathering themselves. There was light packing, phone-charging, a misplaced charger found under a placemat. Brenda helped herself to the last of the chutney, spreading it onto a piece of toast as though nothing had happened. Lena's mother seemed in better spirits. Already dressed and applying mascara by the kitchen mirror.

"I still say it was just one of the neighbours, maybe drunk, wandered up the wrong drive," she offered, more to herself than anyone else.

Theo appeared at Lena's side, hoodie pulled over his curls, rubbing the sleep from his eyes.

"Yo," he said, biting into a slice of banana bread.

"Did you guys hear weird stuff last night?" Lena stiffened.

"What do you mean?"

"Like, Someone moving around. It sounded like upstairs, but I thought maybe it was just plumbing or… I don't know, that creepy delivery guy's ghost." He grinned, but Lena didn't return it.

"No," she said softly. "Not the plumbing."

He raised an eyebrow but wandered off again, half-eaten slice in hand. She glanced across the room toward Dan. He hadn't looked up once.

By early afternoon, the guests had gone. Cars reversed down the drive. Doors slammed. Goodbyes were exchanged with tired, automatic warmth. Then they were alone again. The house was still, but it didn't feel peaceful. It felt, muted. Like something had swallowed the sound and left only shape behind. Dan returned to the study under the guise of catching up on work. Lena didn't follow. She drifted instead into the living room, casting her gaze over the side tables, the bookshelves, the throws still rumpled from yesterday. She paused. One of the cushions on the sofa was reversed, pattern-side down, the corner folded in, as though someone had sat with it and tried to hide the imprint. She crossed to it, lifted it, and turned it over. A faint stain near the seam. Something smudged. Possibly old. Possibly nothing but she hadn't sat there and she knew Dan hadn't either. Her fingers hovered over it for a moment longer before setting it down. Upstairs again, she hadn't planned to come back here but her feet had moved before she'd made the choice. She didn't go into the bedroom. She turned right, into the dressing corridor. The air felt colder here, still, but with a sharpness at the edges, like a room that had been unsealed too recently. She passed the built-in drawers, the linen cupboard. Paused outside the small utility closet tucked behind the stairs. Then she noticed it. The wardrobe. It wasn't quite closed. Just an inch open, like it had forgotten to shut all the way. Lena reached out and touched the edge. The door swung softly under her fingertips. Inside was everything as she left it, clothes, boots, folded knits but something was off. She crouched. Near the base of the wardrobe, behind the shoes, a small vented panel had shifted. A tiny gap in the floorboards, just wide enough to suggest some sort of crawlspace. She stared at it, heartbeat ticking louder in her ears. Lena closed the wardrobe slowly. The click of the latch felt too loud in the silence. She stood there for a moment, listening. Nothing. Her heart still beat a little too fast, but she told herself it was overthinking. She was tired. Off balance. Last night's footsteps had sunk into her bones, and now everything looked like a threat. She ran a hand over her stomach. It grounded her. Then she turned, left the room, and descended the stairs. Dan was in the living room, curled into the corner of the sofa with his laptop perched on his knees. A half-drunk mug of tea sat beside him. The news was playing quietly in the background, low and unobtrusive. When he saw her enter, he set the laptop aside and patted the space beside him. She didn't speak. She just slid in, tucked herself beneath his arm, and let the stillness of the afternoon settle over them like a second blanket. They stayed like that for a while. The scent of the wood burner from earlier still clung to the room, mingling with the last hints of toast and smoke from the garden barbecue. Everything should have felt safe.

"I've been thinking," Dan said quietly, his lips near her temple. "About the baby."

She didn't move. "I always thought I'd be terrified," he said. "But I'm not. Not with you. It feels… weirdly right. Like the one thing we didn't plan is the one thing that actually makes sense."

Lena swallowed against the lump forming in her throat.

"I don't know if I'll be good at it," she murmured.

"You will," he said immediately, brushing her hair back. "You're already better than half the people I know. We'll figure it out." She smiled, though it didn't quite meet her eyes. "You sound confident." "I fake it well," he said, squeezing her hand. The warmth of him, the weight of his arm around her, the steadiness of his voice, it all helped. For a little while, it helped.

As the light began to dim, Lena moved into the office. She had planned to go over her client notes for Monday, emails, meetings, a light social media calendar to sketch out. Something normal. Something grounding. But when she opened the drawer to retrieve her notebook, she froze. The photo frame was gone. The one that had sat neatly on the desk since they moved in. A picture, her hair windblown, Dan squinting into the sun, both of them laughing like they had nothing to lose. In its place, resting at a slant against the back of the desk, was the notecard. The same one she'd tucked away a week ago. Blank at the time. Now it had writing on it. Black ink. Small, neat letters.

"You took mine. Now I take yours."

Her breath caught. The desk lamp buzzed faintly. The house hummed in its bones. She backed away from the drawer and left the office, heart thudding like it had grown too big for her chest. Dan was still on the sofa, laptop open again, fingers idle against the keyboard. She didn't speak. Then he blinked, leaned forward slightly.

"What the hell?"

Lena paused mid-step. "What?"

He stared at the screen. "There's a draft email in my outbox. But I didn't write it."

She crossed the room, stood behind him, watching over his shoulder. It was blank, save for one sentence.

'I can't wait to see you.'

Lena stepped back from the screen like it had burned her. Dan sat still, frowning at the message.

"I didn't write that," he said again, quieter this time.

"It's not just that," she murmured. "My photo's missing."

He looked up.

"In the office. The one in the frame. It's gone and someone left the notecard where it was, with a message."

She swallowed hard.

"It said: *'You took mine. Now I take yours.'*"

Dan rose to his feet. "Okay… okay, just breathe. Let's think about this."

"I *am* thinking, Dan. Someone's been in this house."

He moved to her, hands raised like he was calming a spooked animal. "Alright. Look, just hear me out. It could've been Theo. He was in and out of the study yesterday. Maybe he thought it'd be funny, you know? Leave a message. Move some stuff."

"This isn't a prank."

"I'm not saying it's funny, I'm saying it sounds like something he'd do. He *was* joking about ghosts this morning."

"He wouldn't write that. He wouldn't, say something like that."

Dan hesitated. He didn't argue.

"I'll call him," he said eventually. "Ask."

Lena turned her head away, arms folding tightly across her stomach. He reached for her, gently rubbing her back in circles.

"Hey. Look at me."

She did.

"No one's going to hurt us. I promise. We'll check everything. We'll get cameras if we have to."

She gave a small, half-laugh. "Now you sound like a parent already."

He smiled at her, lopsided and exhausted. "You're not wrong."

Lena nodded slowly, pressing her forehead into his shoulder. The panic didn't leave her completely, but it stopped rising. Just enough to let her breathe again.

An hour later, they were in the kitchen. Dan stood at the stove stirring something creamy, pasta with leftover veg, nothing fancy, just warm and filling. Lena sat at the table, hands wrapped around a glass of water. Her eyes kept drifting to the clock on the wall. The old one. Slightly tarnished brass with Roman numerals. It had never worked properly. The second hand ticked backwards sometimes, or not at all. Yet the time always *seemed* to change. Now it read ***3:25***. It had been stuck at ***3:17*** for weeks.

She frowned. "Dan?"

"Yeah?"

"That clock. It's changed again."

He glanced over. "Probably just settling or ghosts resetting it to factory mode."

She didn't laugh. He brought over two bowls and placed one in front of her, bending down to kiss the side of her head before sitting opposite. They ate in mostly silence. Dan tried light conversation, a story from a campaign briefing, a comment about how they needed to pick up more bin liners, but the energy was strained, stretched thin like skin over glass. Still, they finished the meal. Cleaned up. Let routine distract them from the tension. Later, they curled up in the cinema room, a soft throw across their legs, the lights dimmed low. An animated film played on the projector, bright colours, talking animals, comforting music. The kind of thing neither of them would've chosen before, but tonight it felt right. Light, safe. Lena tucked into Dan's side, her head on his chest. The flickering colours danced across the darkened room. For a little while, the house was quiet again but the clock in the kitchen kept ticking and somewhere behind the walls, someone remembered how to wait. Dan yawned, stretching his arms with a groan as Lena tucked the throw more tightly around herself.

"You falling asleep on me?" he murmured.

"No," she lied. They stayed that way for a while. Neither moved. Eventually, Dan stood and offered her his hand.

"Come on. Let's go up." Lena hesitated for only a second before slipping her fingers into his.

Upstairs, the hallway was darker than usual. Dan flicked the switch, but the first bulb in the ceiling strip blinked and stayed dead. The second hummed and offered only half-light.

"We should replace that tomorrow," he muttered.

They walked in silence to the bedroom. Inside, the covers were still rumpled from that morning. A book lay face-down on Lena's side of the bed where she'd left it, the spine cracked open at a midpoint she hadn't returned to. Dan peeled off his shirt and went into the en suite to brush his teeth, humming faintly to himself. Lena changed slowly. She peeled the day off her body, shirt, jeans, jewellery, each movement feeling a fraction too intentional. When she opened her bedside drawer to place her earrings inside, she noticed her jewellery dish had been moved. Not dramatically. Just rotated slightly. Like someone had been in a hurry, or trying not to be noticed. She stared at it for several long seconds. Then closed the drawer. Dan came out of the bathroom, towelling his face.

"Your turn."

She nodded and disappeared inside. The mirror above the sink was fogged with faint condensation that hadn't cleared properly all day. She wiped at it with a flannel and caught her reflection mid-swipe, tired eyes, hair clinging slightly to her temple. She looked like someone living in a stranger's house. When she returned to the bedroom, Dan was already in bed, one arm behind his head, eyes closed. The lamp on his side cast a warm pool of light across the duvet. Lena climbed in beside him, settling onto her side, facing away. The silence stretched.

"You okay?" he asked softly.

She nodded. But then, after a moment:

"Do you ever get the feeling we're not alone?"

Dan shifted. "Here? In the house?"

She nodded again, barely moving.

"I think," he said gently, "we're just adjusting. It's a big change. And weird things happen in old places."

Lena didn't reply. Dan reached across and switched off the lamp. Darkness filled the room like water. She listened to his breathing even out. Felt the heat of him behind her, felt her own hand rest lightly against her stomach. Somewhere beyond the walls, a house shifted in its sleep and somewhere inside it, something remembered.

CHAPTER FIFTEEN

Lena woke late. The light spilling through the curtains was soft, grey-edged. The kind of morning that blurred the line between sleep and waking. Dan was already up, his side of the bed empty, faintly warm. Downstairs, she could hear the hum of the kettle, cupboard doors, the distant rhythm of the tap. A faint clatter of spoon against ceramic. She didn't move right away. Her body felt heavy. Tired in a way that wasn't physical. Last night's comfort, the laughter during the movie, Dan's arm around her, the soft glow of ordinary things, had faded too fast. Like she'd imagined it. The dread was still there. It had simply been quiet, waiting. When she finally came downstairs, Dan was at the table, flicking through emails on his phone. A slice of toast sat untouched beside him, growing cold.

He looked up. "Hey, you alright?"

She nodded, pulling the sleeves of her jumper down over her hands.

"Did you sleep?"

"Better than I expected. You?"

She hesitated, "Not really."

He stood, came around to her side and pressed a kiss to the top of her head.

"Listen, I've got to pop into town for a bit. Couple errands, and I promised to check in on the campaign rollout in person. You want to come with me?" Lena shook her head. "No. I think I need to stay here or maybe head out for a bit on my own."

Dan studied her, concern flickering behind his eyes. "You sure?"

"Yeah," she said, managing a small smile.

"I think the house and I need a break."

He chuckled at that, but it was cautious. He kissed her once more, squeezed her hand, and left the room. She watched his car disappear down the drive. The gravel settled. The engine faded and then she was alone again. She didn't know what she was looking for, but she knew she wouldn't find it here. Lena pulled on her coat, grabbed her phone and keys, and stepped out into the sharp mid-morning chill. The wind had picked up. Clouds pressed low against the sky like damp cotton. The house stood tall and unmoving behind her, its windows dark as closed eyes. She took the back route into town, less travelled, more winding. The silence was gentler that way. No headlights, no watchers. She kept her hands in her pockets the entire time. The town hadn't changed. It never did. Same crooked rows of brick shops, same leaning lamp posts, same chipped signage and hand-written blackboards advertising homemade pies and loose-leaf tea but something in Lena had shifted. She moved through it like a visitor. A wrong note in a familiar chord. She passed the bakery, the newsagent. The café with the gingham curtains and the peeling chalkboard and that's when she saw him. Tom Calder. Standing at the corner near the war memorial, holding a takeaway coffee and talking to a man Lena didn't recognise. Her feet stopped before she had a choice in it. Tom turned, and their eyes met. For a beat, nothing moved. Then:

"Lena?"

She stepped forward, heart suddenly thudding.

"Tom? What the hell are you doing here?"

He looked momentarily thrown, but recovered with a half-smile.

"I'm on holiday."

"In this village?"

He laughed. "Well, not exactly. Rented a place just outside. I thought it'd be a nice change. Quiet."

She blinked. "That's quite the coincidence."

Tom glanced away, then back again. "Congratulations, by the way."
Lena frowned.

"For what?"

He hesitated. Too long. His smile faltered. "The baby."

The silence hit like cold water.

"I didn't tell anyone," she said, her voice flat.

Tom's eyes widened slightly. "Oh. I, I just assumed. I saw the post, your mum on Facebook, the thing. I thought maybe it was public."

Lena took a step forward. "What post?"

Tom was already pulling back.

"Listen, I've really got to go. Sorry, this is awkward. I shouldn't have…" and then he was gone. Turning sharply, disappearing down the side of the shop, coffee still in hand. Lena stood there, her breath visible in the air. A post? She pulled out her phone, thumb trembling slightly, but there was nothing new. No messages, no tags, no alerts. Just the feeling that her life was moving beyond her control, and someone else was watching it unfold from a better seat. Lena didn't go home. Not yet, Her hands felt cold, even inside her pockets. Her breath misted in the air as she made her way to the local library, a squat red-brick building tucked between the butcher's and the church hall, with ivy curling up its sides and a faded sign that simply read *LIBRARY* in peeling white paint. Inside, it smelled of old paper and furniture polish. Time moved slower here, the way it always did in places made to be quiet. She approached the desk. An elderly woman in a knitted jumper looked up with vague interest.

"I was wondering if you had anything on the Harrow family," Lena said. "They used to own, uh, the old Rosehill property."

The woman's expression didn't change.

"Cemetery records or local history?"

Lena blinked. "Both, if you've got them."

The woman pointed without standing.

"Third row, back corner. Blue binders for burials. Red for family records. Alphabetical, more or less."

Lena murmured thanks and made her way through the aisles. The blue binder was heavy. Dated 1960 onward. She flipped past yellowed pages of typed entries and handwritten amendments. She found them halfway down the list.

HARROW, Charles William – d. 2002
HARROW, Elizabeth Anne – d. 2002
Plot: 18-C, Southside Section
Cause of death: Fire
Noted as closed case

There was no further detail. No newspaper clipping attached, no mention of heirs. Lena ran her fingers along the name, tracing the curve of the H. She closed the binder, gently, and didn't reach for the red one. Not yet. Outside, the wind had picked up. Clouds dragged themselves over the sun like bruises. The cemetery was only a ten-minute walk, through the churchyard and past the low wrought-iron gate where the paint had flaked in long strips. It was smaller than she expected. Tucked into the land like it had been there forever. Trees bowed inward along the edges. Gravel pathways carved sharp lines between mossy stones. She followed the numbering carefully, counting in reverse until she found Section C. Row eighteen was set against the low wall. A single blackbird hopped along the path ahead of her. She scanned the markers, one by one, boots crunching softly beneath her. Then she saw her. Across the path, half-obscured by a tree. Anne. Standing still, staring directly at her. She wasn't holding flowers. She wasn't kneeling or mourning. She was just watching. Lena felt her chest tighten. Anne didn't wave. Didn't smile. Didn't blink. Lena turned without thinking. She didn't run, but her steps were sharp. Purposeful. The air felt too thin. She didn't look back until she reached the main road. By then, Anne was gone. Lena walked quickly, keeping her eyes forward and her breath even. She didn't stop until the cemetery gate was behind her and the town came back into view. Stone facades, quiet windows, the steady beat of small village life. She crossed the road without looking. The air had cooled. That sort of inland chill that made you feel like the sky was too close. She didn't know where she was going, just that she needed not to be alone and then, as she turned past the church, someone caught her by the arm. She flinched.

"Woah, hey, hey. It's just me." Dan.

His expression changed as soon as he saw her face.

"You okay?" he asked, voice low.

"You look like you've seen a ghost."

"I thought I had," she murmured.

He glanced over his shoulder toward the direction she'd come from. "What happened?"

"Nothing," she said, too fast. Then, softening: "Just needed some air."

Dan gave her that look again, the one that hovered between worry and wanting to respect her space.

"Well, come on," he said gently. "Let me take you for lunch. You haven't eaten, have you?"

Lena shook her head. He offered his hand, She took it. The Cracked Teacup sat at the corner of the high street, wedged between a florist and a dress shop that hadn't changed its window since 2007. The café was warm inside, low-lit, the smell of cardamom and vanilla steeped into the floorboards.

"Table for two?" called Cora from behind the counter before she even looked up.

"Sit anywhere, love, Oh! Hello, Dan!"

Dan waved. "Hi, Cora."

Lena followed him past the glass cabinet of pastries and sandwiches, her gaze snagging briefly on a man near the window. Elliot Voss. The dog walker. He was sipping tea with one hand, stroking the back of a brindled spaniel curled under the table with the other. His eyes tracked them as they walked past, flat, unreadable.

"Who's that?" he asked as they sat.

"Elliot," Lena said, unfolding a napkin. "Local. Bit odd. Quiet. That guy who ignored us in the woods," Lena glanced back.

Elliot was already looking out the window again. They ordered tea, then toasties, and Dan did his best to ease the silence between them with light conversation. She tried to listen. Tried to laugh when she should. But the house wouldn't leave her. Neither would the grave or Anne's stillness or Tom's slip. Something was building. She could feel it rising like water behind a door.

After they paid, Lena stood slowly, stretching her arms with a faint groan. As she turned toward the front counter, something caught her eye. A photo frame on the wall. Staff picture. A birthday maybe, balloons in the background, a cake with unlit candles. The uniforms were slightly different. Navy blue with gold trim instead of the now-faded teal and standing toward the back, almost out of sight, Clara. Hair darker. Eyes less tired. Ten years younger, maybe more. Same gloves. Same distance in her face. Lena stepped closer. "Dan." He came to her side.

"That's Clara," she whispered. He frowned.

"Are you sure?"

"She's wearing the same gloves. Same necklace, too."

Cora drifted past behind the counter, carrying a tray.

"That was about twenty years ago, I just opened the place." she said without stopping.

Dan smiled politely. "She cleans for us now."

Cora paused, tray hovering. "Funny."

Lena turned. "Why? What's that mean?"

But Cora only gave them both a look.

"Nothing. She kept herself to herself." And then she was gone, into the back, tray swinging lightly at her hip.

As they stepped outside, the cold returned fast. A low wind cut through the high street, and Dan wrapped an arm around her as they descended the steps. That's when the door behind them opened again.

"Thought about selling the house yet?" came a bright, sharp voice.

Lena turned to see Louise Hale striding into the café in a crimson coat, clipboard in one hand, coffee in the other. She didn't wait for an answer, just smiled, eyes glittering.

Dan forced a grin. "We're getting quite attached to it."

"Shame," Louise replied. "Would've fetched a small fortune at auction." Then she disappeared inside, boots clacking neatly on the tiles. Lena stared at the door long after it swung shut.

The drive back was quiet. Dan had offered to stop by the market, pick up something easy for dinner but Lena had declined. She didn't want to see more people. Didn't want to pretend at normality in front of the butcher or the cashier or the boy who stocked the eggs. The road bent gently through trees still bare with the remnants of winter. Branches arched like ribs overhead. The further they got from town, the more it felt like something was folding back over them. By the time the house came into view, its grey stone against the slope of fields. Lena felt her stomach tighten. Not fear, exactly, but anticipation. The kind that made you check a room twice. The kind that made you listen to silence. They didn't drive straight home. Dan made a small detour just past the old railway crossing, pulling into a narrow lot beside a squat building with a faded sign that read *Gibson's Hardware & General Goods*.

"I won't be long," he said, already unbuckling his seatbelt.

Lena looked over. "What are you getting?"

He hesitated. "Cameras."

She blinked.

"For the house," he clarified.

"I thought it might help. Ease your mind a bit."

Something in her chest softened, but only slightly. The gesture was thoughtful, but it also made everything feel more real. Concrete.

"I didn't ask you to…"

"I know. But something's wrong. I can feel it too, even if I don't know what."

He offered a tired smile.

"Let me at least try to do something."

She nodded once, the smallest motion, and watched him jog across the gravel lot.

Inside, the lights were dim and flickering. The place looked more like a toolshed than a shop, but Dan returned a few minutes later with a brown paper bag tucked under one arm.

"Motion sensors, battery-powered. Discreet," he said, sliding back into the driver's seat.

"We'll put one in the hallway, one near the study and maybe upstairs. I'll do it at the weekend"

Lena didn't answer but she reached over and rested a hand on his knee for a brief second, squeezing gently.

"Thank you," she said quietly.

They pulled up at home just before three. The wind had picked up again, sending small swirls of leaves across the gravel. The trees bordering the property bowed and groaned. Dan unlocked the front door and stepped inside first. Lena hesitated for a moment before following. The warmth hit her first, then the stillness. No notes on the floor, no doors ajar, no immediate sense of intrusion and yet. She shrugged off her coat and hung it slowly, listening. Dan disappeared into the kitchen, muttering something about putting the kettle on. Lena walked into the living room. Everything looked untouched. Except the cushion on the right side of the sofa, slightly indented, its corner pulled as though someone had sat and risen in a hurry. She straightened it without thinking, hand lingering on the fabric. The house didn't feel violent. It felt… attentive. Later, after tea and silence, Dan returned to the study. Lena wandered upstairs to change. She moved slowly through the bedroom, pulling off her jumper, folding it neatly over the chair. As she crossed the room, she noticed something small on the dresser. A silver button. She picked it up. Not hers, not Dan's. Something old, a little tarnished, with a thread still looped through the shank. She didn't remember seeing it this morning. She placed it in the drawer without speaking.

By evening, the clouds had rolled thick over the horizon. The sky looked bruised, and the wind had deepened into something steady and cold. Dan reheated leftover pasta and roasted some vegetables. They ate at the kitchen table with the radio on low, some soft jazz station with intermittent static. Lena watched the kitchen clock again, same as before. Stuck, she wasn't sure anymore. After dinner, they curled up again in the cinema room, choosing something light and familiar, an old series they'd both watched before, easy to half-ignore. Dan rested his head against hers. She could feel the weight of him. His trust and something in her ached with the knowledge that she hadn't told him everything. About Tom, About Anne, About how the grave had almost told her something she didn't want to hear. As the episode ended,

Dan yawned and kissed her cheek. "Come on, let's not fall asleep down here."

She nodded, They moved through the house slowly, turning off lights, checking windows. The routine was beginning to feel ritualistic, like locking the door would somehow hold everything else at bay. Lena paused on the stairs, glancing down the hall. She thought she saw a flicker. Just the edge of something moving. When she stepped back to look, nothing. Just shadows. Just the house. She stared down the hallway for a long time, her breath shallow. Nothing moved, no shadow, no footfall. Just the quiet hush of a house pretending to sleep. Dan had already gone ahead, brushing his teeth in the en suite, humming something tuneless through the open door. Lena turned away from the stairs and followed. They got ready in near silence. She changed into an old oversized T-shirt, brushed her hair in long, mechanical strokes. Dan switched off the bathroom light and climbed into bed with a contented sigh, already shifting to lie on his side. She crawled in beside him and faced the opposite direction. The duvet was warm. The room was still. Dan reached over and gently tugged her close, she let him. His arm settled around her middle, and his breath evened out within minutes but Lena lay awake, eyes open in the dark, waiting for the sound she didn't want to hear. It never came. Eventually, sleep took her. Uneven, shallow. Sometime later, how much later, Dan couldn't say, he stirred. The room was cold. Too cold. He blinked at the ceiling, bleary-eyed, his limbs slow to respond. Then he noticed the door. It was open, wide. The landing beyond was dark, silent. Dan frowned. He was sure he'd closed it. He always closed it. He pushed the duvet aside and stepped onto the cool floorboards, rubbing at his arms as he crossed the room. The hallway stared back at him, black, breathless. He reached out and shut the door with a soft click. Then turned, padded back to the bed, and slipped under the covers again. Beside him, Lena didn't stir. Dan pulled the duvet up to his chest and tried to sink back into the warmth she left behind. But it took longer than it should to fall asleep.

CHAPTER SIXTEEN

The morning passed in quiet fragments. Lena loaded the dishwasher. Folded towels. Replied to emails she didn’t remember reading. The house, for once, seemed cooperative, no creaks, no missing objects, no drafts from doors she swore she'd closed. Outside, the weather couldn’t make up its mind. One moment sunlight slipped across the fields like melted gold, the next it was swallowed whole by thick clouds. She spent a while standing at the upstairs window, one hand resting on the sill, watching wind bend the grass in slow, tired waves. Dan was on the phone for most of the morning, muttering updates, pacing from room to room with his laptop tucked under one arm. Just before lunch, he stepped into the living room with that look on his face. Half-apology, half-business.

“They need me in London,” he said.

“Meeting first thing tomorrow. Imran’s pushing for a face-to-face, something about client-side encryption acting up.”

Lena set down the book she hadn’t been reading. “You’re leaving today?” He nodded. “Train’s in two hours. I’ll be back tomorrow night, promise.”

She didn’t protest. Not out loud. Instead, she followed him upstairs while he packed. Folded shirts, paired socks. Slipped in a small bottle of aftershave without asking. When he zipped the case closed, he paused.

Looked at her. "You sure you'll be okay?"

"I'll be fine."

"You could come."

Lena shook her head. "I've got a few things I want to check on here."

Dan kissed her gently. "If anything happens, anything feels off, call me, alright?"

"I will."

He didn't believe her but he left anyway.

London felt too loud. Even after all these years, the city had a way of crowding Dan's senses, honking taxis, snippets of argument and laughter, the smell of wet concrete and exhaust fumes clinging to the air. It was familiar, but that didn't make it comforting. Not today. He checked into the hotel around 3PM, a boutique place tucked between a wine bar and a stationery shop near Clerkenwell. The kind of hotel that called its towels "artisan" and offered a drink voucher on arrival. Dan declined the cocktail. The lift smelled faintly of citrus and metal. His room on the third floor was sleek, warm-toned, and impersonal, plush grey carpet, clean white sheets, desk by the window. He tossed his case onto the bed and opened the window a fraction, letting in the muffled churn of the street below. The moment his coat hit the back of the chair, his phone buzzed. ***IMRAN – incoming call***

Dan answered. "Hey."

"You at the hotel?"

"Just got in."

"Can I swing by?"

Dan checked his watch. "Now?"

"Now's best." He paused.

"Is this about what we spoke about before?" A beat. Then:

"Yeah. It's weird."

"I'll come downstairs."

Imran was already waiting in the lobby when Dan arrived, perched on one of the oversized armchairs, laptop bag beside him, hair windblown from the cold.

"Still allergic to phone summaries, huh?" Dan asked, sliding into the opposite seat.

"I figured this needed a proper conversation." Imran opened his laptop and turned it toward Dan.

"Here's the traffic we flagged. Access to encrypted dev documents, timestamps, IP trails, all tied to your Cotswolds address."

Dan frowned. "Right, but I wasn't working those nights."

"I know. That's the weird part. Everything's clean. No breach, No VPN redirection. Whoever accessed those files did it from your home IP. No password failures, no alerts."

Dan leaned closer. "When?"

"Every incident we traced happened between 2AM and 4AM."

Dan stilled. "Always the same window,"

Imran continued. "Quiet, efficient pulls. Almost like... someone knew exactly what to look for."

Dan shook his head. "No one else has my laptop."

"You sure?"

"I mean, Lena's been using her own, mostly, and no one else…"

He stopped. His mind caught on something, but the shape of it was wrong. Familiar, but not his. Imran lowered his voice.

"I'm not saying it's her, mate. But if someone has access, if there's someone in the house…"

Dan rubbed his jaw. "We've had some weird stuff lately. Small things, Like someone else is there."

Imran closed the laptop slowly. "Might be time to take that seriously."

Imran clicked once, before he shut the laptop, and stood.

"I'll monitor it from my end. If anything shows up, I'll call."

Dan stood with him, offered a tired handshake.

"Let's hope we're both being paranoid," Imran said.

"Yeah," Dan replied. "Let's hope."

Back in the village, the light had shifted. Grey sky brushed pale gold over the tips of trees. The wind had settled into something constant, no longer gusting, just *present*, like a whisper in every hedgerow. Lena stood at the gate of the cemetery once more, boots rooted in gravel. She hadn't planned to come back. But after the photo, the card, the clock, after all of it, she needed something real. Something old and fixed. She moved quietly, counting the rows, the stones. Her breath left soft plumes in the air. Then she saw it. The grave.

Charles W. Harrow
Elizabeth A. Harrow
Beloved Parents. Taken too soon. Together still.

Lena's stomach turned. *Parents.* She stared at the engraving, heart climbing. The same names from the file at the library. Then, *Anne.* Where she was standing near the treeline, half in shadow, coat drawn tight against her frame. Lena's blood ran cold. Recalling the memory. She was just stood, her face unreadable. Lena turned. Quickly. She didn't stop until the iron gate clanged behind her. Lena didn't go home. Not yet. Instead, she followed the old footpath behind the church, one she'd noticed before but never taken. It curved through the trees, past a rusting fence post and a sagging wooden bench, toward the far end of the village where the houses thinned out. Anne's house stood just before the tree line. Lena had never seen it up close. From the lane it looked unremarkable, stone-built like the rest, with moss crawling up the corners and paint flaking from the sills but up close, it felt, paused. Overgrown hedges choked the narrow front path. Ivy curled tight around the gate like fingers, pulling it inward. The grass hadn't been trimmed in months. A birdbath, long dried, sat cracked and crooked by the porch. The garden didn't look abandoned. It looked *unbothered*, as if the house belonged to the woods more than the village. Lena pushed the gate gently, its hinges groaning in protest. The front door was open. Not wide. Just ajar. Like it had been left that way deliberately. She approached slowly, boots whispering against gravel.

"Hello?" she called, voice soft but clear.

"Anne?" No answer.

She stepped onto the porch, hesitant, and leaned in to knock, when a voice came from behind her.

"You shouldn't walk in uninvited."

Lena jumped. Anne stood by the side of the house, hands tucked into her coat, face unreadable beneath the heavy shadows of the overhanging trees.

"I, sorry," Lena stammered.

"The door was open. I wasn't trying to…"

Anne tilted her head slightly. "You're Dan's partner."

Lena nodded. There was a beat of silence. Then Anne gave a thin, tired smile.

"Come in then. Since you've come all this way."

Inside, the house was warmer than expected. The hallway was narrow, lined with old wallpaper that had begun to peel at the corners. A wooden coat rack leaned in the corner, weighed down with scarves. The smell was one of dust, lavender, and age. Anne led her into a front room where an old armchair sat near a wood burner, a radio quietly muttering static on the shelf.

"I don't get many visitors," Anne said, settling into the chair without inviting Lena to do the same.

"Not since, well. Never mind."

Lena stood awkwardly, hands clasped in front of her.

"I wanted to ask you something," she said.

Anne nodded once.

"I saw the grave. Charles and Elizabeth Harrow. It said, 'Beloved Parents.'" She hesitated. "Were they yours?"

Anne's face shifted, but not the way Lena expected.

She laughed. Dry and short. "Oh no," she said. "God, no. I was already in my twenties when they had their daughter."

Lena blinked. "Daughter?" Anne took a moment.

"Little Grace. Quiet girl. She didn't last long."

There was something final in her voice. Like a door clicking shut.

"But I thought…" Lena shook her head. "I thought you were their daughter. You've been so, odd and distant. Like you couldn't even hear us"

Anne looked at her then. Really looked and for the first time, Lena noticed something in her eyes, clouded, slightly unfocused.

"I'm deaf," Anne said simply. "Or mostly. It's worse some days. I must have not been wearing my hearing aids when you saw me."

Lena felt her stomach drop.

"I wasn't ignoring you," Anne said. "I just couldn't hear you."

The silence that followed stretched like glass between them. Finally, Anne reached for a log beside the burner and tossed it in with practised ease.

"You should be careful in that house," she said.

"Some memories don't like to be forgotten."

Lena didn't ask what she meant. She wasn't sure she wanted to know. Lena didn't linger. Anne didn't walk her to the door, and Lena didn't expect her to.

The sky had dipped a shade darker since she arrived, more soot than silver now, with the edges of the clouds bruising toward dusk. She walked back along the footpath in silence, hands buried deep in her coat pockets, the air pressing damply against her skin. She didn't want to go home. Not yet, not to a house that stared too long at her when she wasn't looking. The bell above the door at The Cracked Teacup gave its usual delicate chime as Lena stepped inside. It was warm, too warm almost. The smell of cinnamon and vanilla clung to the air like memory, and the radio played something crackly and French in the background. Cora was behind the counter, writing something in a notebook with a pencil she kept tucked behind her ear. She looked up and beamed.

"Well, now, look who's wandered back in. Can't keep away, can you?"

Lena gave a faint smile. "Just needed a quiet moment."

Cora nodded as if she already knew. "Sit down, love. Tea's on me."

Lena chose a table by the window, settling into the cushion slowly, like her bones had turned to stone. Moments later, Cora arrived with a pot of tea and a plate with a slice of something warmly spiced.

"Fig and walnut," she said. "Pairs nicely with too much thinking."

Lena took a sip first. Let the warmth fill her throat before she spoke.

"Can I ask you something?"

Cora sat down across from her, eyes alight with curiosity. "Of course."

"The Harrow house," Lena began, choosing her words with care. "Do you know what happened there? The family, I mean."

Cora's expression didn't change, but something behind her eyes sharpened.

"Why do you ask?"

"I saw their grave. It just, didn't feel like the whole story." Cora leaned in, resting her elbows on the table. Her voice dropped, more intimate than quiet.

"Well, some say Mr. Harrow lost his mind. Others say he was broken long before the fire. The house didn't burn to the ground, but the top floor, where their bedroom was, that went up. All three of them were inside. The daughter too."

Lena stared at her. "Do you know why?"

A shrug. "Rumour has it he found out Grace wasn't his. His wife had been seeing someone. The gardener, apparently." She sipped her tea. "Classic, really. Tragic."

Lena said nothing.

"Folk say he snapped," Cora continued.

"Locked the doors. Lit a match or maybe it was an accident, and that just made the story more exciting to tell."

She smiled then, not unkindly. "You know how stories are. People like their tragedies with edges."

Lena picked at the edge of the saucer. "And Grace?"

Cora's smile faded slightly. "She was only eight."

A silence settled between them. Then Cora stood.

"Well, enough of that. You didn't come in here for ghost stories." She cleared the plate gently and turned toward the counter.

"Thanks," Lena said quietly.

"Any time," Cora called over her shoulder.

"Though if you ask me, some houses don't like being lived in by strangers. Not after everything they've seen."

Meanwhile in London, Dan sat on the edge of the hotel bed, laptop open, charger snaking across the duvet like a tripwire. A spreadsheet glowed on the screen, colour-coded and exhaustive, but he hadn't typed in twenty minutes. The room was still. Muted by thick curtains and padded walls. Beyond the window, London churned onward, too loud to hear and too fast to pause. He rubbed at the back of his neck and exhaled slowly. Everything about the house was beginning to press in on him. The missing emails. The camera trigger. The wrong time on the clock. The silence in Lena's voice when she said she was fine. He checked his phone. No new messages. A half-eaten sandwich sat beside his notes. Lukewarm coffee clung to the bottom of a cup. He forced himself to close the spreadsheet and reopen the brief for tomorrow's pitch. Words blurred for a moment, then focused. He adjusted his posture. Began typing. A soft ping came from the system tray, an automatic backup reminder.

As the sun began to settle over Rosehill. Lena walked slowly up the drive. The gravel crunched softly beneath her boots. The house loomed ahead, dark against the deepening sky. Its windows caught the last of the fading light, blank and unrevealing. Everything looked still. The front door gave a quiet click as she pushed it open. Inside, the silence returned like a weight settling across her shoulders. She set her keys in the bowl by the stairs, hung up her coat, and stepped into the kitchen without turning on the radio. She wasn't sure what she was listening for but she listened anyway. The kitchen clock sat on the far wall, just above the spice rack. Lena glanced up. **3:31.** She stared. No ticking. No movement. No sign it had ever changed. Just the time, sitting there. As though it had always known. She turned away, opened the fridge and pulled out the ingredients for a simple dinner, scrambled eggs, half an avocado, toast. Her hands moved on muscle memory. Crack, whisk, stir. Pan on. Bread down. Everything felt too clean. Too easy. By the time she'd eaten, the sky had gone completely dark. The house remained still. No knocks. No movement. No clocks shifting. Just silence.

It was just past eleven when Dan finally shut his laptop. The pitch notes were clean, polished, emailed to himself twice, one copy to work, one to backup. He'd even run through it aloud once in the mirror, like he used to in university when nerves still hit him hard. Now, the nerves felt different. Not about work. Something quieter. Tighter. Like pressure behind a wall. He stood, stretched his shoulders, and stepped into the hotel bathroom to splash water on his face. The mirror was fogged only slightly from the shower next door. A faint hum of pipes lingered behind the walls. When he came back out, his phone screen had lit up. Not a call. Just an alert. A sync. Dan lifted the lid of his laptop again, expecting maybe an auto-update or a calendar glitch. But it wasn't that. His email client was open. The *drafts* folder was glowing. One new message. He hadn't opened it. He hadn't written anything since earlier that day. He clicked it slowly, the pads of his fingers suddenly cold.

No recipient.

No subject.

Just a single line.

Sleep well Daniel x

There was no cursor blinking. No indication of when it had been typed but the timestamp in the corner said **3:31 AM** yesterday. Dan sat back, throat dry. He stared at the words for a long time. Then, without quite knowing why, he shut the lid. Slowly. Carefully and didn't sleep for a long while.

In the Cotswolds, The house didn't make a sound. No knocks, no footsteps. No flickering lights and still, Lena didn't trust it. She walked the rooms slowly after dinner, switching off lamps, checking windows, listening between every movement. Her footsteps echoed more than usual, too sharp against the wooden floors, like the silence had grown brittle. At the front door, she double-checked the lock. Twisted it once. Then again. It clicked sharply into place. Upstairs, she paused at the top of the landing and glanced down the corridor, the same corridor where she thought she'd seen something the night before. Nothing stirred. Just shadows hugging corners. In the bedroom, she stood still for a moment before walking to the vanity chair. It was small, light enough to lift with one hand. She carried it quietly across the room and placed it carefully under the handle of the door. It wouldn't stop anyone, not really, not if someone wanted in, but it was enough to *hear* it first. Enough to matter. She didn't tell herself she was being silly. She was far past that now. Lena changed into her nightshirt, pulled back the duvet, and climbed in with slow, deliberate movements. The room smelled faintly of lavender and warm dust. The window was cracked open just slightly. A breeze stirred the curtains like breath. She turned on her side and rested a hand against her stomach. That was what grounded her now, the small, quiet truth forming inside her. Not fully real, not yet but hers. Still untouched by all of this. Her other hand reached up to brush a stray hair behind her ear. Then, gently, she closed her eyes.

CHAPTER SEVENTEEN

The chair hadn't moved. It stood exactly where she'd left it angled under the bedroom door handle, one leg slightly skewed on the uneven floorboard. Its back pressed tight against the wood, casting a long, thin shadow across the floorboards in the grey-blue morning light. Lena lay still for a while, just watching it. The silence in the room had weight. A muffled, pressing stillness that wasn't quite peaceful. Not quite right. The kind that made her want to hold her breath, in case something else was already doing the breathing for her. She exhaled slowly. Nothing had stirred in the night. At least not that she remembered, no phantom footsteps. No pressure against the door. Just her heartbeat and the creak of the chair when she'd set it in place, half convinced she was being paranoid and half convinced she wasn't doing enough. Dan would've laughed. Called her his *little security guard* but he wasn't here and the silence left behind was more hollow than she liked to admit. By the time she rose, the light had shifted from blue to the pale beige of an overcast spring morning. Outside, the clouds were smeared like chalk across slate. Somewhere far off, a bird called once and stopped. Downstairs, she made tea without music. Without her phone. Just the quiet sound of boiling water and the slow rattle of the spoon against ceramic. She left the radio off. Something about the static unsettled her more than the silence. She buttered toast with slow, deliberate strokes, as if speed might break something. When she sat at the kitchen table, she left one hand curled around the mug and let the steam warm her face. The first bite of toast felt like cardboard. She chewed anyway. The chair across from her was empty. She reached across and brushed the back of it once with her fingertips, then withdrew. The house didn't feel haunted. Not exactly. It felt *inhabited.* Like it had its own slow breath, drawn from the walls and the floors and the dark places behind doors she hadn't opened yet. It was less about what she'd seen, or hadn't, and more about what she could feel. A kind of watching. Not threatening. Just… close. Too close. She stood up before she could think too long about it and carried her plate to the sink. Her half-drunk tea followed. The cup clinked softly in the porcelain basin. She turned on the tap just to hear something moving. Then came the laundry. The basket was waiting at the foot of the stairs where she'd left it the night before. A soft jumble of cotton and jersey. When she reached for it, her fingers brushed something smooth and familiar near the top. Her lavender cardigan. Folded, neat. Warm from the dryer. She froze. She hadn't seen it in over a week, thought she'd left it in London, maybe at her mum's, or accidentally buried it in one of the unpacked boxes still sitting in the guest house but here it was. Clean. Folded. Sitting right on top like someone had just finished the chore. She hadn't done laundry yesterday. She hadn't *washed* that cardigan. Slowly, she pulled it from the basket. Held it up. It smelled faintly of the lemon detergent they used. No stains. No creases. As if it had been plucked from a shelf and placed back without a second thought. Her breath caught in her throat. Was Dan home briefly and forgot to mention it? No. She would've seen the basket shift. Would've noticed the dryer run. Heard it and even if he had, how would he have found it? She looked around the landing, suddenly aware of the silence again. The stillness now felt expectant. Carefully, she folded the cardigan again and tucked it under her arm. She carried the basket upstairs without another word.

The rest of the morning bled into a quiet rhythm. She stripped the guest beds and opened a few windows to let in the stale spring air. The wind pulled faintly at the curtains, just enough to stir the dust on the sills. She put fresh towels in the bathrooms. Rearranged a vase that had been slightly off-centre on the console table. She didn't know why.

Routine. Movement. Occupying the house before it occupied her. It wasn't until just after noon, when she was returning the folded laundry to the upstairs rooms, that she noticed the next thing. The wardrobe in the guest room, the one Dan's brother had used, was shifted slightly off its usual position. Not much, maybe an inch but enough that the edge of it didn't quite line up with the skirting board anymore. Enough that the dust trail on the floor had been broken. She paused, set the laundry basket down gently. Crossed the room. Her fingertips brushed the wood, then slowly gripped the edge. She gave it a careful pull. It moved, easily., too easily for something that heavy and behind it, barely visible in the gloom, was a seam in the wall. Another crawlspace.

Dan woke earlier than he needed to. The hotel room was too quiet, the kind of hush engineered by thick curtains and triple-glazed windows. It made the world feel far away, but not in a peaceful way. More like a pause button had been pressed somewhere just beyond reach. He lay there for a while, staring at the ceiling, hand behind his head, listening to the soft whir of the air vent. Then, finally, he got up. The shower hissed to life as he stepped inside, the water steaming quickly against the cold tile. He closed his eyes and let the heat soak into his shoulders. Tried to focus on the day ahead. Tried not to picture Lena in that big house alone. Tried not to wonder what time it was there, or what the kitchen clock was doing. The meeting was scheduled for 9:30 sharp at the Shoreditch office. Dan took a black cab rather than risk the overground, arriving ten minutes early, coffee in hand, suit slightly wrinkled from the overnight hang. The receptionist offered him a smile too bright for the hour, and he smiled back, only just. He didn't really feel like himself this morning. Didn't feel like Dan from London. He still felt like Dan from the house, Dan with the creaky stairs and the missing photo and the card no one admitted writing. Still, he played his part. In the boardroom, the team gathered around the table, lanyards and tablets and paperless notebooks. A flatscreen mounted to the wall flashed through the introductory slides while someone fussed with the lighting. Dan nodded, greeted, made small talk with a woman from the comms team he barely remembered from a previous project. When it was his turn to present, he stood. His voice was steady. Clear, practised. He went through the pitch like a man flipping pages in a well-worn script, branding strategy, engagement metrics, seasonally-adjusted tone recalibrations. The language rolled out smoothly, shaped by weeks of prep. He even cracked a joke halfway through and got a polite ripple of laughter in return but the whole time, he kept thinking about the emails he had received. After the meeting ended, the rest of the team filtered toward a lunch place two blocks over, some boutique salad chain with biodegradable cutlery and prices no one questioned. Dan made his excuses. Said he had a call to take. Promised to swing by later and never did. Instead, he crossed the road and ducked into a quiet café on a side street, less curated, more normal. A narrow place with a chalkboard menu and smudged sugar jars. The kind of café that still had a worn wooden counter and a bell over the door. He ordered a ham sandwich, a black coffee, and took the window seat. Outside, the sky was a hazy slate, light drizzle painting the pavement silver. People passed with umbrellas tilted sideways, their coats darkened at the hems. Across the street, a newsstand flapped faintly in the breeze. Dan checked his phone, again. One message from Lena. *"All fine here. Can't wait to have you back."* That was all. He read it a few times, trying to decide if there was anything between the words. A hesitation but it looked normal, it read normal though it didn't feel normal. He scrolled through his emails, cleared spam. Flagged a reminder from his bank. Re-read Imran's text from earlier that morning.

Still nothing. No activity overnight. Let's talk later.

Still nothing. Still no one. Still no proof. And yet, the image stayed with him, that open draft email, typed when no one should've been awake. When he hadn't even been *there*. '***Sleep well Daniel x***' He sat in the café longer than he needed to, finished his coffee. Watched strangers cross the street, phones in hand, heads bowed against the rain. The city looked ordinary, unbothered. Everything moved too fast here to notice what was missing. Dan wiped his mouth with a napkin and stood. Slipped his coat back on. Checked his phone again, though he already knew no new messages had arrived. The lobby smelled of fabric softener and brass polish. A woman in a navy uniform behind the desk greeted him with a practiced smile. He returned his keycard and asked them to email the receipt. She nodded, tapping on the keyboard with quiet precision. His suitcase was packed already, parked by the armchair in his room. He wheeled it behind him, the small wheels dragging slightly against the marble entrance. Outside, the rain had softened to mist. He didn't hail a taxi right away. He just stood under the small canopy, watching cars slide past on the slick road, unsure why his chest felt so tight. Maybe it was just missing Lena. Maybe it was more. As he waited for the car to arrive, he caught his own reflection in the mirrored lobby wall. The man looking back at him looked tired. Paler than usual, eyes drawn. Collar slightly crooked but he smiled anyway. Not at himself. At the thought of going home.

Back in the Cotswolds, The panel behind the wardrobe wasn't obvious at first. Lena narrowed her eyes. The house was old, things settled. Floors creaked, paint warped but she hadn't moved this wardrobe. Neither had Dan. and she certainly hadn't cleaned behind it. A memory stirred, of the draft she'd felt in the hallway two days ago, the slight chill when walking past this room. At the time, she'd blamed poor insulation. Now, she wasn't so sure. She pulled the panel open. It didn't creak. It didn't resist. It opened like it had been waiting. The air was stale and dry, like paper that had sat too long in a drawer. She aimed the phone torch beam into the narrow tunnel and saw timber walls and a thin path that curved out of sight, just wide enough for a person to crawl through. A breath caught in her throat. She should've gone back, shut the door and called Dan but her body moved forward before she'd finished that thought. Her knees hit the wood with a muted thud as she crawled in, torch flickering ahead in long, arcing sweeps. The crawlspace bent slightly to the left, and the floor sloped with it. Dust covered everything. She passed a broken plastic doll, half buried in lint. A broken teacup with no handle. Something that might've been a pencil case. She kept going. The tunnel narrowed, then widened again, leading into what looked like an unfinished space above the oldest wing of the house. She pushed through a final bend, ducked her head, and emerged into a larger, open space and stopped. It wasn't a storage room. It was *a nest.*

Blankets and duvets, tangled and matted, were piled into the far corner like bedding. A mattress, stained and slumped in the centre, sagged on its springs. A lantern flickered faintly in the gloom, battery-powered and weak. Around it, a ring of items: empty food wrappers, their food wrappers, notebooks with torn-out pages, and small, personal things. A wooden hairbrush. A cracked iPhone. A chipped teacup that looked like one from their kitchen. Lena stepped in, careful not to knock anything over. Her torch beam landed on the wall ahead. It was covered. Newspaper clippings. Printed screenshots. Pages torn from books. Photographs, *dozens*, taped or pinned in haphazard lines. Among the many photos, there were ones of her, and Dan. One showed Lena reading in the garden, squinting toward the sun. Another caught Dan in profile, looking over his shoulder as he locked the front gate. The resolution was low. Some were grainy, clearly taken through glass. A few had small, jagged corners as if torn from other, larger prints. She took a shaky step forward. There, near the centre of the collage, was the missing photograph from her office. Their photo, the one in the silver frame but now it had been altered. A scratch had been dug across Lena eyes. Below it, written in heavy pen: **"HE'S MINE."** Her breath caught. She turned slowly, shining the torch into the far corner, and saw the peepholes. Three of them. Just wide enough for an eye. One looked directly into the kitchen. Another pointed toward the staircase. The third, aimed into a corner of their bedroom. Her mouth went dry.

She stumbled back, bumping into the edge of a crate. Inside were items she recognised immediately. Dan's jumper from last winter, a teacup from their bathroom shelf, and tucked at the bottom, Her old necklace. She hadn't even realised it was missing. Something cracked behind her. Lena spun. Just beyond the entry point, crouched low in the half-light, was a figure. A woman, hooded. Barefoot beneath a loose cardigan that hung like paper. Her hair was tangled and long, almost ragged at the ends. Her face was pale, chin angled slightly downward as if waiting for Lena to speak first and her eyes, God, her eyes, They *knew* her. Lena staggered back, torch shaking. The woman moved forward a step.

"I wondered," she rasped. Her voice was low, hoarse, as though it hadn't been used in days, maybe years. "How long it would take you to find me."

Lena didn't speak. She couldn't. The woman tilted her head. Her mouth twitched, not quite a smile, but close.

"You found my room, like I found you…"

Lena swallowed, her fingers tightening around the torch. "Who are you?"

The woman's face fell. "You don't know?"

A long pause stretched between them. Lena took a step back. "Grace?"

The woman's lips twitched again. Her voice came out almost gentle.

"He never loved me, you know. Not really. Not like he loved her, but I was still his." She took another step forward.

Lena could smell her now, damp skin and something coppery beneath it with a essence of lavender. The smell of sweat soaked into clothes worn too long. Of breath stale with silence.

"He took them from me." Grace's voice sharpened.

"My home, my mother, my name."

Lena's heart pounded in her throat. "No one took anything from you, "

"You *did!*" Grace's voice cracked, rising suddenly. "You *live* here, in my house! You wear her things. You let him hold you like she let *him* hold her. Like nothing ever happened."

Lena stepped back again, her heel hitting the edge of the wall. Grace's eyes flicked to the exit then back to Lena.

She smiled fully now. "You don't belong here," she whispered. "But I do." and then she lunged.

Lena turned, she didn't have time to scream. Grace's body collided with hers, sharp elbows and frantic limbs crashing forward in a burst of sudden violence. Lena's shoulder slammed into the low cabinet against the wall, a wooden chest stuffed with blankets and a chipped porcelain doll. Pain ricocheted through her abdomen. A short, searing spike that knocked the air from her lungs. She staggered, gasped, instinctively protecting her stomach but Grace was already moving again. A hand fisted in Lena's hair, another at her back.

"No, wait!"

Her plea cut off as her head was driven hard into the wall. A dull, ringing crack. The world split sideways. Lena hit the floor, breathless, hands slack. Her limbs felt distant, boneless, detached from the sharp throb blooming behind her eyes. She saw flickering light. Heard something, the hiss of a breath, the scrape of a rope. Then nothing. Grace crouched over her, panting. Her movements were precise now. Practised. She pulled something from beneath the mattress, a long, fraying length of cord, and began binding Lena's wrists with sharp, efficient knots. Then her ankles an, then another loop around her waist. It wasn't anger on her face now. It was something worse, Focus. When it was done, she leaned close to Lena's unconscious face, brushing a strand of hair from her forehead with surprising gentleness.

"I'm going to make it right," she whispered.

Grace rose as she turned toward the crawlspace exit, and slipped out through the passage. The room fell into soft, swaying darkness and in the stillness, barely audible, a phone began to buzz where it had fallen. Once, then again. The screen lit up. ***Dan** – Just got to Cotswolds Station. Be home soon. x*

CHAPTER EIGHTEEN

The train from London pulled into Cotswolds Station just after three-thirty, shuddering softly on the tracks as if the journey had tired it. Dan stepped down onto the platform, the stone slick beneath his feet from recent rain. The air was damp, the sky the dull pewter of early spring greyness, and a quiet breeze curled through the bare trees lining the edges of the station. He slipped his phone from his pocket and thumbed open his messages. Still no reply from Lena. 'Just got to Cotswolds Station. Be home soon. x' It had been read. That was something. He shoved the phone away and hoisted his shoulder bag higher. The duffel weighed heavier than usual, maybe just from the way he carried it. He found a taxi waiting outside, the only one. The driver, a stocky man with a high-vis vest and half a Greggs wrapper on the dash, offered a nod as Dan got in.

"Heading out of town?"

"Bit past Elmcroft," Dan replied. "Rosehill House."

The driver gave a knowing grunt and pulled away from the curb. They drove in silence for a while, past wet hedgerows and crooked old fences, the rain clinging in mist to the edges of the glass. Dan leaned his forehead against the cool window, watching the countryside blur by. Grass washed dull green by cloud. Stone cottages with mossy roofs. Gateposts that looked like they'd stood since before cars existed. Everything felt slow out here. Weathered. Like the world had loosened

its grip and let the seasons hold sway instead. He thought of Lena. She'd said she was going to spend the day at home, maybe get some writing done or reorganise the guest linen closet, some nesting urge she'd fallen into lately. He imagined her curled up in one of the armchairs in the library, legs tucked under her, the smell of mint tea curling up through the hallway. Or maybe in the kitchen, singing softly to herself as she stirred soup or simmered garlic in olive oil. It was that image, her hair up, her sleeves pushed back, that made his chest ache with something like relief. They were going to be okay. Whatever had been happening, whatever had gone unsaid or unsettled since the move, would pass. It always did. The driver turned up the long gravel lane, tyres crunching softly. Dan glanced up. There it was. The house. Rosehill rose through the mist like a storybook sketch, pale stone streaked with rain, windows soft with amber glow, smoke curling faintly from the far chimney. The curtains in the front room were drawn halfway, light leaking around the edges like the house was exhaling. It looked peaceful. Whole. He paid the fare and pulled his bags up the walk, feeling the familiar crack of uneven stones beneath his shoes. The front door was locked, but the key turned easily. Inside, the air met him like memory. Warm. Slightly perfumed. The scent of dried lavender from the hallway vase, wood polish, and the faint undercurrent of lemon and heat from the radiators. It didn't smell abandoned. It smelled lived in.
"Lena?" he called out, no reply.

His suitcase thunked softly to the floor as he stepped into the entryway, wiping his feet by habit more than need. Her boots were beside the bench. One sock draped over the edge. Her coat hung on its usual hook, creased at the elbows like it had been shrugged off and forgotten. He smiled. She was here. Just upstairs, probably in the bath. Or napping. The silence didn't feel ominous. Not yet. The kitchen was still. A mug sat beside the kettle, steamless, half-full. The tea bag was folded neatly on a spoon, as if it had been removed mid-thought. Her phone rested beside it, screen dark, no notifications blinking. He tapped it. Still unlocked. No new messages. A book lay splayed open on the table. Orchid House. Page folded, spine cracked. He brushed his fingers across it absently and walked into the living room. The throw blanket was folded over the back of the sofa. The fireplace was clean, no embers in the grate. A candle had been burned and blown out, he could smell the leftover wax and smoke. He checked the radio. Off. The silence began to press a little. Not loudly. Just enough to notice.

"Lena?" he called again, louder this time. "I'm home!"

Still nothing. He took the stairs two at a time, expecting to find her in the bedroom, asleep with a book on her chest, or doing something normal, folding clothes, brushing her hair, rearranging the bed cushions. What he found was steam. The bedroom was warm. Too warm. Soft classical music hummed from the radio on the dresser. A plucked cello. A brushing cymbal. Some long-forgotten lounge piece drifting between notes. The en suite door was cracked open. Steam poured from it like breath. The mirror was completely fogged, water trailing down in long rivulets. The shower was running. He tilted his head, puzzled. He hadn't heard movement. Not even footsteps. But there, behind the glass partition, was a figure. Slim. Still. Long dark hair clung to the back of her shoulders. One arm lifted toward the wall. The other down. She was turned slightly away from the door, face obscured by steam and silhouette. Dan hesitated. He smiled. Quiet affection tugged at his mouth. This was so Lena. Head in the clouds. No idea he was back. Probably daydreaming about nursery colour palettes or naming schemes for a garden they hadn't started. He began to undress, quietly. Shirt off. The air in the bathroom was thick with perfume, floral but musty. Not her usual, something more powdery. He stepped across the wet tile, the heat hitting his skin with a damp kiss. He called out softly.

"You're going to drain the whole county, babe." No response.

He reached for the shower curtain. The rings slid across the rail with a soft scrape. Dan smiled, reaching forward. The curtain parted and he stopped. The woman in the shower wasn't Lena. She turned slowly. Hair hanging in wet ropes around her face. Eyes too wide. Lips slightly parted. Her face held nothing, no alarm, no startlement, not even curiosity. She looked at him like someone watching a deer in a field. Patient. Detached. Dan stumbled back. His breath caught in his throat.

"What the… Who are you?"

She said nothing. Water traced paths down her bare arms, threading her collarbones. Her fingers moved, barely a twitch before resting at her side again. Dan reached for a towel, yanking it from the rail.

"Who the hell are you?" he said again, louder now.

Still silence. Then a blink and a voice, soft and colourless.

"I've been waiting so long for you."

Dan clutched his shirt to his chest like armour. His voice, when it came, cracked under its own disbelief.

"What the hell are you talking about?"

Grace stepped out of the shower. Steam billowed around her like stage fog, and her bare feet landed soundlessly on the tile. She made no move to cover herself, no shame, no modesty. Just a calm, dreamlike pace as she moved toward him, water trailing down her body. Her hair clung to her face, to her collarbone. Her lips were slightly chapped. Her eyes, those wide, fixated eyes, never left his.

"You don't remember," she said softly, as though it were something to be forgiven. "That's okay. I do."

Dan took a step back. His heel knocked the edge of the doorframe. She paused in front of the mirror and traced a finger through the condensation. It left a curved line. Meaningless. Childlike.

"I used to listen to you laugh," she said. "Through the vents. In the evenings. The way you looked at her… like she was something precious."

Her tone shifted. Just a fraction. Enough to curdle the air.

"But she didn't deserve that. You know she didn't. She didn't see you. Not really."

Dan's spine locked into place. "You need to stop. I don't know what you think this is..."

"You told her you'd protect her," Grace whispered. "I heard it. Over and over. Always so careful with her. Your voice would get low. Warm. You brought her tea when she was crying. Do you remember that night? She said she didn't want to talk about the picture. You held her."

She tilted her head. "That's when I realised… it could've been me."

Dan's mouth opened, but no sound came out. The lightbulb above them flickered once.

"I dreamed it," she said, stepping closer. "Every night. You and me, in the kitchen. You'd smile. You'd cook. You'd ask me about my day and I'd say it was better, now that you were here."

Her gaze dropped for a moment, just a flicker and Dan moved. Fast. He ducked sideways, bolting past her toward the door, his wet feet slipping slightly on the tile. He hit the bedroom half-dressed, shirt now askew, heart hammering in his chest like it was trying to escape.

"Lena!" he shouted, voice cracking.

The radio was still playing, oblivious. Somewhere below, the floor creaked. Grace's voice called softly after him, lilting and bright.

"You don't have to be scared, Dan. This house is ours now."

Dan stood frozen by the bedroom cabinet side. Grace moved toward him again, slow, barefoot, as if the tiled floor were made of silk beneath her feet.

"The deed will finally be mine," she murmured, eyes distant now, almost unfocused.

"Daddy struck me off the will when I was just a little girl. Said I wasn't his daughter. Said I was a stain. A mistake."

She paused, head tilting with the weight of old memory.

"He was so mean to me. Not like you, you're kind. You'd never shut me away. Never lie to me."

Dan's breath came faster now, chest rising and falling like he'd just sprinted. She stepped closer, ignoring the steam and towel and growing horror on his face.

"My mother… she begged. Pleaded with him not to send me away. Said she'd handle it. Said she'd 'make arrangements.' But I knew what she meant."

Grace's voice dropped into something sing-song. "She meant gone. Far away. Forgotten."

Her eyes brightened suddenly, too much. The kind of brightness that came before breaking.

"I couldn't have that."

Dan backed toward the hallway.

"Lady," he said, trembling. "You need help."

But she wasn't hearing him anymore.

"Whilst they slept," she whispered and then she smiled. A slow, awful smile that spread with terrible grace.

“I took matters into my own hands and oh, how it *burned.*” She closed her eyes.

“It roared, Dan. My childhood, my mother, my father. All of it. Fire in the curtains, fire in the wallpaper, fire in their throats when they screamed. I watched from the orchard, wrapped in a blanket. No one ever suspected. Assumed I died.”

Dan’s stomach turned. He lunged for the door. Grace didn’t follow. As he bolted into the hall, he slammed the bedroom door shut and yanked a chair from the corner of the hallway, wedging it underneath the knob from outside. It wouldn’t hold long, but it might give him minutes. He ran down the hall. His voice cracked the silence, ragged and desperate.

“Lena?! Lena, where are you?!”

No answer. Just the faint echo of the radio, and below, the walls listening.

As Lena lay curled on the wooden floor, the cold had settled into her bones like rot. Every part of her ached, from the sharp throb behind her eyes to the dull, sick twist in her stomach where Grace’s blow had landed. Her limbs were stiff, her wrists bound tight, her breath shallow in the stale dark. And then, there was a sound. Not loud, nothing ever was in here, but just enough to stir something in Lena’s consciousness. It was a voice. Faint. Warped by distance. But real. At first she thought it might’ve been memory. Her head hurt in waves, not sharp exactly more like being underwater too long and then coming up too fast. But the voice came again. Muffled, rising. Echoing through beams and ductwork. *“Lena?!”* Dan. She blinked. The darkness was thick around her, but there was a dull glow nearby. Her torch, lying somewhere near her legs, its beam now dulled by battery drain and the angle it had landed in. Shadows leaned across the space like reaching arms. Her wrists burned. Rope dug at the bone, skin already raw. Her ankles were worse. Cramped. Numb. She had no idea how long she’d been here. It could’ve been an hour. It could’ve been ten. Her mouth was dry. The kind of dry that stuck to your teeth. Another sound above. Fast movement. Floorboards. Then her name again. “Lena, please!” She tried to sit up. Her back screamed in protest, her abdomen twisting in warning. She gasped, quiet, like she’d learned not to draw attention. The pain was different this time. Central.

Taut. She closed her eyes. Tried to breathe. The cold air in the crawlspace had gone stale. There was something at her side. The crate. She remembered it now. The one with Dan's jumper. Her teacup. Her necklace. She shifted again, dragging herself sideways. Her hand landed on something sharp. Plastic or metal. A clip. A pin. She grasped it. Tried the rope at her wrists. She fumbled. The angle was wrong. Her fingers clumsy and slick with sweat, but she worked at it, digging, tugging. Every few seconds, she paused. Listened. Dan's voice was moving. Closer. Down the hall now. She couldn't see him but she could hear the panic now. The edge in his tone that didn't sound like doubt anymore. It sounded like fear. She dug harder. The zip tie cut her palm but the rope loosened. One loop. Then another. She wrenched her hands free with a strangled gasp, the movement pulling hard across her stomach. Her fingers trembled. She reached for the torch and turned it, casting the beam upward toward the wall of photos, the claw marks, the childlike drawing of three stick figures and the word: **OURS.** Lena looked toward the crawlspace's entrance. She couldn't stay here. Not another second and Dan was out there. He was looking for her. She braced herself, hands to the wood, and began to crawl.

The hallway was silent again. Dan moved room to room like a man inside someone else's dream, unsure what was real, what had just happened and what *still* could. He checked the office. Nothing. The small bathroom. Empty. He tore through the laundry cupboard, pulling open doors he hadn't opened since the day they moved in. The house felt changed. Not just because of Grace. Because he *knew* it now, knew it was sick. Full of hidden things and fractured history. It was like the walls had been waiting for someone to peel them back. He moved toward the last guest bedroom on the west side, the one they rarely used. His hand hovered on the knob. The air was cooler here. Still. Pressed.

He opened the door slowly and saw it. The wardrobe stood open, only slightly, just an inch, but enough to see what had been behind it. A panel. Wooden. Old. Shifted. Not part of the original wall. He stepped closer. A sound reached him from the other side. Shuffling. A breath. Then light, dim and flickering, like a dying torch beam sweeping across the inside of a cave. He froze.

"Lena?" he breathed.

No reply. But the light stilled. Then, it moved again. Slower now. Purposeful. And a shape appeared in the gap. Fingers first. Then a hand. He rushed forward, tugging the panel open just enough for her to crawl free. Her hair was matted, her face smeared with dirt and something darker. Her eyes were wide, unfocused. Her wrist bore rope burns.

"Lena, oh my God…" He caught her in his arms.

Her breath hitched, and she collapsed into him, the torch falling from her grip and spinning lazily on the floor. He held her. Pressed his forehead to hers. She smelled like dust and blood and fear.

"You're okay," he whispered. "You're safe now."

But Lena's eyes shifted, past him. Behind him. Dan turned and there she was. Grace stood in the doorway. She didn't move. She just stood there in the doorway, her frame swallowed by the glow of firelight still flickering down the hallway behind her. In one hand, she held the lighter, its silver case catching the light with a casual gleam. In the other, nothing but calm menace. Dan could feel Lena trembling against him, her breath short and shallow. The smell of Grace's perfume, lavender, now carried an acrid undertone of petrol. It hung thick in the air like a threat. Grace's eyes drifted to Lena's hand, where it still rested against her stomach.

"You think I didn't know?" she said, her voice soft and precise.

"Like your mums didn't go on and on about becoming grandmothers... the excited little whispers over wine? I heard everything. Through the walls, through the floorboards. Every giggle, every plan. Like they weren't in my house. Like I didn't still belong here."

Lena's voice broke the silence, hoarse but steady.

"Grace, I'm pregnant..." Grace's mouth twitched. Not a smile. Something more like confusion wrapped in rage.

"That should be mine," she said, and her voice cracked.

"*Mine.* Not yours. You came here and took everything, *everyone.* And now you get to have that too?"

Lena stepped forward, just once. Her legs were shaking, but she kept her hand to her stomach, protective without thinking.

"We didn't take anything from you," she said, gently. "We didn't even know you were here."

Grace tilted her head. Then, her gaze dropped lower to Lena's left hand.

"And that," she said. Her voice sharpened like glass.

"That ring. That promise. That should be mine too."

Dan's hand closed protectively around Lena's.

"We could've had it all," Grace murmured, her voice sweet and poisonous.

"You and me, Dan. The quiet life. The garden. The breakfasts and the bookshelves and the baby... I would've made you happy. You'd see."

Dan stepped forward slowly. "Grace, this isn't the way."

But her attention was fracturing. She started pacing slowly inside the room now, like a cat tracing its territory. Her hand tightened on the lighter, but she didn't strike it. Not yet.

"My mother used to say I was a wild one. Said she'd never have let him keep me if she'd known. But she *did* know. She knew everything and she let him put me in the attic anyway because I wasn't his, because I was the mistake."

Dan and Lena said nothing. So she kept talking.

"She told me I should be grateful. That I had clothes and books. A roof. But I saw how they looked at me. How they closed doors when I entered rooms. I wasn't the daughter they wanted. I wasn't anyone's daughter. I was just… here."

She stopped in front of the dresser and looked at herself in the cracked mirror above it. Her reflection shimmered in the heat, distorted by a hairline fracture in the glass.

"I used to imagine burning it all down," she said. "Not to hurt them. Just to *clear it.* To make room for something new."

She turned back to them slowly.

"And I did."

The silence hit like a drop in pressure. Dan's jaw tightened. Grace smiled faintly, as if the memory were an old song.

"My father said he'd strike me from the will. Said I was nothing to him. That I'd never have this house. That I'd never belong here. My mother begged. Pleaded. She promised to send me away. Said she'd 'arrange something.' I knew what that meant."

Her fingers brushed the wall. Then she looked directly at Dan.

"I couldn't let them erase me." Her voice dropped.

"So I waited until they slept."

Lena sucked in a sharp breath.

"I took the matches from the fireplace. I remember my hands were shaking, but I struck them anyway. One. Two. Three. Tucked between the curtains. The edges of the carpet. The study. Their bedroom."

She closed her eyes. "And then I listened."

Dan felt Lena sway. Grace opened her eyes again.

"They screamed. My mother…God, she screamed for so long. Daddy tried to crawl, but he didn't make it past the hallway. I watched it all from the orchard. Wrapped in a blanket. I didn't cry."

She took a slow, deliberate breath.

"People said it was tragic. Said the daughter died too but I didn't. I stayed here. In *my* house. Waiting for the right family. Waiting for someone who might *see me.*"

Her eyes landed on Dan again. "You were *so* close."

Then she moved. It happened in a blink, her fingers tightened around the lighter, and her body surged forward toward Lena, arm outstretched. Dan threw himself in front of her. The force of it knocked him back a step, Grace clawing past him, trying to reach the belly she saw as stolen. He wrapped his arms around her, gripping her arms as she thrashed and screamed.

"Get out!" he shouted at Lena. "Run!"

"But…"

"Go! Now!"

Lena hesitated, then backed toward the hallway, her hand still at her stomach.

"I'll get help," she breathed. "I promise."

Dan held Grace as she struggled, her fingers scraping his neck. She hissed something he couldn't make out. Then Lena turned and ran. Down the stairs. Toward the night and Grace was still fighting. Dan's grip tightened as Grace thrashed in his arms. She fought like someone possessed, pure, writhing instinct, all teeth and nails and breathless rage.

She was snarling now, muttering curses under her breath, half-formed sentences twisted by fury. "You think this is yours…you think any of this is yours?"

Dan staggered backward, dragging her with him. Her heel slammed into his shin, her elbow into his ribs. He took it, gritting his teeth but then she slipped. One arm came free and she went for the knife she had dropped from her back. He didn't even see it at first, didn't realise it had been tucked into the waistband of her jeans. Just a flash of steel, a sudden pain, and then warmth blooming across his shirt. He gasped. Stumbled. The room tilted. Grace stepped back, panting, the blade wet in her hand. Dan looked down. His hands were stained. Dark, seeping warmth spread through the fabric.

"You should've let me have it," Grace whispered. "You could've stayed. You could've loved me."

Dan slumped sideways into the wall, breath rattling. Grace tilted her head, watching him fall like a dropped coat. The knife dropped from her hand and hit the floor with a soft clatter. She turned toward the window. Her voice dropped to something gentle. Dreamlike.

"It's all going to be beautiful again."

Lena ran. Down the stairs, her knees shaking, ribs protesting with every step. Her bare feet slapped the wood. She clutched the banister with one hand and her stomach with the other. She hit the bottom landing and nearly tripped. The front door was still open. The night waited beyond, cold, endless, alive with wind. Somewhere, an owl called, shrill and sudden. She didn't stop to grab her coat. Didn't stop to look back. She ran across the gravel, her soles stinging. Her breath steamed in the air like smoke but something made her stop at the edge of the drive. She turned. Smoke was rising, faint at first, then darker, thicker. One of the upstairs windows flared orange for a second. The reflection of fire danced across the glass. Her breath caught. Dan was still inside. She should go. Find help. Get to a neighbour. Call someone, anyone but her legs wouldn't move. She saw his face, that last moment, eyes wild, voice cracking as he told her to run. And for a second, just one second, she heard it again: the promise he whispered that morning in bed, when they lay curled around each other like spoons.

"I'll always protect you."

But who would protect *him*? She turned back toward the house.

Upstairs, Grace was humming. It was tuneless, broken, a fragment of something old. A lullaby maybe. The kind sung by women with shaking hands and frayed nerves. Dan lay on the floor near the window, struggling to breathe. His mouth was dry. The coppery tang of blood coated his tongue. The floor beneath him was tacky and warm. Grace moved to the dresser. She picked up the lighter. Her thumb flicked once. The spark hissed. She moved to the corner of the room and crouched beside the baseboard, where she had soaked the carpet earlier. The sharp, acrid smell of petrol rose around her like incense.

"This house was always meant to burn," she murmured.

She lit it. The flame crackled to life. It kissed the edge of the drapes, then crawled. Slow at first. Measured. But eager. Grace stood and stepped back. She watched. Dan tried to move. His shoulder twisted, his hand slipping in blood. He reached toward the door but he couldn't make it. Smoke was already curling around the ceiling. Grace wandered toward the mirror. Looked at herself. Smiled.

"You should've seen me in the garden that night," she said, as if to no one.

"I had my blanket. I watched the flames from the orchard. It looked like a fairytale. Everything glowing. Everything ending."

Dan groaned, barely conscious.

"You're going to be ash, Dan. Ash and silence. That's what this place was always meant for."

She turned toward him again. Her smile was crooked.

"I didn't get to say goodbye last time. But I won't miss that mistake again."

Lena re-entered the house through the back door. The kitchen was already full of smoke. She ducked low, one hand covering her mouth, the other gripping the banister as she climbed the stairs again, slower this time, but determined. She reached the hallway. The air here was worse. The floor beneath her feet felt warmer, groaning as though the house were breathing through its bones. She passed the bathroom. The scent of perfume and burning fabric hit her like a wall. She saw the light from under the door of the guest bedroom. She crept toward it. Inside, through the thin crack in the doorway, she could see Grace pacing now, talking to herself. The fire climbed the far wall. Flames crackled across the bedspread, licking the mattress. Smoke had begun to stain the ceiling and Dan, He was curled on the floor near the wardrobe. His eyes fluttered. Lena's heart nearly stopped. She glanced around. There, a heavy decorative bust on the hallway console. Plaster, not marble, but solid enough. Some nameless dignitary, grim-faced and frowning. She picked it up. Crept forward. One step at a time. The flames hissed behind Grace now, the fire reflecting in her wide, unfocused eyes. Lena raised the bust and waited. Grace stood with her back to the flames, the shadows flickering around her as if the fire itself obeyed her presence. Her dress clung to her skin, sweat and heat giving her the shimmer of something almost celestial. But there was nothing holy in her gaze. Her eyes were fixed on Dan, half-lidded, unfocused, like she was watching a memory and not a man bleeding out in front of her.

"I didn't get to say goodbye," she murmured to the fire.

"Last time... I didn't say anything. But this time, I'll watch every moment." Her voice was soft, almost wistful. A girl at the edge of a bedtime story. Behind her, Lena stood in the doorway. The heat curled around her like a snake, sweat prickling down the back of her neck. The air tasted like ash, like burning varnish and old secrets. She could feel the breath of the blaze growing with every second. A hungry thing. In her hands, the plaster bust. Heavy. Cold. Its chipped edge biting into her palms. Grace tilted her head and stepped closer to Dan. That was enough. Lena moved. She crossed the room in two wide steps, and brought the bust down hard. The sound was brutal, thick and wet and final. Grace staggered sideways, her arms flailing once in the air as if grasping for balance. She turned, eyes wide with something that might've been confusion... or betrayal... or recognition. Lena didn't stop. She raised the bust again and slammed it down on Grace's shoulder, sending her crumpling to her knees. Then Lena dropped to the floor with her. Her face was wild, teeth clenched, tears streaking through the soot on her cheeks. The bust came down again. and again. Grace's body twitched under each blow. Blood sprayed up the wall, onto Lena's arms, across her chest. She didn't feel it. She didn't hear her own breath, shallow and ragged. She didn't think. Only when Grace slumped fully, her head caved in, her limbs limp, did Lena stop. Her arms gave way. The bust rolled from her hands and hit the scorched carpet with a hollow knock. The room was no longer theirs. It belonged to the fire now.

It had reached the ceiling. Flames licked through the beams, painting the plaster black. The smoke poured thick and grey, hugging the ground in a creeping tide and Dan, Dan wasn't moving.

"Dan," she choked, scrambling across the rug.

She reached him, fingers trembling, pressing into his chest.

"Come on, look at me. Please."

His eyelids fluttered. His breath hitched.

"Still here," he rasped.

She let out a sob, part laugh, part cry.

"You're not dying here," she whispered. "I'm not letting this placc take you too."

She hooked his arm over her shoulder and heaved. Her knees nearly buckled under the weight, but she didn't let go. They moved together, one slow step, then another, toward the hall. Behind them, a support beam cracked with a deafening pop. Splinters flew. A drawer burst open as flames devoured the oak frame. Down the stairs. Lena could barely see. The smoke clung to her eyes, made her lungs scream. She kept one hand over Dan's, the other gripping the banister. Every stair was a fight. The living room was a furnace now. Curtains flared, fabric turning to black ribbons as they crumbled. The walls buckled and blistered with heat. The house screamed, wood groaning, glass shattering under pressure. They reached the door. Outside, the night air waited. Cold. Fresh. Real. She kicked the door open with her bare foot. Together, they spilled out onto the grass. Lena collapsed to her knees, Dan slumped beside her. Her hands were burned. Her chest ached. Her face was smeared with soot and blood and sweat. Her stomach throbbed, protective and sore but they were alive. The flames behind them poured out through the shattered windows like fury. The sky glowed orange against the black fields. Smoke twisted into the stars. Lena turned back toward the house, toward the ruin of it. Grace was in there. Gone. A story unfinished. A nightmare sealed behind flames. Sirens wailed faintly in the distance, growing louder. But for now, there was only breath. Only the burn of survival.

THE ASHES LEFT BEHIND

The fire was out by morning, though the smell of it lingered for days. Acrid and chemical, clinging to the lungs. Even with the windows down in the ambulance, Lena couldn't get it out of her throat. Or her skin. Or her thoughts. Dan had stopped responding just before they'd reached the hospital. His body, already weakened by blood loss and smoke, had gone quiet in her arms, but his pulse had held, faint, but steady. That was enough. She'd clung to that. They wheeled him in before her. She followed, barely able to walk, wrapped in ash-streaked linen and shock. A paramedic held her elbow. She didn't feel his hand. They were taken to separate bays. Tubes. IVs. Monitors. A soft-spoken nurse with long lashes and gloved hands. The floor under Lena's bed was sticky with soot footprints, trailing away from her body like shadow echoes. She kept asking the same question over and over: "Is the baby okay?" They ran the scans twice. Then once more, just to be sure and finally, one of the doctors came in and sat at her side.

"He's fine," the doctor said. "Strong. Healthy heartbeat. You did everything right."

Lena broke down for the first time. Not out of fear. But because she hadn't realised until then how close it had all come to ending.

The police arrived just after dawn. A woman in uniform with tired eyes and a notepad stood by her bed. Not aggressive. Just… curious. Controlled.

"There was a body in a hidden room," she said. "Burned badly. We think it was female. Long-term inhabitant. You said her name was Grace?"

Lena nodded.

"Grace Harrow?"

Another nod. The officer made a note.

"The press will get wind of it soon. But you don't have to say anything publicly."

"I won't," Lena said. Her voice was paper-thin. "I don't want to see my name in the papers. Not again."

The officer offered a quiet smile. "That's fair." But it didn't matter. By midday, the headlines were already circulating.

"HOUSE OF HORRORS: WOMAN LIVING IN WALLS ATTACKS COMPETITION WINNERS." "GRACE HARROW DEAD IN FIRE: TRAGEDY AT WINSPIRE'S PRIZE PROPERTY." "THE HOUSE THAT REMEMBERED: A COTSWOLDS NIGHTMARE."

There were photos. Of them smiling outside the gates. Of the fire. Of the body bag being lifted into the coroner's van under the early morning light. Lena's face was everywhere. Dan's too. Old family members were contacted. Neighbours asked to comment. Someone even quoted Cora from The Cracked Teacup:

"She always looked pale. Like she knew something she wasn't saying."

Clara Sheen vanished after the fire. Quietly, Without notice. Miles Fenner issued a public statement: "Winspire is cooperating fully with investigators. We are deeply saddened by the incident at Crescent Vale." Behind the scenes, they reached out. An email. Followed by a call. They offered compensation. Legal support. A lawyer with a voice like silk. Then came the other offer, an alternative property, "should the couple wish to relocate and rebuild their dream." Lena deleted the message without replying.

The insurance claim came through two weeks later. A lump sum. Enough to replace what was lost. Enough to move. The house was beyond salvage. A shell, charred and collapsed. The fire marshal's report was blunt: "Interior consumed. Structure unsound. Probable arson, matched accelerant traces. Fatality confirmed." Dan read it once. Then never again. He stayed in the hospital for four days. Surgery, rest, painkillers. When he was discharged, he still walked with a limp. His side stitched and bruised. Lena helped him dress every morning, bandages swapped out, silence shared. Neither of them had said Grace's name aloud since the night of the fire. They didn't need to.

They moved in with Lena's parents in Surrey for a while. Just until they could decide what came next. Her mother didn't say I told you so, and for that, Lena was grateful. Dan's mother brought groceries every week, without asking. Rory called most nights. Brenda sent books. Theo dropped off a slow cooker and said nothing at all. A month passed. Then another. One morning, Lena stood outside in the garden. Wrapped in a cardigan. Watching the leaves fall. She was five months along. The bump showed now, soft and round beneath her hand. Dan stood beside her, one hand resting lightly on her back. "Where would you go," she asked, "if you could go anywhere?" He didn't answer right away. Then "Somewhere no one's heard of Winspire." She smiled at that. They chose Devon in the end. Near the coast. Not too far from Ruby and friends they hadn't seen in years. A two-bed cottage with a broken fence and a good view. Close enough to family. Far enough from memory. They never reclaimed anything from the house. What hadn't burned had been boxed by contractors and delivered by van, sealed in plastic. They donated most of it. Sold the rest. Kept only the ultrasound photo Lena had carried in her wallet, and a photograph that had been found, half-scorched, in the garden, taken the day they'd won. In the picture, Dan had his arm around her shoulders. Lena was smiling. She still didn't remember the moment it was taken. She kept it anyway. Framed it in a small silver frame and tucked it into a drawer.

Sometimes, when she opened it, she would run her fingers across the edge, still warped by heat. She never threw it away.

And that was how it ended. Not with sirens or shouting or the click of locks. But with quiet. With space. With the hum of something ordinary and in that stillness, something new began.

About the Author:

Jordan D. Martins is a British author whose ranges from psychological thriller to dark speculative fiction. Blending quiet tension with vivid atmosphere. His stories explore human vulnerability, haunting secrets and the unseen forces that shapes our lives. Whether set in modern-day or a forgotten corner of magical history.

Jordan is the author of **This Deed is Ours** and the upcoming novel Duskborn, the first in a sweeping dark fantasy saga. When not writing, he can be found wandering with his dogs, drinking too much coffee and always chasing the next strange idea.

WWW.JORDANDMARTINS.CO.UK

@AUTHORJORDANDMARTINS @JORDANDMARTINS

TURN FOR A

SNEAK PEAK

In the shadows of history, a bloodline endures.

Sage has always known she was different, but when her power awakens in a world where her magic is feared, an ancient families hide behind masks and names. She must confront the truth; she is the last of a forgotten legacy. One that was hunted. One that must remain hidden.

As darkness stirs beneath a fractured magical realm, Sage is drawn into a web of secrets, trials and betrayals where light and shadow are not opposites, but weapons.

Duskborn is the first in a sweeping dark fantasy series exploring legacy, power and the cost of survival in a world built to erase you.

Sneak Preview:

The wind howled through the black woods of Greymoor Hollow, and from the trees hung the scent of smoke and scorched salt. Screams split the canopy, sharp as flint against the brittle silence. That silence had once been sacred, thick with the whisper of rituals spoken in tongues older than any chapel bell. But not tonight. Tonight, there was only judgment. The banners bore crimson crosses. The boots were muddied with soot and blood. Their torches hissed through the fog, a marching line of flame cutting through the mist like divine wrath. They called it justice. Righteous fury. A cleansing. To the families who lived in the Hollow, it was simply The Fall. It did not begin in fire. It began in betrayal. The Tenebrae witches had long known their time would come. Unlike the more common covens scattered across England, those who healed village folk in secret, who bartered luck charms and herbs to midwives and lords, the Tenebrae had always stood apart. Not just because of their magic, but because of what they chose to wield.

They were born of paradox, witches who could cast light and shadow with equal mastery. Who had learned to walk the tightrope of dark magic without falling into it. They drank from the same river of power that twisted others into monsters, and emerged stronger, clearer. Legends whispered that the first Tenebrae, centuries before, had crossed into the Umbravale. A realm where raw, primal magic flowed untamed. Where echoes of creation still crackled in the air. Most who entered the Umbravale were lost to madness. The first of the Tenebrae returned with eyes turned silver and black, marked by balance. They became known as the Duskbound, wielders of shadow and sun. They were not evil. But they were feared. And what is feared is eventually hunted. For a time, the Tenebrae thrived in hidden groves and moonbound sanctuaries. They passed their knowledge in riddles and blood, not parchment. Their magic lived in the bones of their children, not in books. That secrecy kept them safe. Until one of their own gave them up.

To be continued – 29TH August 2025

Printed in Great Britain
by Amazon

62597468R00150